GW01388308

ARGEMOURT

CORINNA EDWARDS-COLLEDGE

Argemourt
Copyright © 2018 Corinna Edwards-Colledge

Printed and bound in Great Britain by Clays Ltd, Elcograf S.p.A

Authors Reach Ltd
www.authorsreach.co.uk

Corinna Edwards-Colledge is also represented in Brighton &
Hove by Storyland Press

www.corinnaedwards-colledge.co.uk

ISBN: 978-1-9999137-3-1

ACKNOWLEDGMENTS

I am grateful to many people for helping me shape this novel, and navigate it through some challenging times both historical and current, in human history and experience.

Thank to Stephanie, Kym and Hayley for giving me unique insights into the qualities and courage required to be an army wife; and the pros and cons of living in a barracks town. Thank you to Douglas W Hawes, author of *Oradour the Final Verdict* for reading Argemourt and making some vital historical corrections. Thank you to my wonderful Beta Readers; Jim Pike, Samantha Penfold, Shani Struthers, V K McGivney, Rebecca Colledge, Gabrielle McCarten and Dan Pye for lending me your skills and knowledge on everything from World War II history to colloquial French.

Thank you also to Barbara Eldridge at the Anne Frank Foundation in Switzerland for allowing me to use Anne's wonderful quote at the start of this book. The fact that she wrote it from her attic hiding place, in the same week that the Waffen SS were leaving their bloody trail of horror through the villages of the Haute-Vienne just adds to its power and relevance.

The following books were invaluable in providing historical background and detail:

Martyred Villages (Sarah Farmer)
Oradour the Final Verdict (Douglas W Hawes)
One Day in Oradour (Helen Watts)
The Voices of Oradour (David M Thomas)

ARGEMOURT

Argemourt is dedicated to the children, mothers, fathers, brothers, sisters, grandparents, lovers and friends that were killed in Oradour-sur-Glane, Argenton-sur-Creuse and Tulle on the 9th and 10th of June 1944.

In hope that one day we will learn the lessons of history.

ARGEMOURT

NOTE FROM THE AUTHOR

Argemourt, and the people I have populated it with, are invented. However, their creation originates in some very real and terrible events from the violent death throes of World War II. The idea for the novel came to me after a visit, on holiday, to the national monument of Oradour-sur-Glane. On Saturday June 10th 1944, 648 villagers were slaughtered by SS Panzer Division Das Reich, a so-called reprisal for Resistance activity in the area. Just the day before, the villages of Argenton-sur-Creuse and Tulle also suffered indiscriminate massacre at the hands of the Waffen SS.

ARGEMOURT

CONTENTS

PROLOGUE

Haute-Vienne, 13 June, 1944

The sun beat down, relentless and blinding. My bicycle bumped skittishly along the dirt track, its tyres trembling over loose stones and the compacted ruts carved out by the daily excursions of Monsieur Bujold's cart. I closed my eyes and let my mind swim through the warm air; trying to ignore the bone-jarring ride, and imagine, instead, that I was as light and tiny as a dandelion seed. After a few seconds, however, my nerves got the better of me and the bike started to wobble, so I opened my eyes again, to a world that was saturated by white light. As my eyes slowly adjusted, the figure of Jacques, on his bike ahead of me, started to take form through the heat-haze.

The sun had fired up his blond hair and his sunburnt, wiry legs moved up and down on the pedals, with a hypnotic motion - simultaneously mechanical and nonchalant. I watched him for a moment, my beautiful brother, my confidant and protector, in a world that had gone mad.

'Hey, Jacques, stop a moment.' The words sounded flat in the thick hot air, but he stopped, turning the bike round ninety degrees and smiling at me. 'I'm so thirsty, can I have a drink?'

'Ah poor little Michèle, is the ride too hard for you?'

I dismounted and pushed my bike a few yards until I was alongside him. 'I can outride you any day of the week *ma puce*, as you well know, now give me the water!'

He took off his rucksack and dangled it above my head. 'Come and get it then little sis, if you can!' I made several grabs for it, but he was too tall and I kept on missing. We went on like this for a minute or two until I landed a well-aimed punch on his solar-plexus and he doubled up, laughing, and surrendered his back pack to me. I found the tin flask underneath our sandwiches, which had been tightly mummified in parchment and string by Angélique. The water was blessedly still cool, I took several deep gulps then passed it on to Jacques. He drank deeply too, his Adam's apple moving up and down behind the skin of his throat. When he had finished he put the flask back into his rucksack and flung it onto his back with a flourish.

'Come on then, back to the pilgrim's hot and weary road. I want to be in Argemourt before Monsieur Baptiste shuts up shop. I fancy a nice cold cider with our picnic.'

I re-mounted my bike. 'I'll race you to the church; last one there is a *crétin*!' I set off quickly before Jacques could get back on his bike and stood up on the pedals, pushing hard. I'd forgotten that it was an uphill route to the church, but I was determined not to be beaten. It was rare that I won any form of test, be it of intelligence, strength or cunning, against my athletic and gifted older brother, so my occasional efforts to do so were heroic - like a mouse banging its tiny fists against the foot of a lion.

About two-thirds of the way to the top of the hill he passed me with a salute and a toothy grin. He had barely broken into a sweat, but I was drenched now. I could feel it sliding down between my shoulder blades, dripping into my eyes and making them sting. *'Merde!'* I shouted impotently after him, but he had already disappeared over the brow of the hill. I knew he could have overtaken me sooner, but with a sense of evil mischief, had let me believe, for as long as he could bear, that I could win.

I stopped to wipe the sweat from my face with my petticoat. If Angélique had heard me swear or seen me defile my skirts in this way I would have felt the back of her hand, but luckily for me she was four miles behind us, so I could swear and misuse my clothes with impunity.

I put my right foot back on the pedal and pushed off. It was hard going, and my chest was hurting, but I could see the top of the hill just fifty yards ahead of me and it spurred me on. Breathing hard I made slow, painful upward progress; but soon the spire of the old church peeped through the treetops, like the sole survivor of a leafy avalanche.

I'll never forget the pleasure of the downward freewheel once I had crested the hill, partly because what followed it was defined by an opposing emotion, one of horror. But for that moment I was full of joy: hair whipping, wind cooling, skirts flapping, feet off the pedals (which were flying round like part of a demonic machine) and I went down the other side of the hill like a rocket. Once at the bottom, I put my feet down hard and managed to slow my pace just before I'd worn through the soles of my shoes, another potential point of apoplexy for Angélique, who was trying against impossible odds to keep us clothed and fed during rationing.

I couldn't see Jacques, and was wondering how far ahead he was, when a lot of things happened at once and my life changed forever - just like that - on a moment as tiny and precise as the point of a pin, the edge of a knife or the depression of a trigger...

PART 1: MICHELLE

'Soldiers and war heroes are honoured and commemorated, explorers are granted immortal fame, martyrs are revered, but how many people look upon women too as soldiers?'

(Anne Frank, 13 June, 1944)

She woke and stared blearily into the grey morning light that had filtered into the room from between the half-drawn curtains. For a moment she couldn't place where she was, or what day it was; but then realisation dawned and the remembering had a bitter edge to it, like the aftertaste of bile in her mouth. The alarm went off on her phone, a shrill *teek teek teek*, and as if the sound was an invitation to be disturbed, Adele burst through the door and clambered on to the guest bed beside her.

'Auntie Jane's up. She's got chocolate croissants,' She pronounced it "crossants" which made Michelle smile, 'and there's crumpets too.'

Jane wasn't actually Adele's aunt, but ever since Michelle came to the barracks town of Anborough, she had been her best friend and the honorary title came naturally. 'That's nice, I'll be down in a minute.'

'Mummy, why can't I go to the funeral too?'

Michelle could feel Adele's weight on the bed against her thigh. She propped herself up on an elbow and replied, through the gloom, to the shadowy suggestion of her daughter's face. 'We've been over this, Chick, because Auntie Jane thinks Beth is too young to go and you've got the very important job of looking after her while we're there.'

'But I was only four when Dad died and *I* went to say goodbye.'

Michelle's chest contracted and she had to force her words out on the top of a shallow breath. 'Everyone's different. Jane knows what's best for Beth, and she'll make sure she gets to say goodbye properly. They'll have Abe's ashes too, remember.'

Adele turned her head towards the window and the whites of her eyes glinted. 'I don't want to be burned into ash,' she said quietly, 'I want to be buried under a tree like Daddy was so you can feed it, and then you go into the berries and the birds eat them and then they fly away with little bits of you inside them and you end up all over the world.'

Michelle didn't reply, but launched herself out of the bed, and the soles of her feet prickled when they touched the thin carpet. 'Right, that's it, I'm up. Go and brush your teeth and get dressed and I'll see you downstairs in a minute.'

Adele sighed dramatically but obeyed.

Michelle went over to the window and drew the curtains. It was a brighter day than she had imagined. The sun was rising from behind the estuary and a flock of gulls were wheeling in the clearing sky, their white feathers reflecting the electric peach light of the dawn. She leant her forehead against the cool glass, and as she did every day, started to talk to Chris. She conjured him, imagined him slipping his arms around her waist, and filled her mind with his voice, imagined it connecting them somehow - across whatever there was now that stood between them: *How am I going to get through this, Chris? I'm doing it for her but I feel like I could break up into a million pieces. I'm trying to be a good person. Am I a good person?*

The sound of laughter came from the living room. Michelle stood at the door and peeked in; the girls were sitting close to each other, watching TV, Adele's leg crossed companionably over Beth's. She went past them and into the kitchen. Jane had her back to her, washing

19

up, but there was a quiet fury in her actions, and water was splashing up onto the counter and down the front of the sink unit. Michelle went up and put her arm around her. Jane was trembling, and there was a sour smell of stale wine coming from her.

'Thanks for staying with us last night, 'Chell, I don't know what I would have done without you.'

She tightened her grip on Jane's shoulders. 'Don't worry about it.'

'I'm sorry I got a bit pissed.'

'It's fine, you know I've been there.'

Jane glanced round at her, her eyes were red and raw. 'Did you have to get me into bed?'

'No, don't worry, you made it up there all by yourself.'

The sound of a wheezing cough broke through from the living room and made them look round. Jane banged her fist against the draining board, and the plates jumped and crashed against each other. Michelle flinched. 'The Asthma's back, I've told the maintenance company a million fucking times about the damp in Beth's room but they don't give a shit! *And* the downstairs toilet's not flushing properly. Our men are out there, risking their lives for this country and they treat us like animals, like fucking animals!'

All of a sudden Jane seemed to fold in on herself, her limbs liquefying. Michelle caught hold of her, just before she spilled onto the floor, with a deep inhuman wail. The sound was brutal and elemental, as if it had erupted from the centre of the earth rather than from Jane's small body. Michelle held on to her tightly, propping her up against the kitchen unit as Jane wept into her neck. She remembered this feeling, the black panic, the ravenous sorrow, the bleakness of the world after it has been broken. There were tears in her own eyes, but she forced them back.

Jane started to talk, but the words ran into each other and gurgled through the wetness of her tears and the mucus that was running from her nose, 'OhmyGodwhatamIgoingtodo? Michelle, pleaseplease, tell me, help me. WhatamIgoingtodowithouthim? WhatamIgoingtodo?'

Michelle heard a movement behind her and turned to see Adele and Beth standing in the doorway looking solemn. 'Mummy will be ok, Beth, she's just feeling a bit sad right now. Go back and watch a bit more telly and she'll be in to see you in a minute, go on, it's ok.' She made a shooing motion with her fingers without letting go of Jane. The girls turned reluctantly and went. Michelle gently lowered Jane into a chair. She had cried herself out now and her face reminded her of a baby mole, puffy and pink and blinking blindly. She fetched the roll of kitchen towel, tore off a few squares and handed them to Jane, who reached out mechanically, took them and wiped away her tears and blew her nose. They were both silent for a moment; the noise of the TV buzzed away in the background.

'It does get better, Jane, that's all I can say to you. I know it feels like you're in hell now, and that's because you are, but it does get better.'

Jane looked up at her blearily. 'I'm sorry, 'Chell, I know this is hard for you too. I...'

'It's ok, I keep saying, you were there for me, and now I'm here for you.'

'I know, and I love you Chell, but some of the bitches here, they pretend to care, but they don't. They can barely

21

bring themselves to look at me. We never fitted in, they never wanted us here, and just because Abe was different and everything...'

'I know, it's horrible, but it's not because of that; everyone loved Abe, it's just because they're scared. They're scared that it could be them next.'

'They're cowards.'

'Maybe. Look, I don't want to piss you off, but do you really think its best that Beth doesn't go to the funeral? It's just something Adele said: that she should have the chance to say goodbye?'.

'I've thought about it, and it's best she doesn't. I have my reasons. She can say goodbye when we scatter his ashes. We'll have all the family around and she can read the poem she's written.'

'When are Pat and Youssef coming?'

'I asked them to meet us at the church. I know they loved him as much as I did, but that's why I can't stand to be around them. Not at the moment. Dealing with Beth is about as much as I can bear.'

'Ok, you know best, you're probably right. I'll make us a coffee and then we'd better get ready.'

The small church was busy and she sensed Jane tense as they walked in. It was the first time Michelle had been in there since Chris' funeral, and she was unprepared for how much it affected her. As they walked down the aisle, Chris and Abe's commanding officer shifted in his seat to look at them, and the action yanked violently on a thread of memory and the past came hurtling towards her, and for a second she thought she was going to faint. She moved away from him and without looking at him, she willed her legs to take her to the front pew. *I can do this, can't I, Chris? I can do it, tell me I can do it.* The benches to her left were full with their regiment, returned from a tour in Afghanistan only the week before, and in a sober Mexican-wave of respect, the soldiers turned and nodded or smiled at Jane, who kept her eyes on the coffin at the end of the aisle.

They took their seats at the front of the church next to Abe's parents, Pat and Youssef, and his sister. There was a flurry of hugging and eye-wiping but Jane seemed to have frozen; her face fixed, her lips compressed into a sharp pink line. Michelle suspected Jane knew she would break down if she let out even the smallest drop of emotion, so she struggled to keep herself in check too. She had loved Abe herself; he was a big gentle man, and a dedicated soldier, just like Chris. He and Jane had had their moments, but they had been devoted to each other, and being apart for months at a time was a huge struggle for them. Where some army relationships could flounder in resentment and the bitterness of wasted sacrifice, Jane and Abe had managed to use the pain of their regular separations as proof and fuel for their love.

She looked across at Jane, so small and alone in the middle of the big polished mahogany pew, and her heart ached. She was the only person there, just for her. Jane's mum and dad were dead, and she was estranged from her sole sibling, Dave, who just didn't seem able to handle the fact that Abe was Asian and a soldier. Michelle didn't really get politics; she preferred to stick to the world around her, one that was small enough to understand, but she knew that Dave had moved more and more to the right and the distance between him and his sister's beliefs had become a gulf that was now too big and deep to cross.

The pews behind them were filling up with local families. Some came over to give Jane a hug, others touched her shoulder from behind making her turn. With each interaction Jane got more and more rigid, as if she was preparing herself for something and couldn't be distracted. Michelle couldn't dwell on it for too long though, she was busy struggling with her own emotions. The echoes of Chris' funeral were starting to haunt her, she could feel her hands trembling and clasped them in her lap to hide it.

Throughout the service Jane stayed immobile, her face fixed and waxen, her stare not wavering from Abe's coffin. At one-point Pat had pressed a packet of tissues into her hands, but they were still unopened. Periodically Michelle put her arm around her, or squeezed her hands, but still Jane didn't respond. Michelle understood though; everyone had their own ways of coping, and this was hers.

After the third hymn and the priest's eulogy, Jane was invited up to say a few words. Mechanically she pulled a few pieces of paper out of her bag.

Michelle hadn't realised she intended to speak and took hold of her arm, 'if you need me to take over at any point,' she whispered quickly into her ear, 'just let me know.'

Jane shook her head then walked steadily up to the pulpit. She glanced out over the rows of mourners and seemed to take in each of them in turn. There was the sound of shuffling and coughing as people tried to get their distractions out of the way before she started. She put the papers down in front of her on the lectern and started to speak. Her voice was surprisingly clear and steady, as if this was a situation she had rehearsed.

'I know what you all want me to say. You want me to say that Abe was a good soldier, that he died doing the one thing he most wanted to do; that he died trying to make the world a better place; that he died doing what he believed in. Well I'm sorry, I'm sorry Pat and Youssef, I'm sorry Squadron Commander Brown, I'm sorry Ben and Suzy and Shane, but I won't say it. I WON'T say it.' There was a sudden silence in the church, as if everyone were holding their breath. Michelle dared herself to look at Pat, and saw that her face was fixed with horror, her mouth half-open.

Jane continued, 'I won't say it, because it *isn't true*. What is true is that Abe died fighting in a war he didn't understand, in a country he didn't understand and for a cause he didn't understand. He is torn away from us all, forever; our lives are shattered, our hearts broken...and for what?' At this Jane stopped and looked out at the congregation again. Near the back of the church someone coughed. Pat was now gripping the edge of the pew's seat, her knuckles white. Michelle wondered whether she should go and try to get Jane to leave the pulpit; could she think up a few things to say herself? But Jane seemed so calm, so certain; what right had she to stop her?

'What is better? What has changed as a result of Abe's sacrifice, and the sacrifice of many hundreds before him, including my dear friend Michelle's husband, Chris, just two years ago? The extremists are recruiting more people than ever, the terrorists continue to terrorise, the countries we went into are virtually destroyed. We learn nothing and achieve nothing other than more death and grief and chaos. So, I ask you this, as we are here, with Abe's ruined body beside us. What is wrong with you men? For God's sake, what is wrong with you?!' Jane's voice rose a pitch and Michelle's heart started to race as there were the beginnings of mumblings and discontent in the congregation. 'We nurture you in our bellies, we raise you and feed you and try to teach you right from wrong, and you grow up and you carve up the world with your need for possession, for power, to be right. War makes men look stupid; it makes fools of you all.'

'Jane, please!' Michelle heard Pat moan beside her, but Jane continued without drawing breath.

'- And you don't care what is destroyed, who is killed - whether it's children, or women - you don't care whose rights are trampled over - so long as you WIN, so long as you're RIGHT.' Jane's voice started to fray at the edges and a tremble passed over her face. 'You bring us war, stupid, stupid war! Is this it? Your greatest gift to the world?! I LOVED HIM, YOU BASTARDS, I LOVED HIM!'

There was a sound like a strangled scream from Pat, and Jane started to sob. The priest moved closer and hovered behind her, unsure what to do. Michelle bolted up to the pulpit, put her arm around her and half-lifted, half-dragged her back to her seat.

'Have they gone yet?' Jane took a deep drag on her cigarette, as if it were, ironically, her only source of Oxygen.

Michelle glanced towards the saloon bar. 'There's a few stragglers, but most of them have gone.'

'Is Beth ok?'

'Yes, she's happy playing a game on your phone with 'Del.' Michelle weighed her thoughts carefully before speaking again. 'Did you really mean all that? Everything you said? That...that Abe and Chris's lives were wasted?'

Jane looked up at her; her eyes were red and, although she hadn't cried for a while, her make-up was smudged. 'You tell me. What did they achieve? Any of them?'

'I...' Michelle stopped, she couldn't bear to think Chris had given his life for nothing. 'I think he was trying to make things better. I think that the people who made these decisions know a lot more than I do; I think sometimes you need to trust in something bigger than yourself.'

Jane looked away and shrugged. 'I'm sorry, it's not fair of me to get you to try and see things my way. I wish *I* didn't see things my way. It's horrible. But whatever you say, I think you can *only* trust in yourself, in those you love; there's nothing else left to trust anymore. Politicians, priests, bankers; they've all proved themselves to be liars, abusers....opportunists.' She stubbed out her cigarette and looked back towards the pub. 'I wish everyone would leave. I just want to go home and crawl into bed. Are you still ok to have Beth tonight?'

'Of course, we'll watch a film and make popcorn.'

'Thanks 'Chell, you've done so much for me. I don't know how I would have managed without -'

She was cut short by the sound of the Saloon bar door slamming shut behind them. Donna Grealy took the two steps down towards the benches they were sitting on a little unsteadily; her eyes were glassy with drink.

'You're full of fucking shit, Jane,' she spat through a lip-gloss-pink sneer. Her mouth worked around her next words silently, as if it needed to practice them. 'You've always thought you're better than us, but you're not. It's about time you got off your high horse and took a proper look at the world.'

Michelle was about to retaliate but Jane took hold of her arm and held her down.

'I'm sorry you feel that way Donna, you're entitled to your opinion. And so am I.'

Donna lurched a few inches closer and jabbed her manicured finger towards Jane's face. Jane looked back at her, without flinching.

'You're a fucking traitor, Jane, and I hope you're first in line when ISIS take over this country. I hope you're the first woman to be lined up and stoned. You've got your head in the sand; you're a fucking coward. Our boys are the only thing between us and them fascist Muslims, and you dare to say that they don't matter!'

Michelle jumped up now, she could feel rage burning in her fingertips, and she felt like punching Donna in the face. But Jane was standing even before she was, and moved in front of her.

'I never said Abe didn't matter, or Chris, or your Darren,' she growled; 'of course their lives matter, Abe's life mattered, but so did the lives of all those hundreds of thousands of innocent people who have died over there. We've not made anything better, we've only made it worse. You must see that, Donna? Open your fucking eyes!'

Donna's face contorted and she compensated for her drunken swaying by grabbing hold of the back of a garden chair. 'You're talking out of your arse, Jane! You shamed your husband today; you shamed all of us!'

Jane's face went white, she opened her mouth and then shut it again. Michelle stood up and got in between the two of them and surprised herself by pushing her finger hard onto Donna's chest. 'You've said enough,' her voice was trembling with fury, 'just fuck off home now and sober up.'

Donna swayed again away from Michelle's finger and had to step backwards to stop herself falling. She turned but shouted over her shoulder, 'Shame on you Jane! Shame on you!'

As Donna walked unsteadily away across the scruffy pub garden Jane suddenly found her voice again. 'YOU'RE JUST FUCKING SCARED!' she screamed after Donna's retreating back. 'YOU'RE JUST AS SCARED AS I AM!'

Michelle could hear the girls giggling, and the occasional thump from Adele's room above her head. Normally these were sounds that would make her smile to herself, but tonight it just didn't seem to bring her any comfort.

She tipped the rejected, unexploded husks of popcorn into the bin and screwed the top back on the lemonade bottle. She moved through her tasks jerkily, as if the only reason she was moving at all was because someone was manipulating her strings. When she'd finished she refilled her glass of wine and sat down on the bar-stool by the kitchen island. She looked down impassively at her chewed fingernails, then up at the framed photo of her wedding on the wall above the dining table. Chris was smiling in that wonderful way of his, with the whole of his big, friendly, handsome face. She wanted to smile back at him, but there was nothing inside her to smile with. *Was it a waste?* she asked his picture, the voice in her head strangely cold and mechanical; *Did you really die for nothing? Abe too? Is this house, this barracks, the whole army, part of something terrible?* There was, of course, no reply, and she found herself shouting out loud: 'For God's sake, Chris, answer my fucking question!'

'Mum?'

Michelle looked away from the photograph and blinked. Adele was standing in the doorway, looking anxious.

'Why are you angry with Dad?'

'I...I'm not angry with Dad.'

'You were shouting at him.'

'I was asking him something and he wasn't answering, so I had to shout, so he'd hear me.'

'What do you mean, Mum?' Adele's voice broke. 'You're scaring me!'

Michelle looked at the little girl again and focused her eyes. She wished she would go away, but then something cleared, and she remembered she was looking at her own daughter, and she saw that silent tears were streaming down her face. The shock of the change in her perception made her feel sick, as if she'd just woken up from a particularly horrible nightmare. 'I'm so sorry, sweetheart, I didn't mean to scare you, I just, you know, I just feel so sad sometimes, but I'm all right now.' She got up and started to rummage in one of the kitchen cabinets, 'There's some more sweets somewhere, let's have a look - '

'Mum, it's ten-o-clock, we don't want sweets, we're tired, I came down because we want to go to bed and we want the story tape on.'

Michelle picked up her phone and looked at the time. Adele was right, it was just past ten. Where had the evening gone? 'Sorry Chick, of course, let's get you two in bed. It's been a long day.

Once the first, clamouring and unbearable wave of grief had passed after Chris had been killed, Michelle had worked hard to keep her pain to herself; partly because she felt that Adele had enough of her own hurt to contend with, and partly because her mum and dad had stayed with her for a few months after the funeral and she had been desperate to appear that she was holding it all together. She had had a probably not completely unreasonable fear, that they might try to get Adele to live with them.

Since then it had become a habit to hide her feelings. It could be as small a thing as turning away to conceal a spasm of grief crossing her face after finding something of his at the back of a drawer; or pretending to be having a bath, just so she could cry and use the sound of the running water to drown out her sobs.

'Your packed lunch, don't forget your packed lunch!' Michelle was in a dark mood, not aided by a hangover and a sense of shame for having let Adele see her in such a state the night before.

Adele ran back into the kitchen and grabbed her lunchbox from the counter.

'Come on! We're going to be late!'

They left the house and set off down the road. Michelle knew she was walking slightly too fast for Adele, and the little girl's feet were barely touching the ground.

'Mummy,' she panted, 'you're too quick.'

'We're late.'

'*Please* Mummy.'

Michelle slowed slightly but tightened her grip on Adele's hand. It was a cool, sunny day, but no amount of sunlight could make Anborough Island look truly cheerful. She'd spent enough time in different Service Family Accommodation on army bases to become inured to it and accept it as the price she paid for being with the man she loved. But sometimes, even she, could find herself depressed by the uniform, indifferently built and increasingly poorly maintained houses; the prefab pubs that you could never rely on to be open when you wanted them to be, and the dingy shop. The only thing that was always consistently good was the schools. They had a higher teacher to pupil ratio than ordinary primary schools, and a special welfare team that had really helped Adele in those dreadful months of incomprehension and agony after her dad's death.

'Here we are!' Michelle attempted to say brightly as they approached the school gates. There was a huddle of mums, including Donna, by the bike shelter, some in running gear. Jane was on her own, about ten yards away from them, trying to peel Beth, who appeared to be having some kind of tantrum, off her legs. If it was possible to "point with your eyes" thought Michelle, that's what the women were doing. She hurried up to Jane's side.

'Hey, Beth, what's up?'

Jane looked up at Michelle, her expression tight and desperate. 'She doesn't want to go into school today. But I think it will do her good.'

Michelle squatted down to Beth's level and smoothed the tear-wetted hair off her face. A small dark brown eye looked at her from behind the swell of her mother's thigh;

Michelle smiled. 'Come on, Beth love, Adele will go in with you, won't you 'Del?'

Adele nodded and reached for Beth's hand. She took it. 'There's clay today.' she said simply. 'You like clay.'

Beth sniffed and moved infinitesimally towards Adele. Jane took the opportunity to stand back and tidy her daughter's hair. Michelle found a tissue in her pocket and handed it to Jane, who wiped the remaining tears from Beth's face. 'There, that's better. Now off you go and I'll see you later.' The two girls headed off together towards the school. A few yards from the door they saw some of their friends and bounded off to meet them.

Jane turned to Michelle and smiled ruefully 'The resilience of children is truly a thing to behold!'

'Tell me about it.'

'Thanks for that, I know I shouldn't care, but I really didn't need Donna and her coven looking on today.'

'Just try to ignore them.'

'I am, believe me.' Jane looked at her shrewdly. 'Are you ok? You look rough.'

'I feel rough, too much wine last night, and then 'Del found me talking to Chris, and I wasn't very nice to her, and now I feel like shit.'

Jane laid her hand on her arm. 'Hey, don't give yourself such a hard time. Life's tough, parenting is tough, you're doing your best.'

'Am I? Sometimes I'm not so sure.'

Jane looked around her and sighed. 'It's this place, I hate this fucking place.'

'It's not that bad is it? They look after us, don't they?'

'Do they?' Jane raised her eyebrows.

Michelle thought about Chris' regular complaints about the outdated equipment he had to work with; of Jane's continuing battle over the damp in her house but felt a sudden need to focus on the positive. 'But they were good to me, to Adele, after Chris' death. And you can stay in the house for ages yet, and Beth's getting extra support in school: all that's good, isn't it?'

'Yeh,'

Jane looked distracted and Michelle wasn't sure if she'd even been listening.

'Look, I need to talk to you, can you come around after work?'

Michelle frowned, 'Sure. but why the mystery, why not now?

'Because there's something I need to do first.'

Michelle's mind wandered, as it usually did at work. She would watch herself wiping tables, restocking the milk and sugar, brushing down the floor - and all the while her mind would be off somewhere else; remembering one of the few, but lovely holidays she, Chris and Beth had had together when he was on his leave, or replaying some childhood adventure; and a noise or a voice would bring her reluctantly back to the present. Making coffee was the only time at work she was truly, mentally there, and training to be a Barista was the only part of her work that afforded her even a modicum of pride. The tangy yet earthy smell of fresh ground coffee as she filled the filter handle, followed by the satisfying pressure of dampening it down; the clunk as she slotted it back into the machine and the frothing of the milk with the steam-wand; these were all part of a ritual she got a lot of pleasure from, but which also required her concentration.

'What about you, Michelle?'

Tracy's musical Geordie accent startled her; she'd barely noticed the table of wives and girlfriends - mostly from Sycamore Row - sitting at the corner table. She put down her cloth and smoothed down her black apron. 'Sorry, I missed what you were talking about?'

'Eyebrow threadin', Kayleigh's startin' up her own business.'

'Oh, right.'

Kayleigh smiled, a little condescendingly Michelle felt, and waved a card in her direction. 'Fifty percent off your first appointment; exclusively for army wives...' her voice trailed off and she blushed, '...well, you know what I mean.'

Michelle went over and took the card from Kayleigh's hand. *And army widows she means, Chris, but she hasn't got the guts to say it.* 'Great, thanks, I'll let you know.' She went back to the relative safety of the counter and stashed the card by the side of the till, mortified to see her hand was shaking. She busied herself with cleaning the shelves under the till, trying to resist the temptation to glance up and see if any of the group were looking at her.

She took out till rolls, dusty glasses and packs of cloths, sprayed the shelf with detergent and wet a cloth. As she scrubbed at the greasy recesses of the shelf, her mind wandered again. It was easy to get caught up in your appearance here, even with hardly anyone around to care what you looked like. There was often so little for the wives to do when their husbands were on tour so most got a job once the kids were in school. The choices were limited though, because you never knew how long you had in a place. It could be six months or six years, so it was almost impossible to find anything decent and most of the wives (and, occasionally, husbands) ended up working on the base, in the pre-school or like Michelle, in the cafe. Jane was a qualified mental health nurse, but even she'd ended up working in a supermarket in the nearest town.

She replaced the items on the shelf and moved on to the next one. She found an old newspaper, a jar of confiscated counterfeit money and several packets of serviettes. She rinsed out her cloth. Once, when Chris was about to come back from a particularly long and hard tour in Afghanistan, she had become obsessed with looking as perfect for him as she could for his return. She'd had gel nails put on and had her hair highlighted, as well as professionally straightened into the current style of straight, sleek hair. Having her eyebrows plucked into neat arches and some new clothes had completed the transformation.

To her dismay their reunion had been strangely stilted and that evening they had almost treated each other like strangers. When, after a couple of glasses of wine, she had finally confronted him about it, he had said that he didn't want to upset her but he really didn't like what she'd done to herself; that she'd made herself look like a doll. She had cried solidly for half an hour and Chris had been mortified and told her that when they spent a long time apart, he would rely on the last picture he had of her in his mind to get him through. She'd changed herself so much that it had made him feel scared and disorientated. What Michelle realised now, with hindsight, was that while they were apart they were on different journeys. Inevitably they would change, even just a little; and when they got back together, it took them both a while to accept that it wasn't quite the same person that was delivered back to them after each absence. *I don't think I've ever been as miserable as I was that day,* she found herself saying to Chris in her mind; *I understand how you felt, but all I wanted was for you to say how beautiful I was.*

She finished off the shelf and went to put the newspaper in the recycling bin. She checked the date, it was from the April before Chris' death. For a second she hesitated, tempted to read it; but instead, gritted her teeth and threw it in the recycling bin. She knew, from bitter experience, that indulging in the past made re-entry to the present almost unbearable.

Jane didn't look at her as she ushered her into the kitchen, heightening Michelle's sense of unease. The house was a mess, the hall carpet scuffed and dirty and the kitchen surfaces a jagged landscape of unwashed pans and up-ended cereal packets. Jane grimaced apologetically as she cleared a pile of magazines from one of the kitchen chairs for Michelle to sit on.

'I'm sorry it's such a mess, I keep meaning to clean up but when I get back from dropping Beth at school I just seem to end up back in bed, and then I wake up and it's time to go and pick her up. I'm going to make a start today though.' As if to illustrate the point she began to pick up some dirty clothes from the floor and stuff them into the washing machine.

'You should let me come over and help you. It wouldn't take us long. It's really hard, to keep on top of things, when you feel like this. But it will make you feel better when you do. I know.'

Jane sat down in front of her suddenly and took hold of her hands, as if she hadn't heard a word that Michelle had said. She looked up at her briefly, then quickly back down at their intertwined hands, Michelle felt the air tighten between them.

'Look, 'Chell, I don't know how to say this; so I'm just going to say it.'

Michelle's heartbeat quickened. 'What is it? What's the matter? Are you ill or something?'

'No, no, it's nothing like that.' Jane let go of her hand, 'I'm leaving, that's what it is.'

Michelle collapsed back in her chair as if she'd been thumped and her mind careened towards Chris. *Oh no, please no, Chris, what am I going to do without her? I've lost you, I can't lose her as well!* 'What do you mean?' She managed to say out loud to Jane, her voice thin with shock. 'Where would you go? The MoD will let you have this place for two years if you want it.'

'If I stay here that long I'll go mad. I can't do it without Abe, I just can't.'

'But you've got me.'

'I know, I know!'

Jane took hold of her hand again and at that moment Michelle realised how much she loved her friend. Her friend who was cleverer than anyone she knew; who could make ancient jeans and a head-scarf look cool; who wasn't scared to get angry at the world; who was always there for her.

'But if I stayed, you would be the only reason that I stayed.'

'You can't mean that! What about the school? About Beth and Adele? They adore each other!'

'IknowIknowIknow!' Jane's covered her face with her hands in distress. Her hands bunched up into fists and she banged them on her forehead before taking a deep breath and laying them flat on the table. 'I'm terrified that I'm not making the right decision, but something inside me, a voice right down deep, is telling me that I have to go. If I can't be myself with Abe, I need to find a different place to be myself with *me*. Can you understand that, even a little?'

Michelle was mortified to find she was crying. 'I do, but...' Her voice sounded like a child's. '...where will you go? I don't understand?'

Jane reached across the table, shook a cigarette out of its packet and lit it. 'Soz, I know I should go outside but...' She lit the cigarette and inhaled sharply. 'I got chatting to this woman, online, I met her through this support group on Facebook. For service widows. Anyway, we got on and we messaged each other off-group and it turns out she's got this big house with quite a lot of land, but no real income, so she wants to share it with another army widow and her child. She's got a daughter just a couple of years older than Beth, and a little boy who's five. She's thought about doing local veg-boxes, fresh juices, relishes, that kind of thing.'

'But you don't know the first thing about gardening!' said Michelle, trying not to let the jealousy show in her voice. 'It could take ages getting something like that off the ground.'

'So, I go back to nursing part-time, the money's not bad, and she's only charging enough rent to cover the bills and give her a bit to put towards the business each month.'

'But where is it?'

'Back near home, in the countryside about twenty miles outside Manchester. It's really beautiful out there. You and Adele can come and see us lots.'

Michelle shook her head slowly; trying to imagine cosmopolitan, feisty Jane slumming it in the wilds of Lancashire. 'It just won't be the same. We won't be able to be there for each other in the same way, we'll -'

Jane propped her cigarette up in an ashtray and clasped Michelle's hands tightly in hers again. '*Please*, 'Chell, I know it's hard, but surely you can see that it could be good for me; for Beth; to have a fresh start? Get away from all the gossip and the bitching -'

'It's not that bad,' said Michelle weakly. 'People look out for each other too.'

'Ok, you're right, but there's a lot of bitching, you know there is. This isn't a healthy environment, you can't *thrive* here, d'you know what I mean?'

'I...I'm not sure.'

'I'm sorry, I know it's a shock. If you'd done this to me I'd have felt the same, but I've got to be selfish; just this once.'

Michelle nodded and hung her head. It felt as if she had been hollowed out, and a familiar numbness crept over her.

Michelle passed through the next couple of weeks, as if she was a ghost, wandering through the rooms of a house full of living people. She felt invisible, and wondered if people sensed her presence as little more than a slight chilling of the air, or a sensation of presentiment and unease. Her familiar routine flashed past her, like the half-snatched glimpses of scenery through a speeding train window: school drop-off - work - school pick-up - cook dinner - tidy up after dinner - help Adele with her homework - drink a bottle of wine by herself - sleep fitfully - get up - school...and so it continued.

She found herself talking more and more to Chris, and more frequently out-loud, without realising. In the shop earlier that week she had started up a conversation with him about what to have for dinner, only to find one of the mums from Adele's class at the end of the aisle looking at her oddly. A small voice from her rational self told her this was bad, that she should get help, but she seemed to lack the energy to do anything about it. Occasionally, in quiet moments, she would catch Adele looking at her with such laser-targeted anxiety that she would feel a quiver in her heart. But even her daughter's obvious concern never quite broke through, and she continued to live her life with a detached, spectral quality. That is, until the letter came.

She had just dumped her shopping bags in the hall and picked up the post from the mat. One of the letters made her heart race. It had an MOD franking mark on it, and the logo of the company that managed the Service Family Accommodation. She opened it feverishly, and skimmed the contents, as if reading it with less than complete care would somehow have an influence on what it said. It didn't. She put the letter down and tried to slow her breathing; the room lurched and twisted unpleasantly. She got up and paced, clenching and unclenching her hands; *it's happened, Chris, what the fuck do I do now? I don't know what to do, help me please!* His silence filled her with rage, she screamed and kicked at the door of one of the kitchen cabinets. To her surprise it cracked and splintered and a wave of jarring pain shot up her leg. Stupid fucking house, stupid cheap useless kitchen! She hated it, she hated all of it. An impotent sob caught in her throat and she sat down at the kitchen table and put her head in her hands. Her phone rang and she slid it across the table. The name and picture on the screen were distorted by her tears. She swiped the screen and picked it up.

'Oh God, Mum, I don't know what to do!'

Her mother sounded startled. 'What's the matter, Michelle? What's happened? Is Adele ok?'

'Yes, yes, it's nothing to do with Adele. I...' She didn't know what to say, she couldn't stop crying.

Her mum's voice was muffled, like she had her hand over the phone then it became clear again. 'Darling, Dad's here too, I want you to take a deep breath and try to tell us what the matter is.'

Michelle tried to do as her mother told her. She took three deep breaths and wiped her eyes with the back of her hand. 'It's the house, I've just had a letter saying I've only got three months left to stay here.'

Her mum was silent for a moment, then spoke again. 'So soon? Has it really been that long since...'

'Twenty-one months, they say it's been twenty-one months. You only get two years, I knew it would happen eventually but - I suppose I thought, stupidly, that they might have forgotten about me.'

'You need to talk to Welfare, you need to try to get an extension. Call them, call them right now!'

'It's no good, Mum!' Michelle stared ahead of her. The room was out of focus, the crushing feeling of despair rendered her almost speechless. 'They'll only give extensions in extreme circumstances. I'd need to prove that I was really ill, that I wasn't coping - but I am, as far as anyone can tell. I've been going to work, getting Adele to school, it's my own stupid fault. I knew this was coming.'

'But what are you supposed to do?'

'They'll inform the council, I'll be given priority on the council housing list.'

'But what will you get? It could be awful! You won't know where they'll send you! How will Adele deal with that? You're in the house you had with Chris, how will she be able to bear to leave it?'

'Mum! That doesn't help! You always knew I'd have to leave here eventually. And how do you think that makes *me* feel? I'll have to leave him too!'

'I'm sorry darling, I didn't mean it that way, it's just - hang on, your dad wants a word.'

Her dad's voice came on the line almost instantly. 'Now, Michelle, I want you to listen to me very carefully.' His tone was crisp and business-like, and a seed of anger burned like a lit match somewhere in her core. 'You and Adele are going to come back home and live with us. We won't take no for an answer. I've never understood why you decided to stay there in the first place -'

'Because it's my *home*, Dad, because I have a life here!'

'What kind of life eh? You tell me that!'

'What do you mean *what kind of life?* My friends, a job, my daughter's school; that *kind of life!*'

'You've stayed there because you didn't know what else to do. You know you have. Pure and simple. You're going to come back here and we're going to look after you, and you can find a proper job, maybe go back to college, and we'll get Adele into the local primary, it's a good school. There's nothing else to be done, you know there isn't.'

'I can't talk anymore, Dad, I've got to go.'

'Michelle -'

She pressed the home button on her phone and cut him off. After weeks of torpor she now felt as if she was full of writhing insects and couldn't bear to be in the house. She grabbed her keys, went into the hall and slammed the front-door behind her. She wasn't sure where she was going, or why, but she just had to move. She crossed the street at a jog and went down the side road towards the edge of the estate. She felt adrenalised and light-headed, and her feet seemed to be floating a few inches off the pavement. She speeded up, she started to run, she kept going until she reached the low fence and the gate that took her out of the estate and onto the footpath across the low scrub towards the beach.

After another couple of minutes, she reached the sand dunes and had to slow down. It was hard going, the sand running away under her feet as she climbed, the tall grasses whipping at her bare calves, but she persisted and was soon sliding down towards the small beach. She stopped, panting, and looked up. Sunlight was fracturing on the pitted surface of the sea, flinging shards of white-gold brilliance into her eyes and making her squint. The beach and sea were deserted, except for the small angular outline of a fishing boat a couple of miles out to sea. She went down to the water's edge, took off her shoes and stepped gingerly into the water. Despite the heat in the air, the cold made her gasp. She shaded her eyes and looked towards the horizon. What was it she was feeling? Fear? Trepidation? Anger? Excitement even? There was a confusion in the depths of her being; a shifting, fragmenting and multiplying of emotion, and attempting to make sense of it was like looking through a kaleidoscope. *I don't know what's happening to me, Chris; I don't even know who I am anymore. Just don't leave me, whatever you do don't leave me; I need you more than ever now.*

'Mummy, I don't want you to go out, please don't go out!'

'Don't be daft Del, I can't miss Auntie Jane's leaving do.'

'I DON'T WANT YOU TO GO OUT, SOMETHING'S GOING TO GO WRONG, I CAN FEEL IT!' Adele was hysterical now; she clung to Michelle's leg, her fingers digging into the flesh of her thigh.

'For God's sake, you're being ridiculous. Kym will be here any minute to babysit, calm down.'

'Mummy please!' Adele was adapting her approach; her voice was a whining appeal now and the sound of it ignited an acidic feeling of frustration in Michelle's stomach. She peeled Adele's fingers from her leg, took hold of her wrists and squatted down to her level so she could look her straight in the eye.

'How often do I get to go out? I'll tell you, hardly fucking ever!' She could hear her voice rising, becoming brittle, but she didn't care; it felt good. 'I spend every hour of every day trying to make a good life for you, working hard, putting you first, and what thanks do I get? This kind of behaviour. Do you want to make mummy unhappy? Is that it?'

Adele shook her head; her tears had stopped and her mouth was clamped tightly shut.

'Maybe you think Mummy doesn't deserve a night out? Is that it?'

Adele stared at her but didn't reply.

Michelle shook her a little and repeated through clenched teeth; 'I said - is - that - it?'

'No, Mummy.' Adele replied in a whisper.

At that moment the doorbell rang, taking them both by surprise. Adele twisted herself out of Michelle's grip and shot upstairs. Michelle went shakily to the door and opened it.

'Hi, Chell, sorry I'm a bit late.' The pretty teenager's face transformed from smiles to concern. 'Are you ok? You look kind of pale?'

Michelle smiled weakly. 'I'm fine, it's ok, come in.'

Kym brushed past her and into the hall. 'So, where's my little princess then?'

'Oh, she's just gone upstairs for a play. I'm sure she'll be down in a bit. There's some coke in the fridge, and some chocolate on the table.'

'Thanks, Chell. I suppose it could be a late one tonight?' She smiled conspiratorially.

'Ha, yes, I suppose so. I'll just go and say goodbye.'

She turned and headed up the stairs, she felt sick. Adele's door was shut, Michelle knocked gently then went in. The girl was sitting on her bunkbed, her legs dangling off the edge. She'd constructed a wall of cuddly toys around her back and had one, her favourite, a soft-toy tiger that Chris had got her after a tour in Afghanistan, on her knee.

Michelle laid her hands on the little girl's thighs, she felt her flinch. 'Sweetheart, I'm sorry, I shouldn't have shouted.'

Adele said nothing but stared fixedly into the tiger's surprisingly sentient-looking plastic eyes.

'I'm sorry, I'm really sorry.'

'You're always sorry, but you don't change things.'

Michelle put her hands on either side of Adele's head and pulled it forward gently so she could kiss her on the forehead. 'It will this time, I promise.'

Adele pulled away and tucked her legs up onto the bed. 'You should go to the party now, Mummy.'

'Yes, ok love. I *am* sorry, I'll see you later. Kym's looking forward to hanging out with you, why don't you put a film on?'

There was no reply.

She was drinking in an unconscious but determined way; glass after glass of luke-warm Sauvignon slipping down her throat like mercury. She wanted the alcohol to obliterate her shame, but it wasn't working, and Michelle felt irrevocably sober.

Jane sashayed towards her through the throng from the bar. The social centre had been made as cheery looking as it was possible for a 1970s single-storey prefab to be. There were balloons in the corners, a banner over the bar saying 'Good Luck You Crazy Bitch!' and star confetti sprinkled over the tables. The seating had been pushed back to make room for a dance floor and the unwanted steel and plywood tables were stacked in the corner like some architect's model for a new modernist tower block. A handful of people were dancing and Michelle could feel the thump of the music in her chest.

Jane sat down heavily on the bench beside her and shouted into her ear. 'I got us another bottle.'

'Shit, I'm losing count, are you sure that's a good idea?'

'Of course it's a good idea.' said Jane, a little thickly. 'It's my leaving do, and no-one's leaving it until they're paralytic!'

'Fair enough, sounds like a plan.' Michelle managed to smile and took a gulp from her wine.

'Whassup?'

Michelle glanced up at her briefly. Jane looked beautiful, her piercing hazel eyes haloed with iridescent pale gold eye-shadow and a perfectly applied retro flick of eyeliner. 'Nothing's up.'

'Don't give me that shit. Whassup?'

'This is your night, a night for fun, I don't want to put a downer on it.'

'The only way you'll put a downer on it is if you don't tell me what the matter is.'

'I was horrible to Adele.'

Jane screwed up her face, leant towards her and cupped her ear.

'I said I was horrible to Adele,' Michelle repeated a little louder.

'Aw we're all horrible to our kids sometimes, it's good for them. It builds character.'

'I mean *really* horrible. Like mean. I feel like shit.' Michelle felt the hot stab of a tear in the corner of her eye and instantly wiped it away. She would not ruin Jane's party with her fucked-up life.

Jane looked at her with a frown, drunk but still astute. 'Ok, so why were you horrible then?'

Michelle sighed shakily and looked blankly over at the row of neatly cropped heads of some of Abe's mates as they leaned on the bar. Donna was there too, with her husband, Dave; but she seemed to be keeping her distance and didn't look over. 'I don't know, because of the house, because I don't know what the fuck I'm going to do. Because I'm unhappy.'

'So, you need to do something about that. Perhaps you should talk to someone?'

'I've done all that though, Jane, a whole year of counselling, remember? There's nothing more to say. I'm worried though, I'm worried that if something doesn't change I could...I don't know.' She was desperate not to cry, but she couldn't help it.

Jane put her arm around her and squeezed her hard. 'Hey, it's ok.'

Michelle made a wet and inarticulate sound of protest through her tears.

'I mean it. You've just...you've just lost your way.'

'Maybe I *should* go back and live with Mum and Dad? Maybe they're right, maybe that's the only way I'll cope?'

'Now listen to me Chell.' Jane disentangled her arm and turned Michelle to face her. She took a serviette from a discarded plate of half-eaten buffet food and gave it to her. Michelle obediently took it and dabbed carefully at her eyes to avoid smearing her make up. 'You know that if you go back to your mum and dad they'll do what they always do. They'll smother you and you'll feel like a child and before you know it ten years will have passed and you'll be in exactly the same place. They're good people, don't get me wrong, but you know how over-protective they are, and they can't bring themselves to let you be a grown-up.'

'I know, I know you're right.'

'Something will happen. Worst case scenario you get a council house for a bit while you get yourself on your feet. We could even ask if you could get one near me? We'll go to the Hub tomorrow and talk to Welfare. Deal?'

Michelle looked up. Her friend's face was aglow with purpose and it made her smile. 'Deal.'

'Ok, now that's enough moping and moaning for one night. Get the fuck up, stop feeling sorry for yourself and come and have a dance!'

They got up, a little unsteadily, and joined the others. Michelle was surprised and relieved to find that the music soon distracted her from her guilt. It was just a cheesy R&B track, but the bass pulsed through her, and moving in time to it seemed to make her tension melt away and she started to enjoy herself. The wine had loosened her up and she moved rhythmically, her hips swaying; she smiled at Jane and they held hands for a moment and moved together. The song was followed by a popular dance track that was constantly playing on the radio at the moment. A second wave of people, mostly husbands, got up and joined them, and their stocky, slightly awkward gyrations were somehow endearing.

Michelle closed her eyes and surrendered to the beat of the music. She experienced a moment of peace and release that she hadn't felt in a long time. She may have to move away, but these had been her people, and they had looked after her. She hadn't wasted the last eight years; she *had* built a home, a life, and she could do it again; with or without her parents.

They danced through the next few songs, until sweat was running down Michelle's forehead and stinging in her eyes.

She nudged Jane, who had started to twerk good-naturedly with Joe, one of the Sergeants in Abe's regiment. 'I'm going to pop out and cool off.' she mouthed and gestured towards the door. Jane nodded and mimed having a cigarette before following her off the dance floor.

The cool evening air kissed the sweat on Michelle's cheek and she sighed. 'That's better.'

Jane took a cigarette out of her handbag and lit it. She took a deep drag and released it, then, mimicking Michelle, also sighed and repeated 'That's better.'

Michelle laughed. 'You need to kick those cancer sticks on the head one day.'

'I know, I know.'

Michelle pushed her damp fringe off her face and looked up at the sky. The stars were out in force. The base was twenty miles from a city and bordered on one side by the sea, so there was little light pollution. One of the few perks of their location.

'You know,' said Jane, breaking Michelle's reverie, 'I've spent most of my life trying my best but feeling like I'm constantly failing, and I'm sick and tired of it.'

'I know what you mean.'

'Now that Abe's gone, I don't know, I just feel angry for feeling that way. It seems like such a waste, because he had no choice in whether or not he could stay here with us. He's gone, but I'm still here; and I feel...' Jane broke off and looked through the dark towards where the sea was, and the light from the social centre windows reflected in her eyes. '...I feel like it's up to me now, to be brave, to stop feeling like that. Because of Beth, I suppose, because she needs me, and I'd rather die than have her grow up feeling like that; to be full of fear and insecurity.'

Michelle wrapped her arms around herself, she'd started to feel cold. 'When Adele was born, do you remember? She came so quick that we didn't have time to get to the hospital and I had her in the bathroom.'

'I remember.' Jane smiled. 'You screamed the fucking street down!'

'When she came out, I sat on the loo and they put her on my belly and she looked up at me and I remember feeling the love and thinking it was like a giant flower, blooming out of me. I felt like I could do anything then, it was amazing, but now...'

Jane put her hand on her arm and squeezed it. 'It *is* amazing, and women do it every second of every day. And here we are, makers of life, dancing with soldiers, the makers of death. It's a bit ironic, don't you think?'

Michelle looked at her, but she couldn't read her friend's expression in the gloom. 'I don't know, I don't think about things like you do.'

Jane snorted. 'Are you serious? Did you hear yourself just then talking about giving birth?'

'That's not the same.'

'Isn't it?'

They stood together in silence for a bit, then Jane stubbed out her cigarette. 'That's weird.'

'What is?'

'The music' stopped.'

They both looked towards the social centre door and strained their ears. Michelle felt a tickle of anxiety in the pit of her stomach. 'You're right.'

They went back inside. As soon as they were through the door, their friend, Mandy, rushed up to them, her face white. 'There's been an attack.'

'What?' Jane pushed past her towards the bar, where the staff were trying to get the big flat-screen TV turned on. 'What kind of attack?'

'A terrorist attack, in Paris. It was in a theatre, they reckon nearly a hundred people are dead. They're trying to get a news channel on now.'

They joined the silent throng that was gathering around the dark TV screen. The atmosphere in the room had become thick with tension. There was a movement to their right and then Donna appeared, her heavily made-up face triumphant.

'And you said that our boys were wasting their time,' she spat in Jane's face, 'You dared to say that we're making things worse - '

'Come on, Donna.' Dave had suddenly appeared by her side, his burly six-foot two frame obliterating the view of the bar. 'This isn't the time or the place, it's Jane's leaving do, for fuck's sake, just let it go. It's not worth it.'

The TV suddenly burst into life with the scene of a Paris street, strung with police-tape and flooded with the flashing lights of emergency vehicles. Donna pushed her husband behind her with surprising ease considering his bulk. ' - Look at it, go on, look at what's happening. Our boys are all there is between us and them. You talked about "grief and chaos", well suck it up, you stupid cow, there it is, right there on that screen.'

Michelle woke up and for a moment, couldn't think where she was. After a while she realised she was in Adele's bunkbed and she lay there for a while, perfectly still, enjoying the warmth and delicate lines of her daughter's little body curled up in front of her. The fug of sleep and alcohol slowly drained away, leaving memories of the evening exposed, layer by layer, and reigniting her feelings of shame. She squirmed slightly and made a small impatient noise, which made Adele stir.

'Mum?' she said sleepily through the dark.

'Hi, sweetheart. I hope you don't mind, I thought I'd come and get in with you when I got back.'

Adele sighed contentedly. 'No, I don't mind. Is it morning?'

'I'm not sure.' She twisted round and looked towards the window. A sliver of peachy-grey light was showing around the edges of the blind. 'Not quite yet, but soon, I think.' Michelle put her arm around her daughter and pulled her in tighter against her chest. 'You were right.'

'About what mummy?'

'That something bad was going to happen.'

Adele's body tensed. 'Is it Granny or Grandad?'

'No, No nothing like that.' Michelle stroked her daughter's hair, which was slightly damp with the heat of sleep. 'There was an attack, in Paris. Some bad people put a bomb in a theatre.'

'Bad people like the kind of bad people Daddy was fighting?'

'Yes, just like them.'

'Did people die?'

'Yes, a lot of people I'm afraid.'

Adele was silent for a moment, Michelle could almost hear her young brain whirring with questions. When she finally spoke the girl's voice was calm and thoughtful. 'Why *are* people mean to each other?'

'I don't know sweetheart, I suppose most people are good, but some just turn out bad. Maybe they don't start that way; maybe they start out good, but things go wrong. Things that twist them inside, that make them sad, or make them hate people.'

'Like that cat,' said Adele firmly.

'Which cat?'

'The one we got from the rescue centre. They said it had been treated bad by people. It was so pretty, it had white socks, but it kept scratching me so we had to take it back.'

'Yes, just like that I suppose.'

'I really wanted that cat,' said Adele sadly.

She must have fallen back to sleep because when she was next aware, the light coming in from around the blind had brightened, and Adele had got out of bed and was playing happily on the floor of her room.

When she heard Michelle stir, Adele looked up and smiled. 'Look, Mummy, I've made a special home for lost cats.'

Michelle leaned over the rail of the bunkbed and studied the scene below her blearily. 'Oh yes, sweetheart, that's lovely.'

'This bit's the hospital,' said Adele, gesturing at a shoe box that had been turned on its side and stuffed with a towel; 'and this bit is the special place where they go to wait for new owners. People come to see them and choose them.' She picked up a Barbie doll and paraded it stiffly past a line of stuffed animals.

'Shit!' Michelle's flesh suddenly chilled.

'Mummy, you swore!'

'Sorry - what's the time? You'll be late for school!'

'It's Saturday, silly!'

Michelle sank back down onto the bed. 'Of course it is, stupid Mummy. You must be starving, I'll get up now and make us some breakfast.'

'It's ok, I went down and got a packet of crisps.'

'Oh,' said Michelle drily. 'That's ok then.'

She turned onto her side and rallied herself for more movement, knowing that it was going to hurt. She sat up and swung her legs onto the rungs of the bunkbed ladder and gasped as her head started to throb. Her mouth felt dry and gritty and she was desperate to get a big glass of water - or even better - of coke, if Kym hadn't drunk it all when she was babysitting.

She made her way gingerly down the stairs, holding tightly onto the banister. As her foot reached the last step the doorbell rang. She made her way over to the door, squinting her eyes against the bright light coming through the frosted glass pane. She opened the door and sighed with relief when she saw it was Jane.

'Thank God it's you. I must look a mess.'

'You look like I feel, but at least I bothered to put clean clothes on this morning and have a wash!'

'Ok, little miss perfect, don't rub it in. I fell asleep in Adele's bed.'

'So I see.'

Michelle smiled ruefully and stepped aside to let Jane come in. 'I'll put the kettle on. I need to start rehydrating; my mouth feels like it's full of sand.'

Jane went past her into the kitchen. 'The joys of a hangover. I'd like to say it was worth it, but that terrorist attack in Paris…it's all that's on the news today; it's so horrible.'

Michelle remembered her conversation with Adele when she'd got in. The little girl's pure incomprehension and her own inability to relieve it made her feel sad and frustrated. She gulped down a glass of water then filled the kettle at the sink and got a couple of cups off the draining board. 'Are you ok? Donna was pretty cruel.'

Jane sighed and sat down at the table. 'Well, it wasn't nice, but it's yet another nail in the coffin of *here*. I feel more convinced than ever that I need to go.'

'I'm sure she didn't mean it, not really.' Michelle squeezed each tea-bag against the side of the cup, watching the dark-gold essence swirl out into the boiling water.

'She did, she meant every word. But I don't care what she says. I know what I believe.'

'I just can't understand it. Why people do these kinds of things to each other.'

'Donna thinks it's just because they're bad people. But she doesn't understand where their hate comes from. We're in this fucking mess because of what *we've* done. What our countries have done. We've made such a mess of things.'

'But there's no excuse for this, not whatever way you look at it. They killed innocent people last night; people with husbands and wives and kids.'

Jane looked over at her with what looked like a mixture of sadness and exhaustion. 'What, and our lot haven't killed innocent people too?'

Michelle didn't answer, she didn't know what to say.

'I just can't stand the hypocrisy, that's all. They see what they want to see.'

'Maybe they think the same about you,' replied Michelle, feeling a pang of annoyance, 'maybe they think you just see what you want to see?'

Jane shrugged. 'Maybe.' She took a big sip of her tea and looked miserably out of the window.

Michelle suddenly felt sorry for her. 'I just don't know, Jane, I try to think about it, even just our tiny bit of it, and I feel lost. Never mind the rest of the world, I'm just trying to keep going, day by day; to not make too much of a mess of everything. I don't even know where I'm going to be living in a few months' time!'

'I know, I'm sorry.' Jane reached forward and put her hand over Michelle's and gave it a squeeze. 'I'm full of shit. Just ignore me. Sometimes I think I worry about the world because that's easier than worrying about myself.'

'What am I going to do though? Where are we going to go? I've not said anything to 'Del yet. I don't know *what* to say. I haven't even told her you and Beth are going away.'

'Don't say anything yet, there's no point, not until you know what the options are. She'll only worry. Worst case scenario you might be able to come with me to Manchester, or get somewhere near your mum and dad if that felt better?'

'No way! Like you said before, they'd drive me insane in no time.'

'Are we going to Manchester, Mummy? Is it a holiday?' Adele had appeared in the doorway, her hair still matted with sleep. 'What *is* Manchester?'

'Oh, hi, sweetheart. It's a city, up north where Aunty Jane comes from. We, err, we're just talking about it.'

'Maybe we'll go there in the summer holidays,' said Jane, brightly. But in the meantime, do you fancy coming swimming with me and Beth today?'

The little girl's face lit up. 'Yes please, and can we have a burger on the way home?'

'Yeh, why not!'

Michelle groaned and put her head in her hands. 'Oh Jane, not swimming, all those bright lights and screaming kids, I can't think of anything worse!'

'Don't be such a wuss, it'll do you good. Now go and get in that shower; you don't want to pollute the water!'

As Michelle had predicted, the swimming pool *was* torture. She still had a banging headache, and the echoing screams and splashes of a hundred kids ricocheted painfully inside her skull. Leaving the girls splashing happily with Jane (who wasn't much of a swimmer) in the kids' pool, she escaped to the full-size pool and started doing some lengths. Slowly, the gentle rhythm of her confident breast strokes started to make her feel better. She hadn't been for a swim in months, and it was good to sense her muscles falling into their well-remembered movements. She counted off twenty lengths then moved into a speedy crawl. She had represented her school at county competitions when she was a teenager, but like so many dreams and ambitions that she had had then, the swimming had slowly fizzled out, replaced by boy-obsessions and the stress of exams.

Once she had counted fifty lengths she stopped to catch her breath. Adele saw her and scrambled out of the kids' pool and came over.

'I'm going to do jumps, Mummy, and you have to catch me.'

'Ok, but let me just get out of the lanes.' Michelle ducked under the floats and swam out into the free area of the larger pool. She stayed underwater until she could see Adele's feet, which were dancing and fracturing the light that filtered through the water. Without warning she burst up through the surface and grabbed the little girl's ankles. Adele screamed with pleasure and launched herself into the pool. Michelle caught her and fell back with a splash. The two of them emerged seconds later laughing and spluttering.

'Mummy, you scared me! That was so funny, you were like a shark!'

'I *am* a shark! And I'm going to *eat you up!*' She burrowed her face into Adele's neck and gnashed her teeth. Adele squealed. Michelle realised that tears had come into her eyes and was glad that the water was hiding them. It just felt so good, she realised, to have some genuine, loving fun with her daughter. It had been so long and the sensation was bitter-sweet because it was also tinged with guilt. *I'm sorry, Chris, I'm sorry that I've let it come to this. Please don't be angry with me.*

'What's the matter, Mummy?'

'Nothing sweets, now you'd better get swimming coz there's a really hungry shark about and it's coming your way!'

When they came out of the swimming baths they were confronted by a sheet of steely rain. The sky was gloomy and curdled with cloud; giving it the feeling of having lowered itself over their heads. The burger restaurant was just on the other side of the leisure centre car park so they made a bolt for it through the rain, shrieking as the deluge drove itself into their faces and down the back of their jackets.

When they were just twenty or so yards from the restaurant, a blinding seam of lightning ripped through the sky followed by a deafening crack. With a synchronised scream of surprise, they all bundled into the restaurant, laughing and wiping the rain off their faces. They settled in a bench seat near the window and watched, smugly, as those outside ran helter-skelter to their cars. It was good to see Jane smiling, thought Michelle, the first time she'd seen a genuine one in weeks.

'Phew, that was close!' Jane picked up a discarded paper napkin and dabbed at her forehead.

'Here comes another one!' said Michelle with a wince as a flash lit up the inside of the restaurant with cold white light. The resulting crash of thunder set off a ripple of gasps and muffled screams. The girls grabbed hold of each other with feverish excitement.

'Right, I don't know about you but storm or no storm, I'm starving. What do you want, you two?'

'A Cheeseburger Happy Meal please, Aunty Jane' said Adele, breathlessly. 'With carrot sticks and a chocolate milkshake.

'Me too.' Chimed in Beth. 'But can I have it with fries and a coke?'

'Ok, coming up. 'Chell, do you know what you want?'

Michelle dragged her glance away from the glowering sky. 'Oh, erm, just a beef burger with a salad and a coffee.'

'Come on, you've got to have fries. Have a poncey salad with your dinner later if you must!'

Michelle laughed and handed Jane a ten-pound note. 'Ok, bossy-boots. I'll have fries please.' She watched Jane head off to the counter to order and distractedly got her phone out of her bag. When she swiped the screen, she was surprised to see that she had two missed calls from a strange looking number she didn't recognise. She was still puzzling over it when Jane returned with a laden tray in each hand.

'What's up?'

'Dunno, a weird mobile number's been calling me while we were swimming.'

Jane put the girl's garish Happy Meal boxes in front of them and then shuffled up to sit next to Michelle. 'Let me see.'

Michelle handed her the phone. 'What do you think it is? Just a scam?'

'Nah, that's a call from France.'

Michelle frowned with incomprehension. 'France? How do you know?'

'Abe went over there for a course once. When he called me from his hotel the number looked like that - starting with a 33.'

'But I don't know anyone in France!'

'I thought your Mum had family there?'

'Not anyone she knows, not anymore. Granny grew up there, but she moved to England in the fifties.'

'And there's no-one else there?'

'I don't think so. Mum's never said anything.'

'Have they left a message?'

'I dunno.' Michelle checked her text history and felt her stomach tighten when she saw there was an alert, saying someone had left a voicemail.

'Aren't you going to listen to it then?'

'Yep, in a mo, I don't know, I just feel a bit funny. It's like in films, when someone knows there might be something really frightening behind a door but they have to open it anyway.'

'Whassup, Mummy?' said Adele through a mouth full of burger. 'Where's there a scary door?'

'There isn't one, I'm only joking. Nothing for you to worry about, love; just a funny phone call.'

'So, come on,' said Jane impatiently. 'Listen to the message.'

Beth looked out of the window with a disappointed frown. 'I think the storm's stopped.'

'The message!' Jane prompted again.

'Ok, ok!' Michelle dialled her voicemail.

It was hot and stuffy in Jane's battered old Polo, and the rain lashed and streamed down the windows, making the car feel like a submarine in stormy waters. Michelle's thoughts were adrenalised and tumultuous. She gripped hard onto her knees and took some deep breaths.

Jane was still shaking her head as she drove. 'It's unbelievable, it's just fucking unbelievable!'

'Mum, you're swearing!' said Beth with gleeful disapproval.

'Sorry, love, but sometimes you just *have* to swear.'

'So, does that mean I can say bollocks now then, Mum?'
Adele giggled.

'No, it DOES NOT mean you can say bollocks!'

They all laughed, the tension in the car reduced, and
Michelle let out a long trembling breath. 'I can't get my
head round it, I really can't. Why would she leave her
house to me?'

'Well, she didn't have kids of her own, and maybe she
felt bad, about losing touch with your side of the family?
She might even have known about Chris. Maybe she
thought you just needed it more than anyone else?'

'Still, it's crazy. I wonder what Mum and Dad will say;
and Danny, he's bound to be pissed off about it.'

The girls, who had been chatting away between
themselves for most of the journey suddenly became quiet.

'Mummy,' came Adele's voice tentatively from the back
seats, 'does that mean we're moving to France?'

'Of course not!' said Michelle, more explosively than
she'd meant to. 'We don't know France, we don't speak
French. It's a crazy idea, but at least we could sell the
house.'

'Don't hold up too much hope of that.' said Jane under
her breath, obviously not wanting the girls to hear.

'Why?'

'It's not like here. It's probably not worth more than
around a hundred grand. It's a working-class area, they're
land rich but revenue poor. Property just doesn't have the
same status over there and it can be hard to sell.'

'How the hell do you know all this stuff?'

'We spent a summer in the Haute-Vienne, with Abe's
lot, don't you remember? A few years ago.'

Michelle nodded and her mind whirred back to the figure Jane had mentioned. 'Still, a hundred grand,' Michelle whispered hoarsely. 'It's more money than I've ever seen and it could mean the deposit on a house.'

'True.' Jane conceded. 'It could really help you move on. I just don't want you expecting a life changing amount of money from it.'

'Believe me, the chance to buy my own house *is* life changing.'

Jane indicated and came off the main road and took the turning to the barracks. Adele's delicate face appeared between the front seats, her big grey eyes wide and curious. 'What was she again? Granny's sister?'

'Not your granny's sister, *my* granny's sister. So, she would be your great, great aunt.'

'Was she nice?'

'I don't know, I never met her.'

'Did Granny meet her?'

Michelle paused, trying to remember. 'I think so, I'm not sure, we'll have to ask her. I think your great granny and her had a row or something. It's all a bit of a mystery.'

'What was her name?'

'Leroy.'

'But that's a man's name.'

Michelle laughed. 'No, that was her second name, I don't know what her first name was yet. They said they'll email me all the details.'

'If she'd been married she would have been Madame Leroy.' Jane explained. 'If she wasn't she would have been Mademoiselle Leroy.'

Adele sat back and started chatting with Beth again, seemingly satisfied.

They were at the main gate to the barracks now. Jane wound down her window and flashed her ID card; a soldier leaned in and smiled at the girls in the back. 'Hi there you two, been behaving today?'

'Yes Dougie.' The girls chorused.

'Don't forget Stacey's party on Saturday, will you?' He nodded at Michelle and Jane and waved them in. The barrier lifted. Michelle watched him as he headed back to the guard-house. Even after all these years she still couldn't get her head around seeing soldiers walking around with guns. It always made her feel a bit funny, vulnerable somehow, which always struck her as ironic.

'It's weird, but I feel kind of sad about it.'

Jane looked across at her then back at the road. 'About what?'

'That she's thought of me, looked out for me like this, and I've never met her. And there'll be this whole house, full of her stuff, and I'll have to decide what to do with it. It's like there's all her life, little signs and objects that tell the story of who she was, and I'm the person who'll be the guardian of that now. It feels...I don't know...like a big responsibility. She was still alive and living in it a couple of weeks ago.'

Jane nodded. 'It is. I see what you mean.' She pulled up outside Michelle's house and put her hand out of the window. 'Wehey, the rain's stopped!'

The curtains in her bedroom were half drawn, and the light in the room was yellow from a nearby street lamp. Michelle shifted onto her back and watched the filigree silhouette of the branches of the tree outside her window move across the ceiling. She tried to collect her thoughts;

she could literally feel the neural firings in her brain, forged by the unexpected news of being left her great aunt's house in France. It was hard to comprehend. Why had this old lady, someone she had never met, and knew virtually nothing about, thought of her in her will, and what should she do about it?

As promised, there had been an email from her aunt's solicitors waiting in her inbox when she'd gone online to check later that evening. It included pictures of the house; one showed a row of three, old looking cottages, white rendered with deep set windows and wooden shutters. Her aunt's house was the one in the middle. It had a small front garden, and at the back, a larger garden with a covered veranda that ended at fields full of wildflowers. There were just two pictures of the interior; a cosy but cluttered kitchen with dark-wood units and a plethora of mysterious cooking implements, and an airy bedroom almost entirely filled with a huge double bed covered with a patchwork quilt. It was like something out of a dream; so different in feel and style to any kind of house she had seen before. She tried to imagine herself and Adele there but found it almost impossible.

She searched her memory for anyone talking about her mysterious great aunt but could find no more than vague recollections of her being mentioned in passing. These generally fizzled out, either because they were conjecture, or because her grandmother would invariably change the subject away from any discussion of her sister.

She turned onto her side, drew the duvet up under her neck and attempted to empty her mind. The feverishness of her thoughts abated a bit, but then the name of the village in which the house was situated popped into her head. *Argemourt.* It was a romantic sounding name, and somehow vaguely familiar. Again, she struggled to place it in her memories, but failed. She sighed in exasperation and turned again, trying to get comfortable. *What should I do, Chris? What would you have suggested we do if you were still alive? Would she have left me the house if you hadn't died? Will I ever know?*

She was woken abruptly by the sound of the doorbell. She reached groggily for her phone on the bedside table and looked at the time; 9 am. Who on earth would be calling round this early on a Sunday? She wasn't sure what time she had finally managed to go to sleep; but the grittiness in her eyes and the heaviness in her body told her that it must have been late.

'I'm coming!' she shouted; but as she struggled out of bed and reached for her dressing gown she heard Adele thunder down the stairs.

'Granny!'

Hearing the word made Michelle freeze. Granny? Not Lou, surely. Chris' parents weren't particularly warm people or into young kids; it had been one of the great sadnesses of his life and the main reason he had got on so well with her parents, who doted on Adele. Michelle and Chris had called Lou and Dennis's annual trips to their house 'state visits', and the need to keep them fed and entertained had always been stressful.

'Mum?' she called rather shrilly down the stairs. 'Is that you?'

'Hello, love!'

Frowning, Michelle descended the staircase; at the bottom she could see her mother, arms around Adele, who held tightly onto her ample waist and beamed.

'Mum, what are you doing here?'

Her mum looked at her, seemingly perplexed. 'What do you mean what am I doing here? Coming to visit my two favourite girls of course.'

'But it's only nine!'

'Well that's old age for you, I'm awake before six every morning, you know that!'

Michelle reached the bottom of the stairs but kept holding tightly onto the bannister. 'But why didn't you call? Why didn't you let me know?'

'Because I wanted it to be a surprise.'

'But I haven't got anything in and the spare room's a mess.'

'That doesn't matter, we've got all day, we can get it sorted in no time.'

'How long are you thinking of staying?'

'Granny says she can stay as long as we like!' replied Adele happily. Michelle felt a tightening in her chest.

'Aren't you going to give me a hug?' said her mother admonishingly.

'Yes, of course.' Michelle went over and hugged her.

'Have you lost weight?' Her mum disengaged from their embrace and held Michelle at arm's length to inspect her.

'Just a bit.'

'It's a good job I've come, you obviously need some looking after.'

'Don't be ridiculous, Mum. We're perfectly able to look after ourselves.'

'Granny, Granny can you cook your shepherd's pie tonight? Please Granny! Yours is the bestest!'

Traitor thought Michelle as she watched Adele jumping up and down in the hallway. She loved her granny, and why wouldn't she? She was a great cook, she made cakes, she spoilt her only granddaughter. Nothing unusual about that. But Adele didn't know the *real* Granny Anne. There was more to her than the cuddly grandparent; as a mother her indulgence and affection was often equally mixed with a streak of manipulative passive-aggression that had set mother and daughter in a constant but suppressed state of conflict.

'So, come on, how about a cup of tea? I drove here without stopping and I'm parched.'

Anne stopped, panting, at the top of the sand-dune. Michelle stopped too and looked back. Her mother was getting rounder every time she saw her, and any amount of physical activity seemed to render her red-faced and gasping for breath.

'Are you getting any exercise back home, Mum?'

Anne looked back at her crossly. 'I get quite enough thank you very much. I've even started going to a local walking group. It's the bloody steroids that make me put the weight on. I've told you that before.'

Michelle turned away and sighed. Her mum had used this excuse before, but Michelle knew it was only half true. Even Anne's doctor had said as much; and he'd refuted her excuse that exercise made her breathless - reminding her that breathlessness wasn't a medical condition in her case, just a lack of fitness. There was no point trying to provoke a rational discussion with her mum about this though. She was pathologically defensive, and if you ever pushed a point that Anne was sensitive about, she would soon end up in tears.

Adele ran down the slope of the dune with a whoop. Early cloud had cleared to leave blue skies with just a few high watercolour-thin wisps of white cloud. Michelle closed her eyes for a second and enjoyed the feeling of the warm sun on her face. *I know, Chris, I know I've got to keep calm with Mum and not get provoked. I'll try my best, I promise, but it's so hard.*

'Come and have a paddle, Granny!' Adele reached out for Anne's hand and virtually pulled her down the last few feet of the sand dune.

'In a minute, poppet, just let Granny Anne get her breath back!'

Adele kicked off her sandals and ran towards the water's edge with her bucket and net. 'I'm going to look for shrimp, Granny, come and see me in a minute.'

'I will, I promise.' Anne sat down on a large granite rock at the base of the dune with a grunt. Michelle settled at its base, cross-legged on the sun-heated sand. She heard her mother shift behind her.

'We've got to talk about what you're going to do.'

'What do you mean?'

'For goodness sake, Michelle, don't be so silly, you know perfectly well what I mean; about where you're going to live. What does Adele think? I bet she'd love it if you came to live near us.'

Michelle looked out to sea and took a deep, steadying breath before replying. She could predict her mother's disapproval at what she was going to say next. 'I haven't told her yet.'

'Haven't told her! Why on earth not?'

'There's no point yet, Mum, we've got a couple of months left.'

'That'll go in no time, you know it will.'

'I think it's better I tell her when I have something concrete to say about where we're going to go. You know what kids are like; they want certainty, they don't like being left hanging; and with Jane and Beth moving too -'

'It's got nothing to do with Jane and Beth; you always knew you were in the same place on borrowed time. Chris or Abe could be moved at the drop of a hat.'

'I know,' Michelle was struggling to keep her voice level. It was uncanny how her mum could find and push all her buttons. 'But I just don't want Adele to handle too much all at once. And anyway, Jane suggested I could try and get somewhere near her in Manchester.'

'Manchester?!' Anne spat out the word with derision, as if Jane had suggested they all move to Lebanon or the Congo.

Michelle got up jerkily, accidentally kicking sand over her mum's feet. 'I'm going for a paddle.' She headed down towards Adele, who was happily kicking her feet through the shallow waves. Sparkling sweeps of water arced into the air creating momentary rainbows. Despite the beauty around her, he heart was beating fast. She could barely last an hour with her mum, how the hell was she going to do several days?

The delicious smell of her mother's shepherd's pie filled the kitchen like a reproach. Michelle had tried to resist dipping in to the remains of yesterday's bottle of wine, not wanting to give her mum yet another reason to claim she wasn't coping; but the effect of the first glass was undeniably calming.

She was about to put the bottle back in the fridge, then thought it was worth asking if her mother wanted one too, to dilute the focus on her own drinking. 'Would you like a glass, Mum?'

Anne eyed her beadily. 'No thank you. Me and your dad only drink on Saturdays now.'

'Oh come on, Mum, one glass. You're on holiday after all.'

Her mum's face softened. 'Ok, just one glass. And you should watch what you have too, it's back to school and work tomorrow.'

'For God's sake, Mum, I'm twenty-nine, not nineteen!'

'I'm just saying. When I came around this morning you were still in bed. It was nine o'clock and Adele was up on her own.'

'It's Sunday! I'd had a shit night's sleep and I was knackered. Adele's independent, you know that. She likes having a bit of time to herself, she gets a snack and she watches a bit of telly and then she wakes me up.'

'She's only seven. You should have been up and made her breakfast.'

'Mum,' Michelle struggled to stay calm, 'I have to do all this on my own, I have done for the last two years; I even had to most of the time when Chris was alive. This is how we do it, it works for us, I get a lie-in every now and then and Adele gets the living room to herself. I really don't need you of all people judging me.'

'Humph.' Her mum looked away but seemed chastened.

They sipped at their drinks in frosty silence for a moment. Michelle studied her mum. It provoked mixed emotions. With an uncomfortable pang of sadness, Michelle realised that her mother was becoming anonymous. Her curvy figure was losing its shape, her thick wavy hair had been styled into a short cut, blow-dried high on the top of the head and highlighted with blond streaks in a way that had something ubiquitously middle-aged about it. Her clothes were like the ones you'd see in lady's clothes-shop windows in well-to-do villages. Maybe that was what she was trying to be, well-to-do; or at least to be perceived to be well-to-do; whatever that meant. Her relationship with her mum had never been easy, but she still missed the energetic, socially busy woman Anne had once been. Since retirement, much of that energy had gone, as if she had lost her purpose.

Eventually her mum shifted in her chair and put down her glass. 'I still don't understand why you wouldn't let us go into the social club after the walk. It would have been nice to see a few people and say hello. I haven't been down here in ages.'

'I told you, it just feels a bit weird. After being there at Jane's leaving do when the terrorist attack happened in Paris.'

'I don't see why. Things like that happen a lot; and this is an army barracks. If anyone knows about what's really going on in the world it's the army.'

'Some people would argue that the army is the least qualified to understand what's really going on in the world.'

Her mother looked at her with what seemed like genuine astonishment. 'Why on earth would you say something like that? You of all people, whose husband died trying to protect us from *all that*?'

Michelle shifted uncomfortably in her chair. She knew she should change the subject but she didn't seem able to stop. 'I've just been thinking that there's more than one way to see things.'

'And how's that exactly? It seems pretty clear to me. There are good people and bad people in the world; and if the good people do nothing the bad people win.'

'I used to think it was that simple, but I'm not so sure any more.' She knew she was straying into dangerous territory but she was feeling reckless. She took a big gulp of her wine. 'Have you thought that maybe Chris died in vain? That he shouldn't have even been there in Afghanistan? He almost said as much himself once.'

Her mother pushed her glass of wine away and looked at Michelle in horror. 'How can you say that? How can you say that about your own husband?'

'Because I loved him!' Michelle was aware of her voice rising. 'Because I miss him, every minute of every day.'

Anne's mouth opened and closed but she remained silent at first. Eventually, she said coldly, 'I don't understand you sometimes, I really don't. You've never been opinionated; and I was glad about that. You didn't even vote in the Referendum! Being opinionated only gets you into trouble and brings nothing but misery. I really don't understand where this is coming from.'

Mercifully, at this moment Adele bounced in. 'How long till tea, Granny? I'm starving!'

'Not long now, poppet. I'll just put the cabbage on.' Anne got up, went to the chopping board and started to slice through the pile of cabbage. Her back radiated tension and her shoulders were high. With continuing recklessness Michelle went to the fridge and refilled her glass of wine. She didn't even bother asking her mother if she wanted another.

Adele sat at the table, seemingly oblivious to the residues of adult conflict in the air and started to doodle absent-mindedly on a magazine. 'Mum.'

Michelle took her fresh glass of wine and sat back down at the table opposite her daughter. 'Yes, love.'

'After Tracy Beaker finished there was something on the news about that bomb in Paris. They said Paris was in France. Isn't that where the house is?' She looked up at Michelle anxiously. 'Paris isn't near the house is it?'

Michelle's mind raced, this wasn't how she had wanted her mother to find out about her Great Aunt's legacy.

Anne turned around sharply; the knife she had been using to chop the cabbage was still in her hand and pointing towards them. 'What house in France?'

Adele started to explain before Michelle could reply. 'The one my great, great, aunt left Mummy. It looks funny, it's all white and it has shutters in the window and a big big garden that goes into a field.'

Michelle felt the colour drain from her cheeks. 'I was going to tell you, Mum, I only found out yesterday?'

'Yesterday?' Anne parroted, her voice barely above a whisper.

'We were in town, getting a burger, and I got a call. Your Aunt Leroy, she's left me her house in France.'

Her mother sat down heavily between them and placed the knife on the table. 'I don't understand, I didn't even know she'd died.'

Michelle wasn't entirely sure why she felt so stressed and guilty all of a sudden. It wasn't as if she'd tricked or cajoled her great aunt into leaving her anything. 'She only died a week ago. She was in her eighties, so the funeral happened quickly. And she didn't have any other family...so...'

'She had me! And what about Danny? Why you and not Danny? He's the oldest. What's he going to say when he finds out?'

'Well it's not really got anything to do with him, has it?' Michelle knew she was starting to get squeaky and defensive. 'He's already got a house and him and Cathy both earn good money. Maybe she thought he didn't need it as much.'

'Aunty Jane says it's probably worth *one hundred grand.*' Proclaimed Adele importantly. 'She said that wasn't very much but Mum and me think it sounds like lots and lots.'

Anne looked at her Granddaughter severely but didn't reply. 'I really just can't believe it. I know Mum and her didn't really see much of each other; I've never understood why, which makes it even crazier. Why you? And why didn't they come to me first - I was her next of kin now Mum's dead after all?'

Why not me? thought Michelle, angrily. *Just for once, why can't it be me?* 'I'm thinking of going to see it.' The words sprang out of her as if they had been waiting, tensed, for her to be ready to hear them. She was not conscious of ever having even thought of it before, but suddenly it made sense.

'What?'

She almost felt sorry for her mum, she was clearly finding it hard to cope with all the revelations.

Adele jumped up in her chair excitedly. 'Yay, Mum! Can we go next week? Can we? Can we?'

'This is ridiculous!' Anne had got up and pushed back her chair violently; causing a screech of wood against tile that made them all jump. 'You've never been anywhere on your own, Michelle! *And* you don't speak French.'

'I did French GCSE!'

Her mum let out a contemptuous snort and shook her head. 'You won't cope! I just don't understand what's come over you! You need to come home, you need to let me and your dad look after you. That's our job.'

'No, it's not.' Michelle looked up at her mother, she felt strangely calm. 'It's *my* job. It used to be Chris's too; but now it's just down to me and I'm going to France. Great Aunt Leroy left it to me; and I need to go and see it.'

'Great Aunt Michèle.' Said her mum, breathlessly.

Michelle's heart skipped. 'What did you say?'

'Her first name was Michèle'

Michelle kept her eyes on the washing up in the bowl as her mum loaded the last of her bags into the car. They had managed one more day and night together, mostly for Adele's sake, because for Anne to have stayed for just one night would have provoked too many questions. As it was, she knew Adele was disappointed but the promise of the trip to France seemed to have distracted and consoled her. It was inexplicable how much the little girl seemed to be excited at the prospect of the house in France. Adele was so unlike herself, and so much more like Chris. She was a free spirit, nothing seemed to faze her. Despite a few emotional breakdowns in the first few months after Chris died, she had carried her grief with a calm stoicism that almost made Michelle feel ashamed of her own messy feelings.

And it wasn't that she had achieved this by wiping her dad out of her life; quite the opposite. Adele had pictures of Chris all over her room and talked about him pretty much every day. The school had been a great help too. There were other kids in the same boat as Adele and they had people there who were trained to give emotional help to the children of army parents. Thank God for that, Michelle thought, for about the millionth time.

She heard her mum coming back into the house and wiped her hands on a tea-towel.

'Right, that's it, I'm off.'

'I told you I'd bring the bags down.'

'I'm perfectly capable of carrying my own bags.'

'Ok, Mum, look, I'm sorry.'

Anne looked at her, her lips closed tight. Her face was flushed but impassive.

'I'm sorry about how it worked out, it was really nice of you to come down.' Michelle faltered. She thought of Chris, and how he had always said how much nicer and more loving Anne was than his own mother, and decided to make a last effort at connecting. 'Look, Mum.' She took hold of Anne's limp hand and squeezed it. 'I do love you, I really do, I don't mean to make you angry, but you really need to start trusting me. You really need to let me be a grown up and make my own decisions. It's not that I don't care, or want you to be worrying, but you're *choosing* to feel like that. Do you understand what I'm saying?' She studied her mum's face intently; despite the anger and frustration she had felt with her over the last two days, she felt the sting of tears in her eyes.

Anne withdrew her hand. 'I never had to worry about Danny, things always work out for him, and now he's got a nice house and security and a happy marriage. But you, I don't know what it is, but it's always been difficult.'

Michelle felt like she'd been slapped. At that moment Adele skipped into the room and Anne's face relaxed into a broad smile as if she'd taken off a mask.

'Ah, there's my little poppet! Now give Granny-Anne a big hug and I'll see you very soon. Maybe Mum will let you come up and stay with us for a bit in the summer holidays, would you like that?'

'Yes please, Granny!' Adele gave her a tight hug then came out of it and took hold of her hands and swung them. 'And you must come and have a holiday in France too! Aunty Jane said it's more sunny there and more hotter.'

'Yes, well, we'll see. Goodbye then.' She went up to Michelle and gave her a dry peck on the cheek. Michelle didn't move. She felt like screaming; like picking up all the crockery on the draining board and flinging it, piece by piece onto the opposite wall, but she didn't.

Adele followed her granny outside and waved as the car pulled away from the pavement. Michelle watched the car go, but her mother didn't turn or acknowledge her.

'That's so weird that she was called Michelle too!' Jane swirled the wine in her glass thoughtfully and squinted against the sun.

'It's Michèle, not Michelle, you say it slightly differently and there's only one "l" in it.'

'Michèle...*Michèle*.' Jane played around with the name, trying out different accents and emphasis. 'But still, it's weird.'

'I know. Mum remembers my nan suggesting it as a name when I was born, but she didn't tell her till a few years later that it was her sister's name too.'

'But I thought they didn't get on, your nan and your great aunt?'

'No-one really talks about it but I think they got...estranged somehow. But maybe there was still love there - or regret or something. Otherwise why would she suggest naming me after her?'

'True.' Jane sighed, closed her eyes and leaned her head against the back of the sun lounger.

'How are you doing at the moment?'

Jane smiled sadly. 'I feel numb.'

'Yes, I remember that feeling; still am like that a lot of the time. I think it's just a way to cope.'

'I'm worried that I won't make it to Manchester. That I might just crack up and they'll put me away or something.' She sounded like she was only half joking.

Michelle reached over and squeezed her hand briefly. 'That's not going to happen. You're going to make it, because you have to, and you love Beth so much it'll give you the strength to do it.'

'I know, you're right. And as you've got to leave anyway, I've got absolutely nothing to keep me here.'

'No, I suppose neither of us have any more.'

They were silent for a moment and Jane lit a cigarette.

Michelle took a deep breath before speaking. 'I'm thinking of going to see the house in France.'

Jane turned around sharply, suddenly animated. 'Brilliant! Yes, you should, you really should. I've been hoping you'd say that, but I didn't want to push you.'

'You think? You really think that it's a good idea?'

'Of course it is! What does Adele think?'

'She can barely contain her excitement.'

'She's a tough little cookie that one!'

'She is, though she doesn't get it from me.'

'So, when are you going to go?'

Michelle suddenly felt a bit sick and closed her eyes. 'Soon. If she misses a few days before half term, it's not the end of the world.'

'Wow, you really mean it, don't you!'

'Yep.' Michelle swallowed down a mouthful of bile and took a series of slow steady breaths.

'You ok? You've gone a bit pale.'

'I'll be fine. It's just a bit scary. I know it sounds pathetic, but I've never been anywhere other than round here and at Mum and Dad's without Chris.'

'You can do it 'Chell, I promise you. You've got more guts than you think, it's not only Chris that Adele gets that from.'

'I don't know about that!'

'Oh shit!' Jane sat up sharply and stabbed out her cigarette. 'We'd better get to school, it's nearly three o'clock!'

'And we're going to roll up five minutes late stinking of booze!'

Jane laughed. 'That'll get the gossip machine going!'

'I know, what are they all going to do when we've gone?!'

The excitable voices of people with a chance at winning a large sum of money, through means that Michelle couldn't quite fathom, came from the TV. It was a daft programme, but Adele always enjoyed watching it. She was cuddled up now, against Michelle's chest, and it felt nice. Michelle brushed a strand of hair from her daughter's face and gave her an affectionate squeeze.

'I think that lady might win, Mummy.'

'Which one?'

'The one with the big red necklace.'

Michelle nodded sagely. The slightly manic gameshow host went over to a board covered with coloured squares and pressed an over-sized button in front of it. A light flickered randomly across the squares then settled on a blue one. *Stick or twist?* said the host; *twist* said the contestant. The host pressed the blue-lit square and a great red cross went across it accompanied by a sound like an electronic raspberry. There was a swell of sympathetic groans from the audience. *I'm so sorry, Natalie,* said the host with a grimace, *it looks like it's just not your day today.* Natalie left with a shrug and a wave to the audience and a new contestant came out to take her place.

'Daddy!' Adele's voice was barely above a whisper.

Michelle gasped. A young man had appeared behind the contestant's podium. He was Chris' double. A slightly narrower face perhaps, and not as tall, but so like him with his strawberry blonde hair, wide mouth and kind, intelligent eyes. But it was his smile that had pinned them both to the sofa: a smile that was slightly crooked - sloping off to the left and creating a dimple on his cheek.

'Daddy!' This time Adele shrieked his name and had started to tremble. Barely in charge of her own emotions,

Michelle caught Adele up and pulled her onto her knee. She held her tight, turning the little girl's face against her shoulder, as if protecting her from the image on the screen. *My God, Chris, what do I do? What do I do for her? This is what death has done, this is what it's left us with! You think the pain has become manageable and then something happens and it's like going through it all over again.*

Adele gripped her mother's body with surprisingly strong fingers, clawing at her, pulling at her clothes. Michelle could feel her whole-body clenching and releasing, as if she were having a fit. She hushed her, stroked her hair, sat forward and rocked her, but still she was inconsolable.

She managed to free a hand and turn off the television. She didn't know what to do. Get Adele to her bedroom perhaps? The only thing she could think of was a change of scene. She struggled up from the sofa and managed to stand. Adele was clamped around her torso, as tightly as a baby monkey when its mother is about to leap through tree tops.

Gripping the banister hard, Michelle managed to stagger up the stairs. Struggling to balance, she then scrambled up the first few rungs of Adele's bunkbed and laid her down on it. When her hands were free, she climbed the rest of the ladder, got in beside Adele and cocooned her small body tightly.

'He did look a lot like Daddy, didn't he?'

Adele didn't reply.

'That happens to me sometimes too; I think I see him, but it isn't him, and it hurts.'

Eventually, after about quarter of an hour, Adele's sobs started to subside. After a few minutes of quiet, she sniffed, and said in a small voice 'I want to leave here, Mummy, I want to get away from here and be somewhere that Daddy has never been. I keep seeing him. He stands in the kitchen and smiles at me; sometimes he's in the garden cutting the grass. I used to like it, but I don't any more. Please Mummy, I want to go.'

The high-pitched ring of her mobile made her jump. She checked the screen, saw it was her brother and turned off the TV.

'Hi, Danny.'

'Hey, Sis.'

'If you're ringing to have a go about Mum, please don't, I'm knackered. Adele had a meltdown because she saw someone on the telly that looked like Chris, and I only managed to get her off to sleep half an hour ago.'

He didn't say anything for a moment, as if what she said had wrongfooted him. 'I don't want to have a go, why do you always think that? It's just that Mum rang and she seemed really upset.'

'*She's* really upset? What about me? She was horrible to me in the end.'

'She said it was like you didn't want her to be there, like you were being deliberately difficult just to make her go.'

'Look, Danny, I know you mean well, but I'm really not in the mood for this. You're just going to have to accept that me and Mum have a different relationship than you and her do. It's more complicated, and believe me, she gives as good as she gets - and more. She's not easy you know. When she's around it's like she's always watching me, waiting for me to slip up or make a mistake.'

'Come on, Michelle, that's not fair, she loves you!'

'Does she?'

'How can you say that?'

Michelle got up from the sofa and stalked over to the window; she was starting to feel edgy, as if she was about to either start shouting or crying. 'It's all right for you, you're the golden boy, you and Cathy can't put a foot wrong. I'm the fuck-up, the one she apparently has to keep worrying about!'

'No-one sees you as a *fuck-up*, how could they? You've coped extraordinarily with what happened with Chris and everything.'

'Have I? Have I really?'

'Yes, you have, and now you've got a chance to start something fresh, have some money behind you.'

She wondered where he was going with this. 'Mum was really angry that she hadn't left the house to you, as you're the oldest.'

'I think it's great she left it to you. So, what are you going to do next?'

Michelle groaned. 'She's told you about that too, about going to France?'

'Yes, and I think it's a great idea, and I've told her that.'

'Really?'

'Yeh, really, and she wasn't happy but it's not her life is it?'

'Thanks, Dan, thanks so much, you don't know how much that means to me.'

'I've been thinking about it all a lot since I heard, about this great aunt, Michèle, and the family.' Danny's voice had become quiet and conspiratorial.

'Right.'

'And do you remember when we were kids and we used to visit Nanny?'

'Yes, why?'

'Do you remember that weird book she had, that used to freak us out?'

Michelle's mind whirred as it went through the library of her memories. 'I'm not sure -'

'It was called *Village des Fantômes*, do you remember now?'

A funny feeling was creeping up Michelle's throat. 'Yes,' she replied in a tight voice, 'we asked Nanny what that meant and she said it meant *Village of Ghosts*. It was about the place that she came from.'

'Exactly,' Danny sounded excited. 'And do you remember what that village was called?'

The funny feeling moved from Michelle's throat and into her chest with an explosion of memory and realisation. She knew now why the name of her Great Aunt's village had sounded familiar. '*Argemourt*, it was called *Argemourt!*'

'Yes! And do you remember she wouldn't talk to us about it. We knew it was a bit weird and sad because it had all those pictures in of the burnt-out church and that freaky SS officer. I can even remember his name; *Stellerman, Sturmbannführer Stellerman.*'

Hearing the name again after all those years made Michelle shiver. She *did* remember the name, and she remembered the photo. A formal portrait of a Nazi officer, ridiculously handsome, in full uniform and with hard, unsmiling eyes. The image had terrified and fascinated her in equal measure. She even remembered, with a flush of shame, that she had had some of her first early-teen sexual feelings looking at the portrait. She knew, in an abstract way, that he was bad; but that only seemed to make him more enthralling. She got up and started to pace the room, her heart racing.

'I knew when I read the name that I remembered it but I couldn't for the life of me remember how or why. And that book, shit, it used to really creep me out. What does it all mean?'

'It means your house is in the middle of a prime World War II tourist site. Thousands of visitors go to it every year; the place is full of guesthouses and lots of ex-pats set up businesses in the town. There could be some opportunities there for you too.'

'I saw that, about it being a tourist attraction, when I searched for it, but I didn't really look into it in detail. Was there some battle there or something?'

'It was worse than a battle. When the Germans knew they were losing the war, in 1944 they destroyed loads of villages and small towns as they retreated. Argemourt was one of those villages. Hundreds of innocent people died.'

Michelle felt dizzy. 'Look, Danny, that's really interesting - and weird - but it's been a hard night and I'm not feeling great. Can I call you back tomorrow?'

'Of course, get an early night. Don't forget to call me though, we've got a lot to discuss.'

'I will.'

'Love you, Sis.'

'Love you too.'

She hung up the phone and felt winded. She leaned on the sill, took deep breaths, and stared distractedly into the dark garden outside of the window. There was a familiar silhouette against the rear hedge, about the size and shape of a man and darker than the rest of the space around it. *What does it all mean Chris?* She said silently to the shape. *Why is this happening to me?* The shape didn't answer. *Maybe Adele's right, darling, maybe it's time for us to be somewhere else. Not to forget you, we'll carry you with us in our hearts, but to move on.* The shape didn't answer, instead it slowly faded away until all that was left to see was the endless black at the end of the garden, and above it, a sky full of diamond-sharp stars.

Michelle fidgeted and fiddled with her seatbelt, worried that she didn't have it tight enough. Adele leaned over, and with slender, dexterous fingers, showed her how to do it. Michelle smiled back nervously and let out a shaky breath.

'It's ok, Mum. More people die in cars than in aeroplanes.'

'Well thanks, that makes me feel so much better.'

The voice of the cabin crew leader came over the tannoy and an air hostess appeared at the end of the aisle to go over the evacuation details. *If anything is destined to make a nervous flyer more nervous, this is surely it,* thought Michelle, and paid as minimum attention to the talk as she felt able, within the confines of her parental responsibility. Adele, clearly fascinated however, hung on the woman's every word.

When it was over, a quick sweep of the plane was made to check that everyone had their seatbelts on; the captain came onto the tannoy to tell them about their expected time of arrival and the weather in Paris, and the plane started to taxi up the runway.

Michelle gripped the arm rest tightly; Adele leaned to look out of the window (an action that made a prickling sensation bloom around Michelle's solar-plexus) and the plane sped up and took a lurching move into a forty-five-degree angle. A second later there was that unmistakable feeling of transition; where what is beneath the plane has become air instead of tarmac.

The air steward appeared in the aisle beside them. 'Can I get you a drink ladies?' She looked kindly at Adele, who returned the kindness with a shy smile.

'Yes,' said Michelle, quickly. 'I'll have a Gin and Tonic please and, Adele, what do you want?'

'A coke please.'

'Lovely.' The air steward repeated the order to a colleague who was behind her in the aisle.

'We've got a house in France,' said Adele suddenly and rather breathlessly. 'My Mum had a great aunt, but she died - and she was very old, a hundred even maybe - and she left us a house and it's all white and has shutters and a garden so big it ends in the countryside, and The World War was there too and so it has a lot of History and so it's special.' Running out of breath, Adele stopped.

The hostess, looked back at her, eyes wide. 'How very nice. Aren't you lucky.' She handed them both their drinks and carried on down the aisle.

'She's beautiful,' said Adele, quietly.

'Hmm.' Michelle was too focused on her G&T to feel jealous of her daughter's obvious admiration. She took a big gulp, and felt the edges of her anxiety soften.

'Why can't we drive, Mummy, when we get to France?'

'I told you, they drive on the other side of the road, and Mummy's never done that before. I just don't feel ready. We can get the train at the airport and it takes us all the way there. The trains in France are really good, Aunty Jane told me, they even have double-decker ones like buses.'

Adele's face lit up. 'Will we have one of those, Mummy?'

'Maybe, let's wait and see.'

A supernatural being scrapes its finger nails across the earth and mountains spring up; the valleys are flooded by water; the water turns to ice and the earth is wrenched apart. A giant silver bird flies through the air, impervious to the drama beneath it, its shining wings blinding-white with reflected sunshine. Then they are in the bustling concourse of Gare Austerlitz station, swept along like leaves floating on the top of a raging river. People stare at them, they laugh and point, and a feeling of dread floods through her.

'Mum!'

Adele's voice cut through her dream and dragged her, disorientated, back into the present. She woke, blinking and feeling suddenly ashamed that she had fallen asleep. 'What is it, sweetheart?'

'We're here.'

Michelle's heart jumped. 'Quick! Before it leaves the station!' She grabbed their bags and took hold of Adele's hand, dragging her to the stairs.

'It's ok, Mum, the train finishes here, there's a map on the wall.'

Ignoring her, Michelle clattered down the stairs to the ground floor of the train, her suitcase on wheels bouncing down behind her. They made it onto the concourse in a jumble, making several people turn and look at them. Michelle studied the platform for a sign saying *Sortie,* frantically trying to remember her GCSE French. 'This way, it's this way.'

They followed the signs until they found themselves in a small but elegant ticket hall with a vaulted ceiling. The hall was busy with people and there was a musical rumble of French being spoken all around them. Michelle handed her tickets in to the inspector and then they stopped for a moment, catching their breath.

'Where do we go now, Mummy?'

'Out of the main entrance I suppose. The solicitor said they'd get us a taxi.'

They negotiated their way through the crowds and aimed for what looked like the main entrance. A pair of ornate doors with heavy brass handles led to a sunny square, and they emerged, startled and blinking into the brightness. The air smelled different, in that way that it often did when you went to a different country; this time, warmed with a hint of dusty sweetness. There was a pretty old clocktower made from some kind of salmon-coloured brick in the centre of the square, and wide, well maintained roads going off in four directions between streets filled with shops, cafes and *Boulangeries.* Michelle looked around for a moment, a little bewildered.

'Over there, Mummy, that man's got our name on a sign.'

Michelle looked over, shading her eyes against the sun. There was a man in a cap, a cigarette clamped in his mouth standing beside a taxi holding up a piece of card that had "Mme M Harvey" written on it. They went over and he sprang into life, putting out his cigarette and opening the boot.

'Bonjour,' said Michelle, hesitantly. 'Pour Madame Michelle Harvey?'

He gestured towards his sign. 'Oui, bien sûr.'

Michelle smiled and they dragged their suitcases towards him. As they drew up to the car he lifted each bag and put them in the boot then opened one of the rear passenger doors with a gallant flourish.

'Merci,' said Adele, sitting on the rear seat and swinging her legs neatly into the car.

'Mon plaisir, petit.' He answered with a smile.

French rap music filled the car as they drove. Michelle and Adele were silent, each looking out of the window at the pretty but foreign landscape that was rolling out beside them. There were modern bungalows, very plain in style but with pretty gardens, fields edged with wildflowers and distant lines of poplar trees; slender and delicate against the hazy summer sky. After a few minutes curiosity took the better of Michelle and she steeled herself for another attempt at speaking French.

'A quelle, erm, a quelle distance?'

The driver looked back at her and grinned toothily. 'About two miles Madame.'

'Oh, you speak English?'

'A little. *Taxi English* you might say. "Not far", "this many miles", "we arrive soon" etcetera.'

They drove on after that in a companionable silence, all the questions that had crowded Michelle's mind suddenly evaporating. She felt Adele squeeze her hand and looked round to see her daughter's face aglow with anticipation and pleasure; something she hadn't seen in a long time.

'Do you like it here?'

Adele nodded, her face serious. 'They have whole fields of sunflowers, Mummy, look!' she said, as if in explanation for her enthusiasm.

Michelle leant across the back seat and looked out of Adele's window. The vivid gold of the flowers stretched as far as the eye could see, their heavy, sensual heads turned worshipfully towards the sun.

'I can't wait to see the house. Can I choose my room straight away?'

'Of course! I think there's three, two larger ones and a little one in the roof.'

'We arrive!' announced the driver cheerfully, making Michelle jump.

The car slowed and they turned off the main road and onto a bumpy track. There was a hedged field to their left and on their right a row of three terraced cottages, set back from the road behind a badly maintained low slatted wood fence, which was punctuated by a gate corresponding to each house. The driver stopped the car by the middle gate and got out. They heard him shouting at someone genially.

Michelle remained sitting, unable to move, but Adele took hold of her hand and tugged at her, until, reluctantly, she got out into the afternoon sunshine.

Michelle blinked and put on her sunglasses. Her heart was beating so fast it seemed to stop her being able to process what she was seeing; she told herself to breathe. The driver appeared in front of her suddenly, wheeling their suitcases, one in each hand, towards the front of the cottage. He was still chatting away in a torrent of French, but not to her. She managed to compose herself and saw that the driver was talking to an old man in a panama hat with a droopy Mexican-style moustache. He was sitting in a rocking chair under the porch of the cottage to her left.

'Alain, Samedi, vous devez venir aux courses.' The taxi driver shouted over to him. 'Ça fait trop longtemps!'

The old man smiled. 'Ok, ok, mais cette fois, tu achèteras la bière!' His voice was gruff, but pleasant.

She followed behind the driver shyly, Adele holding tightly onto her hand. She took a deep breath. 'Bonsoir, Monsieur. Je m'appelle Michelle et...erm..c'est ma fille, Adele.'

The old man put his drink and the newspaper he had in his lap onto an upturned bucket that he was using as a side table and walked over to them smiling. When he got to the line of straggly wallflowers that divided their paths, he took off his hat and bowed. Adele giggled.

'Permettez-moi de me présenter, Je suis Alain, Roi du village de Argemourt et je suis ravi de vous rencontrer!'

'He jokes with you!' said the taxi driver, planting another cigarette in his mouth and shaking his head. 'He is English, he play a game with you!'

'Ah Remy, I can't get away with anything with you around.' When he spoke this time, the old man's voice had a soft twang of Cockney in it, but there was a slightly posh lilt too, which Michelle wasn't sure if he was putting on or not. 'I apologise my dear, I am Alan, and I'm very pleased to meet you, Michelle.' He smiled at her then squatted down to be at the same level as Adele, 'And so this is Adele, I am delighted to make your acquaintance too young lady.' He held out his hand for Adele to shake and she reached out tentatively and took it. As soon as she did, he pumped her hand so vigorously that for a moment Michelle was worried that he may pull her arm off, but Adele laughed and Alan did too, and so Michelle relaxed and smiled.

'Très bien, I will go now.' Remy doffed his cap and headed down the path.

'Should I tip him?' Michelle whispered anxiously to Alan.

'No, don't worry about that, I hear he charged your solicitor an extortionate rate!'

'Oh, ok. She hesitated then followed Remy to the gate. 'Thank you, Remy. Do you have a card? We haven't got a car, so we'll probably need you quite a lot.'

Remy nodded and leaned through the driver's window and retrieved a rather dog-eared card from the dashboard. 'For you!' He presented it to her with a flourish.

She smiled and slipped the card in her jeans pocket. 'Thank you.'

He shrugged and got into his car. When he started the engine the rap music blared out again immediately.

96

He turned the volume up even higher and saluted out of the window as he drove away.

When she headed back towards the cottage a lot of things happened at once. A large shaggy lurcher plodded out through Alan's open front door and at the same time Adele let out a delighted squeal and jumped across Alan's path and threw her arms around the startled dog. Simultaneously Alan shouted in alarm and reached out to hold Adele back but missed her completely. Michelle screamed involuntarily, expecting to see the dog snarl and sink its teeth into Adele's neck, but after a few seconds of terror she saw that in fact, Adele was giggling in pleasure as the dog - which was easily as big as she was - set about washing her face with a large, meaty tongue.

Alan had his hand to his heart and he looked pale, despite his tan. 'I have never known him behave like this! He doesn't generally like children; It's not that he's bitten any - well - not for a while, but he normally wouldn't tolerate a child getting that close to him...let alone giving him a hug!'

Michelle let out a choked laugh of relief. 'It must be hard keeping him away from people? What do you do when you go into town?'

'Everyone here knows what he's like, they know to give him a wide berth. Anyway, he's not really my dog.'

'Whose is he then?'

'He was your great aunt's, and he didn't become grumpy until she died. But obviously,' he nodded his head towards Adele who was now holding the dog's head a little way from her own and staring solemnly into its eyes, 'blood is thicker than water.'

Alan left them so they could have a look around the cottage and settle in but made them promise that they would join him for supper. It turned out that he was the executer of her aunt's will, and her solicitors had given him some money to look after the house and garden while it was empty, and to make sure there was food in for Michelle when she arrived. It was a pleasant surprise, and strangely touching, to find food in the cupboards, wine, milk, cheese and butter in the fridge, and clean bedding on the beds - as if her aunt was thinking about her from beyond the grave.

Adele stalked from room to room, curious and cautious as a kitten that has just been introduced to its new home. She looked through windows, opened cupboards and drawers, inspected under the beds and studied the ornaments on the shelves. After an hour's serious study she declared a pretty room nestled under the roof on the top floor, with a vaulted ceiling, her bedroom. It had a cream-painted single bed with a flowered quilt and a deep-set casement window overlooking the back garden and the fields.

Michelle left Adele happily unpacking her toys and arranging her teddies on her bed and headed downstairs to get her own bag and take it to the largest bedroom. It was a lovely house, and she felt immediately at home. It was cosy but not over-cluttered and it felt like everything in it, from the cushion covers to the pans, had been well used but also looked after. The overall feeling from it was benign and comfortable. She had always been able to pick up the 'mood' of a place instantly. There was one time, she remembered as she started to hang up her clothes, when she had gone to look at a house that was for sale with her mum. It was a 1930s semi-detached on a nice tree-lined avenue and had looked pretty from the outside. As soon as they had gone through the front door, however, Michelle had wanted to get out again. She had followed her mum reluctantly, a growing feeling of foreboding sitting in her stomach. In one of the bedrooms she had absent-mindedly looked into a wardrobe and found it completely empty apart from a doll's head tied by its hair to a clothes hanger. Much to Michelle's relief, as soon as her mum had seen it too, she had taken hold of her hand, and with the most peremptory of thanks to the owners, left the house.

She had just finished unpacking her bag when Adele ran into her room, grabbed her hand and dragged her, excitedly, to the window.

'Look Mummy, there's a ruined castle over there, behind the trees, can you see it?'

Michelle squinted against the light and took her gaze past the field to a lake to the horizon line. There was something, dark and pointed, rising above the silhouetted tree line.

'Yes, I see it, but I think it's a church, not a castle.'

Adele squeezed her hand and looked up at her beseechingly. 'Can we go and have a look Mummy, please?'

'I don't know, it's getting late and Alan said he wanted us round there at seven -'

'It's not that far, please Mummy.'

Michelle smiled at her wearily. 'Ok, Chick, let's go.'

At the end of the back garden they found a half-rotted wooden gate hiding in the hedge. To be fair to Alan, the hedge had obviously recently been trimmed and the small lawn had been cut, but there were a lot of weeds in the beds, and many of the shrubs had bolted. Michelle made a mental note that she would ask Alan if there were any gardening tools about and have a go at tidying it up the next day.

Past the gate there was a footpath of compacted earth running parallel with the row of cottages. Away to their left it disappeared into trees and on their right, it followed the edge of a series of fields.

'I'm not sure how we're going to get there, 'Del, this path takes us in the wrong direction.'

'No, Mummy, look, there's one here too.' Adele gestured for her to come. She was right; it was a bit overgrown, but definitely still a track. It led through the fallow field that bordered their garden, now full of waist-high wildflowers, past the small lake and towards the line of trees that they could see from their bedroom windows. The sun was lower in the sky now and the light was golden. Midges, caught in the slanting rays, lit up like the sparks from a bonfire. It was beautiful but Michelle suddenly felt reluctant to go any further.

Adele pulled at her hand. 'Come on, Mummy, come on, we haven't got much time.'

Trying to ignore her misgivings Michelle followed her daughter dutifully, trying to absorb some of her enthusiasm. As they walked through the wildflowers Michelle raised her arms and let her hands run along the top of them, skimming the lacy heads of cow parsley, cornflowers and other plants she didn't recognise. Birds had started to sing, sending their liquid calls into the soft early evening air, and at their feet Michelle could hear the scratchy calls of grasshoppers. She was being ridiculous, how could there be anything bad in a place like this. She took in a deep breath of the scented air and smiled.

'Mummy, Mummy look it's our lake!' Adele stopped and pointed; it was bigger than it looked from the cottage and the line of trees and dome of blue sky were reflected perfectly in its glossy surface.

'I don't think it's *our* lake, sweetheart!'

'Then whose is it? There's no fence around it. Perhaps it belongs to everyone here?'

'Maybe.'

'Do you think you can swim in it?'

'Hmm, I don't know about that.'

'I'm going to ask Mr Alan when we go there for our tea.'

'You don't have to call him "Mr" Alan, you know!'

'So?' replied Adele, looking serious, 'It suits him. When a man wears a hat like that he looks like a mister.'

Michelle laughed. 'Fair enough!'

'It's not funny, Mummy.' Adele replied, frowning.

Michelle compressed her lips in an effort to stop herself from laughing. 'Ok, sweetheart, I'm sorry.'

They carried on walking and after a few minutes found themselves at the edge of the strip of trees. The path continued into the relative gloom of the wood. Michelle paused for a second, holding Adele back.

'What's the matter, Mummy?'

'Nothing, it's just, I don't know -'

'Come on.' Adele took the lead again, pulling Michelle through the tree line. When her eyes had adjusted to the low light, she could see that the wood was largely made up of old trees; oaks and others she didn't recognise. Their trunks were huge and gnarled and their smooth dark roots plunged with sinewy force into the mossy ground.

Michelle shivered. 'It's a bit spooky.'

'Don't be silly, Mummy, it's not spooky, it's just peaceful.'

They followed the path for another five minutes or so then came across a crumbling old wall. Adele let go of Michelle's hand and ran up to it with excitement.

'This is it, Mummy! It's the castle walls. Let's find a way to get in.'

Michelle stumbled, trying to keep up with Adele, who was darting this way and that trying to find a break in the wall.

'Here! Come here, Mummy, look!'

'Ok, ok, slow down!' Michelle clambered over an old rotting tree trunk and came alongside her daughter. Adele had found a section where it looked like a tree had fallen and knocked down a section of the wall, possibly the tree that she had just stepped over. 'Come on then, little miss curious, let's have a look and then we can head home and have a nice dinner with Alan.' She took hold of Adele's hand again and they went through the gap in the wall together and found themselves in an old graveyard. It wasn't completely derelict, it looked like someone had mowed the grass quite recently, but the most recent grave they found was from 1944, and many went back as far as the 1800's.

After a few minutes studying the graves and trying to pronounce the strange French surnames: *Petit, Dubois, Faucheux, Lécuyer, Desmarais*, they came to a huge yew hedge. At first glance it seemed impenetrable, but after a minute or two they found a wooden door, rusted half-open on old iron hinges. Michelle squeezed through the gap then reached back to take Adele's hand. When she had stepped over the threshold they both stopped and Adele looked up and gasped.

'It's like something out of a fairy story Mummy!'

'Yes, it is.'

The church was made out of two different stones, one the colour of clotted cream, the other a soft grey. The steeple was topped with the skeletal wooden framework of its lost roof, the sides were heavily buttressed and punctuated with round windows, empty of any glass. Although it was much smaller than the castle that Adele had been anticipating, it did have a drowsy, romantic feel to it, as if Sleeping Beauty might be entombed inside the cool stone walls.

Still holding hands, they walked around the church, trying to find the entrance.

After a few yards Adele stopped. 'What are these, Mummy?'

Michelle stopped too and bent down to see what Adele was looking at. It was a series of almost perfectly round holes in the rough skin of the wall. Adele poked her index finger in and it went as far as her knuckle. Michelle passed her finger tips across the wall; there was series of the holes, a few rows deep, peppered along it and level with her shoulders.

With a shiver it came to her what they probably were. 'I think they're bullet holes.'

Adele looked up at her, startled. 'Bullet holes? But why?'

'I think they must be from the war. Maybe there was a fight here or something.'

'Between the goodies and the baddies?'

'Well, yes, maybe.'

Adele looked around her, suddenly pale in the shadow of the church wall. 'I think I want to go home now.'

Michelle glanced around Alan's dining room and made her assessment. She decided it was the room of someone who had not had female influence in his life for a long time. The furniture was handsome, but very dark and slightly too big for the room. There were no plants or flowers, in fact no superfluous decoration or ornament of any kind apart from a row of crime novels on the top shelf of the dresser, some framed photos and two reproductions of old maritime paintings on the wall. Alan's whistling return to the room made her jump, as if he would know what she had been thinking. She sat down abruptly next to Adele and cleared her throat.

'It's really kind of you to have done this for us, Alan.'

He plonked a giant casserole dish onto a woven mat in the middle of the table. 'Oh, it's no bother at all', he said, airily. 'It's been pretty quiet around here since your aunt died, it's nice to have some company.' He ladled fragrant stew into each of their bowls then sat down with a small groan, holding his back. 'Hope you like Cassoulet!'

'Yum.' said Adele decisively then looked sideways at Alan. 'What is it?'

'Traditional French chicken, sausage and bean stew basically.'

Michelle smiled at him. There was something touching about the pleasure he was getting in their company; she suspected he was a bit lonely. He'd smartened himself up too since the morning and was wearing an ironed shirt and an embroidered waistcoat. She looked down at her creased t-shirt and jeans and felt suddenly a little ashamed for not having made a similar effort.

To try to make up for her scruffiness, she decided to make sure she was suitably complimentary about his food and leaned over her bowl to take in the savoury, garlic-drenched aroma of the casserole. Her stomach rumbled, and she suddenly realised how hungry she was. She dug in to the stew wolfishly; Adele was silent, her head hovering over her bowl as she too shovelled the stew in.

Alan watched them with a satisfied smile. 'Slow down, you'll give yourselves indigestion!'

Adele looked up briefly, 'It's yummy!' she said thickly through a mouthful of chicken.

A breeze came through the open French doors and breathed across the bare skin of Michelle's arm, giving her goosebumps. She looked out into the evening garden for a moment, which was fast retreating into warm shadows.

'Where are you from, Alan?'

'The East End originally, my parents ran a pub. Then my granddad died and left my mum a lot of money and she decided the best way to keep me on the straight and narrow was to send me to private school.'

Michelle smiled. 'That explains your accent!'

'Indeed it does,' replied Alan, raising his eyebrows, 'I am half *Cockney-Sparra'* and half *Toff!'*

She laughed at his deliberate switch in accent. 'Did it work? Did it keep you on the "straight and narrow" like your mum wanted?'

Alan took a sip of his glass of red wine then turned to look at Michelle. 'It's hard to say, I don't know what I might have been if she hadn't sent me off to hang out with the rich kids. I became an engineer, it's been a good career, I've seen the world because of it. I've had adventures...' He trailed off.

'I sense a "but" coming?' Michelle felt a bit worried that she might be seen to be prying, but there was something about him that invited questions; the sense that he had a lot of stories to tell.

'Hmm, yes, I suppose you're right. Let's just say that being dumped at boarding school at the age of eight didn't do wonders for my emotional health. Both my marriages failed, and I suspect it was mainly my fault. I've got a daughter too, but I hardly ever see her. Her mum did a bit of hatchet job on me after I left.'

'I'm sorry.'

He took another sip of wine and shrugged. 'C'est la vie. I probably deserved it.'

Michelle decided it would be a good idea to change the subject. 'Tell me about my aunt, what was she like?'

Alan put down his glass and gazed into the distance. His kind, leathery face was almost mystical in the fading light; like a world-weary wizard. 'She was quite a character, but you had to get to know her to find that out. She kept herself to herself, was very private, but she was also fiercely loyal to those she came to know and love. There was a sadness about her, she did talk about it to me once, when she'd uncharacteristically had quite a lot to drink – told me she'd lost her brother in some tragic way in the Second World War, but didn't go in to any more detail. Later I found out that it had been his birthday that night – he'd have been sixty-four if he'd lived. What else can I tell you? Oh, and she never had children; even though she was married. Her husband died in 1980, and she lived alone after that.

'How long did you know her?'

'About twenty years, since I moved here after my divorce.'

'Did she,' Michelle took a deep breath, 'did she ever talk about me or about my family?'

'Yes, she did. I think she was sorry that she didn't have you in her life, I'm not sure why that was - some kind of disagreement with your grandmother I think. It was a long, long time ago though. I bet they couldn't even remember why they fell out in the first place!'

'Did she ever say anything that would explain why she left everything to me? I'm so grateful but I just can't get my head round it. It doesn't make any sense.'

Alan leaned towards her and looked at her intently. 'Does it really not make any sense to you?'

Adele looked from one to the other intently, her spoon frozen half way to her mouth.

Michelle smiled at her and ruffled her hair, then looked back at Alan. 'No, not really, but why not to my brother? He's older; or to my mum, she was her closest relative.'

'I think your aunt probably thought long and hard about what was the right decision, she was that kind of lady, very thoughtful and fair. You share her name, you are widowed,' he glanced at Adele and patted her hand, 'like she was. And knew you were an army wife and probably lived in a Ministry of Defence home. I think those are all perfectly valid reasons.'

Michelle sighed and looked past Alan to the pictures of his family that lined one of the bookshelves. 'I just feel so sad that I never got to know her. It seems such a waste that she could have been a part of my life. We could have holidayed here, spent time with her - '

'Do you have a picture of her, Mr Alan?' They both turned, startled by the clarity of Adele's voice. 'I looked and looked but I can't find any.'

'Yes, yes I do! How silly of me not to think of that, hang on a sec.' He got up with a grunt and went over to the dark wood dresser that dominated the small dining room. From a drawer he pulled out a leather photograph album then sat back at the table. He went through the pages, scanning each image until, with a small exclamation of satisfaction that suggested he had found what he was looking for, turned the album round to face them and jabbed at one of the photos with a thick tanned finger. 'That's her, there, second from left.'

Alan turned on the pendant light over the table and suddenly the scene burst into life. 'That was taken in

2004, on the sixtieth anniversary of the...well, of the village getting into trouble in the war.'

Michelle and Adele bent over and peered at the page. The photo was of a row of four people standing outside what looked like an old church. No-one was smiling. The man on the far right was clearly Alan; he hadn't changed all that much; a bit thinner now perhaps, and with whiter hair. The older woman standing one person to Alan's right was small and elegantly but plainly dressed, at first glance utterly forgettable. However, there was something about her face - her eyes in particular - that drew you to her. There was a sad intensity there and a fierce intelligence. It made Michelle shudder, because there was something else too - a hint of herself - that made the slightly out-of-focus image of the woman unsettling.

'I'll have a look tomorrow and see if I can find any more. And I know she had lots of photo albums - she held on to a lot from her past - so maybe,' Alan turned to Adele and fixed her with a twinkling look; 'this young lady could have a challenge tomorrow, a detecting challenge, to look again and see if she can find them!'

Adele's face glowed and she nodded, clearly enthralled by the idea. Alan stood up and started to clear the plates.

As if on cue the old lurcher padded into the room and Adele squealed with delight. 'What's his name, Mr Alan?'

Alan smiled. 'His name's Jack. Now shall we let him lick our plates or,' he looked at Michelle, 'is that revolting?'

Adele scraped her chair back and leapt up. 'Let him lick the plates! Let him lick the plates!'

Seeing Alan reach for his back as he bent down, Michelle took the plates off him and laid them out on the floor. Jack was over them in less than a second, his broad pink tongue flattening against the porcelain with relish.

'Now, will you ladies do me the honour of joining me on the patio for a nightcap? Do you drink brandy, Michelle? Mademoiselle Adele, would you care for a hot chocolate?'

Adele was crouched on her haunches watching Jack polish the plates. She nodded happily.

'Thanks, Alan, that sounds lovely, let me help you clear up.' She gathered up the casserole dish and their glasses and followed Alan into the kitchen. It was long and thin - galley style, different to hers - but similarly well equipped. Alan was clearly a man who liked the finer things in life.

'Now don't you dare start washing up, young lady. I'll do that later. Just get me the milk from the fridge and we'll make Adele that hot chocolate.

The air in the garden was heavy with the sleepy scent of wildflowers and the resinous smell of Alan's strong French tobacco. Michelle took another sip of her orange brandy and relished the sweet burn of it as it travelled down her throat. Adele was half hidden in the shadows at the end of the garden playing tug of war with Jack and an old rope that was apparently one of his favourite toys. Happy screeches and benign growls came at them through the dark. Alan's jowly face was underlit by a large candle on the patio table between them. His cheeks hollowed as he drew on his cigarette.

'Alan, can I ask you something?'

He turned and squinted at her through a lungful of smoke that unfurled and twisted itself around his face like Medusa's head of snakes. 'Of course.'

'The old church in the photo behind you and Aunt Michèle, is it the one in the woods past the lake?'

Alan turned away. 'Yes.'

She could sense a reluctance in him to say more but she pushed on. 'Did something bad happen there? Me and Adele walked there this afternoon and it looked like there were bullet holes along the wall, and, I don't know, it just felt a bit, well, a bit creepy.'

He stubbed out his cigarette in a faded floral saucer beside him on the table and took a sip of his brandy. 'Did you read about Argemourt before you came here? Did you "google" it or whatever it is they say?'

'A bit,' she felt a bit embarrassed all of a sudden, 'mostly *for sale* sites...' she trailed off. 'I saw some general stuff about it being a historic place, to do with the Second World War, but I was never that big on history. It did sound familiar though, the name, Argemourt I mean, and then my brother reminded me about a book my Nanna had. But I couldn't read it of course, because it was in French.'

'There was a massacre in that church. Pretty much the whole village was killed. Only a handful of people survived.'

Michelle suddenly felt cold and hugged her arms around herself. 'My brother told me a bit about it. What happened?'

'It was the summer of 1944. The Germans were in retreat. Whether it was retribution, or pride, or sheer evil - whatever their reasons - the Nazis destroyed a series of villages in their wake. One because a Nazi Officer had been killed nearby by the Resistance, another in revenge for a tactically important bridge that had been blown up. Here, in Argemourt, it was because of a mistake. Bad intelligence; they thought Argemourt was a secret Resistance stronghold, but they'd picked the wrong village. The one they wanted was ten kilometres to the West.'

'That's horrible. And the church?'

'The men were lined up against the rear wall and shot. The women and children were imprisoned in the church and set fire to. Three hundred and twenty-two people died in one day.'

Michelle was surprised to find her eyes had filled with tears. 'How can people do things like that - to other people? To children?'

'Because they don't see them as people any more. In fact they see them as less than animals. It's what the brain does to justify the horror that is being committed. It's a kind of madness.'

'My friend, Jane, she says all war is a kind of madness.'

'And what do you think? You were married to a soldier?'

With a sharp jolt she realised she hadn't thought about Chris since that morning. 'I don't know,' she replied, a little flustered, 'It used to feel simple, like he was a good guy, fighting the bad guys, but as time's gone on, I feel less sure. It's one of the reasons I had to get away from the base. War was everywhere; even though we aren't fighting one at the moment, it felt like it was still happening, in people's living rooms, in the pub, you couldn't escape it.'

Alan nodded slowly. 'It must feel very different here?'

'That's the weird thing, it's kind of the same but different; alien but familiar, do you know what I mean?'

'I'm not sure, I think so, but I have been here a long time.'

'Like the flowers; some are the same and some are different, and the houses, and the people. I've seen things I recognise, and things that feel totally new.'

Alan reached over and took hold of her hand. 'I am so glad you came. Your Aunt would be so pleased. I have to say, you look right here, you really do, and Adele too.'

With spooky synchronicity Adele appeared at the edge of the circle of candlelight as her name was mentioned. She was flushed but happy looking.

'Jack won the tug of war.' She told them, breathlessly. 'He is super-strong!'

Jack appeared beside her and immediately sank down onto the patio slabs, panting.

Alan laughed. 'You've tired the old boy out!'

Michelle put a hand on his arm. 'And we've probably tired you out too. Come on, missy, let's go, it's late.'

Alan got up with one of his characteristic groans and they went over to him and kissed him. They were about to go back through the house but Alan stopped them.

'You don't need to go that way - there's a little gate - see?' Alan went over to the low fence between their gardens and pointed out that one of the panels was actually a gate with a metal catch. He opened it for them with a flourish. '*Madame et Mademoiselle, par ici.*'

Adele went past, giggling. Michelle wondered if he knew what he'd let himself in for by telling them about this extra access point. He was about to shut the gate when Jack appeared and went to follow Michelle and Adele through it. They all stopped and the dog looked anxiously from face to face.

'Oh dear,' said Alan, 'I was worried this would happen.' He turned to the dog, 'It's not your house any more, old fellow!'

Adele tugged at her mum's hand. 'Please, Mummy, can he come, can he sleep with me? He doesn't understand; now we're back he thinks he should be too!'

Adele's use of the word "back" gave Michelle a shivery feeling in her chest. 'Well, I don't know. I wouldn't want him on the bed.'

'He's got a basket and blanket of his own if that's any help? He always sleeps in it so I'm sure you would be fine?' Alan looked at Michelle and gestured as if to ask if he should go and get it.

Michelle sighed. 'Ok, go on then. But remember, Adele, he's not allowed on the bed!'

Michelle woke up and for a moment was disorientated. She lay there peacefully, expecting to go straight back to sleep, but couldn't. She rolled over and looked at her phone - 4.30am. The rest of the night stretched long and elastic ahead of her, as it used to when she had been woken in the middle of the night to feed Adele. She remembered Jane telling her that 4.30am was the typical time for people to die in the night; the thought made her shudder and decide she might as well get up.

She threw on her jeans and a light jumper, feeling surprisingly alert and rested. As she went past Adele's room to go to the bathroom, she popped her head through the door. So much for Jack's basket. It stood empty on the rug, and the dog was curled up in front of Adele, his shaggy but noble head resting under her chin and his front legs intertwined with the little girl's arms. Despite her initial annoyance, Adele looked so peaceful and content that Michelle smiled. She went over and gently smoothed the little girl's fringe from her forehead and then stroked the old dog down his long nose. He half-opened his eyes and gazed at her, and for a second his look was so full of meaning that she could almost imagine he was trying to communicate something to her.

'Silly old dog,' she whispered to him, 'if you could speak you'd probably just ask me if I've got any sausages.'

She tiptoed out of the room, went to the bathroom to brush her teeth and tidy her hair then down the stairs to the kitchen. She ruminated on what to drink and decided it was too early for coffee so made herself a cup of tea and absent-mindedly covered a slightly stale corner of the previous day's baguette with some butter and jam.

When her drink was made she pottered out into the garden and enjoyed the sensation of the cool paving stones against the soles of her feet. The pre-dawn sky was strangely backlit and portentous. It reminded her of nights as a child, lying in bed, staring at the shifting shadows in the dark corridor outside her room. She would enter a kind of hypnotic state; half-sleepy, half-curious about the bright adult world downstairs.

She finished her tea and put it down on the old wrought-iron patio table, and without thinking padded into the garden and lay down on the lightly-dewed grass. The birds had started to sing; she closed her eyes and listened to them. Undulating layers of trills, beeps and clicks; whistled arpeggios, staccato squeaks, layered and fell over each other in ways that seemed simultaneously random and rehearsed. It was so beautiful that she felt her chest constrict, and a sudden breathless feeling of joy overwhelmed her.

She opened her eyes and watched thin wraiths of blue-grey cloud fray like ageing silks to reveal a peachy sky. She felt like leaping up and dancing, like stripping off her clothes and howling like an animal; there was something so expectant about this morning; about the stirring of life all around her that made her feel wild. She breathed quickly and brought her hands to her face, surprised to find tears running down her cheeks.

She woke again to an unfamiliar sound she couldn't quite put her finger on. After a few confused moments she realised it was a dog barking. She opened her eyes and lifted her head from the sofa and was startled to see Adele looking down at her with wide eyes.

'There's someone at the door Mummy.'

'What?' She rubbed her face and groaned. 'I woke up early and came downstairs for a bit, I must have come in here, sat on the sofa and fallen asleep again.' There was a succession of sharp knocks at the front door and a renewed barrage of barks came from Jack upstairs. Michelle got up shakily and smoothed her hair, the sitting room was warm with morning sunlight. 'Who the hell can that be?'

She went down the narrow hall to the door and opened it. A tall young man with shoulder length blond hair and very tanned skin was smiling at her. He seemed to be caught somewhere between expectancy and hesitancy and was rocking slightly on his heels.

'Bonjour, je suis Paul.'

117

PART 2: PAUL

"That men do not learn very much from the lessons of history is the most important of all the lessons of history."
(Aldous Huxley)

The dream sat heavy on Paul as he woke up. He suspected he had cried out, he was beaded with sweat and felt a vague sense of panic, as if there was somewhere else he was supposed to be. Veronique had turned away from him and was moaning softly in her sleep. He breathed slowly for a few seconds, trying to calm his heartbeat. Honeyed slivers of light were swooping across his ceiling from the headlights of the occasional passing car in the street below.

It had felt so real; the shouts of the soldiers, the feeling of excitement and terror, the final explosion. Over the last two years of his PHD researching the Limousin during the Occupation, he had studied so many stories and accounts; so many old photos and newsreels; that it seemed that the people of the time had moved into his consciousness and had now even evolved to populate his dreams. If he was honest, he liked them being there, even though they scared him sometimes.

He lay in a dozing stupor for the next couple of hours, drifting in and out of sleep and struggling to get comfortable, until dawn infiltrated the room. He woke properly and watched the soft advance of light push back the gloom and reveal the edges of his girlfriend's body and the detritus of life in the room beyond the island of their bed. As if she sensed him looking at her, she sighed, stretched and turned around to look at him.

'Bonjour.'

'Bonjour.'

'What is the weather doing out there?'

'I don't know, I've not been out of bed yet but I think it's another sunny day.'

She smiled.

'I had another of those dreams.'

Veronique turned onto her back and looked up at the ceiling.

'It was different this time, I was with Armand, when he was a young man. We were Maquisards, waiting in the woods at night-time; I didn't know what for, but I could feel the suspense and the fear, it was tangible. And the gun in my hand, cold metal, so real.' He broke off, trying to pull back the threads of the dream, it had been thrilling, and he had butterflies in his stomach as he told Veronique about it. 'And then we were running through the woods and something was burning behind us. I was elated, I felt like I was flying, I watched the dark floor of the forest rush past my feet. It was a feeling like...like...I had really achieved something, really done something that mattered.' He paused again and swallowed. 'And then the dream changed, and we were surrounded by the SS and I heard someone laughing—'

'Your bloody war...*merde*!' The sharpness of Veronique's voice stopped him short. She sat up suddenly and swung her long, tanned legs over the side of the bed. 'It's all you talk about, and now it's all you dream about. It's a beautiful summer's day out there and you're talking to me about the fucking Nazis!'

Paul tried to take hold of her arm and pull her back onto the bed but she shrugged him off.

'Look, I'm sorry, but this work, my work, it matters to me.'

She swung round and glared at him. 'And what about me, do I *matter*?'

'Of course, *Chérie*, come back to bed, please.'

She ignored him and stomped towards the kitchen. 'I'm going to make coffee.'

Paul sighed and decided that the row that was inevitably coming was best dealt with dressed and perpendicular. He got out of bed and pulled on his jeans and shirt and padded barefoot across the polished floorboards to join Veronique in the kitchen.

The two halves of the espresso maker clanged as she ground them together before slamming the pot onto the hob.

'Listen to me.' Paul reached out to put his hand on her arm and felt her stiffen. 'I am sorry, I will try harder. I know it's got a bit out of hand...'

'A "bit"?' Veronique spat back. 'It's become an obsession and you know it!'

'Well, I don't know about that -'

'Well I do, and it has. Death and war, that's all you think about, all you read about. I'm sick of it Paul!'

'It's not like that, Veronique, please, you must understand. I must fight, I have to fight, it's happening again and if we don't try to stop it, if we don't learn the lesson of history, it will happen again.'

She turned around to him, her face tight with anger, and it occurred to him that he would never get the chance to be with someone so beautiful again, and he was letting her slip through his fingers. 'You should try listening to yourself, Paul. You are so pompous! This is *now*, there is no way that something like the Nazis would ever happen again. People wouldn't let it happen, it is ridiculous! You are going to ruin your life with this shit. Can't you see that?'

'How do you know it won't happen again? Why are you so sure?' He could feel the anger rising in him now, she was lying to herself, because it was easier that way. 'Do you think the Nazis just started with concentration camps and goose-stepping? Of course they didn't. It was *drip, drip, drip:* first you start by demonising another group, just because of their skin colour or their religion, and you feed the population propaganda about them, to make people think of them than less than human. If that works, you quietly ignore or encourage the hate crime that follows, you turn them away from your borders, you stick them in detention camps.' He looked at her, searching her face, knowing he was sounding almost hysterical but unable to stop it. 'Can't you see that we are doing that *already?* That they are practising on us, testing us to see if they can get away with it? Can't you see that it is us, now, the people *seeing* the change happening that have to fight? If we don't it will only get worse, and the world, it will slip back into horror and those born after will think it is the natural way of things. All I am trying to do is to try to stop it, to do my bit -'

'Have you heard yourself? And how are you going to do *your bit?*' she replied with a sneer. 'By burying your nose in books?'. By obsessing about your hero grandfather, by organising visits to those morbid martyred villages and poring over pictures of burned bodies? What's wrong with you? Why can't you just enjoy *being alive?*'

He could feel the argument slipping away from him. 'It's because I value life,' he faltered, 'that I have to do this.'

'Well I can't do "this" anymore, Paul, I just can't.'

She pushed past him and went back into the bedroom and started to stuff the few things she had left in his flat into a supermarket bag that had been left discarded on the floor.

He followed her. 'What are you doing? *Chérie*, please stop for a moment!'

She stopped, the half-filled bag trailing in her hand. 'Yes?'

'What are you doing?'

'I don't think I'm going to come back here for a while. Maybe never.'

He went up to her and took her face in his hands. 'Please don't do this, Veronique, I need you.'

She stared at him impassively. 'No, you don't. You're not even *with* me Paul; your soul, your heart, it's somewhere else, looking, always looking. I have to be with someone who is looking *for me!*'

His hands fell back to his sides. He knew that he should want to do anything to make her stay. He should promise that he would change, but he knew he wasn't going to, that he couldn't. 'I'm sorry.'

She looked tearful then, and it filled him with shame. 'I'm sorry too.'

As he shut the main door of the apartments and stepped out onto the street, it suddenly hit him that he was alone again. Veronique had threatened to leave him before, but this time it felt different. He stopped for a moment to study his feelings; strangely, numbness was predominant. Despite her beauty, her elegance and her many talents, something about his relationship with Veronique had felt superficial. He wondered if that was his fault, if there was something wrong with him; he didn't feel qualified to know.

He decided to go to the Human and Social Sciences Library, or CNRS, on the Rue des Saints-Pères. The

library was a good five kilometres from Belleville, where
he lived, in the Latin Quarter, but he could feel ennui
snapping at his ankles and knew the only way to escape it
was to keep moving. He would walk there, and he would
spend the rest of the day working on his doctorate, then
by the time he got home he would be exhausted both
physically and mentally, and could just eat and go straight
to bed and escape the ghost of his impending loneliness.

With this plan in mind he headed north and after a few
hundred yards came onto the broad and busy Rue de
Envierges. It was a hot, dusty day and the buildings and
people around him seemed bleached and drained by the
relentless sun. Within seconds he felt the sweat spring up
on his back and soak through his thin shirt. The image of
the high-ceilinged, cool reading room at the CNRS formed
pleasantly in his mind, like the thought of an iced beer after
a day at the beach.

Five minutes later he hit the northern border of the
Parc de Belleville. Built in the late 1980s, it was the highest
park in Paris and spilled down a steep hill in wide curved
terraces, like a provincial hanging garden of Babylon. The
sun had pulled out the crowds and people sat around on
the lawns and benches in small architectural groupings like
Seurat's bathers. Before making his way down through the
park he stopped at a viewing platform and moved his eyes
across the tumbling panorama of his home city. It spilled
out above a dense belt of trees, a chaos of buildings and
roads ending in a distant blue-grey strip of heat-haze. To
the left there were the tall, bone-white outlines of tower-
blocks; to the right the solitary needlepoint of the Eiffel
Tower.

He turned and headed towards the central walkway which led him down hundreds of steps and through a shaded vine-covered walkway and eventually out onto the Rue des Couronnes. The street was busy with commuters but, thankfully, the shade continued as the sun hadn't yet made it to the strip of sky that ran between the high, flat-fronted apartment blocks.

He decided to stop somewhere for a coffee and a pastry. For a while he drifted, people and places melting into wraiths, passing silently around him as his mind took him into his internal world. He thought of the next stage of his thesis - researching the last Resistance cells of the Haute-Vienne; he thought of how it was going to feel that night getting into an empty bed; he wondered if he should text Veronique - and if he did - what he would say; he thought, for the hundredth time about his grandfather, Armand, and the risks he had taken to fight for a free France; and as it did every time, the thought humbled and shamed him as he compared it with the ease and privilege of his own short life.

Finding himself in front of the Bataclan Theatre jolted him out of his reverie. He stopped for a moment and sighed. The protective screens in front of the building had now been removed, but the image of the colourful old music hall shuttered and closed in with grief behind a moat of wilting flowers was burned in his mind. With every act of terror on his home soil, Paul felt a surge of dread. But his dread was not that shared by many of his fellow citizens - a dread of Islamic extremism and suicide bombs - his was a more political and existential kind of dread; that these attacks would push his country further to the right, and nearer its own kind of totalitarianism and terror.

People were sleepwalking towards it; that was what he truly believed; and it had been one of the bête noires that had driven Veronique away from him. He had enough self-awareness to realise this, but there was no question in his mind that fascism was on the rise again; he could feel it in the bones of himself; and yet there seemed to be nothing he could do about it.

He wandered towards the Boulevard Voltaire, remembering that there was a decent café there. After a couple of minutes, he found it and after ordering an Espresso and a croissant, found a small table in the shade under the awning. He sat down to wait for his drink and stretched out his long legs in front of him. An old man, his face deeply tanned and half hidden behind deep wrinkles, was smoking a roll-up beside him. The scent of it, mixed with the sweet aniseed smell of liquorice papers, was intoxicating. He hadn't had a cigarette in over a week and was only a social smoker really, but he badly wanted one now. He leant towards the old man and smiled. 'Excuse me, Monsieur, but do you think I could have one of your cigarettes?'

The old man looked at him and shrugged before passing him the packet of tobacco and papers. His eyes were black and bright underneath the hooded skin of his eyelids. Paul thanked him, made himself a thin roll-up and passed the tobacco back. His coffee and pastry were put on the table in front of him by a young waiter. He put a little sugar in the coffee and used the small paper serviette it came with to dab the sweat from his forehead and upper lip.

He put the cigarette in his mouth and then realised he didn't have a light. 'I'm sorry, Monsieur, but do you have a light also?'

The old man shook his newspaper out, as if making the point that Paul was interfering with his consumption of current affairs and passed his lighter across to him with a frown.

'Merci.' Paul lit his cigarette and handed the lighter back, squinting as the first plume of smoke from the cigarette drifted up past his eyes.

He took a sip of his coffee and then a proper pull on the roll-up. It felt good. He watched the people as they passed by his little oasis in the shade. Most ignored him, but the odd woman looked his way appraisingly. He was used to this, but also felt a little uncomfortable about it. It wasn't something he cultivated; but Veronique had repeatedly told him, with a glow of pride, that he could just throw on a shirt and a battered old pair of trainers and he was still head-turning. He didn't quite believe it himself and had always looked at stunning Veronique with a vague sense of wonder that he had managed to attract such an extraordinary and exotic being.

As he stubbed out the cigarette he realised it had made him feel a little light-headed and sick and he ate the chocolate croissant without relish. He finished his drink and grimaced as the last bitter grits of the coffee hit his mouth. He got up and took a few deep breaths before walking again, trying to dispel the nausea. He raised a hand in farewell to the old gentleman, who nodded back reluctantly, and stepped back into the loose, chatting crowds.

Forty minutes later he turned onto the Pont des Arts. The broad pedestrian bridge was busy, and barely any of the wooden walkway was visible beneath the movement of bare summer legs, and the pockets of spectators gathering around the painters and artists that had set up their stalls to attempt to reproduce the heat-softened beauty of the Seine. There was something bitter-sweet about crossing the bridge; he and Veronique, in the first heady flush of their relationship, had even put a love lock on the railings; but soon after, every one of the million lovers' locks had been removed by the authorities, as the weight of them was threatening to bring down the bridge. The original bridge had survived two world wars, he thought, and yet this one is nearly destroyed by something as ephemeral as lovers' hubris. He castigated himself internally for his cynicism, but it was hard; now with hindsight, not to feel miserable. They had high hopes when they had started out, but the swift removal of their lock now seemed a sign of the ultimate temporariness of their relationship.

By the time he had reached the other end of the bridge and set off towards the Rue des Saints-Pères, he felt better. What he had said to Veronique, about it being them - the witnesses to change - who needed to fight, was true. People tended to accept the society that they were born into, this was the human way. Within a mere generation, for example, young people didn't bat an eyelid if someone was gay. But it worked the other way too - with evil and intolerance. Without witnesses, without those who could describe and resist the change - what hope was there? He must finish his doctorate, and then, he must tell the world.

Half an hour later, as he plodded up the steps of the library, he realised he felt dog-tired. The building's imposing and angular stone-grey facade loomed in front of him - ever both an invitation and a reproach. An invitation, because it was full of knowledge. In the 80,000 or so books it was home to, there was the story of everything: our wars, our beliefs, our inventions. A reproach, as it stood as a monument to the fact that it was never possible for anyone to know everything. The sum total of human knowledge was exactly that - a sum total - a glorious and flawed universe of individual learning, sacrifice and belief. In the end, all he could hope to do was to add a single star into the inky depths of this infinite universe. As he got older he had realised that he must focus on and study one thing and one thing only, and that was what he had done.

He pushed through the glass doors and was instantly revived by a cooling blast of air conditioning. He stopped for a moment and sighed, feeling the sweat chill and retreat from his skin. He had already emailed ahead to order the books he wanted and stopped off to pick them up before heading to the reading room. Although a million miles from the opulence and grandeur of the reading room at the Bibliothèque Nationale, the one at the CNRS still had for him a slightly magical feel. The simple fact of being surrounded by books, the low light, and the wooden desk tops worn smooth by the passage of a million hands and books spoke quietly but powerfully of humanity's hunger for knowledge and enlightenment.

It was quiet in the reading room; no doubt most students were out in the sunshine, he thought a little ruefully, enjoying being young and free. He chose a desk in the middle of the room, sat down and took out his notes. He had three books; one a social history of the Haute-Vienne region between the wars; another, exploring a more painful subject for the French: collaborators and forced conscripts (the Milice and Malgre Nous) in the Vichy; and the last - an account, partly from personal experience of the massacre at the village of Argemourt at the end of WWII called *Village des Fantômes.*

He settled comfortably in his chair, enjoying that first feeling of expectation and pleasure that accompanied opening a book he hadn't seen before. He went first for *Village des Fantômes,* picked it up and studied the cover. It was stark and disturbing; the outline of a half-ruined church against a blood-red sky. He flicked to the title page: the author was called Michèle Leroy, an elderly lady who still lived near the church where the villagers were murdered. Strange that she should have chosen to stay there, thought Paul. He tapped his finger on the small black and white portrait above the author's biography. It must have been taken soon after the war; a skinny girl in her early teens with haunted eyes, standing in front of a small white-shuttered cottage. It gave him an idea.

The following day was steamy and overcast. When Paul stepped from the air-conditioned comfort of his little Fiat, the air hit him with jungle-like humidity. He locked the car and crunched up the gravel towards his grandfather's door. As ever the front garden was immaculate; velvet lawns on either side of the drive, the planting considered and stylish: yellow flowers contrasted against deep purple shrubs and foliage. It had been his grandmother who had been into gardening, but Armand's subsequent care for it had been an act of homage, even though his increasing frailty had meant hiring a local gardener.

The house was old, built around 1850, and the original door pull had been polished up and renovated. It made a lonely, echoing peal somewhere in the depths of the house, and a few moments later he heard a shuffling step approaching. The door opened and his grandfather beamed at him. At ninety-two, he was still handsome, and dignified in his brogues and waistcoat despite his bowed back.

Paul stooped and kissed him on both cheeks. 'Bonjour, Papy!'

'Ah my golden boy!' His Grandfather patted his cheek. 'Ici, ici! I am making omelettes.'

'My favourite, Papy. You know how to spoil me!'

'Ah you deserve it, Paul, I know how hard you work, now come here and let me look at you.' He pulled Paul gently into the cool hallway and held him at arm's length. 'Can it be possible, Paul, that you have grown?'

This was a conceit they played every time he visited. At 25, he hadn't grown for at least seven years, and although, right up until Paul hit his late teens, his grandfather had been taller than him, age had finally oppressed him into shrinking submission; something that always gave Paul a little pang of sadness.

'I believe I may have, Papy, or maybe it is you who is shrinking?'

'Ha!' His grandfather pointed at him and chuckled. 'I forgive the discourtesies of the young, they know not what they do!'

'Yes, forgive me, Papy. One day I will be as old as you, and hopefully by then I will have learned some manners.'

'Indeed! Come now, let's have lunch.'

They headed down the hall then left into the high-ceilinged kitchen. All was white and old pine and the long sash windows gave the room a feeling of airiness and freshness that always lifted Paul's spirits. His grandfather gestured for him to sit then busied himself with putting a heavy black frying pan on the hob.

'*Only ever cook eggs in a cast-iron pan*, your mamy used to say. Though you must season them properly before you use them - coat them in oil and put them in a low oven overnight. These pans are over fifty years old, a wedding present, so many things have been cooked in them over the years...' He trailed off and his gaze became watery.

Paul smiled at him and said gently; 'She was a wonderful lady. I miss her too.'

Papy nodded and went back to whisking his eggs. 'Is everything all right, Paul? There is something different about you today, you don't seem, well, you don't seem yourself somehow.'

'Veronique left me, but I'm ok, Papy, honestly I am.'

His grandfather compressed his lips and shrugged. 'I am sorry, Paul. She was very beautiful and accomplished, but somehow - ah it is not my place to say.'

'It's ok, let me guess; you think she wasn't quite deep enough, that she couldn't understand my work properly?'

'Hmm. Maybe, something like that.'

'I thought that too, but now, I don't know, I'm beginning to think that maybe it is that I was *too* deep, that I have become my work only, that I pushed her away.'

'Maybe you did,' Papy caught his eye and held it for a moment, 'but then maybe you had to?'

It was Paul's turn to shrug, and then, to change the subject: 'Hey, let me help you.'

'No, no, sit. This is my kitchen, and I am making lunch for you!'

'Ok, Papy! I will *sit here on my skinny arse* as you often like to put it and leave you alone!'

His grandfather put a baton on the table and then stood back with an air of pride. 'I made that baton you know. It isn't as hard as you'd think - but you must leave it to rise overnight and be gentle with it when you knead it at the end or the texture becomes heavy.'

Paul tore the end from the baguette and chewed appreciatively. 'It's good, Papy but be careful you aren't doing too much. You need your rest too.'

'Pah! Rest! I will rest when I'm dead!'

Paul shook his head. 'You'll be telling me you've got chickens next and that's where the eggs are from!'

'You are almost right. They are from Madame Vivier, my neighbour.' He returned to the table with two plates, both filled by a small dressed salad and a folded omelette, perfect pale-yellow semicircles like rising suns. The delicious aroma of ham and melted Emmental emanated from the plate.

'Ah merci, Papy, it smells incredible.'

His grandfather smiled with satisfaction and went to the fridge. He came back with a bottle of chilled Alsace and two slim wine glasses.

'Papy,' he said with mild admonishment, 'you know what the doctor said -'

'Doctor, Pah! Life's not worth living without a glass of wine with my lunch!'

'Ok, maybe one.'

'One? Don't be ridiculous, we're sharing this bottle and that's that.'

Half an hour later they took the end of the bottle of wine and a couple of Espressos out into the garden. Paul felt a deep sense of ease and satisfaction, something he often experienced when he visited his Grand Papa Armand. There was an air of learning and wisdom in the old house: the walls of books and elegant antique furniture all bathed in an atmosphere of peace, quiet and contemplation. True, the sense of quiet had been hard for the first couple of years after his grand-mère, Marie, had died. She had been a force of nature, and unlike his grand-père, a great thrower of parties; a social animal, affectionate and funny. She and Armand had complemented each other perfectly, but as time had gone on after her death, the house had slowly settled into a bricks and mortar expression of its remaining owner - noble, modest and peaceful.

A slightly flat rendition of Trois Gynopédies floated over the fence of the neighbouring garden. 'Ah,' said Armand, swallowing down the last of his wine, 'little Camilla; she is as regular as clockwork - flute practice, every day at 3pm. Poor old Satie must be turning in his grave, but you can't make an omelette, after all, without breaking eggs.'

Paul squeezed his papy's liver-spotted hand and laughed. He was feeling thoughtful and, he had to admit, a little tipsy from the afternoon drinking. He would have to have a catnap in the spare room before he drove home.

'Papy?'

'Oui, *Fiston*?'

Paul swallowed and was surprised to find that there were tears in his eyes. 'Sometimes I feel ashamed.'

Armand frowned. 'Why on earth would you feel like that?'

'Because I worry that I have done nothing with my life. Maybe Veronique is right, all this,' he waved his arm jerkily in the air, 'is just a stupid obsession, a useless obsession with the dead that is taking me away from the living.'

'Death is important, Paul. Without death, without a finite end, life is like sex without an orgasm - just a lot of pointless motion.'

'But it's not just that. I mean, look at you, you were a fighter in the war, you were a *doer*. What am I? I have become a useless intellectual, playing around at the edges of the acts of great people; people who put their lives at risk for the greater good.'

His grandfather put his hand on Paul's arm and squeezed it tightly. 'Listen, there are *doers*, *witnesses* and *explainers*. That is what the world needs. You are an explainer, it is a great gift. Do not squander it through useless self-criticism and lack of faith. You think it is somehow worthier to fight and to kill? Believe me, you are wrong. I am so proud of you, of what you are working for, it is why I have helped to fund you as you do your doctorate. You must reveal your truths, you must tell the story, you must explain why we must learn the lessons of history.'

Paul wiped his eyes with the back of his hand. 'Papy, how did you get to be so wise?'

'I am not wise, I have merely had longer than you to think about things. Let's have that coffee.' He poured the Espressos and added a little sugar. 'Here, this will help to clear our heads.' They clinked their cups together. The sound of the flute practice stopped and suddenly the garden was silent again.

'So, tell me, what are you working on now?'

Paul sat forward. 'Difficult, painful subjects; the true extent of man's inhumanity to man: the martyred villages; mothers and babies shot at point-blank range; people hung from the lampposts in their own town squares; pets' throats cut in front of their owners; children burned alive in their churches. Things I barely know how to contemplate, let alone describe.'

Armand's eyes focused loosely on the middle distance, he looked pale. 'There were some terrible things done in 1944 when the Germans started to accept that they had lost the war. They were like rabid dogs trapped in the corner of a room; vicious and reckless.'

'But what is even worse, what I just can't get my head around, is the Milice.'

His grand-father looked round at him sharply, 'Eh?'

'The fact that some of these atrocities were carried out by our own people. Frenchman on Frenchman. How is that possible?'

'I asked one man that very same question,' replied Armand, barely above a whisper, 'and he said *you just pull the trigger, they drop, and that's it.'*

'Who was that?'

'Ah, no one, Paul. Ignore me, I am just an old man rambling.'

They sat in silence for a while. Paul tipped his head against his chair and watched the mottled shifting of the clouds in the hot air above them. Armand cleared his throat.

'You have to remember how different it was then, Paul. Everyone lived in terror, no-one could escape it. From the soldier to the housewife, you never knew who to trust; you lived in constant fear of saying or doing the wrong thing; you were in constant fear of harm coming to your loved ones. It is terrible to grow up in such conditions, it can deform a man's soul. And for my family, growing up in Alsace, so close to Germany, it was very hard.'

'Surely you're not defending them, Papy?'

Armand looked at him briefly then rubbed his eyes. 'No, of course not. To the Resistance the Milice were more dangerous than the SS and the Gestapo, because they knew the local dialects and geography and could more easily pass themselves off as Maquis. But if you are to *explain*, you must first *understand*. There was a lot of poverty, jobs were hard to come by, and some believed what the Germans said - that their problems, the poverty, were because of the Jews - they bought in to the ideology - just like people are doing today with the Front National, or *National Rally*, whatever they call it now. For some it was just that, ideology, that drove them to it. For others, it was starvation...or terror.'

Paul shook his head and watched a blackbird peck a worm out of the lawn and fly off with it. 'No-one talks about it, I don't think that's right. From films and TV, you'd think every young man in France during the war was in the Resistance, like you, but there's another truth. And we let so many of them go in the Amnesty in 1953, how could we do that? I'm surprised that there weren't riots. I'd rather die than shoot one of my own countrymen.'

'A noble ideal, Fiston, but you have only yourself to worry about; imagine if you had a wife, a child. What if someone said they would be killed unless you joined up; what would you do then?'

Paul shifted uncomfortably in Armand's searching gaze. 'I...I don't know, but many did only have themselves to worry about, and they still did it.'

'That is true, some did it because they were evil, some because they were full of hate, and some - some did it simply because they were weak.'

When Paul got home that evening, he felt exhausted; partly because of the half-bottle of wine he had drunk in the afternoon heat, and partly because he had got emotional. He had wanted to ask Armand so much more about the Milice and the forced conscripts to the SS from Alsace Lorraine, but his grandfather had become very weary and seemed reluctant to talk about it anymore. Paul's research had led him to interview some of the remaining survivors of the Second World War, and if there was one thing he had learnt, it was that pushing people to talk about past horrors if they weren't ready for it, was both unethical and counterproductive.

He undressed and got into the shower hoping it would wake him up a bit. He stood for a long time with his head directly under the jet, enjoying the sensation of the pressurised water hitting his scalp and shoulders and running down his body. His mind felt full from the last couple of days, as if everything that had happened was threatening to overwhelm it. He needed to have a week or so of calm and the chance to sort his head out. As he turned off the shower he found himself wondering for a moment what Veronique was up to; if she was missing him. He thought again about calling her but dismissed the idea.

He dried off and threw on some tracksuit bottoms and a t-shirt and went through to the kitchen to heat up the noodles he had bought on the way home. While he was waiting for the microwave to ping he turned on the radio and went over to the window. His apartment was just high enough for him to see over the tops of the buildings on the other side of the street. The sky was overcast, but there was a rip in the clouds; just over the 10th arrondissement, where a molten sunset blazed through with neon-pink ferocity. On the radio, climate experts were talking about the crisis in the Arctic; that more ice than ever was melting and this meant that some polar bears were starving to death. A sense of melancholy washed over him as if he'd lost something precious; and his breath caught in his throat. The microwave pinged and he changed the radio over to FIP Autour du Monde for some cheery world music instead.

He spent the rest of the evening working; making his way methodically through the new books he had got from the CNRS; logging references, scanning in witness testimonies and allocating information to the different sections of his thesis. The work felt a bit like swimming; for a while he was submerged, moving swiftly and silently - focused entirely on this new world; but then some fact or image or account would jolt him; like the need to breathe; and he would come, spluttering to the surface and back into the lonely reality of his apartment.

Armand had said that for him to *explain*, he must first *understand*. But the more he read about the Milice, the further he was taken away from any sense of understanding. He understood the facts: that the political paramilitary force was set up by the Vichy government and the Nazis to fight the Resistance on home soil; he understood that by 1944 there were around 30,000 of these traitor soldiers; he even understood from various accounts in his books that some (as Papy had told him) joined because of starvation; some in revenge for families killed by the Allies; but however many of these accounts he read, he still couldn't bend his soul towards understanding how one Frenchman could turn and shoot another French citizen in cold blood under the justification of 'war'.

Much of what he read, talked about the process of dehumanisation and how it allowed the Nazis and their sympathisers to see their victims as worse than animals. He didn't believe it was that simple - for him it was also about choice. There was a story about Himmler in the early days of the war, before the genesis of the Final Solution. He had been attending a mass killing of Jews. The unsophisticated and brutal modus operandi was to get them to dig a mass grave then line up in front of it. A firing squad would mow down row after row-and men, women and children would fall backwards into the pit until it was filled. One woman had held her baby out to the soldiers and begged them at least to spare it, if not her. A soldier had promptly and deliberately shot her, through her baby. Apparently, Himmler had fainted. And this, thought Paul, had been a fulcrum, a point of choice. Himmler could have gone from that to challenge the Nazi leadership, to try to rein in the genocide; instead he had teamed up with Heydrich to design the concentration camps - as a way of sparing German soldiers the trauma of 'face-to-face' killings like these.

But even this, this unbelievable, sickening act, made more sense to him than the acts of the Milice. The Germans had already endured years of propaganda, lies and political manipulation. The French had not. In fact, they had been occupied by a terrible enemy and yet some had chosen to side with this enemy; to march with them; to kill with them. For Paul it was an existential crisis; this terrible historical wound in the humanity of his country; and, conversely, the more he read the less he seemed to be able to comprehend it.

That night his dreams were dark and frenetic again. He was in a deserted field at night-time; the only sounds the hoots of owls and the soft rustle of the wheat that moved in eddies around his knees. He knew he was being hunted; he ran, but his legs weren't working properly, and the faster he tried to run, the slower he went, until at last he started to sink, the soft earth tugging at his feet, his heart beating so fast he could barely breathe. And then, he was with the girl with the haunted eyes, Michèle Leroy, just as she was in the picture from her book. She was staring at him, her back against an old stone wall. The sun was bright now and he felt hot and sticky. She opened her mouth as if to scream, but no sound came out. With horror he watched as her mouth stayed open, the space inside dark and hollow. He put his hands out in front of him, shook his head, tried to reassure her that he wouldn't hurt her but the arms in front of him looked strange. He stared down at his feet then reached up and took the hat from his head; everything was wrong. He was in the uniform of the Milice: blue jacket and trousers, brown shirt and a wide blue beret.

Over the next couple of weeks and encouraged by his grandfather's belief in his work, Paul threw himself into the final stages of his doctorate. Only so much could be found out from books and the internet, and the time was coming when he would start his tour of the martyred villages. He had been working on his itinerary for months and had already finalised the details of his first visit. He suspected it was the planning of this tour that had been the final straw for Veronique.

The university had a list of people who rented out their spare rooms to students who were doing research into the Second World War. Some of these households included people who had direct experience of the Occupation or relatives who could share the memories of those who had since died. This process felt right to Paul - families ensuring that the stories of the dead continued to be told. There was a profound necessity, he thought, that this knowledge was passed into the hearts of the young, so that they might hold on to the delicate threads of compassion and tolerance and carry them forward into future generations.

Some of the martyred villages, like Maille and Tulle, had been wiped clean (at least in terms of physical evidence) of the horrors of 1944. However, one in particular, Oradour-sur-Glane, was a national monument, the original village kept exactly as it had been after all 642 inhabitants had been shot or burned alive. Paul had been there once, with his parents on the way to visiting his cousins in Limoges. The crumbling houses and stony roads were strewn with rusted cars, sewing machines and abandoned—prams, decayed and deeply macabre, like the corpses of strange animals. After an hour his mother had gone very white and demanded that they leave. Paul had wanted to stay longer; something about the place fascinated and appalled him in equal measure. He remembered, with a little shiver of shame, that he had taken a small white pebble from one of the graves of the villagers. He had kept it in the pocket of his trousers for weeks, turning it round and round in his hand. Maybe that had been when it all started; this searching, or *obsession*, as Veronique had frequently called it.

And finally, the old village of Argemourt. Surprisingly this was still lived in, and the village had grown, with new shops, houses and a museum springing up in the post-war years. The church, where the main atrocity had happened a mile or so from the centre, was derelict, but still considered as a shrine to those who were murdered. There was something about the pathos of the church, slowly crumbling away back into the earth as the village grew, that had drawn Paul to the place and made him decide to visit there first. And the university had found him a place to stay, in a cottage, still lived in by one of the few survivors of the attack. The idea of this proximity to someone with direct experience of what had happened, both enthralled and unsettled him.

It was another hot and humid day, and despite having all the long windows and the balcony doors open in his apartment, there was no discernible freshness about the air that was coming in to the sitting room. There was a charge in the atmosphere too; a sense of anticipation almost as if

144

the sky was holding its breath. Paul took a deep gulp of his iced tea and tried to focus again on the introduction to his thesis.

"Once, all these villages were normal, bustling places," he typed, aware that he was tense and frowning with concentration, *"like millions of villages all over the world; full of people buying and selling, falling in love, raising their children, squabbling and gossiping. But in the summer of 1944, all that was about to change..."*

His mobile buzzed and vibrated on the desk beside him. He grunted with frustration and swiped the screen to answer it without even looking to see who was calling him.

'Oui?' he said, a little more sharply than he had intended.

'Quoi de neuf, Paul? What the hell have you been up to? Have you joined the Trappists and taken a vow of silence?'

Paul laughed. 'Henri, Salut! No, you know me and religion, no danger of that.'

'Ah, locked yourself away to nurse your broken heart then?

'So, you've spoken to Veronique?' Paul tried to sound nonchalant.

'No, I heard it from Sophie.'

'Did she say how Veronique is?'

'You can quiz her about it all you like when we go out tonight. It's Sophie's birthday, remember? She wants to do pizza then cocktails at Moonshiner. Manny and Nicolas are coming too.'

'Merde, Sophie's birthday, I had forgotten! I'm not sure, I've still got so much to do before I go away - '

'No excuses, we're expecting you. 8 o'clock. Be there or, well, you know what she's like when she's angry! It'll do you good. Remember what happened to Jack in The Shining!'

'Yeh, yeh, *all work and no play*, I get it. See you there.'

Paul came out of Brégeut-Sabin Metro station, crossed the broad and leafy pavements of Boulevard Richard Lenoir and headed down the Rue Sedaine. As he turned the corner he could see his friends seated at a small table under Moonshiner's distinctive black and white striped awning, tucking into sourdough pizza.

'Paul!' Sophie looked really pleased to see him and pushed back her chair as he approached. 'It's been too long!' She threw her arms around him and gave him a tight hug.

Manny got up and fist bumped him, his smiling face perfectly framed by his abundant dreadlocks. 'Where you been, man? It's good to see you.'

Henri got a chair for Paul and gestured for him to sit down.

Nicolas pushed a plate towards him. 'We got you your favourite. Eat! We're all going to need a full stomach - there's a long night of drinking ahead.'

Paul smiled and nodded his thanks. He tore a slice from the pizza and felt his stomach rumble with anticipation. A strand of melted cheese stretched from the base up to his mouth. He twisted it on to his finger and happily licked it off.

'You want a beer?' Henri tapped Paul's plate with his empty bottle of Corona.

'Oui, merci, Henri.'

'Sensible boy.' Said Sophie with a wink. 'We're all having beer to start so we can save some stamina for the cocktails!'

Henri went inside the restaurant to get the beer, bending his tall frame so he could fit through the doorway. Nicolas waved his last piece of pizza at Paul. 'So where have you been, mystery boy?'

'At home, that's all. I've been working hard on my thesis. I go on my trip next week, I've just been so busy.'

'I don't know how you do it; all that reading. I'd go mad.'

Paul shrugged. 'It's not for everyone; but you'd be surprised. Once you start looking into something it can become addictive, there's always more to learn.'

'Isn't that the problem?' Sophie took a swig of her beer. 'Finding out you can never know everything?'

'Yes, but that doesn't mean we shouldn't try. There's so much to learn from the past. There are so many stories behind us, so many experiences. Like my Papy, he went through so much in the war. He risked his life, everything to try to make sure we got to grow up in a free France.'

Manny nodded sagely. 'It's like what that English writer, Hilary Mantel says, "the past is not a rehearsal," he said in heavily accented English; "'it is the show itself." '

They all turned to look at him in surprise. Manny was a laid-back guy who enjoyed a smoke, but every now and then he would come out with something like this. Clearly his thoughts ran deeper than he let on.

'I like that,' replied Paul. 'I may see if I can use it.'

'You're welcome.'

Nicolas shook his long, bird-like face and eyed Manny beadily. 'Where the hell do you get this shit, Manny?'

'I just listen. And when I hear something I like I write it down.'

Nicolas raised his eyebrows but said nothing.

Henri came back and put a fresh tray of beers on the table. 'You've missed some good times, Paul, my friend. The Deen Burbigo gig was incredible, and the anti-racism march; I'm surprised you didn't come to that - it's all linked with what you're studying isn't it?'

'I know, I've been shit. But everything's a bit crazy at the moment.'

There was a deep rumble somewhere in the dark depths of the sky and they all stopped and looked up. There was a flash of lightning, and then another throaty roar that echoed around the grey-stone buildings that lined the street.

'Come on,' said Sophie, stacking their empty plates and picking up her beer. 'It's going to rain like a pissing cow, let's go through to the bar.'

They handed their plates to a passing waiter and headed for the unremarkable metal door at the back of the restaurant that marked the entrance to the cocktail bar. Unless you knew what you were looking for you would have no idea that behind the bustling pizza restaurant, there was one of the most popular drinking dens in Paris. Most Parisians were happy to keep it that way, but the plethora of travel websites was making it harder and harder to keep the secret.

They moved from the sounds of clinking plates and snatches of shouted Italian into the convivial sound of chat and laughter. The bar was dimly lit, and with its Art Nouveau tiled walls and red velvet stools and sofas, it was like stepping back in time into a 1920s speakeasy. Sophie gestured towards a booth underneath a small stained-glass window, and they settled into the plush comfort of the corner seat.

Sophie gathered up the cocktail menus before any of them could look at them and shooing away their shouts of protest, waved for the waiter to come over. 'Hi there, could we have two *Sergeant Reckless*', two *Glasgow Remains* and two *Rien Ne Va Plus*, please.'

'But -'

She cut Henri off before he could finish his sentence. 'Just trust me. You're all going to love them.'

Nicolas looked at her shrewdly. 'That's six cocktails, Sophie, there's only five of us.'

'Two for me.' She said, tossing her curly blonde hair. 'Birthday prerogative.'

Paul laughed and looked at Henri. 'Good luck, she's on a mission!'

Henri put his arm around his girlfriend. 'I love you, Sophie, but if you throw up all that pizza later, you're on your own.'

Sophie dug him in the ribs. 'You have a hard heart, Monsieur!'

Manny, who had been unconsciously banging out a Hip-Hop beat with his hands on the table stopped suddenly and turned to Paul. 'So, what's been keeping you away, Man? What you been studying? Last I heard it was about the Resistance?'

'Really, you don't want to know. It's all a bit dark to be honest.'

'Come on, tell us.'

Sophie leaned over and put her hand on Manny's arm. 'Let him be, this is supposed to be a break for him. The last thing he wants to do is talk about all that shit.'

Paul smiled at her gratefully. 'I'm sorry, Manny, She's right, I'm not in the mood. It's great to be out with all you guys and leave the heaviness behind for a night. And I promise, as soon as I'm back from my trip it's back to the old Paul.'

The flow of conversation was broken as the waiter reappeared with a glittering tray of cocktails. He placed them down in a neat circle, and the candle in the centre of the table shone through them all, lighting up their hearts with gold, peach and pale blue. Sophie picked up each one and handed them out. Paul's was in a tall glass with pomegranate seeds scattered over its topping of crushed ice, like jewels set in a glass crown.

As the others chatted about their drinks and gave each other turns tasting them, he took the opportunity to lean in towards Sophie. 'Henri said you'd seen Veronique?'

Sophie looked up at him, her pretty mouth puckered around her straw as she sucked on the cocktail. She released it and looked down into her drink and gave it a stir. 'Yes, last week.'

'Is she ok?'

She looked up at him again, briefly. 'What are you wanting me to say, Paul? Are you hoping I'll say she's ok so you can feel less bad about the fact that you don't miss her as much as you thought you would; or are you hoping I'll say she's in a mess, because you want to get back together with her?'

Paul sighed. 'That's a good question; and I'm not sure I know the answer.'

She reached up and briefly stroked his cheek. 'Ah Paul, my poor beautiful Paul. I wanted you myself once, did you know that?'

He shook his head mutely, he could feel himself blushing.

'You are so handsome, so gentle. I thought I was in love with you, but there's something about you, a distance. I didn't know how to reach you, and then I met Henri and I knew that *he* was where I was supposed to be.'

'I...I'm sorry, I never knew.'

'Of course you didn't!' She skewered the slice of kiwi in her cocktail and popped it in her mouth.

'Am I really that bad? So distant?'

'It's not as simple as that,' she said kindly. 'If I make it sound like a flaw I don't mean it to. You are a good man, you feel things very deeply, it means that you are often somewhere else in your mind. That's all. Don't feel bad about it, but perhaps, well, I don't know if I should say any more.'

'Please, tell me, Sophie.'

She took hold of his hand and gave it a brief squeeze. 'All of that is good, the thinking, the caring about things; but don't forget to live in the moment too. So long as you're anchored in the present you have a way to get back when you've spent too long in the past. If you lose that anchor, you could get lost forever.'

Paul stared at her, silenced by her words, sorting and analysing them. There was a truth in them, he knew it.

Suddenly Henri got up and raised his glass. 'I propose a toast! Bon Anniversaire to my beautiful girlfriend, Sophie!' Paul, Nicolas and Manny stood up and lifted their glasses, Sophie smiled up at them all happily. 'And to mark this special occasion,' Henri continued with mock gravitas, 'I would like to dedicate this song to you.'

Sophie rolled her eyes and shook her head. 'Henri, in the name of all that is good in this world, please DO NOT sing!'

'Non, je ne regrette rien...' sang Henri, lustily and out of tune; ignoring her.

The rain had stopped and the dark pavement shone glossily under the yellow streetlamps. Henri took a deep drag on the spliff then handed it to Paul. He took a deep drag too, holding the smoke in his lungs for a moment and enjoying the gentle unravelling of tension that was spiralling down from his scalp and into his limbs. He released the smoke with a hiss from between pursed lips and then handed the joint back to his friend.

'That's good shit!'

'Yeh, get it from a friend of mine. Proper old school stuff, not too strong.'

They sat in companionable silence for a while, enjoying breathing in the fresher rain-cleansed air and the sweet, woody smell of the spliff. The storm had rumbled off into the east, but they could still hear it, though much fainter, like the sounds of a distant war.

'Are you really ok?'

Paul looked across at him. 'Yeh, of course.'

'You're not too cut up then, about Veronique? Two years is a long time to be with someone; at least it is at our age.'

'I'm ok, I promise. Of course I'm sad, and I feel lonely, especially in the evenings, you know. But I'll be ok. It would have been hard on her, anyway, when I went away.

And it's not like she could have come with me. I'm researching some dark shit, and she hated all that. Maybe she was the right person, but just at the wrong time.'

'I don't know, maybe.'

'Why do you say that?'

Henri exhaled and passed the joint to Paul again. 'Don't get me wrong, Veronique was lovely, and let's face it, very easy on the eye,' he smirked at Paul good-naturedly, 'but I don't think she was *the one*.'

'Is there ever *a one?*'

'Yeh, of course there is!' Henri replied, animatedly. 'When I met Sophie, I just knew. Simple as that. We fit each other, I mean, not like that - or at least *not just* like that - but with her I feel like I'm home. Do you know what I mean?'

Paul shook his head. 'Fuck, I'm pissed!' They looked at each other and laughed. 'Perhaps we should go back to the others?'

Henri nodded and dropped the end of the spliff onto the damp pavement and ground it out under his shoe.

They stood to go in, and then the air, the furniture around them, the pavement, all trembled, and a catastrophic bang reverberated through them in a jarring wave followed by the silvery, tinkling sound of shattering glass.

'More thunder?' muttered Henri, his face white.

Paul shook his head. He felt suddenly sober and his heart was racing in his chest. The echo of the explosion was still ricocheting, it was everywhere, bouncing off the pavement and the rooftops, tearing the air. Next came the sound of screaming, rolling towards them; faint but unmistakeable.

Henri grabbed hold of his arm. 'Shit!'

With an unspoken but parallel thought they both turned to go back into the bar to get the others but at the same moment the door was flung open and people spilled out onto the street, their faces ghoulishly lit by the lurid glow of their phone screens. Paul and Henri were pushed further out onto the pavement, and the screech of sirens struck up, seemingly from every direction.

Sophie appeared and grabbed on to Henri's arm; she looked terrified. 'There's been an explosion.'

Nicolas appeared too and turned his phone screen towards them, his hand was shaking. 'At the Opera Bastille. The performance had just finished, people were leaving and there was an explosion in the foyer.'

Paul shook his head, he couldn't believe it. 'Are there casualties?'

Manny stood with his back to them, his head lowered. 'It's fucked up, man!' He sounded tearful. 'What's wrong with people? Why can't they leave our city alone?'

'The Opera, it's just around the corner isn't it?' said Henri, urgently. 'We should go, shouldn't we? See if we can help?'

With silent accord they headed back up the road towards the Boulevard Richard Lenoir. Lights were springing on in the apartment windows above their heads and people were emerging, blinking and afraid, from the comfortable depths of bars and restaurants. The friends turned onto the main road, the sound of sirens was getting louder. The Opera was just a few hundred metres away and they started to jog towards it. Paul could feel the adrenalin firing up in his arms and legs, sharpening his mind and his senses. After a few moments they stopped.

The end of the road was obscured by a cloud of dark grey dust, the blue and red flashes of emergency vehicles pulsing through it like the bioluminescence of deep-sea creatures. The sound of the screams was suddenly close, and there was something so animalistic and desperate about them that Paul felt the sudden urge to turn and run in the opposite direction.

They went forward more cautiously, but then a policeman emerged from the smoke, assault rifle in hand; there was a tautness about him that made Paul's stomach clench.

'Go back!' he barked at them.

Henri stepped forward. 'But we thought we might be able to help?'

'No! It isn't safe, the area isn't secured, there could be more. The best thing you can do is go home!'

'But this *is* our home,' said Sophie, her voice small and shaky.

The next morning when Paul woke up, it was to a feeling of unidentified anxiety as if he had done something he was ashamed of or let somebody down in a terrible way. As full consciousness returned and the previous evening played through his mind, he remembered that the feeling was there because someone had brutally attacked his city. For some unfathomable reason they had chosen to slaughter innocent people to pay for the mistakes of their governments - or history - or economics - or whatever they used to justify murder. For a second, he imagined the terror of those inside the opera hall; the terrible sounds, the screams, the suffocating smoke; desperately trying to hold on to your loved ones; losing them, seeing yourself injured - an arm blasted off, a piece of brickwork lodged in your stomach. He reached for his phone, in the panic he had forgotten to let his family know he was ok.

As he leaned over to the bedside table for it, the room started to spin. He breathed deeply and moved more slowly. When he picked up the phone the screen was black. He had obviously forgotten to charge it when he'd got home. He reached down and plugged it in. The floor lurched up towards him and a wave of nausea hit him like a fist. He half fell out of bed and staggered to the bathroom where he vomited up a stomach-full of thin bitter bile.

When he finally made it back to the bedroom, still feeling shaky and light-headed, his phone was pinging and the screen was lit up. He sat down slowly on the side of the bed and rubbed his face. He took a few deep breaths and felt a bit better. He leant over and picked up the phone.

Unsurprisingly most of the missed calls and texts were from his mum. He quickly tapped back a reply: *I'm fine, Mum, don't worry. Sorry I didn't text last night but it was so late. I'll call later.* He threw the phone onto the bed behind him and got up with a groan. The shock of the events of the night before, despite sobering him up in seconds at the time, had unfortunately not prevented his hangover, and his oppressive feelings of anger, despair and melancholy were nourished by a bad headache, dry mouth and delicate stomach.

He spent most of the morning texting Henri and glued to the television; unable to tear himself away from the endless cycle of studio analysis and interviews with journalists at the scene. The same things were said a

156

hundred times in a hundred different ways: the explosion was caused by a suicide bomber; around 30 people were feared dead; police were working around the clock but it was a dangerous and chaotic crime scene; no confirmation yet but there was suspicion that Islamic extremists were behind the bomb.

Paul seesawed between two powerful sets of feelings; his intellectual mind reminded him of the hypocrisies and greed of his own country, of the complicity of the West in its own problems, but this seemed to provide no comfort or context for his emotional mind which whirred uncomprehendingly between anger, sadness and horror at the apocalyptic and savage hate that groups like ISIS held for the men, women and children of his country.

After a few hours, the news started to evolve into fervid conjecture and insincere emoting and he turned it off in disgust. He decided he had to try to salvage something from his day and dragged himself off the sofa to make some lunch. As he opened the fridge nothing seemed to appeal to him and his mouth felt foul and gritty. He picked at a slice of Emmental, but it made him feel sick again so instead he opted for some bread and a tin of soup. The only thing that he felt he could keep down.

He took his lunch over to the little table by the balconette and gazed absently down into the street below. The view was softened by fine rain and the sky was white. He felt a little soreness, somewhere near his heart, as he realised that over the last couple of years he had eaten at least one meal a day at this very table with Veronique. Something that was now very unlikely to ever happen again.

The doorbell rang and he jumped, spilling the next spoonful of soup onto his jeans before it made it to his mouth. He swore and scraped as much of it off as he could with his spoon and went over to the intercom.

He rubbed at his temples, behind them the headache was building to a climax. 'Oui?'

'Bébé! Thank God you are ok!'

'Maman. Come in.' He pushed the key button on the intercom and sighed. Why did she still insist on calling him Bébé? It made him feel infantilised. If only he'd got in touch last night and told her he was ok then, he might have avoided her coming around. He went to his front door and left it on the latch and padded into the kitchen to make coffee. He could smell her before he heard her: a soft wind of Chanel No.5 coming up the stairwell, swiftly followed by the click of heels in the tiled hallway.

She appeared at the doorway of the kitchen, slightly out of breath and pink-cheeked. 'Mon Chéri!'

'Maman.' He went over and hugged her. She hugged back, tightly, then pushed him back to arms' length and cupped his face.

'Darling,' she said, frowning, 'why did you not call me before this morning? I have been worried sick! It is so terrible, so terrible!'

He disengaged himself and briefly kissed her perfectly manicured hands. 'Paris is a big city, Maman, the chances of my having been anywhere near that bomb were tiny. Now, let me make us some coffee.'

'But you *were* near there. Sophie told me!'

Paul span round, annoyed. 'Why on earth did you ring Sophie?'

'Paul! How can you ask that? You didn't call me, what else was I supposed to do?'

Paul knew perfectly well that his mother wouldn't have heard about the bomb till that morning. She and his father were always fast asleep by eleven in the evening, and her regular use of mild sleeping pills meant she never woke till morning. So concerned was she with looking young, that she had invested in an expensive set of pillows that made sure you spent the night sleeping on your back, and therefore, the theory went, preventing wrinkles. As a teenager, he had gone into her bedroom one morning, and had thought she was dead. She was so still, and peaceful looking, the white duvet pulled up to her chest, arms by her side, head perfectly framed by the special pillow.

'If you spoke to Sophie, you *knew* that I was ok.' She said nothing to this and Paul finished making the coffee and carried it, along with cream and sugar, back to the little table and his half-finished lunch. 'Come, Maman, and have a coffee. You look like you could do with one.'

With a delicate sigh she placed her handbag on the sofa and sat beside him. As he ate she poured the coffee, put sugar in her own and stirred it. She sighed again.

'Maman!' said Paul impatiently through a mouthful of bread. 'Please stop sighing! I am ok!'

'I know, I know!' She pouted a little then took a sip of her coffee.

Paul often found his mother cloying in her attentions, but then felt guilty if he challenged her. He put his hand on hers and gave it a squeeze. 'I'm sorry, Maman, but I'm so tired, and a bit hungover. It's a long time since I drank that much - I've been working so hard - and the whole thing was horrible. I'm just so tired!'

She nodded and gazed into the middle distance. Despite the facials, the special pillows, the perfect make up and short, sculped haircut, when she was sad she looked her age. 'Charlie Hebdo, Bataclan, Bastille day, now this. I don't know how much more I can stand. What is wrong with the world?'

Paul didn't know what to say, and they finished their coffees in silence. After a minute or so his mother put down her cup abruptly, as if she had just remembered something.

'And I can't believe you are going away, in just three days, when everything is so…dangerous!'

'Maman, I am more likely to have a Boeing 747 fall on my head than be killed by a terrorist bomb.'

She looked up at him fiercely. 'Not in this city!'

'Well, then, surely I will be safer in rural Haute-Vienne!'

'You are being facetious now. You know what I mean. It doesn't feel like the right time for you to go away – to be leaving your family.'

He made a short, frustrated sound and shrugged. 'I will be less than 200 kilometres away.'

'Even so - '

'Maman!' The name came out like a rebuke, and his mother looked up at him reproachfully. 'Maman.' He repeated, more gently this time. 'I am not a child, and this is important work; work I have spent the last three years of my life on. I must finish it, then I can get my doctorate, and the next stage of my life can begin. That is what you want, isn't it?'

There was a few seconds silence, during which she stirred her coffee sulkily.

'I forgot to ask you,' she said after a while. 'Have you heard from Veronique?'

'No.'

'It is such a shame! She was a beautiful girl, and so accomplished. Is there nothing you can do to get her back?'

Paul shifted in his seat. 'I very much doubt that she wants to be *got back*.'

'Ah, Paul, you don't know that. She was so good for you, she kept your feet on the ground.'

'It's been two weeks, and she hasn't been in touch once.'

'You are the man! You are the one who needs to get in touch with her.'

'Maman, have you heard yourself? You're so old-fashioned.'

She pouted again. 'Mock me if you like but I don't care how *liberated* or *modern* a woman is; she wants to be chased! She wants to be wanted, to be desired.'

Paul chuckled and ruffled his mother's hair affectionately and she immediately smoothed it down again. 'Ok, Maman, I'll think about it. Now please, can you keep your manicured hands out of my business!'

'Oof! You are a cheeky boy!'

'I'm twenty-five years old Maman!'

'Indeed! And still cheeky!'

She got up and retrieved her bag from the sofa. 'I will go now, Cheri,' she said drily; 'and leave you to your lonely little flat and your studies and your hangover.'

'Ah, Maman, so cruel!' He grabbed hold of her and pulled her into a bear hug. At first, she resisted but then sank against him, her perfumed head snuggled under his chin. It was always like this between them: she indulged and cossetted him, he resisted, there was some banter or upset, he would relent. It was almost a flirtation, but the dynamics had been going on for so long that they were hard to resist. If his father hadn't been so polar her opposite, maybe his relationship with his mother would have been different.

She stepped out into the hallway but then immediately turned back. 'You haven't forgotten?'

He searched his ragged brain for what she might be referring to.

'Sunday dinner, you said you'd come?'

'Ah, yes, bien sûr. I'll see you there.'

As soon as he shut the door behind her, and without warning, he found himself weeping. He stood there, his head bent, the tears rolling down his cheeks and darkening his jeans. He hadn't cried like this since he was a little boy, and the thought shamed him somehow.

Paul concentrated on enjoying the simple sensation of the movement of his arms, the forward propulsion, and the water as it broke over the top of his head and down his back. This was his fortieth length; the first twenty he had swum front crawl, scything through the water at an efficient pace; the second twenty had been more leisurely, a well-practiced breast stroke, and he felt as could swim forever.

Although the physical symptoms of his hangover from the day before had finally disappeared, the emotional one still lingered. His mind churned and whirred with moral conflict, and he kept coming back to the same dilemma. He understood the origins of the extremists, he understood his own country's complicity in providing the fertile ground for their stunted and twisted ideologies to grow, but however hard he tried, he could not comprehend what led one human being to destroy themselves in the pursuit of the murder of strangers. At least that was one small mercy, thought Paul, there had been no children at the Opera that night.

It was a Saturday afternoon, but sunny outside, so the municipal pool was half empty. The shouts of the few children that were in the family pool behind him echoed in that strange, tinny way that sounds do at a swimming pool, as if they were all trapped together inside a giant bottle.

He decided to go on to do fifty lengths and pushed himself hard, reverting back to a fast front-crawl, his face emerging, every three strokes, to gasp a lungful of the chlorine-scented air. As he came to the end of his fiftieth length, he was panting. He held on to the edge of the pool to wipe his eyes and catch his breath; and then a strange urge came over him. He put his goggles back on, let go of the side of the pool, took a deep breath and let himself sink slowly to the bottom. With a little effort he was able to effectively sit on the tiled floor of the pool. He looked around him, his mind emptied of thought. The world was now an ultramarine landscape of shifting light; its sky full of pale disembodied limbs; its clouds, trails of bubbling froth left by the rhythmic movement of legs. He felt himself dissolve into this strangely comforting and hypnotic world. He liked its simplicity, its submerged near-silence.

As the seconds ticked on and the single breath he had taken started to be used up, he felt his lungs tighten. Black sparks erupted in his eyes and a growing pressure throbbed behind his temples. Still he didn't move. His body started to feel like it had contained an explosion; his head ached, his chest felt emptied. Still he didn't move. Then a yellow shape appeared above his head, and there was the sound of shouting, muffled and hollowed out as it moved through the water towards him. Suddenly he became aware of where he was, what he was doing; that a lifeguard was now at the edge of the pool, and that if he didn't get out of the water quickly, he would have to suffer the ignominy of the guard jumping in and pulling him out. With a spasm of panic, he pushed himself up and a second later, emerged, spluttering and gulping for air and found himself face to face with a frowning but pretty lifeguard, who hooked her arms under his and dragged him from the pool.

When he stepped out onto the street he was still shaking. The sun was blazing down and the heat that had been absorbed by the pavement throughout the morning was emanating back up towards him. The air-conditioned cool of the swimming pool lobby was still caught in his damp hair, but he could feel it retreating and he started to sweat.

He went over to a raised bed planted with some neglected shrubs and sat down in the relative shade. A sudden urge to speak to Veronique came over him, and before he could change his mind, he took out his phone and dialled her number. After half a dozen rings he was about to give up, but then she answered, and after a silent but obvious hesitation, she spoke, her voice small and cautious.

'Hello, Paul?'

'Veronique. Salut.'

'What is it?'

'I...' he took a deep breath. 'I wanted to check you were ok.'

'Ok in general, or ok because of the bombing?'

'Well...both I suppose.'

'I'm ok. Is there anything else?'

He looked around him, without seeing. A steady stream of busy-looking people passed in front of him but he felt like he was in a different dimension to them. 'I just did something really stupid and I don't know why.'

Silence.

'I was swimming, and at the end, I went to the bottom of the pool, and I just stayed there. The lifeguard says I was down there for over a minute, she had to pull me out.'

'And you don't know why you did it?' She said, with what sounded like a touch of sarcasm.

He frowned. 'No, of course not.'

'Really?'

'Veronique, don't play games with me! What do you mean?'

'*I* know why you did it.'

'Then tell me, you must tell me!'

'Because you wanted to know how *they* felt.'

'*They*? Who are *they*?'

'The dead. You wanted to feel their pain, their panic. You feel guilty; for being healthy, for being safe, for being *alive*.'

A strange tightness took hold of Paul's chest. 'That's ridiculous!'

'Is it?'

They were silent again.

'You need to work this out, Paul. If you don't you are going to destroy yourself. I hope you find the answer you are looking for, I really do. But please don't call me again.'

'Veronique, wait, don't hang up on me.'

There was a catch in her voice. 'I have to go now.'

'I miss you.'

'No, you don't, you just miss the idea of me.' The line went dead.

He got up and wandered off in a daze. Was she right? The feeling of numbness and disconnection continued. He didn't know where he was walking to. The world passed by him in a series of colours and disembodied sounds that made no sense to him. His heart was beating fast and his breathing was clipped and shallow. He turned corner after corner, crossed street after street, losing all sense of time.

'Paul?'

He stopped in his tracks and turned around abstractedly. It was Manny.

'Hey, mate, you don't look good. Quoi d'neuf?' Manny had taken hold of his arm. Paul looked into his dark eyes and shook his head.

'You look like you're about to hyperventilate. Let's go and sit down.' Manny led him across the road to a small, iron-railed public garden. It was planted out with broadleaved fig trees, the shade they cast burnt through with the luminous red of geraniums. Paul followed obediently as Manny chose a bench on the far side of the square. Manny pulled his legs up to sit cross-legged and turned to Paul.

'What are you doing here, man? What's going on?'

'I don't know.' Paul managed to whisper. 'I think I might be having a panic attack.'

Manny nodded sagely. 'I know what you need.' He pulled a small battered tin out of his pocket and opened it. Inside were a row of well-rolled slender spliffs lined up in the tin like anaemic sardines. 'This will calm you down.'

'My head's fucked up. I don't know if that's a good idea.'

'Sure it is, this is good stuff, daytime stuff. Nice and gentle.' He lit one of the spliffs, sucked on it then handed it to Paul. 'My sister used to get panic attacks. You've got to breathe through it, not run away from it. You got to stop and tell yourself it's no big deal. If you run from it, it becomes bigger, scarier.'

Paul took a few tokes from the spliff and tried to pull his ragged thoughts together. Manny was right, he had to stop and think, and breathe. He passed back to his friend. 'I'm glad I bumped into you. I think I would have walked into the night if you hadn't come.'

'You looked like a zombie, man! Your eyes were all glazed over and you were really pale.'

Paul let his arms float up in front of him and let out a low moan.

Manny laughed. 'That's it, man, yeah, just like that.'

Paul laughed too and shook his head. 'It's all going a bit crazy, Manny, I don't know what's happening to me. I feel like I'm holding on by my finger-nails. But to what?'

'Sanity. It happens to us all sometimes. It's a thin line, the line between real life and all the rest of it.'

They let the thought hang there for a while and enjoyed the last of the spliff. It had helped, thought Paul. His mind had calmed down, and his breathing too. He sighed and looked up through the branches of the fig tree towards the eye-watering blue of the sky.

'Maybe I should stop all this, Manny.'

'All what?'

'My thesis, all the stuff about the war, like Veronique said, maybe it's making me ill.'

Manny looked thoughtful. 'Maybe, or maybe it's the world that's making you ill, and your thesis is the thing keeping you well?'

'I hadn't thought of it that way!'

'I tell you what I think. I think what you're doing is real. It's difficult, and it's painful sometimes, but it's real. Look at me, man, I'm just floating around; doing bits of shit here and there, but nothing real. Nothing that matters.'

'But will my work *matter*? What difference will it make, just one more gratuitous, academic look into the eyes of the *Monstre*?'

'Well that's up to you, isn't it?'

They looked at each other intently, and it struck Paul that in Manny he had a true friend and until this moment he hadn't realised it. He'd always thought of him as the 'floater' of the group; the person who had seemed the least serious. But despite all this, his lack of a real job, his seeming nonchalance about life and responsibility, Manny was the only one of all his friends who seemed at that moment to be able to see him as he really was.

Paul put his arm around his friend's shoulders. 'Merci, Manny. I feel a lot better.'

'It's really important to finish what you've started,' said Manny, his voice grave. 'I never did, maybe I never will, but you can. Go on your trip, *look into the eyes of the monster*, learn from it and then tell us what you've learnt. You owe it to yourself, and you owe it to them.'

'*Them?*' questioned Paul, for the second time that day.

'All the people that were twisted by that war, and all the people that died. Show them they matter.'

On his way home Paul did a little shopping, stopping to get some flowers and a good bottle of wine to take to his parents for the family lunch the next day. He felt unburdened and thoughtful, and on his return to his apartment he spent the evening sitting by the open balcony windows, sipping beer and watching the sky change through darkening blue, to golden peach, fiery red and then pale indigo, until the first of the stars winked at him over the rooftop of the apartment block opposite. Manny was right. If he stopped now then everything he had worked towards, everything he had put himself through over the last three years, would be wasted. He must finish what he had started.

The next morning was overcast and surprisingly cool and Paul had a pleasant walk from the Metro through the Jardins du Trocadéro. The Arrondissement de Passy was an affluent area and had been home to Victor Hugo and Molière. He had been born and raised in his family's impressive five-bedroom villa, but ever since he had become old enough to think more critically about the world about him, had always felt a little ashamed of the wealth, privilege and complacency that the quiet upper-class neighbourhood epitomised. Like much of Paris, prices in the area had rocketed to unaffordable proportions, and although his father had bought the house for a modest amount back in the 1980s, his mother often now proudly proclaimed that the house was worth well over two million euros.

He stopped for a moment at the bottom of the steps leading to the villa's impressive mahogany front door. He always felt a little apprehensive before throwing himself into the fray of a family lunch. The combination of his mother, sister, father and grandfather, all in one space, could create an atmosphere so dense with personality, opinion and obstinacy that the emotional oxygen left for him felt as thin as mountain air.

He breathed in deeply, fixed a smile on his face and walked up the steps. With his foot still hovering over the top step the door suddenly opened and his sister's narrow, anxious face appeared.

'Paul, you're late.'

He looked at his watch. 'By ten minutes, Camille.'

'Oui, indeed. Come in.'

He kissed her on both cheeks as he passed her in the hall. Her skin was moist – no doubt from helping his mother in the kitchen. 'Coucou, petite frangine?'

She landed a playful punch on his ribs as he passed. 'One day you will show me the respect I deserve for being two years older than you, darling brother. Hey,' she called down the hall after him, 'I heard about the Opera bomb, that you were just around the corner. I'm so glad you're ok.'

'It was horrible. We're all still pretty shaken up about it. But we were safe, and you can't say that for the poor bastards who were there that night.'

She caught up with him and put her hand on his arm. 'Maman is downstairs, she's fretting over the blanquette de veau. Perhaps you can calm her down.'

'An impossible task, but I shall try. Is Papy here yet?'

She shook her head. 'He rang and said he wasn't feeling well.'

'That's a shame. I saw him a couple of weeks ago and he seemed fine.'

Camille shrugged, 'he's an old man. It is to be expected.'

Paul nodded, but felt his gut twist with anxiety. For a man in his nineties, Armand was an impressive and resilient figure, but, for the first time it struck Paul that he had to accept that his grandfather was moving into the last stage of his life. The thought filled him with melancholy.

He found his mother in the kitchen, reducing the stock for the blanquette. An aroma, rich and creamy, filled the kitchen and made Paul's stomach rumble.

She turned around and waved her wooden spoon at him as if she expected them to start fencing. 'Aha! Mon Cheri! I heard you before I saw you!'

'Oui, Maman, and I smelled you before I saw you. My God, how hungry I am!' He went over and hugged her then handed her the flowers.

'Ah, merci, they are lovely.' She turned from him towards the open kitchen doorway. 'Albert? Ici, s'il vous plait!' His father appeared in the doorway and nodded at Paul.

'Papa, Ca va?'

Albert came over to him and they embraced, a little stiffly. 'I am good thank you, Paul, though I am in the middle of a very difficult case at the moment –'

'I never see him!' declared his mother dramatically. 'Sometimes I think I will forget what he looks like. Albert, fetch the crystal vase from the dining room please so we can put Paul's lovely flowers in it.'

His father disappeared back through the doorway and his mother came towards him and leant in conspiratorially. 'You must talk to him, Paul, about retiring. He won't listen to me, I'm worried he is going to make himself ill.'

'Maman, you know Papa doesn't listen to anyone. If he didn't work he'd go crazy within a week.'

'What nonsense. Please, Paul, can you at least try? You're going to be away, in just two days' time, I will have neither of you, I can't bear it!'

He looked at her eyes, bright and beseeching within their frame of expertly applied kohl and fine wrinkles. 'Ok, I promise I'll try, but not today.'

'Bien sur, today is family time. But, Paul, soon, tomorrow maybe, before you go away?'

Albert came back into the kitchen and his mother started to bustle around and issue orders. 'Paul, take in the rillettes and the salad please; ah, Camille, there you are, can you get the wine.

Paul sank his knife into the glossy veal on his plate, cut off a piece and chewed slowly and appreciatively, enjoying its savoury silkiness. His mother was chatting away happily about her latest charitable work, enjoying, as she always did, having a loyal audience around her. A shaft of sunlight broke through the clouds and slanted through the French windows, lighting up his father's white hair like a halo. He waited politely for her to finish then turned to his father.

'Papa, tell me about this case.'

Albert looked up, as if seeing him for the first time since they had sat down. 'The family insist the girl committed suicide, but it's a murder case as far as I'm concerned, an "honour killing" as they call it in their culture.'

His mother jabbed with her fork at nothing in particular. 'It is most dreadful how they treat their women. As far as I'm concerned we have become far too tolerant.'

Albert nodded. 'I agree, Jeanne, the government is impotent, it has no courage. It is more concerned with avoiding racial tension than with justice. We invite these people into our culture and then they disgrace it.'

'And all this fuss over the ban on hijabs,' added his mother, 'if they are in our country they should abide by our rules.'

Camille shifted uncomfortably in her seat and glanced at Paul. 'But, Maman, would you say that we shouldn't let Sikhs wear turbans or Jews skullcaps? Would you stop Christians from wearing crosses?'

'Pah, come Camille, that is completely different.'

Paul put down his fork and turned to his mother. 'Why is it different?'

'A cross or a skullcap doesn't stop you from seeing someone's face.' Jeanne said defiantly. 'Of course it's different.'

Paul frowned. 'But it is a symbol of faith, an item of clothing or adornment, in exactly the same way. Why is it not the woman's choice?'

'This is a non-issue.' His father said abruptly. 'They can still be worn in places of worship. The *Loi interdisant la dissimulation du visage dans l'espace public* law is there to protect us all, for security. Surely you can appreciate that after your recent experience, Paul?'

The room went silent and suddenly everyone had turned to look at him. Paul paused, feeling both angry and uncomfortable. 'I believe there is no evidence of a link between what Muslim women choose to wear and the acts of terrorists.'

Albert snorted and slammed down his wine glass so that some of the ruby liquid spilt onto the tablecloth. His mother flinched. 'How can you be so naïve, Paul? With all the money we and your Papy have spent on your education, have you learnt nothing?'

Paul felt himself colour. The reference to his trust fund felt like a cheap shot. Summoning all his willpower, he decided to ignore it. 'Two of the terrorists were born in France. How do you explain that?'

'I explain it by saying that it shows that the roots of their religion are opposed to the freedoms that our country has fought for, for hundreds of years. They are incompatible. They can live here, but while they follow Islam, they cannot fully assimilate; and if they cannot assimilate, they should not be allowed to stay. They should return to their home countries.'

Paul was so shocked by his father's answer that for a moment he couldn't speak. Albert was looking at him intently, the expression behind his shrewd grey eyes ambiguous.

'I can't believe you would say that, Papa. Surely you know that a quarter of the world's population are Muslims; what percentage of them are terrorists for fuck's sake?'

'Paul!' His mother cut in sharply. 'I will not have swearing at my table!'

He looked at his mother in disbelief. 'He says these terrible things and yet it is my swearing that upsets you? You cannot believe this too, Maman?'

She lowered her eyes but didn't reply.

'Maman, Papa!' he said desperately. 'Please, you mustn't be pulled in by the lies! This is how it started, before, the war, you know this – with propaganda and fear and hatred of even the slightest difference. You are more likely to have a plane fall out of the sky onto your head than be caught up in a terrorist bomb.'

'And yet,' Albert cut in triumphantly, 'you were caught up in one only a few days ago. And before that Bataclan, Charlie Hebdo, all within a few miles of us.'

'Ok, but we must take some blame too. We are not entirely innocent.'

'Not entirely innocent?!' His mother looked at him, her face flushed. 'I am sorry but I am *entirely innocent*. I have not blown up any children or beheaded anyone!'

'Maman, that is not what I mean and you know it!' Paul's heart was racing, he couldn't believe what he was hearing; it felt as if he had somehow sat down with the wrong family. 'I mean the responsibility of our country, for its actions in the middle east, for the regimes it has supported, the wars it has been part of that were started for reasons of greed instead of justice.'

Albert reached for the wine and started to refill their glasses. 'I am sorry, Paul,' he said calmly, 'we just don't agree and you will have to accept that. The attack last week was the last straw for me. Our country has acted in good faith. Where it has seen wrong in the world it has sought to right it. Now we are paying the price. It is time for us to start to look after *ourselves* again. To look after France.'

Paul watched his father's face in horror as, implacably, he continued to fill up his glass. 'And who is *ourselves*, Papa?' he said softly. 'Just those born in France? Or do you mean just Christians and Secularists? Or maybe you mean just *white* people?'

Albert waved him away dismissively. 'Don't be ridiculous, Paul, you know what I mean.'

'No, Papa, I do not know what you mean.'

'These things are easy for you to feel, you have barely lived, you know little of the real world. You bury your head in books, in the past, and you think that you know, but you do not know.'

'*The past is not a rehearsal, it is the show itself,*' muttered Paul under his breath.

His father looked at him. 'What?'

Paul ignored the question, put his napkin on the table and stood up. 'It did not just happen *then*, Papa, it is happening *now*. It is happening *here*, in this kitchen!' He felt as if his heart was about to stop beating. 'I have to go.'

His mother reached across the table and took hold of his arm. 'Don't be ridiculous, we have not had dessert! It is only politics, Cheri, just silly politics. You must stay.'

He shook her off and headed towards the door. 'That's what they said back in the 1930s, Maman, just politics.'

He ducked into the kitchen for his rucksack, feeling breathless and disorientated. Camille appeared in the doorway, her eyes were red as if she was holding back tears. 'Please, Paul, come back. We can sort this out.'

He moved past her into the main hallway and hurried towards the front-door; he felt as if he couldn't breathe.

Half way down the steps she caught up with him and grabbed his arm. 'Paul, stop for a moment, please!'

Reluctantly he stopped.

'Don't be so angry with them, they don't mean to upset you. They think they know best. I hate it too, but they are still our parents.'

Paul shook his head. 'I don't know those people, Camille, how can they say those things? All this –' he gestured at the broad tree-lined avenue, the grand villas and pebbled driveways, 'they have all this, and yet they have so little space in their heart for others, for those who are struggling and desperate.'

'They're just scared, Paul, with everything that's happening in the world, they're getting old and they're scared.'

'I don't give a fuck if they're scared, we're all scared. It's what you do with your fear that matters.'

'Paul, please, come back to the house.'

He kissed his sister quickly on the cheek. 'I'm sorry, Camille, but I can't. I don't know what to think, I need some time.'

'But you're going away, we won't see you for weeks!'

'I'm sorry.' He turned and walked away from her, imagining he could feel her eyes on him all the way down the avenue. As he turned the corner he quickened his pace. His heart was racing. He didn't know what to think. His phone rang and he took it out of his pocket, expecting it to be his mother, but it was Armand.'

'Papy, thank God it's you. I need to talk to you.'

'Paul.' The tone of his grandfather's voice stopped him in his tracks. It was breathless and panicky.

'Papy, what is it? What's wrong?'

'I need you to come over, now.'

'I've just come from home, from the family lunch. They said you weren't feeling well; Shall we all come over.'

'No!'

'Why not?'

Armand's breathing sounded laboured. 'Just you, Paul, come now, as quickly as you can. No more questions.'

'Ok, I'm coming, I'll get a taxi.' Paul hung up and jogged to the nearest main road, his heart pounding in his chest and his body fizzing with adrenalin. He looked frantically up and down the road for a taxi. After a few agonising minutes he saw one and jumped out into the road in front of it to stop it. 'Arrêtez! S'il vous plait!' The taxi stopped and he threw himself into the front seat next to the driver. 'Rue de Loire, rapidement.'

Paul knocked furiously on his grandfather's front door but there was no answer. He waited a few seconds, tried again, then ran down the side of the house and through the wooden gate to the back garden. It was empty but the French doors were open. 'Papy!' He stepped into the house; the silence was ominous. 'PAPY!' he shouted, then listened. There was still no response. He rushed from room to room, a sense of dread building in his gut. Finally, he found Armand, slumped over the desk in his study. He ran over to him and shook the old man by his shoulders.

'Papy, it's me, Paul. What's happened?'

The old man let out a low moan. Gently Paul pulled him up until his head lolled loosely on to the high leather back of his chair. When he saw his grandfather's face he jerked backwards in shock and had to supress a scream. His nose had been bleeding and a rust-red crust had set around his nostrils and smeared on his cheek. One eye was shut, the other half-open and twitching. The whole of the left side of his face had slipped as if his skin was wax that had been too close to a flame. Paul fumbled for his phone, his hand shaking.

'Fiston...' The voice was little more than a gasp but the old man's right hand reached over and gripped his arm with surprising strength.

'Papy! I think you've had a stroke, I must call an ambulance.'

'Wait, Paul, the letter.'

'What letter?'

Armand's hand suddenly let go of his arm and fell heavily onto the desk next to a sealed envelope with his name on it. Paul picked it up.

'I have it, now, I must call the ambulance.'

'Take it with you,' croaked Armand; spittle was forming in the corner of his mouth and dripping down his chin. 'Show it to no-one. Read it.' The effort of speaking seemed to have drained Armand, and the half open eye fluttered then closed. Paul shoved the letter in his jacket pocket then took out his phone and dialled 15. The call was answered immediately.

'Please, come now, it is my grandfather, I think he has had a stroke, a bad stroke, we are at La Maison Blanche, Rue de Loire, Suresnes...is he breathing?' He leaned over and put his cheek by Armand's twisted mouth. 'Oui, but it's faint.'

They told him to keep Armand warm, and not to move him. He put the phone down and found a blanket on a small sofa in the corner of the study. He tucked it carefully around his grandfather and checked again to see if he was still breathing. Time was sputtering to a stop like a failing

179

engine; his mind and heart were blank and numb. He sat down on the corner of the desk and put his head in his hands.

It wasn't until the following morning that Paul remembered the letter. The rest of the previous day had gone past in an horrific blur. He had sat with his grandfather in the hospital until he heard from the nurse that his parents were on their way. He made her promise to keep him informed about how Armand was doing, then snuck off before they made it to Papy's room. Only a day ago he would have welcomed them coming, been desperate to see them and be comforted by them; but after the disastrous lunch he simply couldn't bear to see them. He felt too raw, too upset, and beset by a horrible feeling that his trust and love had been betrayed by the very people he had never imagined could be capable of it.

The letter lay on the table by his croissant. It was in a good quality, plain white envelope, with his name written on it in his grandfather's elegant but slightly shaky hand. It looked innocuous enough, but he remembered the urgency with which Papy had told him to take it, and suddenly felt like he was looking over the edge of a cliff. His stomach was tight with anxiety. He finished the last gulp of his coffee, its heat and bitterness helping to calm him a little, then opened the envelope.

Dearest Paul

If you are reading this it is because I am either dead or dying. Do not worry about me, being alive is infinitely more terrifying than being dead.

Your affection and admiration for me has been one of the great joys of my life, but I am afraid that I have taken it under false pretences. As you have grown older and found your calling in the voices and stories of the past, the harder it came for me to tell you the truth; something I had intended to do as soon as you came of age.

The fact is that I have been living a lie. It is one of the hardest things I have had to do to tell you this. I know how terribly it will affect you, but I must say it. You describe me, often, as a hero, but I only joined the Resistance towards the end of the war, and in fact, for a while, I was a Malgre Nous, conscripted into the Division Das Reich. I had thought that I could tell you this straight, to resist the need to make excuses for myself, but I am sorry to say after our talk the other day, and as I look sweet oblivion in the eye at the end of all things, I simply do not have the courage to do so. You can call it vanity, you can call it cowardice, you can call it whatever you like. I understand.

I was a very young man, and I spent the first few years of the war in Alsace trying to avoid being dragged into the war, but I had met a girl, I was in love with her, she was pregnant and because of that, when they came for me I felt I had no choice but to join them. If I had refused my conscription they would have deported her. So, to my shame, I fought alongside the Germans. I know what you are thinking, for an Alsatian to fight against the French is worse than being SS, or Gestapo. You cannot imagine it, it is the greatest evil of all, to kill your own countrymen. To this I have no answer except, again, to make excuses for myself like the pathetic man that I truly am. You may not understand this, but not everyone thought the German *occupation was a bad thing. Some even welcomed them. I had lost my mother in the Allied bombing raids of Strasbourg. I was not a political animal, I just wanted a simple life. Thinking back, although my instinct was to hate the Nazis, somehow I was tricked, or maybe, if I am more honest - beguiled. I wonder if you can ever understand that?*

By the time I started to hear rumours about the horrors of the concentration camps, it was too late. I cannot and will not tell you some of the atrocities I played a part in — they will have to go with me to my grave and it is unto my Maker, if one exists, that I must finally answer — but these atrocities have sat in my soul all of my life; and I have no idea if I have gone any way towards atoning for them. Can one ever know if one has done enough good in their life? Perhaps that is the greatest question of all.

Sheets of rain suddenly started to fall in the street outside, startling Paul back into the present. His hands were shaking. He watched through the window blankly as it fell, as hard and targeted as spears, dashing itself against the cars, road and pavement, making the pedestrians below shout and run for cover. He looked back at the letter and picked it up, his mouth was dry.

I have tried to atone, I do want you to know that at least. Eventually, in the summer of 1944 I found out that my girlfriend had died, not from a bullet, but from a terrible flu; the poor child inside, half-grown, dying with her. Perhaps it was my punishment, perhaps it was a blessing that it was not born into the horrors of that year.

When I found out she had died I realised that I had no-one left to protect or send money to. In short, I had nothing to lose. I won't bore you with the details but I managed to escape, to evade the Germans and find a Resistance cell in the Haute-Vienne. It took a while for them to trust me, but they were not unused to Alsatians seeking them out, and I went some way to disrupting the Nazis in the terrible death throes of the war.

And so, after the war I continued to live the lie. I met your grandmother, I put all of my energies and heart into being successful, into giving my son the security and safety that I had not had. I wanted more than anything for him to never have to face the terrible choices that had so blighted me. But I made a terrible mistake. By keeping my secret, by editing my emotions, he grew up to be an austere and cool man; someone I have struggled to recognise as my own flesh and blood. Just recently he admitted to me that he is considering voting for Marine Le Pen. This broke my heart and filled me with shame.

I do not tell you this to hurt you, but in the knowledge that your heart is good, and fierce. I tell you in the hope that you will tell my story too and the story of many thousands of others. The amnesty of 1953 which saw many collaborators released is a cancer that has still not left France. I tell you my story so that I may finally atone for my sins. I wish to declare that I own them, that I take responsibility for them and that I blame no-one but myself. I do not ask you to understand me or not to hate me, I ask only that you add my story to the one you are telling and that you tell it with truth.

Despite all I remain, your ever loving Papy.

Have your heart open, dearest Paul, and be alive.
Little else matters.

Armand

Paul put down the letter and was overcome with rage.
He stalked up and down the apartment, screaming, kicking
and throwing anything that came into his range. He ripped
the sheets off the bed, dashed the cafetière from the
counter in the kitchen so that it smashed against the floor,
splattering the cupboard doors with flecks of sodden
coffee grains, and upturned the little table by the French
doors. After a few minutes he found himself staring into
the mirror in the living room, his face pale and blurred
with tears. 'WHO AM I?' he howled. 'WHO THE FUCK
AM I?!' No answer came and he punched the wall, hard,
with his right hand. The plasterboard dented, and a
crystalline shard of pain shot up from his knuckles to his
elbow. He yelped and cradled his hand then went to the
sink to run it under cold water. The pain and the cold
brought him back to his senses. He hoped that no-one in
the block had called the police.

He went into the kitchen and bandaged his hand, then
he grabbed his rucksack and thundered down the central
stairway of his apartment block and out into the street. He
ran until his lungs hurt and his legs began to shake and
then he got on the bus. He knew he must look like
someone who had lost their mind with his face red and
sweaty and his hair wild and un-brushed, but he didn't
care. Within half an hour he was back at the Bibliothèque
Nationale.

He knew exactly which shelf to go to and was soon in the reading room with half a dozen books on the Milice and Malgre Nous on the desk in front of him. The room was busy - there must have been a big essay deadline looming - but the genial sounds of soft conversation, muted coughs and turning pages did little to comfort him. He felt outside the usual reality that cushioned everyone else in the room. All the markers he had relied on to define him and his sense of self seemed to have been cut away and he had a horrible stomach-clenching sensation of free falling.

He didn't know what he expected to find, he'd already done a fair amount of research on the Milice; from its ignominious beginnings as an army to root out the Resistance in 1943, to the shame and silence that followed after the war. It was a motley, but efficient, army of thieves, fascists, peasants and forced conscripts; he had studied their uniform, he knew their inadvertent but diabolically ironic motto: "Vivre Libre ou Mourir" (Live Free or Die). He had read about the countless assassinations and massacres that they had played a part in. He knew that many forced conscripts, like the Malgre Nous, deserted the German army and fought against them wherever they could; but some had stayed in the Waffen SS, had carried on fighting alongside the Nazis.

But what was different this time - as he read accounts of how Milicien posed as resistance fighters to infiltrate the Maquis; how they had used their very 'Frenchness' to inveigle their way into the trust of local people, leaving many to be tortured and murdered by the SS – how some of the Malgre Nous had played a part in the village massacres of June 1944, was that he no longer had any distance from what he was reading. Every time he looked at a grainy black and white photo of a Milicien with his traitorously jaunty beret on his head, or an Alsation in full German uniform, he thought he might be looking at his own grandfather. Every time he read an account of the assassination of a local Maquisard, he wondered, *was he shot by Papy?*

He lost all sense of time, sitting in the library, reading fact after horrific fact. It was like picking at a scab. It hurt, but he needed to get behind the crust, to properly explore the rich, tender flesh underneath. But after a few hours he couldn't take any more. He remembered Sophie's cautionary words; *You must stay anchored in the present to have a way to get back when you've spent too long in the past. If you lose that anchor, you could get lost forever.* But what was his anchor? A few weeks ago, he would have said his girlfriend, perhaps, his family, in particular his Papy. But now?

When he stepped out of the library the sky had clouded over, and a squally wind rushed up the steps towards him and blew through his hair, making him shiver. He buttoned up his jacket. The tops of the trees that lined the Quai François Mauriac were trembling and whispering in the breeze, and beyond them, the surface of the Seine had become pitted, like goose bumps on skin.

His phone rang, making him jump. He didn't recognise the number and thought it may be the hospital so he swiped the screen and answered it.

'Paul?' As soon as he heard his father's voice his heart started to pound.

'Oui?' he replied coldly.

'We expected to see you at the hospital? Your mother has been there all night.'

'I was there yesterday, I've asked them to let me know if there is any change. He's in a coma, he won't know if I'm there or not.'

'I don't understand you, Paul. I don't understand you at all.'

'The feeling is mutual, Papa.'

His father made a short, frustrated sound. 'Come now, Paul, you are being childish, to let political differences come between us. Your grandfather could be on his deathbed. Some things are more important than politics.'

Paul crossed over the road and sat on a wall at the river's edge. He felt strangely calm. 'That's a cheap shot, Papa. It's not just about politics, it's about your whole attitude. It's dangerous, and it's full of hate.'

'Preaching doesn't suit you, Paul. You think you know everything, but you don't. There is so much you don't understand, that you don't see.'

'In fact, Papa, I am fully aware of how little I truly know. But there are some things I do know. And one of them is that no one race, religion or creed is superior to another. We are all flawed, and we are all human. You have become dangerous; your views are poison.'

'You always were an overdramatic child,' said Albert dismissively. 'We shall just have to agree to disagree. Will you be back at the hospital today?'

'No, I have to pack for tomorrow.'

'What? You are still going away?!'

'Oui.'

'With your grandfather dying? I do not believe you, Paul!'

'He would understand. He wants me to go.'

'How can you say that? You were his favourite, he needs you here.'

'Like you, he was not who I thought he was. I've been lied to all my life.'

There was a brief silence. 'What do you mean?'

'I think you know?'

'I don't know what you're talking about, Paul.'

'Ah, d'accord.' He replied, sarcastically. 'If you say so.'

'You must stay, Paul, you must realise that? Your mother will be devastated.'

'It's what I need to do. I am a grown man and I will only be a couple of hours away; now who is being over dramatic?'

'I simply can't believe that you would leave your family at a time like this.'

'It's exactly it being a *time like this* that makes it the time I need to leave.'

'Well, there is clearly nothing I can say to change your mind.'

'No, Papa.'

'Then I will say au revoir.' His father rang off abruptly.

Dawn was just beginning to lighten up the eastern edges of the horizon when he stopped to fill up the little Fiat at a petrol station on the outskirts of the city. He went into the shop to pay and got himself a small, bitter coffee from a vending machine, and a ham and emmental baguette. He had not slept well and his eyes were gritty with tiredness.

He took the A10 to Orleans and then decided to stay on the meandering and scenic autoroute rather than switch to the more direct A20. The sun rose to a clear and sunny day as he drove along the near-empty road, only occasionally passing a smattering of early-morning drivers. He followed the Seine to Chambray-lès-Toures then continued south to Chatêllerault and Poitiers. Here he switched onto the N417 for the last part of his journey. By now the sun was high in the sky and he felt a lightness in his spirit that he hadn't had in many weeks. He looked briefly at his bruised knuckles and flexed his fingers. It felt so good to get out of Paris. He turned the radio up higher and felt almost excited as the beefy bass of a Kasabian song they were playing accompanied the picturesque fields of the Haute-Vienne as they flashed past the driver's window.

It was just coming up to 10am when he turned off the main road and onto the pitted track that led to the cottages. There were three of them, bordered at the front by the track and fields, and behind them he could see the distant line of a wood and about two miles to the West, the town of Argemourt.

He left the car on the track and got his rucksack and suitcase of books out of the boot of the car. Despite the parlous state of the track, and the fact that the fence and gates that bordered the houses were covered in peeling paint, , the front gardens were pretty and well-kept, and the cottages were charming with their plain white render, timber porches and shuttered windows. He headed towards the middle cottage and made his way up the paved path to the front door.

He knew Michèle Leroy was in her eighties, so when a woman, much younger than he was expecting, opened the front door he was taken by surprise. She looked like she had just woken up, as her wavy light brown hair was unbrushed and her eyes had a smudge of the previous day's make-up underneath them. The loose grey t-shirt and tight jeans she was wearing emphasised her full hips and short but shapely legs; and although she wasn't what he would class as beautiful, she had extraordinarily fine eyes, feline in shape and with a pale iris bordered with a ring of dark grey-green that made them startling to look at. The superficiality of his assessment made him feel a short stab of shame and he smiled and flexed his sore hand in an attempt to stop himself blushing.

'Bonjour, je suis Paul.'

PART 3: ARGEMOURT

"The dead are invisible, not absent."
(Saint Augustine)

Haute-Vienne, 13 June, 1944

Jean pushed his face into the flow of the fountain and drank deeply. The sun was hot on the back of his neck and the air smelt sweet and dusty. He wondered where Lorenzo and Yves had got to. Their morning game of hide and seek had stretched past lunchtime and his stomach was starting to rumble.

He leant over the stone bowl that circled the fountain, cupped his hands in the water then tipped the contents over his head. The chill of the water as it slid down his sweating back provoked a delicious shudder. He sighed, and decided to abandon Lorenzo and Yves; he was bored with the game now, and wanted some lunch.

Just as he was about to get up, a movement in the fountain's pool made him stop. The surface had crinkled, as if it was shivering; and a low rumbling was echoing into the square from all directions. There was something about the sound that was so alien, yet also deep and primal, that his heart immediately started to thump. A shout made him turn, and he saw Lorenzo, white-faced, tearing across the square towards him.

'Allemands, Allemands!'

'What?'

Lorenzo fell alongside him, panting. 'They are coming to the square, dozens of them, in tanks and cars!'

'It is impossible!'

'We must go home.' Lorenzo tugged on his arm. 'Now, come!'

Without stopping to look behind him, and with the momentum of his friend's fear firing his own; Jean sprang after Lorenzo and across the square. He ran so fast it felt like he was flying, adrenalin pumping through him like rocket fuel. When he got home and charged through the door, his mother took one look at his face and seemed to know that something was very wrong.

'Germans are coming, Maman, many Germans and they have a tank.'

The skin on his mother's face tightened, 'We must go to Papa.' She turned back into the house 'Nicole, come now!'

His little sister appeared almost instantly, no doubt picking up on the tone in her mother's voice. 'Listen to me; we must go to Papa now, and you must do as he says.' She took hold of each of their hands and pulled them into the street. 'But remember what we agreed, about where to go if you get separated from me or Papa?' She stopped suddenly and wheeled them round to face her; her expression was terrible to see; fierce and terrified at the same time. Jean felt his stomach clench and Nicole nodded silently, before they were hauled down the street again towards the garage.

When they arrived, it was clear that word had spread. Jean's father, was huddled in the corner with Joseph and Louis, their tools discarded on a nearby workbench. When he saw them, he rushed over, took each of their faces in his hands and kissed them. It made Jean want to cry, though he didn't know why.

'Isabelle, Nicole, Jean, Grâce à Dieu!'

'Étienne, what should we do?'

'We must stay calm, Isabelle. Monsieur Barrot has been here. There has been trouble, with the Maquis, the Germans are most likely searching local villages, looking for them. We have nothing to hide so we have nothing to fear.'

Jean looked up and followed his parent's conversation closely. His papa had always said that he was nearly a man now, and must help to look after his mother and his sister. If he was to do that, he needed to understand.

'But what if the stories are true?' his mother replied. 'About what they did in the other villages?'

'This is a war, there are always stories, always people trying to spread fear; it is a weapon.'

Jean tugged at his mother's sleeve. 'What happened in the other villages Maman?'

'Nothing.' His father knelt down and ruffled his hair. 'Don't worry, Jean, we will be back home in time for supper, I am sure.' Jean wanted to believe him, but his papa's face had changed, like his maman's had. He looked older somehow.

As Étienne straightened up, Jean heard the sound of an engine growling in the distance, punctuated by faint shouts.

Étienne grabbed Isabelle's arm. 'You have our cards?'

'Oui.' She patted the pocket on the front of her apron. Her face was white.

Étienne crouched down again so he was level with the children. 'Écoute-moi, whatever happens, stay by me, and by your mother. Understand?'

Jean nodded. Nicole had slipped her hand into his, he gave it a squeeze. 'Do you hear Papa, Nicole?'

Nicole nodded.

'Unless you lose us, or we get taken, then, you must run. Comprendre?'

'Papa!' Nicole wailed. 'Why would they take you?'

Jean felt tears prick in his own eyes but fought them back. *You are nearly a man now.* But the sound of the engine and the marching steps of the soldiers was getting closer, and more than anything, Jean felt like running.

His maman bent down and hushed Nicole. 'It is ok, ma bichette, that will not happen. Papa is just being careful. He means as I said, if we are separated...by accident.'

'The main thing to remember,' Jean's papa continued, 'is that when we are asked questions, we answer them politely and clearly. We are in the Free Zone, they know better than to cause trouble here. They look only for those that fight them, we are good citizens. They will search the village and then leave.'

At that moment the sound of the vehicle came to a stop. Jean held tightly on to his father's hand. Three German soldiers and an SS Officer in a coal-grey uniform stepped in.

'Out, now.' Barked the officer, in heavily accented French. 'All citizens must go the village square for checks.'

Étienne stepped forward. 'Please,' he said politely, 'can I ask what this is about? Argemourt is a quiet town, we make no trouble.'

The officer strode forward until he was nose-to-nose with Étienne. Jean felt his father push him backwards slightly.

'I said, NOW!' The officer reached down and took hold of Jean's other hand. Jean whimpered and tried to pull away; his wrist twisting painfully in the soldier's grip. His mother let out a small wail and pulled Nicole against her.

'OK, OK!' his father pleaded with the officer, 'Please, I understand, we will bring the children!'

The officer eyed him for a moment then let go of Jean's wrist. 'Sofort, come now.'

As Jean staggered, dazed and terrified, after his mother and father into the street outside the garage, he saw others being flushed out too – from shops, houses and bars. They were people that had been around him all his life, men, women and children he knew by name, but they looked strange to him at that moment. Their faces were rigid with fear, and they walked jerkily, their movements awkward with shock.

When they reached the square Jean saw the whole village assembled there, oppressed into a rough square by a boundary of soldiers. Occasionally there would be a scuffle, or raised voices; usually from the younger men of the village, but every time, a soldier or officer would appear in seconds, gun raised, and the altercation would finish as soon as it had begun. Jean's mother was saying something over and over under her breath, he struggled to hear her, *mon Dieu, je vous en supplie,* she was saying, please God. The words made him feel sick and light-headed.

Eventually the anxious murmur of voices stopped, and Jean saw it was because the deputy Mayor, Monsieur Barrot, had stepped up onto a bench at the north of the square to speak, flanked by two SS Officers. He mopped his forehead with a handkerchief then waved his hands in the air to get their attention.

'Mes amis, mes camarades; please listen.'

The last mutter of conversation dwindled into a wary silence.

'Sturmbannführer Hans Stellerman,' he indicated to the tall officer on his right; 'has assured me that this is a routine check, being carried out in many villages in the area. I, in my turn, have reassured the Sturmbannführer that Argemourt has no links with terrorists of any kind, and that his searches and checks will reveal nothing to incriminate our peaceful village in any way.'

Jean's parents seemed comforted by Monsieur Barrot's words, and his father's grip on his hand lessened slightly.

'Now, to make things easier as the village is searched; the Sturmbannführer has asked that we all make our way, in an orderly fashion, to the church – '

A gasp rippled through the crowd.

'S'il vous plait!' called out Monsieur Barrot again, 'The sooner they can complete their search, the sooner they can leave and we can get on with our day. It is hard to watch your home being searched; it is better this way, there will be fewer problems. Please, everyone, an officer has agreed to talk to Father Petiot, also, and I am sure he will help to reassure our guests that all is well here.'

The rationale of this explanation seemed to calm the crowd again, and they formed, grudgingly, into a rough line that filtered out from the square towards the lane that ran through the woods towards the old church. It was a relief for Jean, just to be moving. He could hear his parents talking quietly and urgently above him; but he focused instead on the hush of the breeze through the high branches and the pools of gold that the sunlight cast on to the forest floor. Nicole was looking around her warily, her eyes bright and startled looking. He would protect her, he reminded himself. Nothing could happen to her, or Mama, with him and Papa around.

When they reached the church the mood suddenly and inexplicably changed. There were thirty or so soldiers waiting for them there, rifles held at hip level. Father Petiot was nowhere to be seen; and the younger children, picking up on the tension in the air, had started to whimper. Orders were shouted in German between the officers and soldiers; which only heightened the swell of unease.

'Étienne, I don't like this, what is happening?'

'It's ok Isabelle,' Jean's father replied, in a gentle voice, 'they are just trying to scare us. Nothing has changed. We have nothing to hide, remember.' Jean wanted to believe his father, but when he looked down, he could see that he was clenching and unclenching his fist. Jean felt the same clenching in himself. How dare they do this to them! He thought, with suppressed rage. How dare they scare his family, drag their Deputy Mayor out into the street like a dog; how dare they go through their things, their homes, as if they owned them.

'ID cards, tout de suite!' A French voice was shouting the orders this time, and the shock of hearing it made Jean turn. The voice had come from among a dozen or so soldiers, going through the huddle of villagers and demanding their cards. When they were presented, the cards were taken and put in a sack. Some people remonstrated, but if they did, they were pushed back, or a rifle would be raised, silencing them instantly. Jean looked away when this happened, his heart pounding.

One of the soldiers reached them and held out his hand. 'Cards!' he snapped. Jean watched, wide-eyed, as his mother reached into her pocket and handed them over.

The soldier barely looked at them, just handed them to the man behind him who threw them straight into his bag.

'I know you!'

The harsh tone of his father's voice made Jean's chest tighten with panic.

'Non, Étienne!'

'Quiet Isabelle! Look! You know him too.'

Jean watched as his mother turned to the young soldier then let out a horrified gasp. 'François? Is that…it can't be… is that François Larrey?'

The soldier seemed temporarily confused and some kind of struggle passed over his face.

Étienne spat onto the ground by François' feet.

Between that moment and his next heartbeat, Jean watched with horror as the soldier rammed the butt of his rifle into his father's stomach. His mother screamed, and Nicole started to sob but the soldier moved on without a backward glance.

'*Mon Dieu, je vous en supplie!*' Jean heard his mother whisper again as she leant over Étienne. 'Please, God, protect us, protect my babies. Please God in heaven.'

Étienne struggled to his feet. 'But he is French, I do not understand, how can he – '

'Please, Étienne, do not cause trouble. Quiet now my love, let us just get through this.'

Jean heard shouting at the front of the group near the church, and then a ripple of movement passed through the crowd, pushing Jean and his family back. For a moment Jean thought about running, of making a break for the trees; but just as he was about to suggest it; soldiers fanned out in front of them, rifles raised. A single gunshot shattered the hush of the forest, echoing flatly through the branches for several seconds. A stunned silence overcame the villagers. 'Women and children in the church!' a voice shouted; 'Men over here by the wall!'

'No. NO!' The word boiled through the crowd, there were stifled screams and angry shouts. Jean's mother held on to him tightly, drew in Nicole and his papa. 'No, no,' she echoed the crowd; her voice a low, terrible moan that scratched at Jean's heart, 'they must not separate us, Étienne, Étienne what do we do?'

'I don't know.' His father said at last, his voice cracking. 'Forgive me, forgive me my love. I don't know.'

When, after many years, Jean finally felt able to look back on that day, he always said; that despite all its other horrors, his father's tears were the most terrible moment of all.

Michelle found herself studying Paul as he drank his tea. It was as if some kind of exotic golden animal had wandered into her living room and she felt like a little brown mouse in comparison. Adele was sitting on the arm of the sofa, clearly equally fascinated, staring at Paul with wide eyes and absently stroking Jack.

'What did you do to your hand?'

He flexed his fingers briefly, looking embarrassed. 'It is nothing, I fell on it.' As if wanting to change the subject he started to rummage around in his old-fashioned leather satchel. 'I must apologise. You see it was a surprise to me.'

He looked up at her and smiled and she noticed that he had a gap between his front teeth. She couldn't decide if it made him look wolfish, or boyish. Maybe a bit of both.

'To see you, I mean, I was expecting to see an old lady. I was looking forward to meeting your aunt, you know, to hear her stories...' he broke off, looking a bit embarrassed. 'But I don't mean that it isn't nice to meet you...' he blushed slightly then bent his head over his bag and pulled out a crumpled piece of paper. He put it on the table in front of Michelle. 'Here, you can see, the arrangement was made with your aunt weeks ago.'

She picked up the letter and glanced at it. 'It's in French.'

'Ah, oui, pardon.' He smiled toothily and pointed at a logo in the top right-hand corner. 'This is my university, they have an arrangement with people, like your aunt who live near historical sites, for students to stay with them for their studies. You can call them and they will confirm it.

I can give you the name of my tutor, she speaks English too.'

'Your English is very good.'

'Thank you, I spent a year in England for my degree, I lived in Brighton.'

'And you will pay me one hundred euros a week?'

Adele's eyes widened at the mention of money.

'Oui.'

'I have to admit, it'll come in handy, I've not been working and I'm hardly rolling in it.'

Paul frowned. 'Pardon, what is this *rolling in it?*'

Adele spoke for the first time since Paul had entered the house. 'Alan says that we have to watch out for Jack as he likes to roll in poo sometimes when he goes out for a walk.'

Paul looked more confused than ever.

Michelle hid a smile behind her hand and raised her eyebrows at Adele. 'In this context it means I'm not rich, I am not *rolling* in money.'

'Ah, I see.' Paul looked relieved.

'How long did you want to stay?'

Paul shrugged. 'A few weeks, I think, this is OK?'

'Yes, that's fine.' Michelle took the last sip of her tea. She felt self-conscious and was desperate to get out of her scruffy clothes and have a shower, but her curiosity was getting the better of her. 'So, you never met my great aunt?'

'No, but I spoke to her a few times,' he looked down at his hands, 'she seemed like a very nice lady, I am very sorry to hear that she died.'

'Me too, it's sad that I never got to meet her; and then she leaves me this house, and I'll probably never really know why.'

He nodded, then seemed to remember something. 'And of course,' he said eagerly, 'I read her book as well.'

Michelle looked up sharply. 'Her book?'

'*Village des Fantômes*, do you know it? It is about the history of what happened here, of what happened in - '

'Argemourt, yes I know.' She felt suddenly a little light-headed and realised she'd had nothing to eat since the end of a stale baguette hours earlier. 'I remember it, my Nanna had a copy at her house and it used to spook me and my brother out.'

'Spook…out?' enquired Paul, tentatively.

'It scared them.' Adele had suddenly appeared, her elbows on the table, face in her hands, looking at them intently.

'So, my Aunt Michèle wrote that book?'

Paul nodded and reached back into his old satchel. 'Here.'

'That's crazy, my nan never told me, why wouldn't she tell me that?'

He put the book on the table in front of them. Adele's expression was bright with curiosity. Michelle reached out to it slowly as if it might burn her; looking at the cover, the outline of the old church against a stormy dark-red sky stirred feelings of apprehension and nostalgia. She opened it randomly and scanned the pages; it was in French.

'There is a picture of her.' Paul turned the book around to face him and fanned the pages through his slender fingers. 'Here.' He turned the book back towards her and pointed.

Michelle looked down and her heart stopped in her chest. It was a picture of the cottage, her cottage. The picture was in black and white, and the plants in the front garden were different, but other than that it looked exactly the same. In front of the cottage stood a skinny girl that must have been her aunt. She could have been in her early teens but it was hard to tell because she was so thin. There was a sadness in her expression and a frown was compressing her features. But what struck Michelle was how much the girl looked like Adele: delicate features, poker-straight dark hair with a severe fringe, and, more than anything, those large, wide-apart eyes that could look so solemn that sometimes it was hard to believe that it was truly a child, and not someone older, looking out from behind them. It was incredible, Michelle thought; she must have looked at this picture a hundred times as a child, yet it had held no meaning to her. Now though, it was the opposite.

She spun the book round on the polished table top until it faced Adele. 'She looked a bit like you, don't you think?'

Adele studied the picture intently with her characteristic frown. 'A little bit,' she conceded.

'Can you see it?' she pushed the book back to Paul.

He looked down at the page and back at Adele a few times, and Michelle smiled to herself as she saw her daughter's cheeks colour.

Paul sat back in his chair and nodded at Adele. 'Oui, she does.' He seemed to consider his next words carefully. 'They both have the eyes of great thinkers.'

Adele beamed. Michelle looked into her daughter's big grey eyes and felt a surge of love. *He's right,* she thought.

And he's the same, his mouth might smile but his eyes are serious. It was going to be an interesting few weeks.

She closed the book and got up. 'We'd better show you your room, it's only little I'm afraid, the box room really. Adele took the room in the roof that I think my aunt probably meant for you to have, but there's a bed and a chest of drawers in it and a little sink.'

Paul stood up too and slung his satchel over his shoulder. 'That will be fine. I will be out a lot of the time with my research. Perhaps you will permit me to study in the living room sometimes? I have a lot of books and will need a desk or table.'

For a heartbeat, Michelle wavered, did she really want someone invading her new space like this, another person that she would have to talk to and engage with? She wasn't sure if she liked the idea. *A few hundred Euros*, she reminded herself. *That's enough to keep you in food for another month until you sort something else out.* 'Of course, that's fine.'

'I'll try not to get in your way. I appreciate your kindness, particularly as you did not think you would be having a guest!'

'Really, it's fine.'

Adele went over to Paul and took hold of his hand. He looked startled, as if he had had little to do with children in his adult life. But whether he liked it or not, Adele had clearly taken to him, just as she had to Alan. Michelle felt grateful that there were some nice men in Adele's life again, but she hoped that she wouldn't get too attached to this pretty young man; he wasn't staying long and Adele was stoic but sensitive too. Jane always said she was like a little dog, once she had decided she liked or hated someone there was little that could be done about it.

When she had first seen Jane at a playgroup when she was just a toddler, she had gone straight over and sat on her knee, and that had been it.

Adele tugged him towards the hallway. 'I'll show you your room, Mr Paul.' she said, with charming formality.

'Ah, merci.' He smiled awkwardly but relented.

Paul unpacked his modest possessions, arranged his books on the top of the dresser and hung his coat and satchel on the back of the door. It was a pretty little room, the plaster walls were whitewashed, but there was a texture to it, and an unevenness that added to the room's charm. There was a small, old enamel sink by the window with jointed steel legs and a crossbar that had a hand towel draped over it. He went over and tried the taps, they both worked. Handy for brushing his teeth, and, he thought a little guiltily, he could pee in it at night if he couldn't be bothered to walk down the hall to the cottage's only bathroom.

The window was a small wooden casement with a deep sill on the outside on which someone had put a glass tealight holder. The curtain was heavy lace, and the soft but comfortable old bed was covered in a deep green satin quilt which looked handmade. There were a couple of old pictures of the village on the wall, which took his attention for a while, and a pretty watercolour of a lake in summer, its edges fringed with reeds and wild flowers. It was signed "Jacques, Août 1938". *Poor Jacques, whoever he was,* thought Paul, *sitting by a lake on a beautiful August afternoon, and no idea that a terrible storm was coming.* He yawned and lay down on the bed. The sun was shining through the lace curtain and projecting an intricate pattern onto the ceiling. He studied it idly, a sense of peace overwhelming him, and then he felt his eyes close.

He was cycling down a hill, the sun was warm on his back. His feet were held out either side of the bike, the pedals whirring round so fast that they were little more than a blur. He was laughing, a warm wind was blowing through his hair. He felt alive and happy and as if life was a simple thing that he knew the edges of. The track underneath him was bumpy and pitted and scattered with small stones. Every jolt and dip in the track shot up his spine through the solid old leather saddle but he didn't care, it just made him laugh even harder. He was coming to the end of the track now, but suddenly there was nothing there. The world had simply ended, no sunlight, no track, no trees, no flowers, just a black endless hole.

'Mr Paul?'

He murmured and shaded his eyes against the sunlight in the room as he struggled out of his dream.

'Mr Paul?' The voice was a little louder now, but still hesitant. He pushed himself up onto his elbows and looked ahead. The head of the large scruffy dog he had seen in the living room was poking around the side of his door and studying him sombrely. For a crazy second, he thought it must have been the dog that was talking to him, but then the little girl, Adele's, face followed the dog to peep around his door. 'Sorry, Mr Paul, but Mum says do you want some lunch?'

He smiled. 'Just Paul, please. And I, can I call you Adele?'

She nodded then darted back behind the door, the dog close on her heels.

He went over to the little sink by the window and splashed his face with water. He looked into the mirror above the sink as he dried his face. The glass was slightly frosted and liver-spotted with age, creating the impression that he was staring back at himself from another time; the thought made him shiver.

When he got downstairs he saw that Michelle had showered and changed. Her hair was still damp, making it look darker, and she'd put on a little make-up, a nice olive-green shirt dress and a pair of battered converse pumps. She looked nice. He wondered how old she was. If she was older than him, as he suspected, he couldn't tell by how much.

He ran his fingers through his hair and found himself laughing.

She looked up at him and frowned.

'I am sorry, I am laughing at myself.'

Michelle smiled as she tore up a fresh baguette and put the pieces on an old wooden chopping board on the dining table. 'Why?'

'When Adele came to me just now, I could hear her, but I couldn't see her. The old dog was looking around the door and I thought it was him who was speaking!'

Michelle laughed too, and her striking eyes lit up, emphasising the dark rim of her iris. 'He does have that kind of face, old Jack. Some dogs do, as if they're about to talk, or like they understand a lot more than they are letting on.'

'Yes, and then some just look exactly what they are, completely stupid!'

She gestured for him to sit down. 'I don't know what the arrangement is, about food I mean. You know, whether it's full board or anything like that? But either way you've had no chance yet to go to the village or get any food so you must have lunch with us.

'Merci, you are very kind.' He looked around at the bread, cheese, charcuterie and bowl of little tomatoes. 'It looks very nice.'

'She shrugged, a little apologetically. Some stuff gets delivered every day, like the bread, but I've not done a proper shop yet – we've eaten with the neighbour, Alan, and he's given us some fruit and veg from his garden, so it's just what we've got around I'm afraid.

'Thank you, I am very grateful.'

Michelle went to the hall door and shouted up the stairs. 'Adele, it's ready!'

The sound of the girl's feet pattered down the stairwell behind the wall and then she appeared in the doorway, slightly red-faced.

'Come and sit-down, sweetheart.' Michelle pulled a chair out for her daughter. Adele sat down and Michelle absently smoothed her hair then bent down to kiss the top of her head. *They are so close, so natural.* He thought with a pang of guilt. He felt bad about how he had left things with his Maman, but he was equally angry with her too.

When Michelle sat down he started to fill his plate. He hadn't realised how hungry he was. The last thing he had eaten had been the meagrely filled baguette early that morning. 'You know, I like to cook. If you are happy for me to do so I could give money towards your shopping and make some of our meals?'

He looked across the table at Michelle. She didn't seem to know how to answer and glanced up at him before replying.

'Ok, thank you, that would be nice. I'm an ok cook, but just simple things really. I wouldn't want to take up your time though, if you're supposed to be studying?'

He smiled. 'Not at all, it is important, as my family and my friends keep reminding me, to take a break from learning.'

Adele chewed a piece of ham thoughtfully, her grey eyes steady, assessing him. 'But you're a grown-up, why are you still in school?'

Paul laughed. 'Not in school, Adele, I am doing what in your country you call a PhD. It is learning that only grown-ups do.'

'It means he will be a professor when he's finished.' Michelle said to her daughter.

'Ah, no, not quite, just a doctor!'

Michelle coloured slightly.

'But not a medical doctor, and I would need to teach too,' he added quickly, wanting to distract from her obvious embarrassment, 'and probably do another higher qualification. It's complicated, even for me!'

'What are you going to be a doctor in?' replied Adele, seemingly unaware of her mother's discomfort.

'I am studying things that happened during the Second World War. Some bad things, I'm afraid, done by bad people.'

'Like the things that happened at the church?'

Paul looked at the little girl, surprised, then over at Michelle. 'She knows about what happened here?'

Michelle picked up the last piece of bread and started to tear it up into little pieces. 'Yes, we found out a bit about the history of the village before we came here, and the neighbour, Alan, told us some more last night.'

'The Nazis put all the women and children in the church,' Adele said solemnly, 'and then they killed them.' She looked at him steadily. There was something old beyond her years about this little girl.

'Oui.' Paul replied, unsure of how much to say. 'But what makes it even more horrible is that not all the bad people were Nazis, some of them were French people.'

'The same as the people in the church?' Adele looked sceptical.

'Oui, the same.'

Michelle shook her head. 'But why would they do that? To their own people? The Nazis were the enemy?'

'It is hard to explain.' Paul sighed and pushed his empty plate away. 'By 1944 France was so damaged. It was cut in two, many of its people were hungry and lived in fear. Some men did it because the Nazis threatened the lives of their families, some were given the choice to join the Nazis or be deported as slave labour, some did it because they believed the same things as the Nazis believed –'

'But to kill your own people,' Michelle cut in, 'to kill children. I'd rather die.'

'This I feel also, but how can we know for sure. It is easy for us to say that *we* would rather die, but if it means your wife, your child...' He trailed off, uncomfortable with where the discussion was heading.

'I suppose.' Michelle replied sadly. He felt bad that he had led the conversation into such dark places.

'Mum, let's take Paul to the church.'

'I don't know, sweetheart, Paul is probably tired.'

He felt his heart quicken. 'No, I am fine. I slept this morning. How far is it to walk.'?

Michelle looked reluctant. 'Not far, about a mile.'

Adele sprang up from the table. 'Come on, Mum, Jack needs a walk too.'

'But we don't have a lead for him or anything.'

'Alan says he doesn't even have a lead. He knows everywhere around here, he can't get lost.'

'Ok, I suppose we could.'

'If it is any trouble, please do not worry, I am sure I could find it.'

'No, it's ok, it's not easy to find, we kind of got there by accident. We'll show you this time and then you'll know where it is.'

'Thank you, you are very kind.'

'It's really spooky,' Said Adele, smiling widely. 'There's bullet holes in it and everything!'

There was a tautness, an expectancy about Paul that Michelle could feel as they walked. His shoulders were slightly raised and he was looking fixedly at the track. Adele was running ahead of them, occasionally hiding in the tall wildflowers that had taken over the meadow, then bursting out, provoking a barrage of happy staccato barks from the old lurcher.

'I don't know if she's going to kill him or give him a new lease of life!'

'Pardon?' Paul looked across at her distractedly.

'Adele – and Jack.'

'Ah,' he managed a small smile, 'Oui.'

They fell into silence again. The afternoon was warm and muggy, the deep blue sky peppered with islands of high white cloud. The sun was hanging lazily midway to the West, casting their shadows thinly across the track ahead of them.

She took a deep breath, unsure if she should speak to him again. 'It must be a funny feeling?'

He broke out of his reverie again and turned to her, his expression neutral. 'What is funny?'

'Sorry, no, I don't mean that. I mean you must feel strange, perhaps, going to see the real place that you've studied for so long?'

He nodded. 'Yes, it is hard to explain. Perhaps I could say it in French, but in English…?' A few sentences of rapid French exploded from him and then a struggle passed across his face. 'It is like, I am coming home, but coming home to somewhere I have never been.' He glanced at her again. 'Do you understand this?'

'I think so, I felt a bit like that too when I came here. I never met my aunt, but she left me this place, she meant for me to have it, and in a way that makes it feel like I sort of knew her after all, even though I didn't…' She trailed off, unsure of what she was trying to say.

'When you just read about something in a book, you build a picture in your mind. You look at an old photo and you build a picture, but neither of these pictures are the real place. When you see it, it is somewhere entirely new, almost unexpected. That is why it is so important, for my thesis, to come, to see with my own eyes.'

They were interrupted by a happy shout from Adele who was a few yards in front of them.

'Our lake, we're by our lake!'

They caught up with her, Jack was bent over the water's edge, drinking deeply. 'Be careful with him, Adele, he's old. You don't want to tire him out.'

Adele leant over the dog's shaggy back and hugged him. 'He's ok, he likes it.'

Paul wandered over to stand next to Adele and crouched down until he was at her level. 'So, this is your lake?'

Michelle went over and stood behind them. 'I don't think you can quite call it that! I'm not sure who owns this bit of land, if anyone. Perhaps I'll find out when I visit the solicitor next week.'

He looked up at her. 'Can you swim in it?'

'I don't know, we were going to ask Alan, but we forgot.'

He straightened up and looked longingly at the shimmering water. 'I would like to swim in it if it is safe.'

She had to admit, with the delicate willow trees reflected on its surface, and the fringe of wildflowers and reeds, it did look inviting. 'We'll ask Alan if he knows. We love swimming so it would be a really nice thing to do, especially while it's so hot.'

Paul looked up at the sky, squinting against the brightness of the sun. 'And the forecast says it is going to get hotter.'

Adele looked excited. 'Do you think Jack can swim too?'

Michelle laughed and stroked her daughter's hair. 'Probably, we'd soon find out anyway.'

They carried on along the path, Adele again leading the way. 'You get into the wood here.' She gestured for them to hurry up. She was clearly enjoying being their guide.

'Ok, speedy Gonzales, we're coming!' She smiled apologetically at Paul, but he looked miles away.

As they entered the woods a group of wood pigeons launched out of the trees hooting softly and making the branches above them shiver. They tramped for a few minutes through the dark ribbon of woodland until they came across a barrier of crumbling brick wall.

'There's a broken bit.' said Adele, running off into the shadows. After a few seconds she reappeared and took her mother's hand. 'It's this way.'

Paul followed, his heart vibrating with trepidation. He breathed deeply, the air was rich with the smell of warm earth and a sweet back-note like distant blossom. After a minute or two they came out at a clearing in the trees. The line of the old wall had been broken by a fallen oak tree, and Adele was already clambering through the breach, nimbly navigating her way around the rotting tree trunk and scattered bricks.

She gestured for them to follow. 'Come on, it's easy!'

Michelle went after her daughter and Paul followed more cautiously, watching his footing on the tangle of old branches and rubble. It was so hot that the exertion had made him start to sweat. He wiped his forehead with the sleeve of his shirt.

After they were all on the other side of the wall Adele looked back. 'Jack, come on, Jack.'

The old dog's face appeared on the other side of the wall, peering anxiously at them.

'Come on, Jack!' Adele squatted and patted her thighs. 'It's ok, Jack, it's easy, I told you.'

The dog sat down stubbornly.

Michelle took her daughter's hand. 'Come on sweetheart, he's old, he probably knows he might hurt himself if he tries to climb over.'

'He can do it!' Adele replied fiercely and started to head back through the gap.

Paul laid a hand on her shoulder and she stopped and looked up at him. 'Dogs can sense things, Adele. Things happened here, bad things, maybe he feels it.'

'You mean like ghosts?' the little girl replied, wide-eyed.

'Fantômes? Non, just energy. You know if a stone is in the sun all day, even after the sun has set the stone is still warm. Maybe it is like that.'

Michelle looked at him oddly and came over to take Adele's hand again. 'Come on, you said yourself that he can't get lost here, he'll wait for us.'

They turned and Adele looked reluctantly back at the lurcher. 'Wait there, Jack, don't go home, we won't be long.' The dog sighed and lay down, resting his head on his paws.

They walked on; a number of old graves, in varying states of disrepair, started to pepper the grass, which Paul was surprised to see had been recently mown.

'Look, one's got flowers on.' They followed Adele to a newer-looking grave, she was right, a small bunch of white roses in a glass jar had been balanced on the earth in front of the headstone.

Paul bent down and read. *Pierre Valéry, 1900-1944.* Then there is an inscription from Saint Augustine, I will translate for you, it something like *the dead are not gone, just invisible.*

Michelle grimaced. 'That's a bit creepy.'

Paul stood up and stretched. 'What is this *creepy*?'

'Erm, you know, like a bit spooky, makes you feel a bit funny?'

'A moment please.' He got out his phone and tapped the word into his French-English dictionary app. 'Ah, oui, in French we would say, perhaps, *effrayant.*'

'Eff-ray-ont.' Adele repeated haltingly, as if trying the word out.

'Oui, effrayant.'

They wandered away from the grave and towards a huge yew hedge, at least ten feet high, and, like the grass, recently trimmed and shaped. The neatness of it looked incongruous against the dark tangle of the wood.

'There's a gate.' Adele took hold of her mother's dress and tugged, then looked up at Paul. 'Come on, it's this way.' He followed them along the line of the hedge, brushing his fingers against the dense bottle-green foliage; a deep, astringent pinewood scent was released, and it carried something nostalgic and ancient in it. After a minute or so they stopped, there was indeed a gate of sorts, an old wooden door, rusted half-open on its hinges and set deep in the hedge. They squeezed through, Adele leading and Paul bringing up the rear.

As he passed through the door and saw the walls of the church rise up ahead of him, it felt to Paul as if his heart had stopped. He had read so much about this place, studied so many pictures, that to be actually standing by it was utterly overwhelming; almost, he imagined, like meeting someone famous or revered. Adele was chattering away excitedly to Michelle, he turned away from them and started to walk around the base of the church. The walls were hugely thick and buttressed, made out of two types of stone, one cream, one slate grey, hewn into huge slabs. He laid his hand on one of them and closed his eyes. His head swam and his breath quickened, he released his hand and walked on.

After he had turned the second corner at the Western end of the church he looked down the flanking wall to the church's tower. The tiles of the roof had long since fallen away, revealing a wooden skeleton topped by a battered weathervane that pierced the treeline. Paul looked up. The tower created a stark silhouette against the blazing blue sky, but his eyes started to water against the sudden brightness and he had to look back down to the wall. A number of small, deep set round windows ran the length of it, the leaded glass shattered and darkened by something that could have been soot. Below the windows, he noticed, with a sudden nauseous lurch in his stomach, the stone was peppered by a line of holes. He went over and touched them, his fingers trembling; the bullet holes that Adele had mentioned.

He remembered his dream, the one with the girl. It was this church he had dreamt of, he had wanted to reassure the girl, to tell her not to be afraid of him, but then he had realised that he was dressed in the uniform of the Milice and the girl had opened her mouth to scream –

'It's ok.'

Startled, Paul looked down to see that Adele had come up beside him and taken hold of his hand.

'It's ok to cry.'

'But I'm not…' His other hand went up to his cheek. She was right, he was crying.

'When my dad died the counsellor said it was good to cry. She said it can't take all the bad feelings away, but it takes a little bit away, every time you cry.'

She was looking away from him, as if trying not to embarrass him by seeing his tears, and the sensitivity of the action in someone so young touched him.

He squeezed her warm hand briefly then let it go. 'Your counsellor is right. Maybe that is why I have been crying so much recently. And this place, it is so sad.'

Adele nodded sagely then smiled and all the seriousness left her face and her voice in an instant. 'Come on, let's go home. I want ice-cream!'

Michelle glanced over at Paul as he hunched slightly over the steering-wheel. 'Thanks for this, it'll be really good to see the town and do a proper shop.'

He took a while to answer. 'It is no problem. I need to get a couple of things too.'

He was driving a bit too fast, and in a slightly jerky way that made Michelle feel nervous. She was surprised. Paul seemed so quiet and thoughtful that the boy-racer driving style didn't fit; perhaps it was just a French thing.

He turned to her quickly then back to the road. 'Adele likes Alan I think?'

Michelle smiled. 'Yes, you'd think they'd known each other for years rather than forty-eight hours. She's really taken to him.' she wondered if Paul was concerned that she had left her daughter with an older man she barely knew. On the outside it did look odd, but she could feel in her bones that he was a good person and she trusted Adele's instincts too. 'He was good friends with my aunt, they'd known each other for years, and he's nice to Adele, she enjoys his company.'

Paul nodded, but kept his eyes on the road. 'She is a very wise little girl, she sees everything.'

Michelle wasn't sure what he meant. 'She's been through a lot, I'm just grateful that she seems to have come out of it ok.'

'And you?' He glanced over at her again.

She was silent for a moment. 'We've *both* been through a lot.'

'Adele said,' he paused, and Michelle noticed his hands tighten on the steering wheel, 'I am sorry if it is wrong of me to mention it, but she said that her father had died?'

She turned to look out of the window, at the green and gold of sunflower fields flashing past, and a familiar ache started up somewhere near her heart. 'Yes, he was a soldier, he died in Afghanistan.'

'I am very sorry. It seems that we are both touched by war, but in different ways. My experience, it does not compare to that, but through my research I have read many millions of words about war.'

'And has it helped you to understand it?'

He laughed in response. 'Non! In fact, sometimes I feel like the more I know of it, the less I understand!'

'Same here.' They looked at each other for a second, both smiling.

'Ah, bien, we are here.' He gestured at the road, which had become a broad avenue, lined with slender silver birch trees. The pavements were laid with a pale stone slab, which reflected the heat and the light of the sun, creating a floating shimmering skin. The roads were wide and framed on both sides by shops, houses and municipal buildings made, too, out of the pale cream and grey stone they had seen at the church. The buildings had flat fronts, and small shuttered windows. Many had tubs and hanging baskets filled with flowers.

'It's really pretty, and bigger than I expected.'

'Oui, it is not so much a village now. The centre is old, but there are suburbs too, more modern. Ah, I see the supermarket.'

He parked the car along the side of a pretty square. A small fountain glittered at the centre of it and behind that Michelle could see the garish sign of a supermarket. They got out and walked over to the fountain. There was a plaque by it with an inscription which Paul bent down to read.

'It says the water is from a spring, deep underneath the village. You can drink.' He leant towards the fountain, cupped his hands and brought them to his mouth. He drank deeply and filled them again. 'Ah, it is very good.' He gestured towards the tumbling water.

She knelt on the low stone wall that surrounded the fountain and angled her head so that the water could flow straight into her mouth. She pulled away sharply. 'Shit, that's cold!'

Paul laughed. 'Of course! It comes from deep below us, where the sun cannot reach!'

More carefully she copied Paul and used her hands to cup the water. 'You're right though, it is very good. So crisp and clean.' She straightened up and saw the picture of a saint engraved beside the writing on the plaque. 'Who's that?'

'Saint Nicholas. The patron saint of children…and bakers.' He laughed, 'A strange combination – it makes me think of an old fairy story, the one where the witch tries to cook some children in a pie!'

'You mean Hansel and Gretel?'

'Oui! That is the one.'

She looked back at the plaque and read in faltering French: *La Fontaine des Larmes.* "Larmes" means "tears" doesn't it?'

Paul shaded his eyes against the lowering sun and read from the rest of the plaque. 'Oui, it says it is called this for the children. There is a legend, that many years ago this was a well, but a child fell in and died, so they filled the well and used pipes for the water to come up instead. Then, after the war, they renamed it the Fountain of Tears for all the children who died at the church.'

Despite the prettiness of the square, and the sun slanting through the fountain and fracturing the water into diamonds, she felt suddenly sad. 'Come on, let's get that food and go back. Adele will be wanting her ice-cream.'

Paul saw Michelle wince as Adele hacked again with her blunt knife at the spring onion she had on the chopping board in front of her.

'You should give her a sharper knife, people cut themselves more with blunt knives.'

'If you're an experienced cook, maybe, but not if you're a small child.' She stood behind Adele protectively and took both of the little girl's hands in her own. 'Look, like this, hold the onion still in your left hand then cut with your right. Don't just bash the knife down though, slice it through,' she brought the knife down at an angle against the green and white flesh of the spring onion, 'like this.'

Adele nodded, her forehead creased with concentration. Michelle finished chopping the rest of the spring onions into thin slivers, just like Paul had asked and handed them to him. He could hardly see her through the steam that was rising from the old cast-steel wok that he had found in a dusty corner of the kitchen.

Adele brought her contribution over too and put it next to him with an air of ceremony. Paul noted ruefully, however, that it now looked more like a half-chewed twig than shredded spring onion. 'I thought you were going to make us a *French* meal.' She said, with what sounded like a hint of approbation.

Paul looked down at her and smiled. 'And at home, do you always eat English food? Or do you perhaps sometimes eat pizza, or spaghetti?'

Adele nodded.

'And me, I do not always eat French food. I like Thai food too, but it is hard, always, to find the ingredients I want, which is why I take this always with me. My mother says I am crazy. "Only one pair of shoes," she says to me when we go away, "but six sauces!" ' He gestured at a huddle of jars and packets on the counter. Adele picked one of the little pots up, unscrewed the lid and sniffed. Her face immediately creased up with disgust. 'Eugh, this smells like dirty socks!'

Michelle took it from Adele and, sniffed at it too. 'That really does smell disgusting. What is it?'

Paul laughed. 'It is fermented shrimp paste. But please, do not worry, it does not taste as it smells.'

'Thank God for that.' Michelle put it back on the counter. 'What's next?'

'It is nearly ready, I am just soaking the noodles. You, perhaps could watch the chopped peanuts in that small frying pan? They must not burn.'

Michelle gave the little cast-iron pan a shake, releasing a hot, earthy smell that made Paul's stomach rumble.

'Adele, love, do you want to go and pop over to Alan and tell him that dinner is nearly ready?'

Adele called to Jack and headed out of the front door. Paul studied Michelle as she tipped the roasted peanuts into a ramekin, weighing up whether or not he should speak. She had pulled her hair up into a loose bun and the line of her neck and stray wisps of light brown hair that curled against it made him feel an unexpected rush of protective affection.

He took a breath. 'Michelle,' he hesitated, 'since the village, you have been quiet, are you ok?'

She glanced up at him and smiled thinly. 'I think so. It's just, I don't know, it's hard to explain, it's the history of this place, what war does, it's like I can't escape it.'

He nodded and tipped the rice noodles and beaten egg into the wok with the vegetables, hoping she would say more. She leant against the counter beside him and looked abstractedly into the middle distance.

'Since I met Chris, war, it's always been there. I could live with it at first, I thought our army was a force for good, that Chris' and my sacrifices meant something; because we weren't alone, you know?' She looked at him for a moment, frowning slightly, 'It's not just the soldiers who make sacrifices, but the people they leave behind too. All I've done for years is work in a café, because I'm not anywhere long enough to build a career. And it's the same for all my mates too. They're all nursery nurses, or care workers, or they just stay at home. And then there's all those months, when the men aren't around, when you have to keep everything going, and then they come back and expect everything to carry on as normal, but it can't.' She stopped, laughed slightly as if she was embarrassed.

He dared himself to reach out and gently touch her arm. 'Please, go on.'

She turned to the cupboard and started to take out bowls and glasses but carried on talking. 'And then Afghanistan happened, and it became something else. People were dying, my friends, all those poor ordinary people half the world away. And now, this, finding out what the Nazis did to the people in the village. It makes me wonder if there's any hope. If we will ever stop hurting each other.' She turned towards the wok, picked up a beansprout and chewed it, her eyes fixed somewhere beyond him.

He turned the heat off under the noodles and wiped his hands on his apron. 'I think about it all the time. About why there is war, about why people do evil things; and the only way I can understand it is to see evil as a monster. Sometimes the monster is a country, or a race, or a political party. But wherever it comes from, it is like the Trojan Horse; inside it is made of many many people, each doing small things of evil, each turning their little wheels, but together they make something much bigger and more terrible.' When he looked up he found she was looking straight at him, her piercing eyes fixed on his face. They stayed like that for a second, just looking at each other, but the spell was almost instantly broken by the front door crashing open and Adele bursting back into the room with Jack and the neighbour, Alan, in tow. On closer inspection he looked older than Paul had thought when he'd seen him in his garden that afternoon, but he had an air of crumpled bohemia about him in his linen granddad shirt, pressed chinos and deck shoes.

Paul took off his apron and walked over, holding out his hand. 'Bonsoir.'

The older man took his hand and shook it vigorously. 'Bonsoir, Paul. I'm Alan. It's kind of you to invite me.'

Paul smiled and gestured to the table. 'Michelle and Adele are surprised by my Thai cooking, I hope you like it and weren't expecting coq au vin!'

Alan laughed and patted Jack's head, who was happily pawing at his legs for attention. 'I've spent half my life travelling the world, working everywhere from Saudi Arabia to Brazil. I can eat and enjoy pretty much anything; although the kebabs made with skewered baby chicks in China didn't do much for me.'

Adele looked at Alan, horrified. 'They didn't do that! That's horrible!'

'I'm afraid they do, on some of the street stalls away from the tourists. Is it really any worse than you eating a beef burger though if you think about it? Most beef comes from very young cows and bulls.'

'It's not the same!' Adele said, stubbornly. 'They're just babies!'

Alan ruffled her hair. 'It's ok, Adele, believe me even if we're hypocrites in the west when it comes to meat, then I'm one of them. I couldn't eat it. Oh, I nearly forgot.' He held out a bottle of wine wrapped in plum-red tissue paper. 'A small contribution to the evening.'

Michelle took the bottle of wine from Alan and kissed him on the cheek. 'Thanks, Alan, that's kind of you. Now, shall we all go and eat?' She looked around and smiled, with what seemed to Paul like forced brightness. 'Paul's cooked us a lovely meal and we don't want it to go cold.'

Paul picked up the wok and Michelle grabbed some glasses. He turned to Adele, 'Can you get the bowls and forks?' The little girl nodded, seemingly happy to be asked to contribute.

'Can I take anything?' Alan hovered by the door.

'Ah, just the chilli sauce please.' Paul nodded towards the small red bottle on the counter.

They trooped out of the kitchen and into the little dining room. Michelle had lit candles, tall ones for the table, and a number of tealights on the shelves and fireplace, and the room had a warm, comfortable feel to it. Paul felt a little rush of contentment and peace, something he hadn't felt in a long time. These were new people, and they seemed like good people. He didn't have to worry about their history together, or their opinion of him; there was no guilt, or anger, or resentments between them, they could just be people and talk together as equals, and the realisation of that brought something back to life in his heart.

The few glasses of wine she had drunk had gone to Michelle's head, and she was struggling to make sense of the strange mix of emotions she felt as she watched Adele, Alan and Paul chatting happily. Adele was glowing as she talked, her cheeks flushed and her eyes bright. Michelle told herself to relax, to feel grateful that her little girl was enjoying the moment and taking a break from the long shadows that had fallen over her life. Another part of her was full of caution and fear; what if Adele was hurt again? Abandoned again? The vehemence with which she fought inside to crush this thought inadvertently led to her gritting her teeth and shaking her head.

Adele looked at her across the table, frowning. 'Are you alright, mummy?'

Michelle felt herself blush. 'I'm fine, sweetheart, I just think it's time you went to bed now.'

For a second Adele looked as if she was going to protest, but then a smile crept over her face and she looked up at Paul, shyly. 'Will you read me my story tonight?'

Paul looked startled and glanced over at Michelle. As their eyes met she realised what was causing her unease. It was the memory of how she had felt when he'd talked to her about the Trojan horse. The intensity with which he thought and felt, the passionate way he spoke to her had stimulated something that she didn't feel able to face.

She attempted to look nonchalant and took a sip of her wine. 'If Paul doesn't mind, but just one book 'Del, it's late.'

Adele beamed and pushed herself out of her chair. As she headed towards the door she went over to Alan. 'Night, Mr A, I'll come over tomorrow for our snail hunt.'

Alan took the little girl's hand in his and bowed his head gallantly. 'I shall await the visit from my fair neighbour with a beating heart!'

Adele giggled.

Michelle looked from one to the other. 'Snail hunt?'

'Yes!' replied Adele, a little breathlessly, 'We're going to find them in the garden and make them a house and then we're going to cook them and eat them with garlic like the French do. Aren't we, Alan?'

'Oh yes, absolutely.' Alan looked at Michelle and winked.

Adele smiled with satisfaction and then headed for the hall. Paul followed behind, looking terrified. Again, she thought, he was obviously unused to the attention of children, and this was probably one of the things that drew Adele to him. There was nothing she hated more than being patronised by adults who felt they knew how to talk to kids. She pulled Adele towards her and kissed the top of her head. 'I'll come up in a bit and give you a kiss good night'.

They headed out of the room, Adele holding Paul's hand. Michelle listened to the faint sound of her daughter's high voice behind the wall as they headed up the stairs; then when the sound stopped, she sighed. Alan leant forward and put his hand over hers. He looked tired and somehow a little defeated in the golden tremble of the candlelight.

'What's the matter?'

She squeezed his hand briefly then looked away. 'I don't know, it's hard to explain. It's a bit like…it's something to do with this place.'

Alan leaned back in his chair but said nothing.

'And I'm worried about Adele.'

'She seems fine to me, happy in fact.'

'Yes, well, that's just it. I'm worried that she's going to end up getting hurt.'

'Why would you think that?'

'Because of Paul. She's really taken to him, but he's only here for a few weeks. I don't want her to like him too much. He's going to go; and she's had enough loss in her life.'

Alan looked at her curiously. It made her feel uncomfortable so she took a sip of her wine.

'Adele is a clever girl. She knows he's only here for a while and she's making the best of it. You never know, who, in the end is going to stay, and who is going to leave. I know it's hard, but I think you need to trust her, and trust yourself, that you have the strength and the love to keep her safe.'

Without warning Michelle felt a pressure build up behind her forehead and then tears brimmed hotly in her eyes. She wiped them away and took in a long shaky breath. 'It's this place, it's like it's opening me up. And it hurts Alan, but not always in a bad way. Does that make any sense at all?'

When Paul woke up the next morning, he felt refreshed and contented. He sighed, and stretched, his hand moving across the top of his sheet into a sliver of warm sunshine that had escaped through the join of the curtains. He let it lie there for a while, enjoying the sensation, and letting his mind wander. He heard the gentle whisper of the treetops in the woods, and the birds singing. His mind drifted happily, and to his surprise, the image of the line of Michelle's neck materialised, and then, the memory of the warmth of Adele's small hand in his. He had escaped into something wonderful, something real, it made him realise how relieved he felt to be away from his own family.

He turned onto his side and decided to doze a little longer. Outside his door he heard Adele chattering away to the dog as they headed down the stairs. It had taken him by surprise when she'd asked him to read her a bedtime story. At first it had made him feel uncomfortable. Was it 'appropriate' for him to be in a bedroom with a little girl he hardly knew? Would she expect him to 'do voices' when he read? He had no nieces or nephews and had had little to do with young children, so he had felt woefully unprepared. In the end it had been a moving experience. The book was Roald Dahl's 'The Twitts' and was surprisingly fun to read. Without Adele even having to ask, he had found himself making up voices for each of the characters, and she had laughed at his accent. And then, after he had read a whole chapter, she had leant her head on the side of his arm and closed her eyes, and the trust and simple warmth inherent in the action had made his breath catch in his throat. What were they doing to him, these women?

He stretched again and decided his mind was too busy for him to sleep any more. He needed to go to the museum in town and do a day's solid research. He was getting distracted, he was here for a reason, and he owed it to the victims of the massacre at Argemourt to tell their story accurately and with a serious heart.

He decided his shower could wait till the evening and settled with brushing his teeth and having a quick clean with a flannel at his little sink. He dried his face and opened the curtains. The morning sun was high in the sky, and he could see past the garden to the meadow beyond. The surface of the lake was draped with diaphanous shreds of mist. It was beautiful, and sad, that the heart of Argemourt, despite being surrounded by such pastoral prettiness, was a place that had lived through such horror. He shivered at the thought.

The sensation of Adele's hot toothpaste-minted breath on her cheek dragged Michelle up and out of her dreams. They dissolved instantly, but left Michelle with an inexplicable feeling of anxiety. She reached out sleepily and stroked her daughter's hair.

'Morning, Chicken.'

'Morning, Mummy.'

'What time is it?'

Adele shrugged. Michelle reached for her phone and groaned; 9 o'clock. 'I'm sorry, it's late, you must be starving.'

'S'ok, Paul helped me get a bowl of cereal, but he said it didn't look like real food.'

'Really?' Michelle snorted. 'Because a great big buttery croissant and a massive dollop of jam is better for you?'

Adele reached over and tenderly cupped Michelle's cheek. 'I'm going to Mr Alan's now to hunt for snails.'

Michelle propped herself onto one elbow. 'Are you sure it's not too early?'

'No, he says he's always awake early since he got older and he gets bored.'

'Oh, ok, is Paul in?'

'No, he's gone to the town, he said he's got to do some,' Adele squinted up at the ceiling, clearly thinking hard, 'ree-search, yes that's what he said. He won't be back till tea time either.'

Michelle felt relieved. 'Oh, ok, great.'

'Mum.'

'Yes, love?'

'After lunch can we look for Great Auntie's photo albums? Mr Alan says that she had loads.'

'Yeh, ok, of course we can.'

There was the sound of snuffling and Jack appeared next to Adele, his long noble face resting on the covers. Adele patted his head. 'Come on, Jack, time to go.' She turned and headed towards the door and the dog padded faithfully behind her.

'Will you be back for your lunch.'

'Yes, Mummy.'

They left the room and Adele pulled the door closed behind her. Michelle felt suddenly bereft, and nearly called Adele back, but stopped herself. The little girl was happy, and it wasn't her job to make her mum feel better. A wave of sleepiness came over her and she pulled the covers up around her face. She recognised in herself a creeping and familiar sense of indifference. It was like a favourite duvet. If she let it, she could wrap herself up in it and disappear inside for days. She never wanted that to happen again and knew she had to fight it.

She dragged herself out of the bed and struggled to make sense of her emotions. What was wrong with her? Since she'd come to France, she had felt a heaviness lift from her soul almost immediately; but now it felt like it was sneaking back. She rubbed her face; no, it wasn't that heaviness was coming back exactly; more that she felt a kind of low anxiety; guilt almost; but she couldn't put her finger on why.

She stood up, headed to the bathroom and splashed her face with cold water; hoping it would somehow make her feel more alive. As she straightened up she looked into the mirror. The face that looked back at her was pale and nondescript; she had become a ghost. When had that happened, she wondered? When had she become a ghost of herself? She would put some make-up on today, she decided, some lipstick and mascara to define her features. She hated the blankness of the face that gazed back at her.

Down in the kitchen a few minutes later she went through the motions of making herself some breakfast. She put the coffee pot on the hob and filled a bowl with muesli. *I'm sorry, Chris,* she found herself thinking, *I haven't spoken to you in a while. And I feel bad, because I only seem to talk to you when I want something, or when I feel confused; but I don't know what's happening to me, it's all so different here, Chris, can you help me?* There was, of course, no answer. She poured her coffee and then a wave of anger came over her and she found herself crashing the pot back down onto the counter with such force, that some of the coffee lurched out of her cup and over her hand. She winced and went to the tap to rinse her burning fingers. 'I'm sorry, Chris;' she said aloud this time, 'I'm just so fucking fed up of being on my own!'

Paul reversed the Fiat into a spare parking space and stopped the engine. He scanned the broad, leafy boulevard, the *Musée de la Mémoire Argemourt* was about fifty yards away under the shade of an old beech tree. He locked the car and slung his rucksack over his shoulder. There was a simmering, nervous feeling in the pit of his stomach. The Musée was a modern building, constructed from the same pale local stone as the old municipal buildings on either side of it. The name was carved out simply in thin, elegant capitals on a large white stone slab that was mounted above the heavy wooden doors. The sun shining through the undulating leaves of the beech, cast a dreamy, underwater light on the building's façade.

He double checked the opening hours on an etched glass sign to the right of the entrance, then leaned his weight against the doors. They opened easily with a soft 'whish' as if a vacuum had been released. There was something about museums, a quality, that made Paul feel as if he was entering a sacred place. Maybe it was the humbling knowledge that they contained learning and treasures beyond your comprehension; maybe there was something in the disconcerting truth, that in the main, they catalogued the doings of those who were now dead.

The entrance hall was a perfect square, painted white from floor to ceiling, with tall, slim wooden doors leading off on three sides. On the wall to his left a simple sentence had been written in large grey letters, first in French, then in English and German: "For the people of Argemourt. For those who have been, for those that are, and for those that will be. We will never forget." He stood looking at the sentence for a long time, then heard a faint cough behind him.

There was a *bureau d'information* to the left of the central door, he walked towards it. A small man, with neatly combed black hair and piercing blue eyes, looked up at him as he approached.

'Bonjour, Monsieur.'

'Bonjour. I wonder if you can help me. I am a student, studying the Martyred Villages and I am staying in the village, in the home of Michèle Leroy, with her great niece. Is there a tour? A map I can use?'

'Bien sûr, I can help you.' The man lifted a small two-way radio from the desk and spoke into the microphone. A voice replied, broken up by static; the man seemed satisfied and put the radio back on the desk. 'Voila, my colleague is on her way to take over the desk. If you would like to follow me.' He stood up and gestured towards the door on their left. Paul squinted at the man's ID badge. 'Ah merci boucoup...Gérard."

Gérard smiled and led Paul towards the door. The wooden surface had been polished to a high shine, revealing a sinuous and intricate tracing of whorls and eddies in the grain. He pushed the door open and it made the same hushing noise as the front-door had when it opened.

'The museum is in three parts,' explained Gérard as he followed Paul into the first room; 'each part is behind one of the three doors. The first part explains the series of events that led to the massacre; the second contains artefacts of those that died, alongside the few accounts of those that witnessed, or came close to witnessing the massacre first-hand; and the third explains why Argemourt has survived as a town; why people stayed. It is, if you like, a tale of defiance.' He cocked his head like a bird and seemed to be studying Paul keenly.

'Yes, I see, thank you. And is there a library? Historical records?'

'Oui, so long as you can show me identification and proof of your student status, I can book you a session in the archives. Also, come back to me before you leave, I have something that I think you might like to see.'

Paul nodded and smiled, resisting the temptation to ask Gérard to explain further.

'Maintenant, I will leave you to explore on your own. Please come and find me if you have any questions.'

'Oui, merci, I will.'

Gérard turned and left the room, and the door sighed shut. Paul took a deep breath and looked around him. The wall on his left was filled, floor to ceiling, with an enlarged old photograph of the village. He recognised some of it, including the square and the fountain, but there were fewer buildings bordering the gardens, and the essence of the light in the image suggested that little was built up behind them; unlike now. On the remaining three walls there was a timeline, with boards of text and more framed images, marking the tragic progression of events that culminated in the massacre. In the centre of the room; a dummy dressed in a full SS Officer uniform, stared blankly into the room like a sinister sentinel. Paul suddenly felt a little light-headed and walked slowly and carefully over to the image of the village.

The orientation board beside it said the picture was taken in 1939; a year before the occupation. Several people had been caught in the shot; a mother pushing a large black pram; a young man in a cap with a cigarette in the corner of his mouth; a number of people sat outside a small bar with the name 'Baptiste's' painted crudely above the door on a wooden board. All of them, frozen in a moment of blithe innocence and ignorance of what was to come. Paul wondered what had happened to the young man in the picture. Had he been sent out to fight? Had he returned from battle, or from the Resistance, to find everyone he had ever known, slaughtered? And the mother and baby? The child would have been about five when the massacre happened. Had it, with its mother, finished its short life screaming in the burning church?

Paul's stomach churned and he leaned against the wall for support. *I am pathetic*, he thought to himself scornfully; *all I have to do is look at what happened; these people had to live and die through it; I need to pull myself together.* He closed his eyes briefly; he could hear the blood pumping in his ears with a cold, rushing sound. A chill realisation came with it. Argemourt was the first of the Martyred Villages that he had actually visited; there was Oradour-sur-Glane, Tulle, Maille, Argenton-sur-Creuse and Vassieux-en-Vercors still to come. He had been stupid, naïve, how could he have taken it for granted that he was strong enough to face these terrible truths? But he had, and it was too late to go back now.

He moved on to the next wall. The timeline ran on two levels; the top one charting life in the village from the start of the war, occupation, the establishment of the Vichy government, right through to D-Day, and then the massacre. The lower timeline showed the development and progress of the 40th SS Panzer Division 'Odin' led by Sturmbannführer Stellerman, culminating in it being sent North as part of a drive to hold back the advancing Allied forces. And then, the day itself; June the 13th, 1944, this point in the timeline marked by a larger interpretation board that joined both levels together. He bent forward to read it.

"Sturmbannführer Hans Stellerman and his division were one of many commanded in the second half of 1944, to advance North to strengthen the Nazi front in the Battle of Normandy following the D-Day Landings on the 6th of June. During this time his Panzer Division (called 'Odin' after the Norse god of war) was diverted towards the Limousin to root out a Resistance cell that had been wreaking havoc with Nazi operations in the area. Stellerman, had, by this time, already gained a reputation for levels of cruelty and brutality, that were extreme even by SS standards; and followed in the footsteps of other Panzer and Waffen SS divisions that had already carried out massacres in the villages of Oradour-sur-Glane, Tulle and Argenton-sur-Creuse.

On June 13*th*, the same day that Germany launched 11 V1 Flying bombs on Britain, Stellerman's 40*th* Panzer Division arrived in the town square at Argemourt. They were commanded to go there following incorrect intelligence that townsfolk were harbouring the leaders of a particularly notorious and successful Maquis. With barbaric and indiscriminate zeal, Stellerman ordered his troops to raid every house in the village and have every resident; regardless of age or gender; to congregate in the village square. After a show of checking ID papers to flush out the Maquisards, all 322 residents were marched towards the village church. The men were separated from the women and children who were forced into the church. The men were then lined up against the church walls and shot. For the women and children in the church, already screaming in horror at the sound of gunshots, worse was yet to come. The SS smashed in windows on the Western flank of the church and sprayed the inside with bullets; before throwing in incendiary devices; burning many of the women and children alive; including three babies.

Only four residents of the town survived the attack; the bar owner, Jean Baptiste, who was saved by a metal flask in his jacket pocket; a brother and sister saved by Matilde Montande, who hid them in her home, and a seven-year-old boy who managed to escape the church shortly after witnessing his father being shot. Around a dozen villagers also survived as they were not in Argemourt during the time of the attack. Some others, who lived in neighbouring farms and villages, came perilously close to dying in the massacre, including writer Michèle Leroy, whose book 'Villages de Fantômes' remains the most comprehensive account of the terrible events of that day.

Unlike some other of the Martyred Villages, Argemourt itself was not razed by the Nazis. Theories for this include the fact that the village church, where the massacre was carried out, was half a kilometre from the town itself; others that Sturmbannführer Hans Stellerman wanted to avoid the approbation of the wider German army; such as Sturmbannführer Adolf Diekmann did following the massacre at Oradour-sur-Glane.

Stellerman escaped justice by dying on the battlefields of Normandy just weeks after the attack on Argemourt. Some officers from his division were tried at a military tribunal in 1953. In the same year, some 10 members of the division, who were identified as Malgre Nous, were pardoned in an amnesty, which caused much anger in the region; an anger that has carried on in the hearts of some of the survivors and their families.

However, the town of Argemourt, continues to grow and prosper – perhaps the best act of defiance against the horror and inhumanity that the massacre symbolises.

In those that are, in those that have been and in those that will be, burns the memory of Argemourt; and with it the hope – delicate and tender though it is – that Man shall one day learn the lessons of history."

Paul blinked back tears and once again found himself staring into the expanding black hole of his incomprehension. How? *How?* He moved, unsteadily into the second room. In here the tall windows were heavily shuttered, and the only light came from a series of display cases set in glass-topped cubes at intervals around the room. He went over to one and rested his hand on the glass. His fingers were trembling. The case was filled with items of clothing; a cloth cap, an apron, a pair of brogue-style shoes, a battered trilby hat, a shredded and soot-stained chemise. All bore the dusty, faded quality of items from an archaeological dig. They made his stomach turn.

There were no information or interpretation boards by the cases, just the cases themselves and their heart-breaking contents. Every item had a sense of tragedy and abandonment about it; the crushed and twisted wire frame of a pair of glasses; a torn scarf stained with age-browned blood; a pair of lady's nylon stockings, melted at one end into a blackened stump. Paul's mouth filled with bile and he rushed out of the room and into the sudden brightness of the entrance hall. He stood for a moment, his hand over his mouth, feeling utterly bewildered then turned to the information desk.

'Where are the toilets?' he managed to say to Gérard.

'Please,' Gérard came over to him and took hold of his arm, 'come and sit down for a second and you will feel better.' He led him to the welcome desk and pulled out his swivel chair. 'Many feel as you do now. It is hard. Sit and close your eyes and take deep breaths. If you feel dizzy put your head between your knees. I will be back shortly.'

Paul did as he was told and the nausea slowly started to subside. Just a few moments later Gérard returned with a steaming drink in his hand.

'Some tea, with sugar. It will make you feel better.'

Paul reached out for the cup gratefully. 'Merci.'

Gérard leant against the welcome desk and fixed Paul with his bright, intelligent eyes. 'So, you are a student.'

'Oui.'

'Studying our town?'

Paul took a sip of his tea. 'And the others.'

Gérard nodded. 'A difficult subject.'

'Yes, I feel pathetic, I'm sorry, I can't believe how weak I am when faced with this...this...'

'Horror? Sadness? Despair? Rage?'

'Oui.' Paul acknowledged.

'You mustn't be too hard on yourself. You care, and that is important. If you didn't feel then you could not do justice to this subject. If a surgeon did not feel they could not do their job, they would cause damage at every operation; however, they learn to control their feelings; that is the only difference. You will learn to do this too, this is your first visit, it will get easier. To me, now,' Gérard gestured at the doors to the exhibits, 'these are old friends. I give them stories, I keep them alive. I honour them and that makes the sadness bearable.'

'But do you ever...has it made you,' Paul struggled to express what he wanted to say, 'can you comprehend?'

Gérard was silent for a moment. 'I comprehend that people can become so twisted and destroyed that they commit great horrors; yet I comprehend that there are also people who will risk themselves, and the lives of those they love, to protect the rights and safety of strangers; I comprehend that humanity requires constant vigilance; that sometimes small acts of kindness feel like the only weapons against the darkness...ah —' he broke off, sounding frustrated, 'Je ne sais pas!'

'Moi non plus!' Paul said, in solidarity. They looked at each other and smiled.

Gérard's expression suddenly changed. 'Ha! Pardonne moi, I almost forgot!' He went to a small filing cabinet behind the welcome desk and took out a book. 'For you, you must have it.'

Paul took the book from him and turned it over. He recognised the cover image instantly; though the title font had been changed. 'Michèle Leroy's book, thank you, but I have it.'

'Ah non, you do not have this one. It is a new edition; Madame Leroy produced it before her death, we have just received our copies from the publisher.'

Paul turned the book over and studied it closely. 'What has changed?'

'It has some new accounts, from survivors and their families, that have come to light only recently. And there is a new prologue and epilogue too, you should read it.'

Paul nodded, 'I will.'

'You know why she wrote this book?'

Paul shrugged, 'She lived near the town, she wanted to tell the world about it? Make sure it wasn't forgotten?'

'Non, well, that is not all. Her brother, Jacques, died in the massacre. It was a tragedy, they didn't even live in the village but on the outskirts, in the very cottage you are staying in as you know.'

'Then how did they get caught up in it?'

'They were cycling that day, going for a picnic. Jacques wanted to stop in the village, at the bar, for some cider. He was ahead of Michèle, and when she got to the top the hill behind him, she saw him surrounded by SS soldiers. She went into the trees, hid her bike, and crept closer. She heard him trying to joke with them, saying what a beautiful day it was, "No, no I am alone," he kept saying in answer to their questions; and then suddenly they shot him, just like that, in the middle of the track that runs past the church and into the town. Michèle saw him collapse onto the ground – she said it was as if he was a puppet and they had cut his strings – and then she hid. She could not move, she was there for hours, hidden in the bushes. It wasn't until the local mayor sent out search parties that she was found, many hours later.'

'How horrible. Poor Michèle.'

'Until this edition I had only heard the account from a relative of her husband. I do not know why she waited so long to tell her story; perhaps she felt ashamed that she did not try to help him. But what could she have done? She would only have been murdered too, and then, we would never have had her book, and so many people would never have known what really happened here. I believe she wrote the book for her brother. An atonement, perhaps.'

'In her house, there is a picture in the room I am staying in, a watercolour, it is signed by a *Jacques*.'

'Then that will be by him, by her brother. I am sure of it.'

'And her old dog, it is called Jack, as the English say it, you know?'

Gérard nodded. 'Despite all the years that have passed, she had not forgotten him.'

'Yes, it is so sad.' Paul got up and reached out to shake Gérard's hand. 'Merci, you have been so good to me; I have learnt so much, and your kindness, I will not forget it.'

'It was my pleasure. I will see you again?'

'Bien sûr. Very soon, I have much to learn!'

Gérard smiled and released his hand. 'Au Revoir.'

Paul put the new edition of *Villages de Fantômes* into his rucksack and headed out into the street. The air had changed, thick with heat and static as it pressed against his skin. The sky was hooded by an enormous dark storm cloud and the town had fallen into silence. He turned his back on the brooding sky and walked briskly down the road towards the little Fiat.

It was quiet and peaceful in the garden and Michelle jumped at the ringing of her phone. She smiled though when she saw the contact picture of Jane on her screen; a crop of a larger double-selfie they'd taken at a regimental dinner; one that had started properly enough but descended into drunken ribaldry once the officers and their wives had excused themselves.

'Hey! I'm so glad you called!'

'I thought it was about time, I'm missing you down here you know!'

'Yeh, I'm sorry. It wasn't great timing with you getting ready for Manchester and everything.'

'Ah don't worry about me; I've been kept entertained. It's been like a soap-opera here. Jodie and Sarah had a bitch-off on the wives' Facebook group; didn't you see?'

'I've not been on it, can't bear the idea of seeing anything from home at the moment to be honest!'

'God it's brilliant; you should go on and see. The admin tries so many times to get them to sort things out but it keeps kicking-off again, and then everyone's DM-ing each other about whose side they're on. Take a look; if you had any doubts about getting out of here, it will get rid of them straight away!'

Michelle laughed. 'It's nice to know some things don't change.'

'Anyway, how are you? What are you up to right now?'

'I'm sitting on the patio in Aunt Michèle's garden in the sunshine!'

'Lucky bitch! Where's my little 'Del?'

'She's made friends with the neighbour, she's over there, hunting snails. She keeps appearing in the garden and showing me them over the wall; but she's gone inside now making a house for them.'

'That's great, so they've got a kid her age next door?'

'No, it's an old English guy in his sixties!'

'You're kidding?'

'Nope. They've hit it off big time. He's really sweet, a bit like an honorary uncle; and he was friends with my great aunt; he's been looking after her old dog; though it's moved back here now thanks to Adele.'

'Ha! I bet you didn't think you'd get a new pet into the bargain. Is the house really in the middle of nowhere then? Is there anyone else about?'

'The house on the other side of us is a holiday home and its empty at the moment so apart from Alan, no. Well, except... there is someone else too.'

'...Ok, who's that?'

'A young student, called Paul. He's from Paris.'

'When you say *young*, how young?'

'Oh, I don't know, a bit younger than me. It's his PhD or something, he'd arranged to stay here with Great Aunt Leroy while he researches the history of the village; something like that.'

'So, you let him stay with you instead?'

'Yeh,' replied Michelle, airily, 'he had all his papers and everything and the money's useful.'

'Yeh, I bet; and what's he like?'

'He's, erm, he's quiet and thoughtful. He's a bit stuck in his head, if you know what I mean, one of those types that's always reading and end up not seeing what's happening in front of their eyes; but he's nice, I suppose. He cooked for us all, for Alan the neighbour too, and Adele likes him.'

'Sounds like you've fitted a lot in to your first few days!'

Michelle laughed. 'Yeh, I suppose so, but today, I don't know, I feel a bit shit.'

'How do you mean?'

'Kind of unsettled, you know what I mean? Like everything feels a bit weird.'

'That's just change; that's what change feels like at the beginning, but it doesn't make it wrong, and that feeling goes in the end.'

'I know, but it's more than that; it's like I feel bad, like I'm letting Chris down somehow;' she sighed, 'I don't know, it's hard to explain.'

'It's ok, honey, I know what you mean. But you've been on your own for two whole years now; it's ok to move on, and its ok to be around new people. Maybe it's just that, maybe you feel like you're leaving him behind somehow?'

Michelle heard Jane stifle a sob. 'Shit, sweetheart, I'm sorry, I've been wittering on about myself the whole time. It must be really tough for you up there with the move to sort out and all that.'

Jane let out a shaky sigh; 'It's just, it's just harder than I thought, leaving this place. I mean, I hate it, in lots of ways I really do hate it; and without Abe or you, what's the point? It's just; it feels like everything Abe and I did together, making a home, having Beth, all that, it all happened here. On the one hand I know that if I don't leave, if I don't take up this opportunity in Manchester, I'll go mad, I really will; but on the other hand, I feel like I'm abandoning Abe, and our memories. It's like I'm being torn in two.'

'I understand. But you're doing the right thing, Jane, I know it. You're too big for that place, too clever, too independent. You could never be what you need to be, what you *could* be there. When Abe was around, you could argue it was worth it, but now?'

'I know, I know you're right.'

'And you're not leaving Abe, he's in your heart, he's in your memories. He'd want you to do this, you know he would.'

'You're right. And it's the same for you. Chris would be proud of you for what you've done, and he'd want you to move on. To open yourself to new things. Maybe it's time for you to let *him* go a bit?'

They were silent for a while.

'I'm sorry, 'Chell, I didn't mean –'

'No, it's ok, you're right. I think that's why I suddenly feel bad, because being here has done that; I've spoken to him less, my mind's been busy on other things. But maybe, maybe that's not so terrible?'

'No, it's not so terrible, love. I remember, about ten years after Dad died, I felt really funny one day; I couldn't put my finger on it, and then I realised; I'd forgotten that it was the anniversary of his death. I felt really shit about it, I even worried that he might haunt me because of it, but then Mum told me it was great; because it was a sign that I could just love Dad and remember him in the good ways and not have him dying as the main thing that defined him and his memory. She said it was good, and it was natural.'

'She was very wise, your mum.'

She heard Jane start to cry again. 'I miss her, I miss them both so much. It's so hard doing all this on my own, without any family, I mean there's Dave, but he turned out not to be the brother I thought he was.'

'Look, why don't I come back? I could put all this on hold for a couple of weeks, help you out there?'

'No! I mean it 'Chell, I don't want you to come back. It means so much to me that you're out there, doing what you need to do and building something new. I'd hate for you to stop doing that because of me. You doing it first is giving me strength.'

'Ok, but promise me, you'll come up here soon and take a few days out at least? We'd love to have you here, and it will give you a break.'

'Yes please, that sounds great. You and 'Del, you mean so much to me.'

'Don't be daft, you're literally my sister!'

'Yeh,' replied Jane drily, 'your crazy, communist, alcoholic sister.'

'Don't be daft! Just crazy – and only at the moment.'

'You cheeky bitch! Hey, talking about crazy relatives, what about your mum?'

Michelle let out a humph of exasperation. 'She keeps texting me to tell me in lots of different ways about how mad I am to be doing what I'm doing, that she doesn't understand what's got in to me, and that if I was putting Adele first I'd take the money from this place and go and live near them.'

'Well that decides it then; you're staying there!'

'Would it be that crazy, Jane? I mean, Adele really likes it here, there's a little primary school up the road, and I could train to do TEFL?'

'So, you're really thinking about it? About staying?'

Michelle realised then, that although she hadn't thought seriously about staying there, or had any kind of reasoned conversation about it in her own mind, she obviously had started to think about it on some unconscious level. 'I don't know, Jane, maybe? At least, I'm not ruling it out.'

'When do you have to be out of your house here?'

'In a couple of months.'

'You've got plenty of time to try it out, to think about it then.'

'Exactly.'

'So, what does he look like?'

Michelle was nonplussed for a moment. 'Who?'

'You know, the French guy, the student?'

'Talk about changing the subject!'

'Sorry! Come on, I'm curious.'

'I don't know, well, he's quite tall, and skinny. He's got really blonde hair and tanned skin, and he's got a bit of a faraway look in his eyes.'

'Fuck me, 'Chell, you struck lucky there!'

'Oi, watch it! It's not like that. But he's nice to talk to sometimes, and like I said, Adele seems to approve of him.'

'Shit. Sorry, I've got to go.'

'Ok, love, you ok?'

'Yeh, just forgot, I've got to pick Beth up from her mate's before her mum goes out.'

'Thanks for calling, I can't tell you how good it is to hear your voice.'

'And you, look after yourself 'Chell, and ring me, ring me in a couple of days.'

'I will, I promise.'

'Bye.'

'Bye.'

She hung up the call and smiled. Jane always made her feel better, thank God she had such a good friend.

'There's going to be a big storm Mummy, look.'

Michelle started at Adele's voice, and turned to see the little girl on Alan's side of the fence, pointing and looking fixedly up at the sky.

'See, there's a great big cloud coming.'

She followed her daughter's gaze and saw that the sky had been slashed in two – on one side vibrant cornflower-blue; on the other, a deep curdle of cloud in battle-ship grey. She shuddered, although the air had become hot and syrupy. 'Best come in now then love. Have you finished your snail house?'

'Yes, it's got two floors, and a kitchen and a bedroom!'

'Wow! Clever you! Why don't you bring it round and we can have a nice lunch?'

Adele looked at her fearfully. Michelle couldn't understand why then it hit her and she laughed. 'Don't worry, silly, I don't mean we'll eat the snails!'

Adele smiled with relief. 'And then can we look for Auntie Michèle's photos?

'Yeh, why not.'

As Michelle turned to head back into the house the cloud burst and a sheet of thick, heavy rain hurtled out of the sky, bringing with it a smell like sun-warmed hay. Adele squealed and ran towards Alan's patio door.

'Meet me out the front,' shouted Michelle through the hiss of the rain, 'I'll bring the umbrella.'

Back in the house, Michelle wiped the rain from her eyes and grabbed the big old black umbrella, that had remained, unused and unwanted in the hallway since she had arrived. She opened the door and unfolded it, gesturing to Adele, who was sheltering under Alan's porch, holding her 'snail house' protectively against her chest. Jack was huddled beside her, sniffing at the air without enthusiasm. 'I'll come over to you.' She stepped over the strip of flowers that separated the two paths, rain running into her sandals and between her toes. She reached out for Adele's hand and Jack followed after them, his head bowed.

When they got back into the cottage they laughed and shook out the old umbrella before leaving it upside-down in the porch.

'It's like jungle rain!' said Adele, beaming. 'It's good you had that or the snails might have drownded.'

'You mean *drowned*.'

Adele frowned at her. 'That's what I said, *drownded*.'

Michelle smiled and stroked the wet fringe away from her daughter's eyes. 'Come on then, show me this snail house.'

Adele trotted into the kitchen and put her treasure on the counter. It had been made from an old fish tank, with layers of sand, soil and leaf mould. The snails were exploring happily, leaving their silky trails up the side of the glass. 'See, that's their bedroom,' said Adele, pointing at an old plant pot lying on its side, 'and that's the kitchen,' she continued, pointing at a pile of dandelion leaves.

'It's wonderful!'

'Alan says I can keep them in it for a few days so long as I keep putting leaves in and make sure it doesn't dry out.'

'Hmm, it's a good job it's got a lid then.'

'Mr Alan knows everything, Mummy, and he's been all over the world.'

'I know, he's really interesting isn't he.'

Adele turned and look at her. 'I think it's sad.'

'What is, sweets?'

'That Mr Alan doesn't see his little girl.'

'She's not a little girl anymore, she must be in her thirties by now.'

'I know, but even so. He has a room upstairs, that he says is for her when she stays, but she hasn't been for three years. And he's made it really pretty, and it's got photos of her in and an old teddy-bear that he let me play with.'

'That is sad.'

'But why wouldn't she want to see him, Mummy? She's got a dad, and she doesn't want to see him.'

Michelle sat down and pulled Adele onto her lap. 'Grown-up lives are complicated. Maybe he was just working all the time when she was little and she never really got to know him; maybe her mum felt like she had to do all the work?'

Adele squeezed her hands into fists. 'But he knows that now, and he wants to make it better. She doesn't understand. If I had a dad and he was alive I would see him.'

'Yeh, baby, I know.'

Adele looked up at her again, she looked anxious. 'I did something, Mummy.'

Michelle's heart missed a beat. 'What, what did you do?'

'I stole something from Mr Alan.'

Michelle pushed Adele off her knee. 'What? What did you take? You've got to go over there right now and say sorry and give it back!'

Adele's face crumpled and tears ran down her cheeks. 'I was going to give it back, honest, Mummy, I was just borrowing it!'

'That's no excuse –'

Adele reached into the pocket of her jeans and pulled out a battered envelope, not improved by having been hastily stuffed into her pocket.

'What is it?'

'It's from a letter Mr Alan sent to his daughter that she sent back.' said Adele, between sobs, 'It's got her address on it. I want to write to her and tell her how nice he is and make her come and see him so he's not so sad all the time.'

'Oh sweetheart!' Michelle pulled her daughter into a tight hug. 'I'm sorry I shouted, I didn't understand. But I'm not sure that's a good idea. Let me think about it. I'll copy down the address and if you do write to her I'll help you. But you must put that envelope back where you found it tomorrow. Can you do that?'

Adele sniffed and Michelle felt her head move as she nodded against her chest. 'Good girl. Now come on, let's have some lunch and then we'll go on that photo hunt.'

The sound of the front door slamming made them both jump. Paul appeared in the doorway to the kitchen, his face pale and his blonde hair plastered darkly by the rain to his face. 'Excuse moi, I need to get my books.' He went past them to the deep sill by the kitchen window and grabbed a handful of books he had left there. He didn't seem to notice that Adele had been crying or that Michelle was holding her, in fact he didn't seem to notice anything at all.

'Can I get you some lunch? We were just about to have some?'

'Ah, non, merci, I must work,' he shouted back at them as he headed up the stairs.

Paul shut the door behind him and threw his bag and books on the bed. For a few moments he just stood there, feeling the rainwater from his hair run down the sides of his face. Through the window the deluge continued, a curtain of shifting grey, smudging the view of the world outside and giving the room a shrouded quality. He went over to the little sink, dried his face with the hand-towel then sat on the edge of the bed to take off his wet trainers. He had the strange sensation of being on a boat; with the sounds of a wild sea outside his cabin and an uncomfortable rolling feeling inside him.

He took Michèle Leroy's book out of his bag and flicked through it in an attempt to distract himself from these strange sensations. From the chapter listing he could see, as Gérard had told him, that there was a new prologue and epilogue, and some previously untold accounts from the time of the massacre. He lay back on the bed and opened the book at the first new chapter; it told the story of a young woman from Lyon, who had been staying in Argemourt for the summer as a nanny for children of the town's doctor. She had not managed to escape the horrors of that day, but the children of her younger sister had seen *Villages de Fantômes* in a local bookshop and got in contact with Michèle Leroy's publisher. They sent copies of letters she had sent to her family while she was staying at the village. No-one knew exactly what happened to her that day, but her charred bones had been found amongst the countless other women and children in the church.

He looked up from the page. He could hear Michelle and Adele coming noisily up the stairs. Adele sounded breathless and excited; he listened to them stomp off into one of the other bedrooms then cast his attention back to the book. He read about the lucky escape of Argemourt's vet; out on a job in an outlying farm; the fate of a group of school children, unlucky enough to be at a pond on the edge of the village for a biology field trip; of eighty-year-old Matilde Montande, who bravely hid a brother and sister in her cellar, saving their lives. Matilde, however, died with the other women and children from the village in the church. She had stayed in her kitchen so she could cover the trap door to the cellar with a rug and had been discovered. As he read, he continued to hear Michelle and Adele, passing outside his door, heading up and down the stairs, chatting animatedly.

He turned to the new Epilogue. After just two lines he was completely absorbed in what he was reading and the sounds of mother and daughter dissolved into a background world that he was barely aware of. He had never heard this story before, how had he not known of it? Stories of SS officers and their cronies risking their necks by helping those they were attacking were rare. And for this officer, a Malgre Nous, did this final act of compassion show a level of internal conflict and guilt that burned in the hearts of most of the forced conscripts?

There was a hurried knock at the door and then it flew open. Adele and the old dog almost fell into the room and Adele came over to the bed. 'We've been looking for Aunt Leroy's photos,' she said, breathlessly, 'and we've found loads of them, and there's a letter too, from my mum's granny, but we can't read it coz it's in French –'

'Please!' responded Paul, emphatically. 'I am working right now, you cannot just come in here like this! I must not be disturbed!'

The colour drained from Adele's face and she ran from the room. The dog gave him a reproachful look from under its shaggy brows then trotted after her. He sighed with exasperation.

Michelle appeared in the doorway, arms crossed, glaring at him. 'Don't you dare, ever, talk to my little girl like that again! You chose to live in this house, with a family; you can't pretend we aren't here. And if you don't like it you can go and get yourself a tent and pitch it up by that fucking church and wallow all you want.' She slammed the door.

'Merde!' Paul threw his book onto the quilt and rubbed his face with his hands. Frustration and guilt battled inside him and he felt suddenly exhausted. He knew he had to apologise, to try to find somewhere new to stay now would take up a lot of time, and she was right, this wasn't a museum or a library, it was a home. He fought to summon up the energy to move and forced himself up from the bed.

He found Michelle and Adele in the small sitting room, an array of old photo-albums in front of them on the coffee table. Adele was sniffing slightly, her face red; Michelle still had her arms crossed and looked furious.

The sound of the rain outside brought back the sensation of being on a boat; *we are all at sea*, he found himself thinking.

He took a deep breath. 'Please, Michelle, Adele, I am very sorry.' There was no response. He sat down in the armchair in front of them. 'The things I am studying, they are difficult and sad and sometimes I let them get too deep inside of me. But you are right; it is no excuse, you have taken me into your home and I respect that, I do, and it has been so good these last couple of days to spend time with you.' He reached his hand out towards Michelle, she hesitated and then took it. Her hand felt warm and strong in his. 'Please, Michelle, will you accept my apology?' Her look softened a little and she nodded silently. 'Merci, and you, little Adele,' he released Michelle's hand then reached out to the little girl, 'will you forgive this stupid, grumpy man?' Adele took his hand but her face was sombre. 'And now, show me this letter.'

Adele let go of his hand and wiped her eyes. 'Here it is.' She handed him a one-page letter written in small curling script on a sheet of delicate airmail paper.

'We think my granny sent it when Great Aunt Leroy got married.' Michelle pushed a strand of hair behind her ear. 'It's dated March 1955, but that's about all I can make out, apart from a few words.'

Paul lifted the letter towards the weak grey light that was coming from the rain-darkened window. 'I will do my best to translate it for you, but the writing is difficult to read.' He studied it for a few moments. 'She says something like, *"Dear Michèle, I received your letter informing me of your wedding to…Dieter…"* I think that's the name.'

'Yes,' said Michelle, 'that's him, there's some photos of them and it says their names and where they are. Holidays, things like that.' She flicked through one of the old leather photo albums on the table in front of them. 'This is him.' She turned the album around. There was a picture of a young couple; Michèle Leroy looked pretty in a floral summer dress, and beside her, with his arm around her shoulders, was a tall, thin man with a shock of dark hair and deep set, intelligent eyes. Paul nodded and returned to the letter.

"I am sorry but I cannot attend." He squinted at the close text, struggling to decipher it. *"You tell me Dieter and his family spent the war in Switzerland, because of their communist beliefs, but he is still a German, and could have decided to join the Allied forces to fight, but he didn't. Our own brother dies, but you marry a man who hid away and chose not to fight. This causes me great pain, and although I love you, dear sister, I cannot give my blessing to a union that includes one from the very race that murdered our friends and neighbours just 11 short years ago."* He rubbed at his eyes. 'Sorry, it is hard to read.' He bent down towards it again, there were only a few sentences left. *"You break my heart with this marriage, and if you love me at all, you will not visit us in England on your honeymoon as you have suggested and will respect my wishes. Despite this, I wish you only well, and can only say, in sadness, that from this day on, you remain my sister in name only. Yours, Cécile."*

Paul put the letter back on the table.

Michelle picked it up and carefully put it back into its envelope. 'That's so sad. You can't help who you love, and he wasn't a Nazi or anything.'

Paul sighed. 'It is hard to explain, what people felt after the war. A year before your grandmother wrote this letter, many Nazis and collaborators were released under an armistice. Imagine how that felt, for people who had witnessed horrors like Argemourt, who had lost children, parents, siblings, husbands and wives to the Germans. It created a bitterness, an anger, and for some, that feeling is still there.'

Adele frowned. 'But it wasn't his fault, what the Nazis did.'

'No,' Paul conceded, 'I agree, but all your great grandmother could see was that he was German.'

Adele made a huffing sound and got up. 'She was silly, to not see her sister because of that. If people die you can't ever, ever see them again. They're just gone. But Great Aunt Michèle wasn't gone.' She stopped, as if thinking of something but then her face cleared. 'Mum, I'm going to go upstairs and play on my iPad. I've got to level 10 and now I've got two hundred jewels so I can buy the dragon I wanted.'

Michelle smiled at her daughter and squeezed her arm. 'Ok, sweetheart. When it stops raining we'll take Jack out for a walk.'

Adele stopped at the doorway. 'And Mr Alan says we *can* swim in the lake. It used to be for the sheep and the cows from the farms to drink in the summer but no-one knows whose it is now that the farms have gone. He says lots of kids swim in it when it's hot. If it's sunny tomorrow can we go and swim?'

'Yes, of course darling. If you want to.'

She turned to Paul. 'And will you come too?'

'Oui, I love to swim.'

Adele smiled and left the room, Jack trailing faithfully behind her.

'She's only young, she doesn't understand.' Michelle picked up one of her aunt's photo albums and started flicking through it. 'In the letter my granny says Michèle had a brother. Do you think he died fighting in the war?'

'In a way he did.'

She tipped her head to one side. 'What do you mean? How do you know?'

'The man in the museum told me. He was called Jacques, he died on the day of the massacre, he got caught by the Nazis on the edge of the village.'

'That's awful.'

'Michèle was with him but a little behind. She saw the soldiers get him, he saved her, I think. She heard him keep saying that he was alone. She hid in the woods, but not until after she saw them shoot him.'

'Poor Michèle, I never knew about him. Something else Granny didn't tell us. So many secrets. Like Adele says, it's such a waste.'

'That's what war is, I think, a terrible waste.'

'I don't know how you stand it, studying this stuff all the time. The history, the sadness and the anger, everything that happened here, sometimes it feels like it's just too much.'

Paul leaned back in his chair and rubbed at his eyes. 'Sometimes I wish I was still a child and could switch the difficult feelings off like she does and just go and play on my iPad.'

He felt Michelle's hand rest lightly on his knee for a moment and he took his hand down from his face and looked at her. She smiled briefly then leant back against the old sofa. 'You look tired, Paul.'

'So do you.'

'I feel it, but I don't know why. I'm sleeping ok it's just...I don't know...this place. It feels like there's this big story, all this history, and its pressing around me. Sometimes I feel like it's trying to tell me something, or get me to go a certain way,' she looked up at him again, 'does that sound crazy?'

'No, not at all.' As he looked at her then it suddenly occurred to him how incredibly pretty she was. Not as beautiful as Veronique; or then again; maybe she was. Somehow Veronique had become more ordinary looking the longer he had known her; with Michelle the opposite seemed to be happening. Her face, that he had at first (apart from her eyes) thought quite plain, was he saw now, not plain at all. There was a depth, a profoundness to it, and her expressions, and he wondered, now, how he could ever have been stupid enough not to see it. 'I think for places like this; where terrible things happen, an energy is left. Not just from the events, but from the reckoning afterwards: the grief; the surrender of some, the defiance of others. They say that all fascism needs to succeed is for forty percent of a country to be behind the leader who is trying to introduce it. In the last election the *Rassemblement National*, what you know as the *Front National*, got twenty percent of the vote. You could say we're half way.'

Michelle looked shocked. 'Really, I can't believe it.'

'I am oversimplifying, maybe, but this is why I feel such a weight, such a responsibility. It is why I keep studying.'

'So what do we do? How do we fight it?'

'Ah, that is, what you call, *the million-dollar question*. A man I met today, the concierge from the museum, he said something that I keep thinking about; he said that sometimes, it feels like small acts of kindness are the only weapons we have against the darkness.' He stopped and shook his head, 'Ah, now it is me who is sounding crazy!'

'No, I like that, about the small acts of kindness. I think that's true. I don't know much about politics, about history, but when kindness goes, it feels like there's nothing left.'

'Yes, I feel that too. Your great aunt's book, a new edition has just been published, there are accounts I have never seen before, and the last chapter, the epilogue I have just started reading, it is from a Malgre Nous; a conscripted French soldier who was part of the Nazi division that carried out the massacre, here in Argemourt. He tells a story of how he saved a young boy, on the day of the attack. It was one act of kindness in a day of unimaginable horror. But it makes a difference, it gives us hope.'

Michelle shook her head sadly. 'It's just so horrible. I can hardly bear to think about it. Do we know what happened to the little boy?'

'Non, it says Madame Leroy and her publishers tried to find him but they could not. Perhaps he was killed later in the war, perhaps he is somewhere, living a quiet life and trying to leave it all behind.'

'If he was alive, he'd be an old man now.'

'Exactement. It would maybe be unkind to get him to remember. And survivors, of such horrors, they can struggle, they can feel great guilt.'

'If I lost Adele, I'm not sure I would want to go on.'

Paul envied Michelle at that moment, to have a love as great as that; he felt suddenly lonely. 'But we are lucky, we do not live in such times and she is safe.'

Michelle glanced at him, frowning. 'I hope so.'

The next day was the hottest since their arrival in France, and the moisture of the previous day's rain was rising out of the warm earth and pressing against Michelle's skin. Adele was excited, bouncing alongside Alan, who was bringing up the rear of the little party, carrying a picnic basket. Paul was a little ahead of her, his distinctive lope making his blonde head bob up and down. She felt a little nervous of stripping down to her swimsuit in front of him and was glad she had brought a light pashmina with her so she could cover up between swims.

A haze of tiny insects danced around the tops of the tall grass and wildflowers that hemmed either side of the dirt track, their movements strangely choreographed to the abrasive sound of crickets. Michelle breathed deeply, enjoying the throb of life around her, and tried to dispel the lingering feeling of strange melancholy that had overwhelmed her the day before.

Paul paused on the path in front, and when she caught him up he fell into step beside her. 'When I was young, my grandpapa would take me to a place like this.'

She smiled; she could imagine the little golden boy with sunlight shining through his pale hair.

'We would fish, and swim. It was good to get out of the city. He knew everything; how to gut fish, to make a bow and arrow, to suck out a snake-bite, to start a fire from just two pieces of wood. He was my hero then.'

'But he's not anymore?'

Paul shrugged. 'It is difficult, I found out he wasn't who I thought he was.'

Michelle sensed he didn't want to say any more so changed the subject. 'When me and my brother were little, Mum and Dad would take us on these really long walks in the countryside. I loved it when it was sunny and nice, but even when it rained, when it was freezing, they'd still make us go. When it was like that the only good thing about hiking was Kendal Mint Cake.'

'*Kendal...Mint...Cake?*' he repeated, hesitantly.

Michelle laughed. 'You wouldn't have had it here. It was a Northern thing, you know, from the North of England?'

'What kind of cake was it?'

'Well, it wasn't really a cake, it was more – a bar – you know – like chocolate. But it was just a brick of pure sugar that tasted of peppermint.'

He looked at her, dubiously.

'I know it doesn't sound nice, but it was, trust me!'

Paul raised his eyebrows at her and smiled.

'Mummy, Paul.' Adele appeared beside them, slightly breathless. 'Mr Alan's made us scones and he's got jam and cream too!'

'Ah, there you go, Paul, another English delicacy for you to try – a cream tea!'

Paul still looked unconvinced. Alan and Jack caught them up, Jack was panting, Alan looked red-faced. Paul reached out to take the hamper from his hand. 'Please, Alan, it is my turn to carry it now.'

'I'm perfectly capable of carrying it,' replied Alan, a little defensively.

'Oui, of course, but it is a hot day, and it is only fair that we share it.'

Alan yielded the basket and then took off his panama hat for a moment to mop his face with a handkerchief. 'Ok, thank you, Paul, it *was* starting to feel a bit heavy, I have to admit. I think I may have overdone it by bringing two bottles of wine!'

Michelle squeezed Alan's arm, feeling a sudden rush of affection for the old man. 'We're going to all end up falling asleep under a tree somewhere!'

'Exactly, just what I have planned for myself while you nutters go swimming!'

After a few more minutes walking they reached the lake. The surface was still, reflecting a fringe of willows and reeds and bright blue sky. A pair of ducks glided lazily across, breaking the glossy surface up into an infinity of delicate ripples. Adele whooped and immediately started to strip down to her swimming costume.

'Hang on, young lady!' Michelle laid a restraining hand on her daughter's arm, 'You have to let me get in first, you don't know how deep it is!'

Alan laid out a chequered picnic blanket in the shade beneath one of the willow trees then came over. 'This side is the shallowest, Adele, just make sure you stick to the bit between these two trees, and don't swim out to the centre, it's very deep there.'

Adele nodded solemnly then opened up the rucksack she had been carrying to reveal a pair of deflated arm-bands. 'I can swim, but it's easier when I wear these. And I've got my goggles too so I can look under the water and see the fishes.'

'Are there any fish in it?' said Michelle, feeling a bit squeamish about the prospect of them brushing against her legs.

'Of course!' Alan took off his hat again and fanned his face with it. 'Fishing is the second biggest sport in France you know! There's carp and trout in this lake, but you need a licence to fish in it.'

Paul chuckled. 'Despite our zealous public servants in France, I doubt one would come all the way out here!'

'Perhaps not, young man,' Alan raised his eyebrows, 'but if one of the locals saw you, you'd be in trouble!'

'Ah, oui, thank you for the warning, Alan!'

'I'm ready, Mum, come on, come on!' Adele was hopping on the spot, her now inflated arm-bands wedged half way up her arms. Self-consciously Michelle started to get undressed, she could feel herself blushing and turned away. *I'm being ridiculous,* she admonished herself, *he's just a friend, he's not going to be looking at me like that. Just enjoy yourself.* After she had got down to her swimsuit, she took Adele's hand and they ran towards the lake's edge, Adele squealing with delight.

'Don't stop!' said Michelle breathlessly, 'when we get to the water just jump straight in, if you do it slowly it will be harder!'

'Ok, Mummy!'

They broke through a few straggly reeds and with their next step they were in the water. The shock of the temperature – much colder feeling compared to the sultry air – made Michelle yelp. 'Don't stop!' she shouted to Adele and continued to pull her into the water until she was at waist height and Adele, gasping and smiling, started to doggy paddle, her fluorescent orange armbands bright against the deep blue water. Michelle let out a whoop of pleasure and dived, it felt so good, the cool caress of the water against her skin, the sudden buoyancy, the pull of her muscles as she broke back up through the surface of the water.

'It's wonderful!' she shouted back at Paul and Alan, who were laughing and watching them. 'Come on Paul!'

'Ah, maybe in a minute.'

'You chicken?'

'Am I *what*?'

She made clucking noises and waggled her arms; Paul smiled in recognition then wagged his finger at her.

'Ah, you say I am lâche! We will see!' He pulled off his t-shirt in one fluid movement, kicked off his espadrilles and dropped his shorts to reveal his swimming trunks. He was deeply tanned, thin, and lean; so different to Chris, who was stocky and muscled from the army's fitness regime. The comparison made Paul look vulnerable somehow.

Adele squealed with pleasure as Paul dived past her and into the water. 'Paul, Paul, I'm swimming too, look!' she called after him as he broke into a fast front crawl.

He made it a third way across the lake then swam back to them. 'Show me again, how you swim...ah, très bien! Now, lend me your goggles, ma petite Adele, I must hunt fishes.'

Adele giggled, Michelle swam over to her and held her while she took off her goggles and handed them to Paul. He adjusted the strap and put them on. He looked ridiculous. They were bright pink and way too small for him, but he didn't seem to mind.

'Now, if I do not return within one minute,' he said, suddenly serious, 'you must call for help. The carp in here,' he paused and held his hands out by his sides, 'are this big!'

Michelle felt Adele wriggle, maybe she wanted to stop him, but before she could, he had taken a deep breath and dived. Michelle knew it was a game, but when he still hadn't come up after thirty seconds, Adele was clearly worried.

'Mum, why hasn't he come back? Is he ok?'

'Of course, darling, he's just mucking about.'

They waited another ten seconds until Michelle started to feel anxious too. Adele was frowning, but then she screeched, and Michelle felt something grab her ankle and screeched too. Paul burst up out of the water in front of them, his hair slicked back from his face and laughing.

'That wasn't funny!' said Michelle, trying to sound serious, but failing.

He pointed at her and howled with laughter again; 'It is *very* funny, you should see your faces! Adele, did you feel the giant carp? He came over and bit your leg, I saw him!'

Adele's eyes were wide, 'You didn't see him, it was you!'

'Ah, non!' Paul replied, frowning, but with the hint of a smile, 'it was the giant carp, I had to wrestle with him to stop him eating you, that is why I took so long!'

Adele looked cautiously into the darkness of the water. 'Is there really one?'

Paul laughed again and ruffled her hair. 'Non, I only saw a few tiny fish, and Mr Carp, he will not bite. Put on the goggles and see for yourself.'

He took them off, adjusted the straps again and handed them back to Adele. She put them on. 'Mummy, will you hold me and I'll look?'

Adele lay over her arms and put her face into the water. Michelle could feel the muscles of the little girl's stomach tensing as she twisted and turned and she felt a rush of love. It was so good to see her happy, to see her living the kind of life a child *should* have, swimming in the summer sunshine, with friends, laughing, forgetting her worries.

They swam for another quarter of an hour and then started to feel hungry so scrambled back up the bank to join Alan in the shade. One of the bottles of wine was propped in a cooler against the trunk of the tree, and glasses had been laid out. The scones, jam and cream were together on a tray, and there was a selection of cheeses, cured meats and fruit and two batons of bread. Michelle tied her pashmina around her and sat cross-legged beside Alan. He poured her a glass of wine and she took a deep gulp, enjoying the cool slip of it down her throat. 'This is amazing, thanks so much Alan.'

'It's the best day of my life!' said Adele, suddenly and simply.

Michelle looked at her daughter and felt her eyes fill with tears. Alan glanced at Adele, then away again, his expression unreadable. *He's thinking of his own daughter* she found herself thinking.

'Here's to the best days of our lives!' said Paul, raising his glass.

Michelle and Alan brought their glasses up to meet Paul's. Adele popped the straw out of her mouth and her bottle of Orangina came up too. *'To the best days of our lives.'*

They ate and chatted for a while and a deep sense of wellbeing came over Michelle, taking her by surprise. She had felt so much, changed so much, in the last few days, it made her wonder if the last two years of her life, the grieving, had been a kind of hibernation. And now, here she was, coming out of the cave, blinking into the brightness of the light.

'Are you alright, Mummy?'

'Yes, of course, sweets.' She looked down at Adele and stroked her hair. Paul and Alan were deep in conversation.

'You looked far away, Mummy.'

Michelle smiled, 'I was just thinking.'

'About what?'

'About how nice it is here.'

'Can we stay all summer?'

'I don't see why not.'

'We could see if Auntie Jane and Beth want to come.'

'Yes, I'm sure they will, I mentioned it to Auntie Jane when she called me.'

Paul downed the last of the wine in his glass and stretched. 'I must go back and do some work soon, but first, one more swim!' He looked at Michelle and Adele. 'Are you coming?'

Michelle shook her head. 'I've had too much to eat, I'd sink like a stone!'

Paul laughed. 'Ha, who is *chicken* now?' Before she could answer he had jumped up, taken off his t-shirt and run back into the lake. She watched him as he dived then surfaced again, his long brown arms carving the surface of the water as he swam, expertly, towards the lake's centre.

'I think Paul is right.' Alan grunted with effort as he pulled himself up to start packing the picnic hamper. 'Time to go back, it's long past my nap time!'

Michelle wiped out the wine glasses with a napkin and laid them carefully in their allotted spot in the picnic basket. 'I'll tidy this lot up, Alan, you sit down.'

'No, no, I'm fine. Finish your cake!'

'To be honest, I couldn't eat another mouthful.' She glanced out at the lake, Paul was at the centre now and looked to be turning around. But then, he seemed to falter and disappeared from view. Her hand froze, half way to putting the remains of the batons back in the hamper. 'I'm not sure he should have gone out so soon after eating.'

'What's the matter, Mummy?' Adele put down the daisy chain she had been making and followed Michelle's gaze. 'Where's Paul gone?'

Michelle started to stand, frantically searching the surface of the water for a sign of him. With a surge of relief, she saw him break the surface, but it was short-lived. He gasped and thrashed his arms and then sank again. 'Shit, shit!'

Alan grabbed her arm. 'What is it?'

'It's Paul, he's in trouble.'

Adele started to sob. 'Mummy, Mummy, what do we do?'

Michelle threw off her pashmina. 'I've got to go after him.'

Adele grabbed hold of her leg. 'No, Mummy! Don't! You said you'd sink!'

'I'm sorry,' said Alan, putting his arm around Adele, his face white, 'I'd go in if I could, but I can't, I wouldn't even make it to the middle and you'd end up with two people to save.'

'It's ok, I'm going, I'm a strong swimmer, I've done a life-saving course.'

'NO, MUMMY, NO!' Adele was screaming now.

'Alan, please take her, I've got to!'

Alan nodded and gently prised Adele from Michelle's legs. As soon as she was free she ran towards the lake, so flooded with adrenalin she felt like she was floating. She hit the water and started to swim, her eyes fixed on the centre of the lake.

He broke the surface of the water and took a deep, searing breath that burned in his lungs. His head was a chaos of thoughts and words, but there was no sense to anything. One minute he was swimming, steadily and confidently, the next there had been a stabbing feeling in his side and his legs had stopped working.

He tried to cry out, frantically moved his arms, trying to keep afloat, but it was as if his legs were made of lead and inexorably, terribly, he started to sink again. Just before the water closed over his head he caught a sight of Michelle, standing at the water's edge, Adele screaming and clinging onto her mother's legs, the old dog barking furiously.

His first thought, crazily, as the water closed over his head and the light from the sun began to dim, was that this reminded him of what had happened at the swimming baths, just a week before. He wondered if it had been a premonition? Or some kind of strange unconscious suicidal practice run? Just as he had in the baths that day he felt again, that strange sense of calm. It lasted for a few seconds, and then, as the final traces of the last breath he had taken when he broke the surface started to run out, it was replaced by a sense of rising panic. He was still sinking, he couldn't believe how deep the lake was. He looked down into the gloomy depths below him, hoping against hope to see something there he could push up from, and then he saw it.

It was a face, the pale face of a young man in dark uniform, looking sightlessly at him from a tangle of dark water and the algae-covered carcases of unidentifiable, rusting machines and fallen branches. There was something about the face, something familiar; *NO!* His mind screamed, *no, it can't be!* He struggled then, and pushed down with his hands. There was a tiny bit of movement in his legs, and he thrashed them about, and finally, he started to move up, ever so slowly. The effort was excruciating and the impulse to open his mouth, to breathe, was so strong that it took every ounce of his sense of self-preservation to resist it. Just at the point that he thought he could stand it no more, that it would be better to open his mouth, let the cool water flood in and stop this agony, he felt something grab him and pull him upwards.

He broke the surface again, gasping and gulping for air, the water streaming down his face. He heard the sound of a faint shriek from the other side of the lake and a hand pushed the hair out of his eyes.

'I have to get you on your back! Come on, you need to help me!'

'Je...Je l'ai vu.'

'I   don't...understand   you. Roll...onto...your...back...now!'

He nodded in the direction of Michelle's voice but he couldn't see. Everything was a blur of colour and light.

'That's it, I've got you. Kick if you can but keep your arms still.'

He felt her behind him. She slipped her arms under his and then he felt the surge of water as she kicked away. He couldn't speak, his head and lungs were in agony. He stared sightlessly up at the sky, panting, the sun hot on his face. Time seemed to contract, and in what seemed like seconds they were back at the shore and he felt the drag of wet earth and pebbles underneath his heels.

'I can't...pull you anymore,' panted Michelle.

He rolled over onto his hands and knees, she was sitting ahead of him, her face red with exertion. Adele came hurtling down towards them.

'Mummy! Mummy!' She flung herself at Michelle and started to sob. 'I thought you were both going to die, Mummy!'

'It's...ok,' mumbled Michelle, between deep gulping breaths. 'We're ok.' She looked at Paul, briefly, then, and he felt something tug in his heart.

Alan appeared and flung towels over both of them. 'Thank God you're both ok! What happened, Paul?'

Paul shook his head. 'I got cramp...my legs stopped...I could not...'

'Ok, ok, don't speak any more, just stay there, both of you, until you feel better. I'll get some water. He headed, a little unsteadily, back up the bank. Paul reached out and took Michelle's hand. 'Thank you. I don't know how to say it, you saved me.'

She glanced back at him with an expression he couldn't read, 'I had to.'

The sun beat down on them as they walked back to the cottage but Paul felt cold. He shivered and pulled the picnic blanket tighter around his shoulders. They had been silent since leaving the lake, Alan and Jack a little behind them, Michelle beside him with Adele clinging tightly to her mother's hand.

Michelle touched his arm lightly. 'Are you ok?'

'Oui, I think so.'

'You seemed fine, and then all of a sudden – '

'It was like something pulled you down,' said Adele anxiously, looking first at Paul and then her mother.

'Non, I was just stupid. I should not have gone back to swim after eating all that food and having wine.'

They were silent again for a while.

Michelle looked at him. 'Did you see anything? In the water I mean? Did your foot get stuck or something? There can be a lot of stuff at the bottom of lakes like this. It happened to a friend of mine once, she got her foot stuck in a tree root.'

'Did she get away?' asked Adele, her eyes wide.

'Yes, she was fine, but it was scary for a few seconds.'

'Non, I did not get stuck. There was some rubbish, a rusty bike, some kind of old agricultural equipment I think; but it was just cramp.' He looked down at Adele, 'Your mother was very brave, helping me like that.'

Michelle blushed. 'It was nothing, it wasn't far to swim, these things are always scarier when they're happening, but afterwards, when you look back, you realise it wasn't that bad.'

He didn't say anything. He was remembering the face he saw in the water, it had been Armand's face. The face he had seen in an old photograph from during the war, his grandfather with a few men from the local Maquisard, but the face in the lake had been wearing German uniform. In his panic some neuron had obviously fired in his brain and thrown up the image of the very thing that was haunting him; his grandfather's betrayal, and the wider betrayal of the Milice and Malgre Nous against their own people. He felt foolish now and made a pact with himself to never mention what he had seen.

Jack trotted up beside him and nuzzled his hand before looking up at him with his big expressive eyes.

'He knows you feel bad.' Adele said simply.

'Do you still want to stay here, after today I mean?'
Michelle put her arm around Adele and they snuggled
deeper into the old floral sofa. The screen of the television
cast an aquatic light into the darkened room.

Her daughter was silent for a while, clearly thinking.
'Yes, it was scary when Paul couldn't swim, but it was still
a nice day, and anyway, you saved him.'

She had, Michelle thought, she *had* saved him.
Thinking back, she was surprised by the certainty she had
felt when she had run towards the water; not going after
him had simply not even felt like an option. She could
sense Adele's pride, emanating from her like a warm aura.
She wondered at it. She had spent so long feeling the
constant drain of worry that she was letting her daughter
down, that she wasn't a good enough mother, it was
liberating to let those feelings go, even if it was only for a
day. But then a different thought clouded over her
contentment; in many ways she had taken a terrible risk,
what if she had got into trouble too? Adele would have
been an orphan. The thought made her feel sick.

'Mum.'

Michelle twisted round to look at her. 'Yes, love?'

'I know I asked you not to go in. I was just scared,
that's all. I know you had to go in.'

It was if she had read her mind. 'Thanks, sweetheart,
it's kind of you to say that.'

'I mean it, Mum. He could of died! And then
everything would have been ruined.'

'What do you mean?'

'It would have felt horrible, staying here, we'd have to
go back.'

'Would that be so bad?'

'I don't want to go back.' Adele stared stubbornly at the television.

'Why? Why do you like it here so much?'

Adele shrugged. 'I don't know, it's just –' the little girl's face was screwed tight with thought, '- it's just that here everything feels more real.'

'But won't you miss your friends? School?'

'I'd only really miss Auntie Jane and Beth, and they can come here in the holidays lots. And I'll make new friends and I can learn French, and then I'll be bi...biwhatsit.'

'Bilingual?'

Adele looked at her and nodded.

Michelle laughed, 'You never cease to amaze me young lady!'

'What do you mean?'

'I mean, that you're special.'

The door swung open, making them jump, but it was only Jack. He padded over to them and jumped up onto the sofa, folding his lanky body into a small space by Adele's feet and settling down with a sigh.

'Do you think he's ok?

'Hmm?'

'Paul, do you think he's ok?'

'Yes, he's fine, he said he was going to call his family and then do some work.'

'He must have been really scared when he was under the water.'

'I know.'

'I want to be a really good swimmer, Mum, like you. Will you teach me?'

Michelle took her hand and kissed it. 'Of course I will. But not in the lake, OK? Let's find out where the nearest swimming pool is.'

Adele smiled. 'No, not in the lake. I won't go back in the lake until I'm as good as you and can save people if I have to.'

'Well let's hope you never have to!'

'I bet he really likes you now.'

'What do you mean?'

'Paul, he must really like you now you've saved his life.'

'Hmm, I'm not sure it works like that.'

Adele looked up at her, sneakily through the corner of her eye. 'I am.'

'Non, Maman!' Paul sighed with exasperation and rubbed at his face with his free hand. 'I cannot come back right now. I have told you. I just want to know how he is.'

'Then come, Paul, come and see for yourself!'

'I can't!'

'What is this *can't*?! I do not understand you, Paul, you are my son but I do not understand you.'

'I am sorry, Maman, but it is just the way it is. Will you tell me or not? It is a simple question, how is he?'

'He is the same.' His mother sounded angry. 'Nothing has changed. He clings to life, he is silent, he waits for you.'

'Please, please do not say things like that.'

'It is the truth. He always loved you the best, and you betray him.'

'I...betray him?!'

'Yes, why do you answer me like that.'

'Maman, you know nothing.'

'You're scaring me, Paul, what do you mean?'

He was tempted to tell her then, to tell her about Armand's letter. He was sure his father knew, but not his mother. If he told her now it would be coming from a mean place, a place of spite and self-interest. He swallowed the compulsion down.

'It doesn't matter.'

'Tell me what you mean, this instant!'

'I'm sorry, Maman, I have to go. I can't do this. I will be back in two weeks, as planned. If there is any change in Papy, let me know.'

'I –'

He hung up the phone, cutting off his mother in mid-sentence. He felt sick. But not in his stomach, sick in his heart. He got up and went over to the little deep-set window and stared out at the view beyond his room. The sunset was bruising the sky with oranges, blues and greys, and a light mist shrouded the fields and lake beyond the garden like a gathering of ghosts. He shivered again; he felt a little feverish, as if he was coming down with something. *I need a drink,* he said to himself.

Paul headed down the stairs. He could hear the sound of the television, and behind it, no doubt coming through the open French doors, the faint sound of the birds singing to the dusk. When he went into the sitting room, Michelle was there, curled up with Jack on the sofa, her back to him. The television was on some random French chat show. He walked round to the front of the sofa and saw that she was asleep. Jack opened one eye, inspected him benignly for a second then closed it again with a little snuffling sigh. Paul stroked the dog's head, it was a sweet old thing.

ARGEMOURT

Michelle looked peaceful, her hands folded under her
cheek, her head resting on one of the threadbare old velvet
cushions. A strand of hair had come loose from her
ponytail. and worked its way into the corner of her mouth.
He felt tempted to move it, but resisted. Instead, he knelt
down and retrieved the remote control. from the floor by
the sofa and turned off the television.

For a moment there was only the sound of the birds
out in the garden. He straightened up and stood there for
a moment, listening. He heard movement behind him and
turned; Michelle stretched, then looked at him blearily
through her half-closed eyes.

'Oh dear, I fell asleep.'

'I'm not surprised,' he replied gently, 'after today.'

She rubbed at her face, dislodging the strand of hair and
sat up. Jack grunted his disapproval, changed his position
then promptly went back to sleep again. 'And you, you
must be exhausted.'

He shrugged. 'You would think so, but it feels
impossible that I would sleep.'

'Why?'

'Too much,' he hesitated, 'in my head.'

She smiled but looked sad. 'I know what you mean.'
She yawned. 'What's the time?'

'Nine o'clock.'

'Already? God, I've been asleep for ages'.

'I was wondering, I don't want to seem rude, but is
there anything to drink?'

'There's plenty of wine in the fridge. Alan seems to
have an endless supply, he keeps giving me bottles!'

'I was thinking maybe something stronger.'

'Ah, purely for medicinal purposes, hey?'

'I'm sorry, I don't understand?'

She laughed. 'It's a saying, an English saying – it just means when you want a strong drink to make you feel better.'

'Ah, oui, exactement!'

She got up and stretched. 'Aunt Michèle has a drinks cabinet in the dining room. Let's have a look.'

He followed her into the adjoining dining room watching her body as she walked. She was so small and neat that it was crazy to think that she had had the strength to swim out across that lake and literally tow him back to the shore. It added a new kind of beauty to her, something beyond the physical.

'Here we are!' She knelt down by an antique polished mahogany cabinet, opened it, then disappeared behind the doors. Her hand emerged periodically with different bottles, each clouded by a thin layer of dust. 'So, what have we got…ah, some Pernod, Advocat – yuk – Campari, and…' she appeared briefly from behind the cabinet, 'what's this?'

'Yellow Chartreuse, it's nice in coffee, but very sweet.'

'Hmm,' she opened the bottle, sniffed at the contents and her forehead wrinkled, 'maybe.' She went back to inspecting the contents of the cabinet, 'Ah, bingo. What about this?' She stood up and handed him the bottle, 'Even I know that Courvoisier is good!'

'Ah, très bien!' He blew the dust off the bottle, 'this is perfect!' Michelle picked out a couple of crystal cognac glasses from a shelf above the cabinet and they headed back to the sitting room.

She paused by the kitchen. 'Should we have ice?'

'Non, this is an XO, *extra old*, for me it is best served straight, just warmed by your hands.'

'Ok, you're the expert.'

She went back to the sofa and tucked herself neatly in the corner. At first Paul didn't know where to sit, Jack was taking up the other end, he would have to sit quite close to her. After another moment's hesitation he joined her on the couch, trying to ensure there was a couple of inches of space between them. She didn't seem to notice his discomfiture. She held out her glass and he poured a generous measure of the golden liquid into it.

She held it to her nose and sniffed. 'Mmm, smells lovely.'

'Eau de vie.'

'What's that?'

'It means *water of life*, it is what we call brandy.'

'Waters of life,' she looked thoughtful, 'I like that. French is so much prettier than English.'

'I don't know, maybe in some ways, but English is incredible.'

'How? I suppose it's bound to be ordinary to me, It's the only language I really know, but I've always thought it must sound quite ugly to other people.'

'Non, not at all, it is one of the greatest languages. Do you know you have about three times as many words in common use than we do?'

'No! I don't believe you!'

'It is true, we have about 40,000 words in French, you have over 200,000. Some say you have too many words to ever truly count.'

'That's incredible, I never knew that.'

They were silent for a while, but it was an easy silence. The singing of the birds outside, now slowly diminishing as darkness overtook the garden, was sweet and strangely melancholic. Paul rolled each sip of cognac around in his mouth, savouring the rich flavour and the velvety warmth as it slipped down his throat. 'This is just what I needed, merci, Michelle.'

She smiled. 'No problem, I needed it too.'

'I am sorry, if I frightened Adele. I felt so bad, after she said it had been the best day of her life.'

'It's ok, she's fine, and it doesn't seem to have affected her, except that now she wants to be a really good swimmer!'

'Like her Maman.'

Michelle looked a little embarrassed. 'Ha, yes, I suppose.'

'You have swum a lot?'

'I did it at school, then I represented my county a few times.'

'You must have been good.'

'I could have been, if I'd stuck with it.'

'Why did you stop?'

'The usual reasons, I became a teenager, I stopped being interested in anything except boys and going out!'

'Ah, oui, I know what you mean. Though for me, of course, it was girls. And, I have to admit, I was always a bit of a – a *swot* – is that what you call it.'

She laughed, a musical laugh with a pleasant edge of roughness to it. 'Yes, that's it, I was never a swot though. I could have done with being a bit more of one, then I would have done better at school.'

'It is not for everyone.' He reached over to the coffee table to get the cognac and refilled their glasses.

'But it's been good for you. With your studies and everything, it must be really interesting. All I've ever done is shit, boring jobs. Like I said the other day, it's hard to get into anything when you never know how long you're going to stay at a place.'

'Yes, that must have been difficult.'

She seemed thoughtful then, her gaze softly focused on the dark garden beyond the French doors. 'And now I feel like a blank page. A blank page that I don't know what to write on.'

Her words made something tremble deep inside him; it was a nice tremble, but it left him with a feeling of unease. He wondered at what to say. 'Maybe that is what we all are, a story being told, erased and rewritten every day.'

She glanced at him, a little shyly he thought. 'That's a good way of looking at it. If it *is* like that then nothing that's happened to me so far is wasted.'

He suddenly felt quite emotional. He swallowed. 'Non, nothing is wasted. Even the most terrible things, perhaps, so long as we learn from them.' They fell silent again. Despite his promise to himself to mention nothing of what he saw in the lake, he could feel the words rising inside him, bubbling and pressing at his consciousness. He wanted to stop them emerging but he couldn't. 'In the lake,' he said, more abruptly than he had meant to, 'I did see something, just as Adele said. It didn't, it didn't *pull me*, but it shocked me.'

Michelle turned to him sharply and the low light of the standard lamp beside her caught in her startlingly dark-rimmed irises, giving them a nebulous glow. 'What do you mean? What did you see?'

'I...' he took a deep breath. 'I saw my grandfather.'

'Is he dead? You mean like a ghost?'

'Non, he is in hospital, he had a massive stroke, just a few days ago.'

'My god, how horrible. Is he, did you check – you hear about people seeing things like this when someone dies.'

'I called my Maman just now, he is still alive, but in a coma, there is no change.'

'What did it do, the thing in the lake I mean?'

He was relieved that she wasn't ridiculing him. 'Nothing really, he was just there, at the bottom of the lake. He was looking at me,' he shivered as the pale, sightless face came back into his mind, 'but he was also not looking at me. It was very strange.'

'Shit, no wonder you freaked out. What do you think it was? Did it feel real?'

'Oui, very real, almost ordinary, but it is impossible. For many reasons. It was not him as he is now, it was him when he was a young man.'

'That's weird.'

'Oui, but in a different way it makes sense.'

She turned so that she was facing him and crossed her legs under her, suddenly alert. 'How?'

'Because it is linked with all I am reading and writing and researching.'

'Because he was in the war?'

'Oui, and also...' He hesitated again, if he told her why, there was no going back. 'It is not so simple. All my life, he has been my hero, he fought in the Resistance, he was tall and handsome and he seemed to know about everything. He was another parent to me. My mother…she loves me, but too much, do you know what I mean?'

Michelle shrugged. 'Can't say I've got that problem with my mum. I think I know what you mean though, she suffocates you with her love, is that what you're saying?'

'Oui, exactement. And my father, he has always been, distant, I feel I have spent all my life trying to impress him but failing.'

'That's a feeling I *can* empathise with, but maybe everyone feels a bit like that about their parents?'

'Yes, that could be right. I am not trying to say I have had a difficult childhood, in many ways I have had a privileged one, but I am trying to explain, about my Papy.' He bolted down the last bit of cognac from his glass, 'it is ok?' he gestured towards the bottle, 'to have another?'

'Yeh, so long as you get me one too.'

He reached over to fill her glass but was surprised to see his fingers were shaking slightly.

Michelle gently cupped his hand as he poured, steadying it. 'It's difficult for you, telling me this stuff?'

'Yes,' his hand was tingling pleasantly where she'd touched it. He poured his own drink then put the bottle down, hoping she couldn't see how she had affected him. 'I have told this to no-one. Only my Papa knows what I know. At least, I think he does.'

She looked concerned, 'You don't have to tell me, if you don't want to?'

'Non, it is ok. I think I need to tell someone.' He stroked one of Jack's shaggy ears and the dog whinnied in his sleep. 'When Papy had his stroke, he called me. I went to him, he was very ill, but he was desperate to give me a letter. I was shocked, and upset, I went with him to the hospital, I forgot about the letter until the morning. When I read it, everything that my belief, my history was built on, they all went.'

Michelle leaned forward slightly. 'Why? What did it say?'

'He told me that he had only been in the Resistance at the very end of the war. For most of it he was a Malgre Nous.'

'*Malgre Nous*?' she repeated, frowning.

'I told you about them, remember? They were French people who fought for the Nazis.'

'Yes, and I still can't understand why they would do that?'

'Like I said, it is not a simple answer. Most were forced or threatened into it. A few were taken in by Nazi propaganda, some wanted revenge because their families had been killed by Allied bombs.

'What about your granddad?'

'A bit of all of those reasons, perhaps.'

'Did he, you know, did he do things? Bad things?'

'Oui, he does not go into detail about them, but he says he has spent the rest of his life trying to make up for them. But knowing he cannot.'

'How horrible, he must have felt torn apart inside. How did he not show it?'

Paul shrugged. 'I don't know, I hadn't thought of that. He was from a different generation, people who had been through the war had seen terrible things, people expected them to have secrets, to hide a lot of their feelings. And France, she did not want to speak of these things, to tell the story that sometimes her own people had also been part of the murder and the torture. Betrayal did not just live in the Vichy, in the government; but also in the towns and the villages. In the very heart of the country.'

'What a terrible thing for you to find out. I'm not surprised that you saw something. It makes sense now, you were terrified, when you got the cramp in the water; some part of you must have thought that you might be about to die. Your brain plays the thing that hurts the most, like a video. Do you know what I mean?'

'Oui, I had thought the same thing. The brain is an amazing thing, and we know so little about it. I read, once, that the brain lives for up to ten minutes after death. For that moment, you are only soul, for that amazing ten minutes your body has gone but *you* remain.'

Michelle looked pale. 'In some ways that's a nice thought, that maybe we do go on in some way. But not for Chris, not for how he died. I hope his brain didn't go on like that.'

'Ah, merde! I am sorry, I did not think.'

'It's ok, don't worry.'

'If it does go on, I would like to think that at that time we are set free, that the pain of the world leaves us. That we rise like a bird.'

She smiled at that. 'Don't they say that? They did some experiment, and they found that people's bodies got lighter straight after death, by about the weight of a bird.'

'That is beautiful.'

'Yes, it is, isn't it.' She yawned. 'I think I'm going to have to go to bed. I just suddenly feel like I've hit a wall. I'm sorry, it's been really good to talk to you. Really.' She uncrossed her legs and sat up.

Without any sense or warning that he was going to do so, he watched his hand move towards her and gently, briefly, touch her cheek. 'Thank you. For talking with me, for listening. '

Her hand went up to where he'd touched her, but he couldn't read her expression. 'That's ok.' She said, quietly. 'I'm glad you're here. I think it would be lonely otherwise.'

'Merci, Michelle, bonne nuit.'

'And to you.' She got up and stretched. 'Would you put Jack out in the garden,' she said, sleepily, 'he'll need a wee.'

'Of course. And afterwards?'

'Just leave the hall door open. He'll find his way up to Adele's bed, or mine.'

She looked at him, briefly, and smiled. 'Thanks.'

He watched her leave the room, then put a last shot of Cognac in his glass. 'Wake-up, old boy.' He rubbed the dog's back. 'Time to go out.'

The dog lifted its head and looked at him blearily. Half of its face was squashed up where it had been leaning on the sofa, revealing a few large, yellowed teeth. He got up and went to the French doors, 'Allez, chien!' he gestured, and eventually Jack struggled up and off the sofa and padded past him into the garden. Paul followed, swilling the cognac slowly in his hand, feeling the warmth of his skin move into the glass.

Jack disappeared into the deeper shadows at the bottom of the garden. Paul took a deep breath from the sweet but muggy evening air and looked up at the sky. Stars pierced the perfect blackness with icy precision, and in the Western corner of the sky, he could see the glowing belt of the Milky Way. He sipped his cognac again. He hadn't eaten anything since their picnic at the lake and he was starting to feel a little light-headed. But it wasn't just the cognac that was making him feel giddy, he knew, it was also the memory, of when Michelle had steadied his hand, and the fact that she hadn't flinched when he'd reached out to touch her cheek.

For the next few days Michelle avoided spending any time alone with Paul and he seemed to have thrown himself back into his studies, which made it easier. The sense of low-level unease seemed to have returned to her, and she wasn't entirely sure why. She suspected it had something to do with their talk a few nights before. In the end she had pretended to be tired, so that she could excuse herself, and go upstairs. But it wasn't because she hadn't enjoyed talking to him, perhaps it was because she had enjoyed it too much. And then Paul had reached up and touched her cheek. She knew it was just because he was feeling emotional, that he was grateful to her for listening to him; but it had woken something up in her that she didn't feel ready to deal with.

She threw herself into practical things. She called up the housing company at the estate and confirmed her date for vacating the house at Anborough and was surprised at how unemotional she felt about it. She spent a lot of time with Adele, walking Jack, exploring the town and organising things at the cottage, and as the first week went by, she felt more and more certain that she was going to stay at Argemourt, for the foreseeable future at least.

On the Thursday, a warm mist settled over the fields and roads, bringing with it a strange hush that made the cottages feel as if they had been transplanted into the middle of a placid ocean. As Michelle stood by Alan's door, Adele's small hand neatly tucked within her own, the soupy air pressed so closely around them that even the gate at the end of the garden path looked out of focus. She knocked, and after a few moments Alan opened the door, a pair of reading glasses perched on the end of his nose.

'Ah, my two favourite mesdemoiselles, enter please.' He smiled and gestured down the hall. 'Come in the kitchen, I am attempting to make bread, and it's not going well.' They went past him and into his little kitchen. A recipe book was propped up against his utensil jar and the counter was covered in flour and dough. 'Would you like a cup of tea?'

'Yes, lovely, thanks, Alan.'

He knelt down with a grimace, 'and for you, little Adele, a lemonade perhaps?'

'Yes, please, Mr Alan, and then can I go and finish my jigsaw?'

'Of course.'

'I never knew she was good at jigsaws until you got her started.' Michelle laughed. 'I don't think I've done one with her since she was little.'

'I have to say,' Alan put the glass of lemonade in Adele's hand, 'she is quite a precocious talent!'

Adele smiled happily. 'I've done the big T-Rex now, but I've still got some trees to do, and the Dip...dip – '

' – lodocus,' finished Alan.

'Yes, the Dip-lod-ocus.' She took a sip from her lemonade and went out to the living room.'

'Was it your daughter's?'

Alan put the ball of dough he had been kneading back onto the counter. 'Hmm?'

'The jigsaw?'

'Oh.' He went back to the dough. 'Yes.'

Michelle was about to say more but thought better of it.

'I wanted to ask you, about schools.'

'Oh yes?'

'Adele wants to stay here, and I think we will. At least for now, to see how it goes. Great Aunt Michèle's solicitor got in touch and it turns out she left me some money too, not a lot, but enough to pay to have my stuff put in storage back in the UK for a bit and give me a bit of spending money till I sort out getting a job.'

'That's great news!' Alan looked genuinely delighted.

'I don't seem to need much money to live here, the food's cheap and I'm miles from the kind of shops that make me spend, and Adele seems happy doing simple things like walking Jack and playing in the garden. And I thought, that maybe I could work in a café, somewhere it would be useful for them to have an English speaker?'

He dusted off his hands and came and sat next to her. 'That could be useful. Quite a lot of tourists come here, because of the history.'

'That's what I thought, I'm a trained barista, and I know the ropes, and I've booked in for French lessons at the nearest college. I think I'll have to sort out a little car though.'

'You can always share mine, I hardly use it.'

She smiled and squeezed his hand. 'That's really kind, thanks Alan.'

'You said you wanted to ask about schools?

'Yes, could you help me? You speak French and it would be good if you could talk to the local one for me, see if it's possible for Adele to start there?'

'Of course.'

'You know this is all Adele's idea really!'

'Well, that's wonderful, it really is. And Paul, have you talked to him?'

She felt her cheeks redden. 'No, but he's only here for another week.'

'He may want to stay longer if he knew *you* were staying?'

'I doubt it. He's got lots of other places to visit.'

'He likes you, you know that don't you?'

'What do you mean?' She stumbled over her words. 'He doesn't, that's crazy, we're completely different?'

'Are you? Are you really?'

'Yes! He's well educated, he comes from a well-off family, he's young – '

'But what about the ways that you are the same?'

'I don't know what you mean!'

Alan picked up his cup of tea, leaned back in his chair and scrutinised her. She shifted uncomfortably in her chair. 'You must have seen the way he looks at you?'

She snorted. 'Honestly, Alan, I don't know what you're talking about.'

'There's an intensity, when he looks at you. His eyes follow you around the room.'

A light, fluttery feeling started up in her stomach. 'I can't – '

'Can't what?'

'Chris, I . . .' she wasn't sure what she had been about to say.

'You loved him very much, that's obvious. And you've done him proud, the way you've looked after Adele, the way you're working now to build a new life for yourself.'

'You don't know anything! I've done a shit job, of all of it!' she tried to stop them, but tears ran down her cheeks. 'Until now.'

Alan reached behind him for a roll of kitchen towel, tore off a piece and handed it to her. 'Here, it's ok.'

'I'm sorry.' She wiped her cheeks and blew her nose. 'It's just sometimes, I know I've tried my best, but other times, I'm ashamed. I've behaved badly to her too.'

'You've been grieving as well, dealing with your own pain.'

'It's no excuse.'

'Yes, it is.'

They sat quietly for a moment. Mist moved lazily against the glass of the kitchen window. Michelle dried her eyes.

Alan squeezed her hand briefly then reached for his tobacco pouch. 'I'm sorry, I never normally smoke in the house, but I don't think I can do this unless I have one.'

'It's ok. But what do you mean, *do this?*'

'I need to tell you something.'

A sense of dread spread through her chest. 'What is it?'

'I'm dying.'

'What?'

'I've got bowel cancer. I've tried all the treatments but they haven't worked. They offered me another round of Chemo but I said no. I want to be as well as possible for whatever time is left to me.'

'Shit! Alan. I'm so sorry!' She felt her eyes fill with tears again.

He smiled thinly. 'It's ok, I'm kind of used to the idea now.'

'How…I'm sorry, that's a stupid question.'

'How long? Don't worry, it's the only question really; I'm not entirely sure, months? A year if I'm lucky?'

'Oh God, oh Alan! I can't believe it.' When she had decided to stay at the cottage, Alan being next door, to advise her, to be there for Adele, she had taken all that for granted. *Stupid* she shouted to herself internally *stupid woman, you should have known not to rely on anything!*

'Please, don't tell Adele.'

'Of course, I won't. Is there anything, anything at all I can do?'

He looked at her strangely. 'Just two things.'

'Tell me.'

'Number one, carry on being my friend. Number two, give him a chance.'

'Him?'

'Paul. He's confused, he's a bit lost, but he's a good man.'

She put her head in her hands. She felt exhausted.

'If there's one thing I've learned, through all this, it's that there's no time to waste.'

'I…'

'You don't have to say anything. It's ok, just think about it, please. Think about Chris, what would he want for you? Would he want you to be happy again or would he want you to be alone for ever?'

Adele burst into the room. 'I finished it!' She looked at their faces and her expression dropped. 'What's the matter?'

Alan got up and clapped his hands. 'Nothing, young lady, nothing at all. Now come on, let's have a look at your masterpiece!'

When they got back to the cottage Michelle went straight to the laptop and opened it up. 'Adele, come here darling. I need your help.'

Adele came over, frowning. 'What is it, Mummy?'

'I've had an idea.' She typed Facebook into the browser. After it had loaded, a week's worth of notifications flooded in, she ignored them and went straight to the search option. 'What was the name of Alan's daughter again? God I completely forgot to remind you to take that envelope back! Can you get it? It's in the kitchen table drawer.' A few moments later Adele returned, her eyes wide.

'Are we going to write to her, Mummy?'

'Better than that, we're going to see if we can find her on Facebook.' She took the envelope from Adele and typed the name into the search box and pressed enter. A list of people and their profile pictures filled the screen. 'Can you remember what she looks like, from the pictures in Alan's house?'

Adele nodded and studied the faces carefully. After a few seconds she pointed excitedly at the screen. 'That's her, just there!'

'You're sure?'

'Yes, Mummy. That's her.'

'Ok, great. Let's send her a message?'

Adele beamed. 'Can we do that?'

'Yep.'

'But you said that we shouldn't write to her.'

'I thought about it some more and I decided you were right.'

Adele leant her head on Michelle's shoulder.

'So, come on then, what shall we say?'

Paul drove cautiously through the mist that was clinging to the warm surface of the road. He went through the presents he had bought, he was happy with Adele's, and the one for Jack, but Michelle? Would it seem too personal that he had got her things that she would use in the bath? Would she take it the wrong way? All of a sudden, he felt stupid and transparent. Why hadn't he just bought her that pretty serving bowl he had seen at the craft fair? It was too late now though, he told himself. He would have to stick to what he had got her or not give any presents at all.

He pulled up outside the cottage, took a deep breath and headed up towards the front door. Before he could put his key in the lock the door sprang open and Adele nearly fell into him, Jack at her heels.

'Oh, hi, Paul! Me and Jack were just going to call for Mr Alan. We're going to go for a mystery mist walk!'

'Ah, that sounds exciting! What happens in a mystery mist walk?'

'Mr Alan is going to hide things and I have to find them.'

'Chocolate, I hope?'

Adele smiled, toothily.

'I have got some presents – '

'Ooh presents! But it's not my birthday.'

Paul shrugged, he was feeling more and more uncomfortable by the minute. 'Non, but must we only have presents on our birthday? Can we go inside a minute?'

Adele called Jack and they went into the house together. Before the front door had even closed, Adele ran ahead and down the hall into the kitchen.

'Mummy, Mummy, Paul has presents!'

Paul headed awkwardly towards the kitchen, he could feel himself colouring. 'Really, it is nothing!'

Michelle appeared in the kitchen doorway, wiping her hands on her apron. 'Presents?'

'Oui, I just wanted…' He trailed off, the words eluding him. He took a breath. 'I just wanted to say thank you, for all you have done.'

Michelle's expression tightened. 'You're not leaving?'

'Non, not for at least a week.' Was it his imagination or did she look relieved when he said that? 'But you have done so much for me already, and I was in Poitiers, studying, and they had a craft market and I thought…' He rummaged in his bag, 'Ici, Adele. My sister had one of these when she was your age, and I thought you might like it.' He pulled out a box containing what looked like a wooden ladybird with three hoops sticking out of its head and a bag of different coloured balls of wool.

Adele took it and looked it over. 'What is it?'

'It is a knitting doll. It has a needle with it too, you thread the wool through the hoops with the needle and it makes a knitted rope.'

'Yes!' Michelle's face brightened. 'I had one too! I used to make scarves for my Sindy dolls with it!'

Her mother's enthusiasm seemed to rub off on Adele and she smiled and gave Paul a brief hug. 'Thank you. I'm going to go and set it up now.'

'Avec plaisir!' He ruffled her hair. 'And I have for Jack too.'

Adele paused, 'What is it?'

'Two things.' He reached into his bag and pulled out a large triangle of paisley cloth. 'It is, how you call it, a *neckerchief* I think, he wears it.' He knelt down and called, 'Jack, ici!' The dog padded towards him and gave Paul's face a brief lick. Paul tied the cloth around Jack's neck, positioning the point of it against his shaggy chest. 'There, he is very handsome, no?'

Adele giggled and put her arms around the dog. 'It really suits him!'

'And he has this, I stopped at the butchers on the way back and got him a bone. I hope he is not too old for it and his teeth are strong!'

'He's got really strong teeth,' Adele confirmed. 'He always wins when we play tug of war.' The dog looked from the girl to Paul and back again, as if he knew they were talking about him.

Paul unwrapped the big beef bone and held it towards Jack. The dog sniffed at it, took it gently from his hand then headed into the sitting room. Adele followed him.

Michelle smiled. 'He'll be wanting to take it into the garden to bury!'

'Do dogs really do that? I thought it was a myth.'

'No, they really do. Our dog, when I was a kid, would always bury his bones. Then weeks later he'd come up with his face covered in earth and really stinky breath. I think they like them better when they've gone off a bit.'

Paul grimaced. 'I am glad I am not a dog!'

She fixed her gaze on him. 'You didn't need to do this you know.'

'Oui, I know, but I wanted to.' His heart started to beat a little faster and he struggled to not let the sudden feeling of breathlessness show in his voice. 'And this is for you. After I got it, I was worried that it might seem – ah – well – here it is. They are made from local lavender, I thought the smell was very lovely.' He passed her the bath oil and salts in their woven basket. She took it, a little shyly he thought, and opened the bottle of bath oil. She held it under her nose and breathed in.

'It really does smell beautiful, thank you. This, all this, it's really kind of you.'

They looked at each other for a beat, and Paul found words coming out of him, words he had not even thought of to say, and yet, here they were. 'Tomorrow…I was wondering, perhaps you would be interested in coming to the Musée de la Mémoire, in the village; and afterwards, perhaps, we could eat at the bistro on the high street, I hear it is good?'

She was silent for a second, he held his breath.

'Yes, ok, I've been meaning to visit the museum, and I thought Adele would find it interesting too.'

'Ah, I was not thinking Adele.'

She looked at him, her eyebrows raised.

'You see, I think it could be upsetting for her, some of the things there, the things you see, perhaps she is a little young? But it is up to you of course.'

'No, you're right, let her be a child while she still can. I'll ask Alan if she can stay with him.' She fell silent and her gaze settled in an unfocused way down the hall towards the front door.

'Are you OK? Michelle?'

She blinked and looked at him. 'Yes, sorry, it's just something Alan told me yesterday. It's playing on my mind.'

'Something?' He shrugged. 'Something that has worried you?'

'Yes, about him, that he's really not well. Cancer.'

'Merde. Is he having treatment?'

'He was, it didn't work.' She looked away from him and a tear ran down her cheek. 'He says he may only have months.'

Paul didn't know what to say. He wanted to reach out and comfort her but he wasn't sure if she wanted him to. 'I am so sorry, I know you have not known him long, but I see that you have become close.'

She brushed the tear away. 'Yes, look, don't say anything to Adele, will you? He doesn't want her to know, and I don't think there's any point either. You never know with these things, he could do better than he thinks.'

'Oui, of course, I will say nothing.'

She smiled at him and touched his arm briefly. 'Thank you for these, they're lovely. I'll take them upstairs.'

She headed up to the bathroom, leaving him alone in the hall, his heart thumping.

He spent the rest of the afternoon reading then had a nap. When he woke up the sun had started to set, and the room was flushed with peachy light. He yawned and stretched, he could hear the faint sounds of Michelle and Adele in the garden. He lay still and tuned into them for a moment. Adele was obviously having fun with Jack, screeching, calling his name and laughing. Michelle's voice was low and insistent, as if she was talking to someone.

He got out of the bed and stretched again, his fingertips brushing lightly against the low, plastered ceiling. The room's little casement window was ajar and a light breeze was blowing the lace curtain into the room like a swirling skirt. He went over and pulled it to one side. The mist had cleared, and he could see Adele at the bottom of the garden playing a game that involved hiding Jack's beef bone then telling him to find it. He couldn't see Michelle, but he could hear her, she must have been standing just outside the French doors and under the little porch that was beneath his bedroom window.

'I know, it's really sad isn't it.'

The words drifted up to him, so clearly it was almost as if she was in the room with him. Sound was funny like that, he thought, the way it rose. Without thinking he leant against the wall, so he couldn't be seen from the outside, and turned his head towards the open window.

'I didn't know what to say to him.' She continued. 'I mean, what do you say to someone who knows they're going to die?...No, don't worry, he's gone into town....Yeh, I know, and I can't tell Adele either...' Her voice had become a bit ragged, as if she was getting upset. He felt awful, listening to her when she didn't know, but he couldn't tear himself away from the window. 'I just didn't think I'd have to go through anything like this again, do you know what I mean? I thought, for fuck's sake, surely I've been through enough loss....Yeh, that's true, you just don't know.'

'Mummy, Mummy,' Adele shouted from the bottom of the garden. 'Watch Jack, watch!'

'Oh yeh,' Michelle shouted back, a sounding distracted, 'isn't he clever!' Her voice lowered again. 'She's hiding this bone that Paul got for him, in the bushes, and he keeps diving in to find it. He's ruining my plants but I haven't got the heart to stop her...What's that? Oh, he seems fine. He got us all presents today, which was sweet...yeh, it's worked out all right...it's just...well, it's difficult, I'm not sure how to say it –'

Paul's breath had shrunk high and tight in his chest; he felt terrified and excited at the same time; terrified that she was going to say something that embarrassed him, about how awkward he'd been when he gave her her present, or how grumpy he'd been the day before; excited that she might say something nice, and how that would make him feel. He held his breath.

'- the thing is, it's something Alan said when he told me about being ill, he said there was two things he wanted me to do for him, and one was *give him a chance*...yeh, I presumed that was what he meant too, and it's just, well, I haven't thought in that way for years, you know? I mean, I haven't even,' her voice dropped to a whisper which he had to strain to hear, *'touched myself like that* since Chris died...exactly... it's the last thing on your mind...but, oh God, Jane, I don't know if I can say this, even to you, I feel so shit about it...ok, ok...he's touched me a couple of times, just little things, nothing like that, just my cheek or my arm - nice, gentle - and it's like something's woken up in me; does that make any sense at all?' She was silent for a while, obviously listening to her friend's answer. '...Thanks, love, I needed to hear that. I just keep asking myself, *what would Chris think? What would Chris say if he was here* –'

He turned away from the window, breathing hard. He had *woken something up* in her. To hear that was disconcerting, and arousing in equal measure; but, *merde*! he thought, *I do not have the time, the space to feel for someone like this.* But there it was. Veronique, in all her long-legged, bronzed, slender beauty, had never made him feel like this; like his insides had been taken out, shaken, re-arranged and put back inside his body. But, Michelle - a series of images of her flashed through his mind: Michelle stroking her daughter's hair; Michelle, her expression thoughtful and a little sad; Michelle with her slim, strong arms around his chest, pulling him through the water to the bank; Michelle's startling eyes catching a slant of sunlight - she did make him feel like that. It was the last thing he had expected to happen, especially after just a few days; but it had, and somehow, he knew, that there was no going back.

The doorbell rang, making Michelle jump.

'Sorry, Jane, I've got to go. That must be Alan, I'll give you a call in a day or two. Thanks for listening…I will, I promise. Bye, love, bye.'

She hung up the phone and put it on the coffee table by the sofa as she headed to the door. It was Alan, he looked a little flushed, and there was an air of something about him, as if he was excited.

He handed her a bag with the garish logo of their nearest supermarket on it. 'Here you go, the few bits and pieces you asked for; and a whole trout, it was on offer.'

She laughed, she'd never cooked a whole trout in her life and didn't have a clue where to start. 'Thanks, Alan, will you come in for a bit? I was going to make a coffee.'

'Just what I need, thank you. Where's Adele?'

'In the garden playing with Jack. Happy as Larry.'

He followed her into the kitchen and the sense of supressed animation came with him, charging the air around them. She decided to let him come out with it in his own time. She filled the espresso pot with ground coffee and water and put it on the hob.

'Do you want your milk hot?'

'Ah, no, don't worry.'

She put a couple of small cups on the counter and got the milk out of the fridge. After a minute or two the pot started to gurgle and the kitchen filled with the aromatic, smoky miasma of brewing coffee.

'Ah,' Alan breathed deeply, 'I love that smell. It takes me back to the pub when I was a boy.'

'Really? What about the smell of stale cigarette smoke and spilled beer?'

He laughed. 'Yes, well, that too; but Mum would always make a fresh coffee to drink when she put float in the till in the morning. I'd sit at the bar and do my spelling or times tables practice with her until it was time to go to school.'

She poured the coffee out and stirred in a splash of milk. 'I bet it was really interesting, growing up above a pub.'

'It was, until she inherited, then Mum bought a boring little mock-Tudor semi in an estate around the corner. I hated it, but for her it was the height of luxury.'

She sat opposite him at the little kitchen table and took a sip of the coffee, enjoying the stimulating burn of it as it went down her throat.

He took a sip too, looking at her over the rim of the cup. When he put it down he cleared his throat, 'I've got some good news.'

She smiled. 'What's that?'

'I had a chat with Delphine at the café in town. Luck would have it that she has a couple of free shifts. She speaks excellent English so she could tell you people's orders – until your French gets better. She needs a barista, and she's happy for you to start on a trial basis.

'That's wonderful! Thanks Alan!'

'It would just be about ten hours a week for now, but it could soon pick up. When do your French lessons start?'

'In a couple of weeks.' She felt ridiculously excited. It had been lovely, spending the first week at the cottage and sorting out things at home, but it would make such a difference to feel part of something bigger and start to join in the life of the town.

'The school stuff is a bit more complicated. You'll need to make sure you have been fully signed over as the owner of the house before you can apply. And there's no bilingual or international school nearby, they're only really in the cities, so unless you're prepared for her to have a two-hour round journey to school and back every day, you'll have to go for the local primary. There's a bus that picks up around here or it's only a ten-minute drive away. They aren't oversubscribed, so there wouldn't be a problem with getting in, but you'd have to really think about the language barrier.'

'Yes, I see what you mean. But she's still so young, she could pick it up really easily couldn't she? And if she starts after the summer holidays, she'll have had a couple of months to get started.'

'True,' Alan conceded, 'and I've got a contact for you. There's an English expat teacher there, I got her number from Delphine so you and Adele can go and have a chat with her.'

'Thanks so much Alan,' she leant over and kissed him on his cheek, 'what would I do without you?' When she sat back down the unintentional meaning behind her words hit her and she blushed.

He didn't seem to notice and gave her hand a squeeze. 'And there's one more thing.'

The shadow of a strong but unidentifiable emotion passed over his face. She braced herself for whatever was coming next. 'What is it, Alan? Are you ok?'

For a moment he didn't seem able to speak and his eyes filled with tears. 'It's my daughter,' he said at last, 'she called me this morning. I've always put my phone number on my letters to her, but I didn't think I'd ever hear from her again. And then she calls me, just like that.'

'That's…that's wonderful, Alan.'

'Yes, yes it is. She wants to come and see me, next week. And she's bringing my…my –' he broke off, shaken by a sob. Michelle passed him a square of kitchen towel and he wiped his eyes. 'She's bringing my grandson. I have a grandson!'

Michelle felt herself welling up in sympathy. 'Oh wow! How old is he?'

'Eighteen months.'

'That's a lovely age.'

'I'd like you to be there, you and Adele, when she comes. Would that be ok?'

'Of course, if that's what you want, but wouldn't you rather see her on your own?'

'No! I'm terrified, I don't know what I'd do with myself, what I'd say. If you were there at first, it would really help me.'

'Then we'll be there.'

He blew his nose and laughed. 'I must look ridiculous.'

'Of course you don't, look at me, you've got me going too!'

'You didn't...' he paused and looked at her keenly, 'it wasn't you, was it?'

She raised her eyebrows. 'Me?'

'Who got in touch with my daughter.'

She smiled at him. 'Don't be daft, how would I have done that? Pass me your cup, I'll top up our coffees.'

He looked like he was about to reply but seemed to think better of it. She took the opportunity to change the subject. 'It's not as if you haven't done me enough favours already, but could you do me one more?'

'Of course, if I can.'

'Paul thought I might like to visit the museum in Argemourt tomorrow. It's open till six, so we thought we'd go in the afternoon, then maybe go to the Bistro for some dinner.'

'Sounds like a lovely idea.'

She felt her face get hot and busied herself with the coffees so that she didn't have to look up at him. 'So, I was wondering if you'd mind having Adele for the evening?'

'Of course, I'd love to. I've got that film channel thing on the TV, we could pick something and make some popcorn.'

She smiled at him gratefully. 'Thanks, Alan, that's great.'

'No problem at all. I'm just glad.'

'About what?'

He winked at her. 'That you took my advice.'

She closed the book and lay down next to Adele. The last traces of dusk etched the edges of the pale curtains with faint light. The window was slightly open, letting in the rasping sound of crickets.

'Mum?'

'Yes, love.'

'What did Alan's daughter say to you?'

'Not much, the Facebook message just said thanks for getting in touch and that she would think about what to do next.'

'Did you reply?'

'Yeh, I said it was great to hear back from her and I asked her not to tell Alan that we'd got in touch with her.'

Adele shifted onto her side and propped her head on her hand. 'Why?'

'I don't know, maybe because if he did know it might make it feel less special?'

Adele frowned, a face she always made when she was thinking hard; then she nodded. 'Ok, I won't say anything then.'

'He asked me today if she'd got in touch because of us, but I managed to not say yes or no, but it was hard!'

'Do you think she'll be nice?'

'Yeh, of course, why wouldn't she be?'

'Because she's not seen Alan for ages, and she didn't answer his letters.'

'It's complicated, love; with families sometimes. Even Alan says it's his fault too, because he was away so much —'

'But Dad was away so much too, and I never didn't write him a letter.'

She smoothed Adele's hair back from her forehead. 'I know, and he loved your letters so much, more than anything, but we don't know what it was really like for Alan and his daughter. Grown-ups can get angry, or hurt, and it can make them behave badly and say bad things. They don't mean to make things worse, but sometimes they do.'

Adele flopped back down onto the bed with a 'humph!' and grabbed a giant stuffed dinosaur and hugged it to her chest. 'That's what Stacey Milligan in my class is like. When she gets angry she's really mean.'

'Yes, well, that's not quite the same. Anyway.' She sat up and straightened Adele's covers. 'Time to go to sleep young lady.'

'What are we doing tomorrow?'

'Well, I thought we could do some more knitting with the present Paul got you, then we're going to go into town, Alan says there's a woman there who needs help in her café, and I thought we could go and see what the school looks like.'

'Is there lots of children there?'

'No, it's only little. But apparently it's shut tomorrow, they do that here in the smaller schools in the countryside, they just do four-day weeks.'

Adele eyes lit up at that, Michelle noticed.

'So at least see what it looks like from the outside, and I've got a number for a teacher there, an English lady, so

I'll have a chat with her and then you can go back another time and see it properly. Oh and,' she attempted to keep her voice light, 'Alan has asked if you want to go to his and have some popcorn and watch a film?'

Adele's face lit up. 'Yes, Mummy, can I?'

'Of course, sweets.'

'Are you watching the film too?'

'Well, actually, Paul's asked me if I'd like to go into town and get some dinner.' She watched Adele nervously.

A subtle smile crept across the little girl's face then disappeared as quickly as it had come. 'Yes, that's a good idea, Mummy.' she replied, in the grown-up voice she sometimes adopted since Chris had died, 'You go and have a nice time, you deserve it.'

When Paul woke up the next morning it was to an unsettling, but also arousing feeling of anticipation. He lay in his bed, sweaty and entangled in his sheets, trying to sort through a blizzard of thoughts and sensations. The reality of the day ahead of him was somehow thrilling. Instead of being, like it normally would, a series of chores and necessities to be got through; it felt mysterious and ephemeral, waiting for him to conjure it into whatever he wanted.

He knew he was too distracted to write anything that day, so he decided instead to work on the references and appendices to his thesis. He could put the radio on and work through them methodically but without the need for intellectual thought. He sprang out of bed, energised by the plan, and went for a shower.

As he stood under the warm water, he focused on the sounds around him. The clicking of the cottage's old pipes

and patter of the water as it hit the enamel bath; the happy
barking of Jack in the garden, the faintly melodic chatter
of Michelle and Adele in the kitchen; the diminishing roar
of a plane going overhead. For a heart-achingly short
moment he felt insanely happy, as if anything was possible;
as if, after all, people were basically good, that there was
hope. He let the feeling shimmer through him with a sigh
that twisted, without warning, into a sob in his throat. He
turned off the water and crouched in the bath for a
moment, holding tightly onto the side. There was a knock
on the door.

'Oui?' he shouted back, his voice ragged.

Me and Mum are going to the town. We're going to
see the school, and Mr Alan says that Mum could get a job
in the café so we're going there too. Mum says do you
want anything?'

'Ah, non, merci, Adele. I am fine.'

He heard the floor boards creak as she stepped away
from the door, then return again followed by another little
knock.

'I've put something in your room.'

'OK, I will look in a moment.'

'It's a present.'

'That is kind, ma petite, merci.'

He listened to her go down the stairs and then to the
front door closing. He stayed crouching in the bath and
ran the tap so he could splash his face with cold water.
What was happening to him? It was as if he was
disassembling, frantically trying to grab hold of the pieces
before they fell away and were lost for ever. But then, he
reflected, there were new pieces being added too. What

313

he wasn't sure about was how they all fitted together or what he would be if they did.

He got out of the bath carefully, aware that he was feeling a little light-headed. Food was what he needed, and a strong coffee, to weigh down his insubstantial feeling body and clear his mind. When he got back to his room he found Adele's gift. It was a multicoloured tube of knitted wool, no doubt made with the knitting doll he had got her. Adele had sewn a couple of small buttons on one end and written him a note in green crayon. *This is a rainbow snake. I am making a whole family. This one is called Jimmy-snake.* She signed it off with her name and a large lop-sided X. He smiled at the little offering and put it on his bedside table.

When he'd dressed and gone downstairs, he found the French doors open and Jack asleep, half in and half out of them, his face and shoulders in the sunshine that was bathing the patio, his back legs in the shade of the living room. He raised his head a few inches and blinked sleepily as Paul approached. He rubbed the old dog's face; Jack licked his hand then laid his head back down in the warm light.

Paul went through to the kitchen and was grateful to see a bag of fresh croissants on the counter. A quick perusal of the fridge rewarded him with Emmental cheese, a tomato and some thinly sliced ham. He turned the radio on and put fresh coffee in the espresso pot. The sun was beaming through the window above the sink making the drying cutlery and glasses sparkle. He stepped forward into the light and stayed there for a second, eyes closed, enjoying the warmth of the sun on his skin. *This day,* he thought to himself. *I've never known a day feel like this before.*

314

Adele bounced happily across the empty playground. Michelle and Louise, the teacher that Alan had told her about, followed a few steps behind.

'It was really kind for you to open the school up and show us. I didn't expect you'd be able to do that, and particularly at such short notice.'

'That's ok.' Louise smiled. She was older than Michelle, perhaps in her early forties, and had a pleasant, slightly hippy look about her. 'It was good to hear from you, it will be really nice to have more people from home here and hear some English accents.'

'I bet you almost forget how to speak English!'

'It's true, I can go months only speaking in French, but you'd be surprised how quickly it comes back. It's a funny thing, language, once you've learnt it, it never really goes, it just kind of goes to sleep somewhere deep in your brain waiting to be woken up.'

Adele appeared beside them, a little breathless. 'It's got a treehouse Mummy, over there, see?'

'Oh yes, that's lovely.'

'And there's a pond, but it's got a fence round it.' She turned to Louise. 'We have a pond at the park near my granny's house and it gets baby frogs in it and one year we got petals from the rose bushes and we put the baby frogs on them and we raced them.'

Louise raised her eyebrows. 'Wow, I'd love to see a baby frog racing on a rose petal!'

Michelle shook her head affectionately. 'My dad started singing *I am sailing*, it was actually quite funny.'

'Wait till I tell Granny that I'm going to go to a French school!'

'Well, let's wait and see first before we say anything to Granny. It's not decided yet.'

Adele bounced off again to explore a multicoloured spiral that had been painted on the playground.

'That's for *Escargot*,' shouted Louise after her, 'it's a kind of round hopscotch, you have to hop into the centre of the circle then backwards out of it.'

This was a challenge Adele clearly could not resist, and she immediately started hopping.

Louise turned back to Michelle. 'You shouldn't have a problem getting in, it's a small community school and it's generally undersubscribed.'

'I know, I just need to get my proof of residence at the cottage sorted. It's more that I don't want my mum knowing yet. She doesn't exactly agree with us moving here, she thinks I'm mad!'

'Ah, I see.'

'I want everything to be sorted and certain before I say anything to her. We didn't exactly part company on good terms when I left England. And she doesn't approve of Adele missing school.'

'I'm sure she'll come around, and you can reassure her that there are three other children from the UK here already. A boy, Brandon, he's in the equivalent of year six, and two girls who would be in the same year as Adele, Tilly and Charlotte.'

They stopped in the shade of a tree in the corner of the playground to get out of the sun. Adele was inelegantly hopping backwards out of the *Escargot* spiral, looking like she didn't have a care in the world.

'Would your husband like to come and see the school too?'

'Unfortunately he's not here. He died two years ago.'

Louise touched her arm lightly. 'I'm sorry, I didn't mean to –'

'It's ok. He was in the army. That's another reason we're here, when I inherited the cottage from my great aunt, I'd been given notice to leave our house in the town, well, it's kind of a village really, attached to the barracks. You get to stay for two years, but then they expect you to have sorted something else out. They'll help you get social housing, what there is of it, but that's it. It's funny how it happened like that. I found out I'd inherited the cottage right after getting the letter saying I had to leave.'

'I knew her you know.'

Michelle's heart quickened. 'My great aunt?'

'Yes, Madame Leroy. She used to come to the school and do a talk about what happened at Argemourt in the war. They do a segment on World War II in year six and she'd come and do a talk.'

'What was she like?'

Louise squinted up through the lacy branches of the tree with a faraway, gaze. 'At first glance she was the kind of person you'd pass in the street and not notice. But once you got to know her you couldn't believe you had ever found her ordinary. She dressed very simply, she was quiet, but once you got past that she had a fierce intelligence, and when she talked about that time, with the kids, she'd have them all spellbound. Sometimes even in tears.'

'It's terrible, what happened here. I can't get my head around it.'

'I know, it is incomprehensible. I think that's why Madame Leroy came here every year, to make sure the

317

children knew. To keep telling the story, to make sure no-one forgets.'

They said goodbye to Louise then did the short drive from the school to the village. Alan's car was an old but luxurious Saab, with leather seats and air conditioning. She had been anxious about driving it, she'd only really driven a couple of cars in her life, but it was surprisingly easy. The café, as Alan had told her, was down a pretty cobbled lane that led off from one of the corners of the village square. A few wrought-iron tables and chairs marked the entrance, framed by a riot of red geraniums spilling from window boxes and tubs.

They went inside, making a bell over the door tinkle. There was an older couple sitting in the corner, reading newspapers. A pretty young woman with black curly hair, red lipstick and thick-rimmed trendy glasses came out from the back of the café, wiping her hands on a tea towel.

'Bonjour, que puis-je faire pour vous?'

'Bonjour, je suis Michelle, je suis…erm…un ami de Alan? Tu…Delphine?'

'Ah oui! Hello, yes Alan told me about you.'

Michelle smiled with relief at the switch to English. 'Yes, I've moved here recently from the UK, I have a lot of experience working in cafes and he said you might need some help?'

'That's right, and you are a barista too?'

'Yes, I've done the training, I can show you my certificates.'

'Bon! Could you start next week? As it is summer now we are getting busy, especially in the afternoons. Could you do perhaps, Wednesday and Friday afternoon? From, say noon till four?'

'Yes, thanks, that would be perfect!' She looked down at Adele. 'Alan has said that my daughter, Adele can stay with him until she can start school, so yes that should be fine.'

Delphine smiled and reached her hand over the counter. 'Then we have a deal?'

Michelle took her hand and shook it. 'Yes, we do!'

'Why don't you take a seat outside and I will bring you something. You should know what we do here before you work for us after all.'

'That would be lovely, thank you.'

'You drink coffee?'

'Yes please,'

She looked down at Adele. 'And for Mademoiselle?'

Adele straightened her shoulders. 'Do you do milkshake?'

'Oui, framboise? Chocolat?'

'Erm,' Adele screwed up her face. 'Chocolat, s'il vous plait.'

'I will bring it,' she gestured to the outside seating, 'please sit.'

They went outside and sat in the shade of a red and white striped parasol. A skinny ginger cat strolled up and wound itself around Adele's ankles. She reached down and stroked its back then sat up and frowned. 'Mummy.'

'Yes, sweets.'

'It's a funny day today. I feel happy and sad. It's like this cat, it's really friendly and purry, and that makes me feel happy, but it's also really thin, like it's a stray and doesn't have a proper home to go to and that makes me feel sad.'

Michelle reached over and squeezed Adele's hand. *Bittersweet, that's how I feel too.* 'I know what you mean, it's like everything's new, and that makes me feel happy and sad too.'

'Here we are!' Delphine appeared at their table with a tray and decanted two drinks and a range of tiny pastries, glossy with fruit and custards. 'Enjoy.'

As they drove out of the village half an hour later, they passed the museum: it looked elegant, yet strangely alone on the quiet sun-lit street.

Paul could hear the ambient hum of Paris in the background of Camille's phone call: car horns, animated chatter and a gentle rushing sound like the wind through leaves.

'One moment, Paul, I'm just going to find a bench and sit down.'

'Where are you?'

'Parc Monceau, I finished work early. It's a shame, I missed the Magnolias this year.'

'Are you ok?'

She sighed. 'Oui. But it has been a hard few days. Maman and Papa are hardly speaking, and Papy, well, he is the same.'

He felt a rush of shame. 'I'm sorry that you are dealing with it on your own.'

'Indeed!' He could hear the irritation in her voice. 'And why am I on my own? Why are you not here? Papy is your hero, you've always said that. Sometimes I thought you loved him more than Papa. I do not understand!'

'I know, I know, I'm sorry.' He sat down at the little rusted wrought iron bistro set on the patio and rested his forehead in his free hand. 'I know it's hard. I wish I could make you understand.'

'Then try!'

'I don't know if I can.'

'Maman knows something is going on. That's why her and Papa aren't speaking. She says you both know something, but that you're keeping it from her. It's driving her crazy.' She stopped, and he heard a pigeon hoot in the background. 'It's driving *me* crazy!'

'I don't know what to do, Camille...*merde*!'

'Paul,' her voice had softened, 'whatever it is, just *tell me*. You've always said that secrets are bad. You're my brother, we've always told each other everything.'

'Ok, ok. Just, wait a minute.' He put down his phone and looked up at the blue perfection of the sky, as if it could give him some answers. It didn't. He picked up his phone again. 'Camille?'

'I'm here.'

He took a deep breath. 'Ok, I'll tell you, but I have one condition. Don't talk about it to Maman or Papa. I don't know for sure if Papa knows this or not and it shouldn't come from you if he doesn't. If they must be confronted with this we'll do it together, when I'm back.'

'Ok, ok, I get it, just tell me what it is, you're scaring me now!'

'Hold on, I have to read you the letter Papy gave to me. It's upstairs.' He held the phone to his ear and went inside. It took his vision a while to adjust to the relative gloom of the living room.

'What letter?'

He bounded up the narrow stairs, two at a time. 'He had it with him,' he said, panting, when he'd reached the last step, 'when he called me to his house, when he was having his stroke. I didn't read it until the next day, I forgot about it because he was so ill, the hospital and everything.' He went into his room and took the letter from where he'd been keeping it, inside the back page of one of his books. 'I have it.' He held it in his hand for a moment, he hadn't looked at it since he'd arrived. Even just holding it made him feel anxious.

'Merde, Paul, tell me what it says!'

'Sorry.' He read her the letter, she didn't interrupt and when he'd finished there was silence.

'Camille? Are you still there?'

'Oui.' She sounded like she'd been crying.

'I'm sorry, you see now, why I haven't said anything to you. Maybe I shouldn't have. But it's been so lonely not telling anyone, at least, not anyone who knows him.'

'It is so terrible. So terrible in so many ways.'

'I know.'

'And you think Papa knows?'

'I'm not sure. If I'd been with him, when I suggested he knew something about it, I think I would have known, from his reaction; but over the phone? I couldn't tell.'

'I won't say anything, but it's going to be really hard.'

'I know, imagine how it has been for me the last week.'

'But you're not here. I am.'

'I know, I'm sorry.'

She sighed again. 'I don't know what to feel.'

'I still love him, love isn't something you can just turn off or on like a light; but other than that, I don't know how

I feel about him anymore either. Everything was so tied up with respecting him. I don't know how to unravel it.'

'So, you are staying there?'

'Yes, I am staying here. I'll come back for a few days if there is any change in Papy. If not, I'll see you in a couple of weeks, like I'd planned. But it will only be for a little while, then I must go to the next village.'

'Has it occurred to you that he's waiting for you?'

Paul stood up and looked out of the window. A pink-breasted wood pigeon landed clumsily in the top of the tree at the bottom of the garden, making the branches sway. 'Papy?'

'Oui.'

'I had thought about it, but then maybe I'm waiting for him too.'

'What do you mean? To do what?'

'To make sense to me.'

He heard a snort of impatience, a sound he was used to from his sister. 'Paul, you think too much, you really do.'

'I know.'

'I'm going to go now. But be careful, Paul, think about how you will feel if he dies before you come back. Think about that.'

'I will, I am.'

'Ok. Then I don't know what else to say. I need to think.'

'I'm sorry, Camille, I love you.'

'I love you too.'

She hung up. He put down his phone, went over to his little sink and splashed his face with cold water. He felt better for having talked to Camille; there was a sense of relief that someone else in his family knew, someone he could trust. But he also knew his burden was lighter because he had passed some of it on to her. But what else could he do? He heard the front door open and the soprano chatter of Adele as she came into the hall. His heart lifted in his chest. He dried his face off quickly and went downstairs to greet them. Jack bounded into the hall and launched into a frenzied licking of Adele's face; Michelle was closing the door behind her and smiling.

'Hello!' he said cheerfully.

Michelle looked across at him, a little hesitantly he thought. 'Hi.'

'How did it go?'

Her expression brightened. 'Brilliant! I've got a job at the little café off the square, and we went and had a look at the school. There's a teacher from England there, and she doesn't think we'll have any problem getting Adele in.'

'That sounds fantastic!'

'I played Escargot,' cut in Adele, excitedly, 'it's like Hopscotch but it goes in a circle —'

'Ah, oui, I remember playing that in school.'

'- there's a pond, and a picnic bench, and the teacher says there are two girls from England in my year too.'

'That is very lucky.'

Adele and Jack ran into the living room, leaving him and Michelle alone in the hall. Michelle picked up the bags she'd put down on the doormat. 'I'd best put these away.'

'Let me help.' As she moved to go past him he reached for the bag in her nearest hand.

'Oh, ok, thanks.' Their fingers tangled together briefly as she transferred the bag to him. He could smell the heat of the sun in her hair; he felt a buzzing, somewhere near his heart.

'Alan came around.' He said, a little breathlessly as he followed her into the kitchen.

'Was it about tonight?'

'Oui, he said he could drop us in the village, so we do not have to drive.' She looked up at him but he couldn't read her expression. 'He thought, as we are going to the Bistro, we would be having a drink?'

'Ah, of course, that's kind of him.'

'And to come back, it is such a beautiful day, we could walk?'

She looked up at him again and something about her face had softened. 'Yes, I suppose we could. It's not that far is it?'

'Non, three, or four kilometres.'

'Ok, great. When do you want to leave?'

'The museum closes at six, so, in an hour perhaps?'

She smiled. 'Perfect. I'll just have a shower and get Adele ready.'

'Yes, of course.' He thought frantically about the meagre bag of clothes he had brought with him. There was only one pair of pants that weren't shorts or jeans, and nothing even remotely smart for the bistro later. 'I...I said I would let Alan know, excuse me.' He put her bag of shopping on to the counter then hurried next door.

'Un, deux, trois, quatre, cinq, six, sept...' said Adele in a sing-song voice from the back seat of the car. Paul was teaching her to count to ten in French.

Michelle kept stealing glances at them in the rear-view mirror. He was very patient, and Adele would look at him with rapt concentration each time he repeated the words. He looked quite smart in his borrowed white linen shirt and waistcoat. Michelle was touched that he had gone to her neighbour to ask for something to wear, and she had taken care with her own appearance too, blow-drying her hair for the first time in weeks, and putting on her favourite summer dress, a fifties-style one in delicate blue gingham that Jane had found her at a vintage fair.

She turned to Alan. 'It's really kind of you to give us a lift.'

'No problem at all. It means me and Adele can get some treats for the film too, doesn't it, Adele?'

Adele bounced up and down on her seat happily. 'Oui, Monsieur Alan!'

'Ah, sounding like a little native already.' Alan replied, making Adele beam with pleasure.

'I feel a bit like a teenager getting dropped at a date by her parents.' As soon as the words had left her mouth, Michelle realised what she'd said and blushed. From a quick glance in the rear-view mirror again, it looked like Paul hadn't noticed. She let out a long sigh of relief. Alan turned to her and winked. She smiled and shook her head then decided it was safer to be silent for a while and just look out of the window. The fields, that she had come to know well over the last week, rushed fluidly on the other side of the glass. A gravelly-voiced French singer was playing on Alan's car stereo; the song sounded old, 1950s or 60s perhaps, and it made something about the scene outside the car feel nostalgic. Just over a week ago she had still been living at Anborough. How was it possible that her life had changed so much in such a short space of time? How was it possible that both these new people were now in her life, filling the car with kindness and friendship? In what felt like the first time in ages she found herself talking to Chris. *So, what do you make of all this? I think they're good people, don't you? And Adele likes them. But I'm scared too, about her losing them, because she lost you, and she still misses you every day. She seems ok, but how much more could she take?* She thought of Alan's illness, he hadn't mentioned it since the first time he'd told her, but she needed to know more. She needed to know how long. She needed to prepare herself. She needed to prepare Adele.

The fields outside her window had now been replaced with a sparse assortment of shuttered farm houses and villas. After a couple more minutes they were on the broad road that marked the entrance to the town.

'If you're going to the shop, Alan, you can drop me and Paul at the square and we can walk from there if that's easier?'

Alan turned in his seat briefly to look at Paul, who nodded his assent. 'Ok, if you're sure.' He manoeuvred the car into a parking space on the southern end of the village square and they all got out. The afternoon heat was a shock after the air-conditioned cool of the Saab, and the air smelled of hot paving stones and drying grass.

'Bye, Mummy!' Adele skipped over to her and flung her arms around her legs. Michelle reached down and lifted her up. Adele burrowed her face into her neck and they held each other for a moment.

'See you later, sweetheart, have a lovely time with Alan, be good, and remember you can't have him running around all night!'

'I won't, Mummy, I promise.'

She went over to Alan and kissed him on the cheek. 'Thanks, Alan, it's really kind of you.'

327

'Nonsense! We're going to have a much better time than you two,' he reached down and ruffled Adele's hair, 'aren't we?' Adele nodded, smiling.

'Merci, Alan.' Paul shook Alan's hand.

'Well you don't look as good as me in that waistcoat and shirt, Paul, but you don't look bad.'

Paul laughed. 'Oui, bien sur, I do not have your...panache, it is true.'

Alan nodded gravely and tapped his tummy. 'That's not the only thing you've got less of! Let me tighten that.' He went around to Paul's back and adjusted the waistcoat, Paul's cheeks coloured, but Alan seemed to be enjoying himself. 'Much better! Now you look good enough to escort this lovely young lady. Anyway, enough of all that.' He took Adele's hand and turned towards the supermarket. 'Au revoir, mes amis!'

She watched them, the old man with his slightly stooped back and the little girl bouncing along beside him, cross the yellowed grass, with a creeping sense of melancholy.

'What is it?' Paul had appeared beside her, frowning.

Michelle sighed. 'I don't know. It's been a funny day today, a good day but a funny day too, and just then, looking at them, I felt...I suppose because of what I know about Alan, it feels so sad.'

'Oui, and, Adele, she loves him I think.'

'Yes, I think she does. Someone else she loves and is going to lose.'

They were silent for a moment then Michelle turned and briefly squeezed Paul's arm. 'We'd better get to the museum soon, hadn't we, or we won't have much time there.'

'Oui. Let's go.'

They walked together for a few minutes in a surprisingly comfortable silence. Michelle studied the people they passed. A couple of older men on a bench, their skin dark and weather-beaten, a heated conversation being carried out from behind the roll-up cigarettes clamped in their mouths; a young punk girl with several piercings in her cheek and green-tipped hair; a middle-aged couple carrying bags of shopping, stopping for a moment to share a kiss.

'I wonder, as I watch them.'

Michelle turned to look at him. 'What?'

'How many of them are descended, from the original inhabitants of Argemourt.'

'Yes, I see what you mean. Probably not many, not directly.'

'No, so few were left. Perhaps from the farms nearby there are some?'

'Yes, perhaps.'

'Ah, we are here.'

They turned the corner and the museum appeared on their right. Just as she had earlier, Michelle felt the strange air of silence and loneliness that seemed to surround the place. She tried to identify where it came from; was it from the simplicity and gravitas of the building's design? The dappled light cast by the tall birch trees that lined the avenue? The fact that every time she had come down this road it had been empty? She suddenly felt quite anxious about going in.

'Are you coming?'

She realised she had stopped in the middle of the pavement. 'Yes, of course, sorry.' She picked up her pace again and they went up the few stone steps to the entrance where Paul stopped and looked at her solemnly.

'It is difficult. Some of the things you will see.'

Annoyance flared in her. 'I was married to a soldier for years, Paul, and I'm a widow; I've got more experience of war than you. I think I'll cope.'

Paul looked flustered; 'Of course, I did not mean, I am sorry.'

She reached past him and opened the door. Inside the museum she was surprised to see a group of young students gathered around the information desk, clipboards in hand.

'Merde.' Paul had appeared beside her. 'I was hoping it would not be so busy.'

'It's ok, it's what it's here for isn't it?' She gestured to the inscription on the wall to their right *'For the people of Argemourt. For those who have been, for those that are, and for those that will be. We will never forget."* To make sure people don't forget?'

'Oui, you are right.'

He looked a little dejected now and she felt guilty. 'So where do we go? Talk me through it.'

He smiled and his expression brightened. 'Bien sûr. This way.' She followed him to a door on the left of the desk and they moved past the gaggle of students. On the other side of the door there was silence and the light was low. There were a couple of people in the room, but they didn't look up when Michelle and Paul entered. On the wall immediately to their left she saw a huge image of the town, blown-up to the extent that the people in it were life-size. She went over to read from the information panel. She felt the warmth of Paul's body behind her.

'I think about this picture a lot.'

She straightened up. 'Just before the war started, it's so sad.'

'It makes me think of disaster movies. You know? At the beginning everything is normal and happy. People, they go about their business, not knowing what is around the corner.'

'Yes, I know what you mean, it feels just like that.' She shuddered slightly.

They were in the final room now and Michelle's expression had started to show her distress. 'I'm sorry, about giving you a hard time earlier,' her breathing sounded disjointed, as if it was catching in her throat, 'I didn't realise how it would affect me.' He put his arm around her and she leaned against him, ever so slightly, it made his heart beat faster. He wondered if she could feel it.

'It's ok, it upset me like this too, when I first came. These things are hard to comprehend.'

They were standing in front of an account by one of the first people to uncover the remains in the church; a municipal fire warden called Enrique Bardot. It was a particularly devastating record. He described how the bodies of women and children were melted into grotesque intermingling shapes, the agony of their deaths expressed through their twisted limbs; that some bodies appeared whole, but when touched, disintegrated into a human shadow of ash; how, unbearably, every now and then he would come across something mysteriously untouched by the flames. A child's shoe, a lock of hair.

She moved away from him gently. 'It's just, the cruelty, the horror of it.' She dabbed under her eyes with the tissue he had given her. The tears had made them bright, and despite the sense of tragedy and incomprehension he knew she was feeling, he couldn't take his eyes off her.

'It is impossible to understand. Maybe these things happen because not everything needs air, and light and food to grow; some things need only darkness and starvation.' As he said them he didn't know where the words had come from. He'd just felt the need to speak, to try to help her with her feelings.

'What do you mean?'

'That when people are hungry, when they live in fear or anger, it can twist them.'

'But these Nazi officers, they weren't hungry, they weren't afraid!'

'Non, maybe, but they came from a place of fear and darkness and anger.'

She shook her head. 'Still, whatever you come from, to do that...' she gestured towards Enrique's account and a small sob escaped her '...to women and children. You must be evil.'

'Oui, perhaps. Come. Let us go. I could do with a drink.'

'Yes, me too.'

She took his arm, a small act of comfort, perhaps, but it made him swell inside. As they entered the main entrance area, Paul heard his name called. He turned and saw Gerard walking towards him through the last few students that were studying the books for sale.

'Attendez.'

He stopped and turned. 'Salut Gerard. This is Michelle, the great niece of Michèle Leroy.'

'Ah!' Gerard reached for Michelle's hand in both of his and clasped it tightly. 'It is a pleasure to meet you. Your great aunt was a hero of mine. An extraordinary woman.'

Michelle looked a little taken aback. 'Thank you, that's lovely to hear.'

He released her hand and held his arms out wide. 'It means so much to have you here for the anniversary.'

'The anniversary?'

'Oui, it was on this day, seventy-four years ago, that the massacre happened.'

A chill crept up Paul from his feet to his scalp. How could he have forgotten? 'Of course.'

Michelle had gone white. 'You mean on this date? This is the actual date?'

'Oui, Mademoiselle.' Gerard replied gravely.

Suddenly Paul felt the need to be out in the fresh air. He took Gerard's hand and shook it vigorously. 'Merci, Gerard. I must come back and talk to you, when I have finished the book.'

'Oui, please do. Have a good evening.'

'Merci.'

Paul put his hand on Michelle's back and propelled her gently out of the museum. When they had stepped back into the warm evening sunlight they both looked at each other and blinked, like two animals that had emerged from a burrow.

'Fuck.' Michelle's eyes were still bright, but haunted. 'It was on this day.'

'Yes, I cannot believe I had not realised it.'

'When he said it, I felt all weird. Like that expression, do you have it in France? That someone has walked over your grave?'

Paul laughed, he felt light-headed. 'Non, but it is very expressive!'

She took his arm again. 'Come on, let's get that bloody drink and something to eat. I think we've earned it.'

When they reached the bottom of the steps she stopped. 'Which way, to the Bistro?'

'One moment.' He took out his phone and clicked on the maps app. He gestured to their right. 'This way, it is just a five-minute walk. There are four places to eat in the evenings in Argemourt, but this one is supposed to be the best.'

'Adele's still not got over the fact there isn't a McDonald's!'

Paul shook his head. 'Ah, McDonald's, at least there are still some places that they have not colonised!'

'Maybe they didn't think massacres and burgers were a good combination.'

They both stopped and looked at each other for a second. Michelle had her hand over her mouth and looked horrified. 'I can't believe I just said that!' The images that had been suggested by the fireman's account flashed unwanted in Paul's head, then the image of a burger being flipped, and the juxtaposition was at once so horrific and so absurd that a huge bubble of laughter welled up inside him then forced itself out with a snort. She looked at him, her eyes wide, and then they started to water and for a horrible moment he thought he had made her cry, but then she started laughing too. They both howled, the hysteria bending them double, forcing them to hold on to each other for support. Paul's lungs were aching, he took a few deep gulping breaths, trying to calm himself. Michelle was obviously struggling too, she was wiping her eyes and gasping.

'I haven't laughed that much in ages.' They looked at each other for a moment, then looked away. Paul started to walk down the road again, suddenly feeling a little embarrassed – or exposed perhaps? He couldn't decide which. 'Me neither.'

She fell in to step beside him and took his arm again. 'I remember, I got a terrible attack of the giggles at my gran's funeral. The angrier my mum got, the more I couldn't stop myself, it was awful!'

Paul smiled and looked down at her. 'Sometimes we laugh because we have to, because there is nothing else we *can* do. It releases the tension.'

'Yes, that's it, that's exactly how I feel! Like there was something I had to let out. My chest's still aching!'

They laughed again, quietly this time, and Paul focused on enjoying the warmth of the lowering sun on his face, and the pleasant sensation of Michelle's strong but slender arm in his. The town was beginning to rouse itself from its afternoon torpor and the pavements were slowly filling up with families and couples coming out for the evening.

'I've always liked this about European cities.'

'Hmm?'

She looked up at him then gestured at the street. 'The way that everyone gets together in the evenings, you know, to go out and eat or walk and enjoy the air. It just doesn't seem to happen at home, but maybe that's just because of the weather.'

'Have you lived in many places? With your husband being in the army?'

'Oh, I see what you mean. Well we lived in Germany for a bit because of Chris, but mostly we've just moved around in the UK. I was thinking more of when you go on holiday, when you notice those little things that are different to how they are back home.'

'Oui, I know what you mean.'

'Have you travelled a lot?'

'After university, I travelled for three months. Around Asia, mostly. And when I was ten we spent two months in Africa, at a nature reserve when my father did some legal work for a charity out there.'

'I would have loved to have travelled when I was younger. South America is the place that's always fascinated me, but there's no way I could ever have afforded it.'

He thought of how easy it had been for him to travel, how Papy had given him ten thousand Euros when he turned eighteen, and he blushed. 'Some people say there is more to learn by truly getting to know your own country than by travelling abroad.'

'Ha!' she said contemptuously. 'The only people who say that are those that have the money to afford to travel, to make those that haven't feel better!'

'This is the street.' He was glad to be able to change the subject. 'It is there, see it? With the green sign?'

She peered down the road. 'Yes, I see it, great, I'm starving.'

The restaurant was already half full, and generating a pleasant low hum of conversation. A slightly flustered looking middle-aged man with red cheeks and a goatee beard came up to them.

'Bonsoir.'

'Bonsoir, Monsieur. J'ai réservé une table, mon prénom est Paul.'

'Ah, oui, pour dix-huit heures?'

'Oui.'

'Par ici, s'il vous plait.' He led them to a table by the window. It was a nice spot at the front of the restaurant, and a folding window that ran the width of the room had been pushed back to let in the warm evening air. Michelle smoothed down the full skirt of her pretty blue summer dress then sat down in front of him.

'I am sorry that I did not say before, but you look très jolie tonight.'

She smiled and looked down at her hands for a second. 'Thank you. And you,' she looked back up at him with a small smile, 'you look very smart…in Alan's clothes.'

He laughed. 'Thank you, I think!' He picked up his menu. 'Do you need help? To understand what things are.'

She was frowning down at the menu, 'Yes, I think so, I know what some things are, but not a lot.'

'I spoke to Alan, and he recommended the Poulet aux écrevisses, it's a speciality of the house.

'I know poulet is chicken, but what the hell is écrevisses?'

'Ah, it is, not lobster, not crab, what is the other one…' he huffed with frustration, '…that looks like a big prawn?'

She put her hand over her mouth, she was laughing at him, he laughed too. He wanted to reach over the table and kiss her, the pull was so strong it almost took his breath away.

'I think you mean crayfish!'

'Ah, oui!' he managed to say, in a relatively normal voice. 'That is it. Crayfish.'

'I have to say, it sounds a bit weird, chicken and crayfish. I've heard of *surf and turf* but never chicken and seafood.'

'Will you trust me? I have had it only once before, in Paris, but it was delicious.'

'Ok, I trust you. What are you going to have for your starter?'

He scanned the entrées, he was finding it hard to concentrate, but he was starving. 'Ah, the carpaccio I think.'

'Isn't that raw beef?'

'Very rare, seared on the outside.'

'Hmm, not sure I fancy that. Rillettes, isn't that a bit like a pate?'

'Oui, a little. The meat is cooked slowly with wine and herbs, then it is chopped fine and sealed under butter.'

'Yum, that sounds lovely. I'll have that.' She spread her hands over the menu and looked up at him. 'Thank you.'

'For what?'

'For being kind, to me and Adele. For getting us presents for taking me to the museum, and here.'

'Please, it is nothing.'

'I feel a bit embarrassed to say it, but when you arrived, I was really unsure about it all. About sharing the house. I almost asked you to find a B&B in the town. But actually,' she turned towards the window and her eyes glazed over for a second as if she'd gone inside herself, 'it's been good this last week to have you around. It's helped me and Adele get through being somewhere so different, it's helped to make sure we're not lonely.'

'I cannot imagine you and Adele ever being lonely if you have each other.'

'Actually, we've had some difficult times. I've not always been a good mother to her.'

He was about to speak but the waiter appeared, smiling, his hand hovering over his order pad grasping a freshly sharpened pencil. He must have heard them speaking in English as he greeted them in the same language. They ordered the food and a bottle of local red wine and he nodded his approval. When he had gone, Paul turned back to Michelle and risked putting his hand over hers. He was relieved when she didn't pull away.

'It must have been hard. To be on your own, after your husband died.'

She smiled thinly. 'It was, I did my best, most of the time, but other times it overwhelmed me. I lashed out. It's hard to admit it but in the months before I came here it was getting bad again, I was drinking too much and I wasn't there for Adele, not in the way I should have been.'

'But it must be impossible, to be a good parent all the time. None of us have known that, surely?'

'True, but it doesn't stop you telling yourself that you should be perfect.'

'I do not know. I am not a parent, but one day...'

'Tell me more about your parents.'

The waiter appeared with their wine. Paul was glad of the interruption so he could gather his thoughts.

'Would you like to try it first, Monsieur?'

'Non, merci, please just pour it.'

The waiter nodded curtly and filled both their glasses. Paul took a mouthful of his and swallowed it gratefully. He felt a little wired and strangely excited and needed something to settle him down.

'You were going to tell me about your mum and dad?' Michelle prompted.

'It is hard to describe.'

'Why?'

'Because your relationship with them can change so much, from when you are a child to when you are an adult. Recently it has been very difficult, I feel I do not know them anymore. They have almost become strangers.'

'How do you mean?'

'Their politics. They have become very far right. Do you know what I mean?'

'Yes, I think so.'

'Very intolerant. We have terrorism in France so now they blame all Muslims. They try to say it is because of feminism, or fairness or legitimate security of the country that they have changed their views, but at the bottom of it all it is just racism and moral laziness. I cannot stand the hypocrisy.'

'But I remember you talking about your mum, you said she loved you too much? Surely however much you disagree on all that they are still your parents? She's still your mum?'

He thought for a moment. She was right, of course, but in his heart, he was struggling to feel it. He tried to think of his Maman as he remembered her rather than how she was now. 'She is quite something, very glamorous, very elegant. She has always been very affectionate, she has, I think the expression is, *put me on a pedestal*, no?'

She smiled. 'Lucky you, I'd say my mum was more likely to put me in a ditch!'

'I am sorry to hear that. I complain about the way she is, but I know I am lucky. In many ways, I know she loves me so much.'

'I think my mum probably loves me, but sometimes, the way she acts, makes me doubt it.'

'Ah, she must love you!' He had not meant to say the words with such vehemence. He felt himself colour.

'It's not her fault, it's just the way she is. She dotes on Adele though.'

'Dotes?'

'It means,' she looked up, 'it's like Adele can do no wrong, you know? She loves her but she also spoils her a little.'

'Ah like all grandparents I think.'

'Yes, I suppose so. It winds me up a bit though, you know, when she's so critical of me all the time.'

'Oui, I can understand that.'

'I think you had a very different upbringing to me.'

'In what ways do you think?'

'Money, class, opportunities.'

He shrugged. She didn't sound angry or resentful, more a little sad, but he felt embarrassed nonetheless. 'I suppose I have. But class, it does not mean so much here as in the UK. And some things are universal, non? Like grief, like love?'

Her eyes were steady as she held his gaze. 'Yes, that's true. However different our experiences are, in the end, we're pretty much all motivated by the same things. All trying to be happy.'

Happy, what was happy? *Right now*, thought Paul, *happiness is sitting opposite Michelle in her blue dress.* The waiter appeared and put their starters in front of them. Michelle looked at hers with evident satisfaction.

'They look delicious!'

'Oui, they do.' He stabbed a sliver from the delicately sliced beef onto his fork and ate it. The meat melted in his mouth leaving a savoury tang of rich buttery stock and wine. They were silent for a couple of minutes, both busy with their food. Paul was trying to take his time, to savour it, but he was ravenous.

Michelle cleaned the inside of her ramekin out with a hunk of bread. 'Mmm, that was lovely. So rich and such simple but lovely flavours.'

'Perhaps, then, *this* is happiness, non?'

She looked a little flustered at that and he instantly regretted saying it. 'But then how do we define happiness?' he started again, trying to move away from the intimacy of his last words. 'Is it just contentment? How do we define it when it is so based on context and circumstances? When the environment it exists in is constantly transforming? It is like…' he reached out towards the open window and closed his fist, 'trying to take hold of air!'

She had put her head in her hands and looked amused. 'You speak fantastic English, but sometimes, Paul, I just don't understand you.'

'Ah, I do not believe that. I think you know exactly what I mean.'

She chuckled. 'Ok, I suppose I do, really, but sometimes it's like your PhD is speaking rather than you.'

He looked down at his plate, discomfited. 'Perhaps that is true. My friends often say I seem far away, too stuck in my studies.'

She reached over and touched his arm briefly. The contact sent a shimmer of pleasure down his spine. 'I'm sorry, I'm teasing really. I like listening to you. It challenges me. I suppose I've got a bit of a chip on my shoulder because I never got to finish college.'

'It is not too late.'

'No, it isn't. And I don't really have anyone else to blame. It's always easier to give up on yourself than try to do your best, to be the best that you can be.'

'That is very true. So, have you thought what you might do now?'

'Well the first thing is to learn French really well, then who knows what I might be able to do. Working in the café is just a start.'

'Of course.'

'I want to keep it simple though, do you know what I mean? Since I got here, I've watched Adele, and she's adapted perfectly. Her whole pace of life has changed and she's loving it; just pottering in the garden and reading, and playing with Jack and watching films, things like that.'

'I think simplicity in life is the most important thing we can all strive for, but also the most difficult.'

'But why?' Michelle said passionately. 'When you're a kid everything is simple, why does it have to change so much?'

He shrugged. 'Because a child does not have to worry about sex or money or work?'

'True, I thought about that, but they still have worries: school, their friendships. I suppose what I mean is that we should learn from them. They focus on each thing they do with total attention. They throw themselves one hundred percent into what they are doing then, *at that moment*. They know what they like to do and they do it as often as they can, without guilt or self-criticism.'

'And you say I speak like a PhD!'

She looked at him, her head on one side. 'Touchée!'

'Ah you are speaking French already!' She laughed at that.

'You know, you put yourself down a lot, say that you are not intelligent, not educated, but you are one of the most intelligent and thoughtful people I have ever met.'

She looked embarrassed, he'd touched a nerve. He looked out of the window trying to think of how he could change the subject. A skinny tabby cat walked nonchalantly past the front of the restaurant. It stopped briefly, sat and looked at him, then immediately started to wash its genitals. 'Here is a perfect example!' He gestured towards the cat and her gaze followed. 'That cat is living in the moment! It decided it needed to wash its *derrière* so it stopped right there and then to do it!'

She giggled, all her previous discomfort seemingly gone. 'So, we should all be more like cats… and kids!'

'Exactement!'

He watched her take a sip of her wine then look back out at the cat again. It was now on its back, revealing its furry belly to the last slanting rays of the evening sun. Her expression was enigmatic; there was a sadness there, but also a ruefulness, as if she was thinking of a private joke. She shook her head slightly then looked behind him.

'Ah, here comes the famous chicken and crayfish!' The waiter placed two large steaming bowls in front of them. An extraordinary sweet-savoury cloud engulfed him, pulling him in. He let out a sigh of pleasure.

'I will just get you some more bread.'

'Merci.'

He looked down into the casserole. The creamy surface was embellished with a golden glaze of melted butter, and the face of a crayfish peered out at him reproachfully. His stomach rumbled. Michelle had taken her spoon and was tasting the broth.

'Oh my God, that's incredible!'

Paul tore off a chunk from a bowl in the middle of the table and dunked it in the fragrant sauce. 'Oui, it is incredible. I am glad we followed Alan's advice.'

'Ok,' she looked at him and there was a hint of mischief in her eyes, 'I know what happiness is, it's this casserole!'

As they were about to leave the restaurant, the head waiter rushed up to them.

'Excusez-moi, Monsieur, Dame -'

Michelle turned around and gestured for Paul to stay.

'I am very sorry but I completely forgot, Monsieur Alan, he called and paid for this.' He held out another bottle of the local red wine. 'I forgot to give it to you when you ordered, and now you have paid, but please, accept this with my apologies.'

He looked stricken and his skin was covered by a fine layer of sweat. Michelle felt sorry for him. 'That's no problem, don't worry, we'll take it with us, thank you.'

Paul reached out and took the bottle. 'Ah, Alan, always thinking of us!'

They said their goodbyes and stepped into the sultry air outside. The sun had almost set and the light of it was reflecting with peach-gold brightness off the windows of the houses and shops that lined the street.

Paul raised the bottle in his hand. 'So, what are we going to do with this?'

Michelle laughed. 'I feel a bit like a teenager who's snuck out of home late. Maybe we should go and sit on a park bench?'

'Ah, I am sure we can do better than that!'

'Hang on, I'd better check in with Alan.' She fished around in her bag and pulled out her phone. 'Ah, that's lovely, look at this picture he's sent me.' She turned the phone around so Paul could see the screen. 'She's fallen asleep on the sofa with Jack.'

'They look very cosy!'

'I can just go and lift her up when I get back and carry her to bed.'

'So, no need to rush?'

She looked up at him. His expression was boyish and hopeful. It made her smile inside. 'No, no rush.'

They wandered towards the town square. The aroma of sun-baked paving stone and the sweet smell of flowers from the nearby pots and window boxes wrapped itself around her. With her full belly, wine-softened senses and the easy, loping presence of Paul by her side Michelle felt a sudden and profound sense of contentment. They passed the square then crossed over to meet the broad dusty road that snaked its way back towards home. A stab of pain burned in the corner of Michelle's eye, forcing her to stop, short, in the middle of the pavement. Her eye was watering furiously and she could barely see. She felt Paul's warm hands squeeze her shoulders.

'Are you all right Michelle? What has happened?'

'Shit, there's something, in my eye.'

'Which one?'

'The right one.'

'You need to open it.'

'I can't!'

'Please, trust me, even if you have to hold it open. It is important. Your eye cannot flush it out unless you open it.'

'Ok, ok, I'll try.' She used her thumb and forefinger to prise open her eyelid. It kept trying to close and hot salty tears were streaming down her cheek.

'Let me look.'

He put a hand on either side of her face and tipped her head back. She could just about make out the look of concentration on his face through the smear of her tears.

'Ah, oui, I see it. It looks like a piece of ash.'

'Ash? How could that have got there?'

'Can you not smell it? A farmer must be burning his field.'

She breathed in deeply, she *could* smell it, faint, acrid and smoky. 'Why would they do that?'

'It clears the land for the next crop and gets rid of any fungus or disease.'

She blinked hard, tears running down her cheek. 'Can you get it out?'

'It is best if you do it yourself, but I will help you.' He tipped her head to the left. 'Blink now, several times, to move it to the bottom corner of your eye…that's it; now, use the tip of your finger to get it.'

Gingerly she brought her finger up and dabbed at the corner of her eye. Immediately the burning stopped and she knew she had got it out. She held up her hand. 'There's the bastard. Got him!' A small flake of dark grey was suspended in a glistening dome of tears on the tip of her finger.

'Très bien!'

'Thanks, it really hurt!'

'No problem.'

They were standing very close to each other now, Paul's face only a few inches from her own. Her heart was beating fast, she thought for a moment how nice it would be to kiss him, but then something caught her eye. She grabbed his arm. 'Look!' It was a small white enamel sign attached to a weather-beaten wooden pole. The lettering was dark blue and read:

EGLISE ORADOUR-SUR-GLANE
MONUMENT NATIONAL

His tanned face paled as he read the sign. 'We must go. There is a path, see?'

She stepped forward and peered into the relative gloom; it was more like a tunnel than a path, the trees and shrubs untended and overgrown, creating an arched cathedral roof of knotted branches. 'It doesn't look like anyone's gone down it in years.'

'Yes, which is strange, as the museum is often busy. People must go to the church too when they visit. Perhaps there is another way that is used more often. A route to it nearer the museum.'

'Yes, perhaps.'

'But we must go, mustn't we? It is the anniversary, it means something.'

'Yes, I suppose we should. If my great aunt was here she'd be going today. We should pay our respects.'

Wordlessly they stepped off the road and on to the path, Paul leading. As soon as they were on it, the quality of the sound changed, and a dreamy silence enveloped them. The smell of the burnt field was getting stronger, but there was another smell too, a sickly-sweet smell, that probably came from the white flowers that studded the darkening green of the bent trees and bushes like tiny stars. They didn't speak for several minutes, and at some point, without her knowing who had instigated it, they were holding hands.

The further they walked the more a sense of otherworldliness overtook her. It made her feel detached and a little breathless, as if the air around them had thickened. 'I feel really strange.' Her voice fell flat and toneless in the cloistered hush of the tunnelled path.

'Oui, me too.'

Just when she was about to suggest that they turn back, they came out into a clearing that she recognised from their previous walks to the church. It was eight-thirty now and they probably only had about an hour or so of light. The thought made Michelle feel anxious. However, despite the fading light, they easily found the old wall that marked the boundary of the church and after following it for a few yards, came across the broken gate.

They both stopped, as if nervous about what they would find on the other side. It was Michelle, this time, who stepped through first. When Paul had followed her she took hold of his hand again. 'Look!'

The low beams of the dying sun were slanting through a gap in the branches in front of the church, creating a pool of gold on the woodland floor. In this almost supernatural light, the old church felt like something from a fairy story. Michelle almost expected to see its door open, and a procession of goblins and sprites come dancing out into the glade.

'We should sit here.' Paul said, a little breathlessly.

'Yes, it's perfect.'

They passed into the glade. Michelle sat, cross-legged on the grass and Paul lay on his side, his long legs stretched out. She picked up the bottle of wine. 'Shit, it's got a cork!'

'Aha!' Paul reached into the front pocket of his canvas knapsack 'Voila!' with a flourish he produced a swiss army knife and pulled down a corkscrew from within the polished red handle.

'You're a life-saver!'

He smiled toothily and opened the wine; the cork made a satisfying 'pop' as it came out. He took a swig and passed it to her. 'I am sorry, I would wipe the top with my sleeve for you, but it is not my shirt!'

She laughed, 'that's ok, my mum always said you don't want things to be too clean. She's always going on about all the asthma and eczema these days being down to antibacterial cleaning products!'

'She could be right!'

'Yeh, she could.'

He put the corkscrew back into his knapsack then pulled out his hand suddenly. 'Merde!'

'What?'

'Look what I have found!'

'What is it?'

He opened out his palm and inside it was a what looked like a large roll-up cigarette and a small lighter. 'It is a present from my friend, Manny. I had forgotten it was there!'

'He gave you a cigarette, for a present?'

He smiled at her and shook his head. 'This is not just a cigarette.'

'Oh, you mean it's a spliff or something?'

'Oui! But good stuff, nothing crazy.'

'I didn't know you smoked?'

'I don't, just this, every now and then.' He surprised her by immediately putting the joint between his lips and lighting it. He took a long, slow pull on it, smiled, his eyes closed, then slowly released the smoke. It billowed out of his nostrils and curled around his golden head. For a moment he looked like some kind of god emerging from a fire, and it made her heart flutter.

He took two more drags then passed it to her.

'Here, try it.'

'No, it's ok.'

'Don't be afraid.'

'I'm not afraid!'

'Have you never tried it before?'

'Not for years. Not since I was a teenager.'

He looked at her and his expression suddenly changed, from mild amusement to something intense and undefinable. He reached out and stroked her cheek. 'You look so beautiful, just now, like this. You look...wary, like an animal, I cannot explain it.'

She was unable to reply, and to disguise the tumult of her emotions she took the joint off him and inhaled. The second the smoke hit her lungs she could feel it. A floaty sense of wellbeing, that started with a prickle in her scalp then seemed to flush down her body. She took another drag on it then passed it back. She let the smoke out slowly, tipping back her head and watching it insinuate itself towards the branches and the sunset-bruised sky.

'Do you like it?'

'Yes, I think. I don't like the taste though.'

'Here, have more wine, to take it away.'

She tipped the bottle back and swallowed. 'I've got the strangest feeling.'

He sat up and passed her the joint again. 'What is it?'

She sucked on it, inhaled, and immediately started to feel light-headed. She let herself melt into the sensation. 'Like I'm not real, like I'm in a story or something.'

'It's this place, it's because we *are* in a story.'

'Yes, I suppose we are, but isn't that how it always is? Isn't all our life just a story?'

'But some stories are more powerful than others.' He said quietly. 'Most stories happen then die. Others have such joy, or pain in them that I think they last forever.'

Who is this incredible man who has appeared in my life? She found herself thinking. *What should I do? Where are we going?* She felt reckless and strangely excited. *I could die tomorrow* her internal voice continued, *I could die next week, what am I waiting for?* 'Do you know what I think?' she said, more passionately than she'd intended.

'Non, what?'

She got on to her hands and knees and crawled towards him like a cat until her face was close to his. She could hardly believe what she was doing, it was as if someone else had stepped in to her body and taken over. 'That my friend, Jane, is right. It's all men's fault, all of it, all the war and fighting and the cruelty and the need to control, it's all men. All of it!'

'Oui,' he replied vehemently, 'you are right!' He took hold of her face and kissed her, hard. She put her arms around his neck and they fell back onto the grass, their bodies rammed against each other, chest, groin, thighs, intertwined and connected. There was an inevitability about it, something that made utter sense and locked her to the moment. She wanted him, she needed him; feelings she hadn't had in so long that the shock of them being ignited so suddenly made her feel like she had been transported to some kind of parallel universe, where anything was possible.

Seemingly without any kind of conscious decision or action they were now both half dressed. She was undoing his trousers, she was pulling them down, he was struggling out of his underpants, his expression urgent and somehow beseeching. Then her dress was off and beside her on the grass, quickly followed by her bra and knickers. For a moment she stood there, naked, looking down at him. He was spread out on the ground, as if she had flattened him, just by looking at him, only his cock was erect, and the sight of it sparked a kind of madness inside of her.

She stood over him then slowly lowered herself down. He gasped as she enveloped him and bent forward as if it hurt. She pushed him back onto the grass and pulled herself up, until only the tip of him was in her. He cried out.

'Vas-y! Vas-y!'

'No! Wait!' She hovered above him, teasing, lowering a little then up again. He was moaning now, low and urgent. She held back as long as she could then sat down on him hard.

'Michelle!' He pushed his fingers into her hair and pulled her face down towards him. They kissed again, she pressed herself against him, their hips rocked a few times and then the orgasm hit her and she cried out, a strange animal cry that sounded utterly alien. A second later and he came too, the sound beautiful and ragged, and at that moment the fact of their being together felt like the most natural thing in the world.

They rolled onto their sides, still connected, and panting. Paul wiped the sweat from her forehead and smoothed back her hair. 'Oh Michelle, Michelle.'

'Shh.' She kissed him briefly and ran her hand down the valley of his spine. 'We don't need words right now. No words.'

He nodded and smiled and after a few more moments they pulled themselves apart and looked up at the sky, now a deepening blue.

She propped herself up on to her elbow, sniffing. 'The smell of burning, it's stronger now.'

He raised his face and closed his eyes. 'Oui, you are right. The wind must have changed.'

This strange turn of events unsettled her and she started to pull on her clothes. Wordlessly, Paul followed suite. He shoved his foot into his shoe, hopping on one leg, his shirt on but still unbuttoned. After he'd finished dressing he stopped, his head on one side, and pointed towards the church.

'Look, there is a light.'

As they approached it she saw that he was right. There was a thread of brightness around the edges of the door.

Paul took a deep breath, then his fingers tightened around the handle and turned it. The heavy wooden door swung open and Michelle peered down into the gloom; a large lit white candle was inside a glass lantern on the altar. She glanced around cautiously; fingers of anxiety scratching at her insides; but there was little else to see. In one corner, some rubble, in another, a fallen beam from the ceiling, blackened to charcoal, and at the far-end of the nave she saw the dull glow of the candlelight reflected off the melted dome of the fallen church bell. She gasped. The shape of it resembled the back of huge slumped man.

Paul looked at her, concerned. 'Are you ok?'

She nodded her head but couldn't speak.

Still holding hands, they went over to the altar, there was a brass sign to the left of the candle, Paul translated it for her.

' "*On each anniversary day from 1945 to the present, this candle is kept lit to commemorate the murder of some 322 villagers of Argemourt by soldiers of the 40th SS Panzer Division Odin and members of the Malgre Nous.*" And then they list the names of those who died.' He glanced at her and the reflection of the candle flame trembled in his pupils. 'Shall I read them?'

She let go of his hand and sat down on the plinth of the altar. She felt weak and feverish. 'Yes.' She closed her eyes and focused on his voice.

' "*Men and boys of Argemourt, murdered by firing squad outside the church: Luc Briel, nineteen; Maurice and Albert Fitou, fifty-three and twenty-nine; Salazar Petite, eighty-one; Lorenzo Capalletti, twelve years…*' "

As each name was read out, Michelle pictured them, one by one, lining up against the wall of the church. It must have taken several rounds for the firing squad to work its way through all the men from the village, and she tried to imagine the profound terror and disbelief of the men as they watched the soldiers assemble their machine guns and waited their turn. The wretchedness of having their futures torn from them, as cold-eyed officers chatted and smoked nonchalantly nearby must have been unbearable. She felt the horror in their hearts as they imagined what awaited their wives, mothers, daughters and sisters inside the church. *Surely, they will take just us, the men* - they maybe thought, with a last, futile grasp at hope – *what could they want with women and children?* But they probably didn't know in their town with just a couple of telephones and a German war machine that specialised in hiding its atrocities; that the Nazis had already made a sport out of the murder of women, children and babies: in Oradour-sur-Glane, Tulle and Argenton-sur-Creuse. She felt, with a kind of shame, that however hard she tried, it was impossible for her to imagine even the tiniest fraction of the emotion that must have been burning through those men. Even so, her eyes filled with tears and her heart ached.

Paul paused, his voice breaking as if he was fighting back tears. 'Un moment, I am sorry.'

'It's ok. Stop if you need to.'

He sniffed and cleared his throat. 'I should go on, it says now: "*Women and children, murdered with incendiary devices and machine-gun fire: -* " ' Michelle went and stood beside him and stroked his back. 'It's ok, I'll do it.' He nodded and turned away. She bent down and peered at the commemorative plaque, struggling to decipher the engraved names in the gloom; "*Anna Babin, sixty;*" she read, *"Marie Séverin, twenty-one; Clara Guillory, nine-months; Angélique Fitou, seven…"* ' *Seven years old,* she thought, *just like Adele.* ' *"Camille Breton, Sarah Sénac…"* ' She went on until the list had finished. Her throat was dry; over a hundred names. It was incomprehensible. A hollowing wave of despair pressed down on her and she sank onto on the altar plinth. Paul sat down beside her and held her to him. 'How is it possible, Paul? So many people, so many innocent people? What was going through their minds, the soldiers? What was going through their hearts? How did they sleep that night…or *ever again*?'

'Je ne sais pas.'

'I want to go home.'

'Oui, let's go.'

She pushed through the gate and up the path towards Alan's back door. It was ajar, and as she entered the living room, she could see Alan in the glow of the standard lamp, slumped in his chair, his head on one side. She tiptoed around to the front of the sofa, Adele was there under a blanket, with Jack stretched out between her back and the sofa. Michelle smiled and stroked Adele's hair, and then the rough cheek of the old dog, who grumbled gently in his sleep.

She went over to Alan and knelt beside him. He was so still. Too still, she reached out a trembling hand and pushed him gently, nothing happened. With a mounting sense of panic, she pushed him again, her heart thumping in her chest. This time, he grunted and shifted in his chair before opening his eyes and staring at her blearily.

'Oh God, oh thank God!'

He reached out and put his hand on her shoulder. 'What on earth's the matter?'

'I'm sorry it's so late, I hope you weren't worried.'

'You look…extraordinary, what's happened to you? What time is it? Are you ok?'

'Never mind that, I thought you were…' a sudden impulse came over, something urgent she had to say to him, 'listen to me Alan.' She said in a fierce whisper, 'You're not allowed to die, ok? I mean it, there's enough dead people in the world, and you're not going to be one of them!'

'Michelle, my dear, I'm ill, I'm afraid there's nothing I can do about it.'

'I won't hear that!' She gripped his hand tightly. 'I mean it, you didn't have us before, you didn't have your daughter, and grandson. You need to *live* for us. You hear about things, people get better, they find things that help – cannabis – healers – special diets. We're going to try them Alan, we're going to *try them all.*'

He laughed softly, 'That sounds exhausting!'

'I mean it, we're not giving up.'

'Ok, ok. I'll try anything, but not more chemo. I've done all I'm prepared to do of that. I'd rather have one last wonderful summer with you and be well, than let that stuff make a ghost out of me again and live through a decade of summers. Ok?'

'Ok. It's a deal.'

'So, tell me, what's happened. You look different, I can't put my finger on it.'

'Nothing, really. Well, maybe, sort of, but not right now, OK? I just can't.'

He smiled, a compressed and knowing little smile, then nodded.

'Shall I take Adele home?'

'No, no, leave her. I'll send her over after breakfast. She did say that if she fell asleep she didn't mind staying there until the morning. I said I'd have to check with you.'

'Ok, thanks Alan, we'll catch up in the morning. When I've had a chance to have some coffee and something to eat.'

'Yes, of course. But you promise me you're ok?'

'I promise.'

When Michelle came back into the cottage she was empty handed.

'No Adele?'

'She was fast asleep on the sofa with Jack. She looked so peaceful. Alan said to leave her and he'd send her back in the morning.'

'He is a good man.'

'Yes, he is.' She reached up and touched his face, and the skin of his cheek buzzed beneath her fingers. He took her hand and kissed it.

'I'm so exhausted.'

'Oui, me too. I'll leave you to sleep.' Reluctantly he let go of her hand and headed towards the stairs.

'Wait.' She took hold of his arm, and the breath caught in his throat. 'Will you come with me? Hold me? I don't want to be on my own.'

'Of course. Come.' He took hold of her hand and they went upstairs. They got straight into bed, only bothering to take off their shoes.

Michelle turned around to face him, her eyes the only part of her he could see in the darkened room. 'Thank you.'

'For what?'

'For being here.' She kissed him, lightly, then turned over. He curled himself around her back, his knees fitting snugly into the crook of hers, his left arm wrapped around her back and waist. Holding her like this felt so good. He zoned in on the gentle movement of her back as she breathed, and the movement became hypnotic. He thought he was too stimulated to sleep, but was surprised to find his thoughts soon twisting into bizarre hypnagogics, and then the oblivion of sleep.

An intense smell of burning, and then a light, blinding and bloody, saturated the interior of the church with red. Paul was standing by the altar, staring towards the door, his throat tightening around a scream. A group of soldiers, in Wermacht and SS uniforms, were lined up in front of the doorway, saturated by the ghastly red light. They stood, staring out in front of them, and the expression on their faces made Paul double over, fighting back a wave of scalding nausea. Each was distorted into a mask of agony, each mouth a gaping, silent but shrieking black hole, the eyes wide – lids peeled back. Despite the revulsion he felt, he found himself looking at them again, drawn, with a kind of fascinated horror, to inspect each one. Then he stopped, and it felt like his heart had been torn from his chest. There, again, was the face from the lake – the young face of his Papy framed by his dark green field cap and tightly buttoned jacket. But this time, his expression, too was grotesque and tormented. 'Papy! No Papy!' Paul screamed, but his voice was lost in the roar of flames.

They were surrounded by blinding, choking smoke. Michelle pushed as far back underneath the altar as they could go, still clinging tightly to Adele. She could feel the frantic movements of her daughter's chest as she struggled to breathe. Everywhere the air was black or red, ash or fire, an unbearable heat pressed down on them, Michelle kept breathing but it was like the air was a lie, and instead of oxygen, her lungs were filled with bitter choking smoke.

Should she run? She leaned forward and looked out, her eyes stinging and watering so much that she could hardly see. The shapes that emerged from the gloom were a visceral portrait of Hell; bodies writhing and crying out; a devastating sea of flesh, burning clothes and outstretched hands. The sound of gunfire stabbing through the smoke, followed by the dull, fleshy thuds of bullets entering burning legs and chests. There was nowhere to go. Adele was still pressed against her chest, sobbing and gasping. They were going to die. The truth of it struck deep in the nerves of her soul; like a pin jammed into the root of a damaged tooth. The last job that remained for her, she realised at that moment, was to comfort her daughter until death came.

She looked down, smoothed the hair from the girl's forehead, and realised – with a rush of insane relief - that it wasn't Adele after all; she at least still had a future. The realisation gave her strength, she held the little girl tighter and started to whisper a ragged prayer into her ear. It was a prayer she hadn't said since school assemblies somewhere miles and years away from here, in another world, perhaps.

Something dragged her out of her dream, and she emerged from it with a whimper like an injured dog. As her eyes adjusted to the gloom she could see the shape of Paul standing by the window.

'What is it?'

'It is impossible.' His voice was barely more than a whisper. He sounded scared. 'The ropes holding the bell burnt, the bell fell. Most of it melted in the heat of the fire.'

'What do you mean?'

He turned to look at her and his face was bleached white by moonlight. 'I heard the bell, the church bell.'

She got up and stood beside him. As she turned to look out of the window she heard it too. A profound, resonant toll, that seemed to vibrate through her bones. It set her heart beating so hard that it almost hurt to speak, 'You're right, I saw it too, it was burned and broken. Maybe there's another church, nearby?'

'Maybe. But to ring the, bell, at this time?' Tension radiated from him and his eyes were wide.

She looked back out of the window towards the church, and a steely filament of cold shot down her back. 'Look!'

He turned to follow her gaze. 'Merde!'

Faintly, but undeniably, a plume of smoke was rising from the dark tree-line of the horizon.

'It looks like it is coming from the church.'

She nodded, she couldn't speak. Her tongue felt like it had swollen to fill her whole mouth.

He took hold of her hand. 'Should we, is it crazy, I mean, should we go and see?'

Again, she nodded, again she couldn't speak. She must be mad, but she knew they had to go. Silently they sat beside each other on the bed and put on their shoes. Before they left the cottage, Michelle found a couple of torches in the cupboard under the stairs, and gave one to Paul. She was grateful for the reassuring light, and the weight of it in her hand, though what she was afraid of, she didn't know.

They ran virtually the whole way there, no doubt fuelled by their adrenalin, Michelle thought. Within minutes they were at the shadowed boundary of the forest. She was about to rush on in but Paul held her back. He motioned for her to turn off her torch.

'What is it?' She whispered, struggling to speak through the blooming ache of a stitch that had started in her side.

'We should be careful. It may be people.'

'People?' Of course, what else would it be? She had thought that maybe the candle had fallen over; or...what else? She didn't know.

'It could be far-right thugs, Nazi sympathisers. There are more and more here now, they deface Jewish graves and memorials; terrible things; maybe, because of the anniversary...?' He trailed off.

'Then let's go without the lights. We'll sneak up, and if it is them, we can call the police. We must stop them, mustn't we?'

The look on Paul's face moved from fear to determination. 'Oui, we must. Come.'

He took her hand and they moved, more carefully now, into the woods. Dawn was clearly waiting on the other side of the horizon, and the tone of the sky had changed, infinitesimally towards light, just enough for them to see by.

After a few minutes they came to the churchyard wall. Paul laid a restraining hand on her shoulder. 'Attendre. Let us listen first.'

They stopped, Michelle held her breath. She couldn't hear anything except the faint hiss of the trees moving in the mild air. And then it came again, the teeth-jarring clang of the church bell.

Paul's hand tightened on her shoulder. 'Come on!' he hissed.

Stepping through the broken gate into the churchyard was one of the hardest things she had ever done, but she did it. Once over the over side, they stopped, looked and listened again, but the clearing in front of the church was empty and silent.

They moved forward hesitantly, Paul was holding her hand so hard that she couldn't feel her fingers any more, but she didn't care. They continued towards the church, that was when Michelle saw that the doors were open. Paul took a few more cautious steps forward and shone his torch inside. She could barely look. She had the sudden memory of a time when she was a little girl, and there had been a scratching in the chimney breast of her room. The fireplace had been blocked off, and she had lived with the terror of the noise for two days. Eventually when her parents noticed that she hadn't been sleeping, she came clean. Her dad had knocked a hole in the plasterboard then shone a torch in to the black space beyond. She had been too terrified to look until he had reassured her. Even then, leaning forward to see what was illuminated by her father's torch had been one of the most heart-stopping moments of her life. When she had finally plucked up the courage to look in, it had been to see a bedraggled, but still alive wood pigeon; blinking uncomprehendingly.

'Rien, I see nothing.'

She stepped forward, 'No, look, isn't that smoke?'

A soft gathering seemed to be happening in the dark at the back of the church; the beam of the torch picking up a swirling and massing of grey. Michelle couldn't tear her eyes away; there was something mesmerising about it, like staring into the dancing flames of an open fire.

Paul gasped and dropped the torch. 'Regardez,' he was pointing into the church, 'les gens...The people!'

She looked back at the smoke, and started to see something different in its movement. It no longer seemed random, but organised; the momentum of its forward movement took on the rhythm of a slow march. She blinked and looked again, not believing what she was seeing, but it became undeniable. In the smoke there was a slow, silent procession of silvery shapes, watercolour thin and solemn. They passed through the church then spilled down the steps; Michelle flinched, but each figure dissipated before it reached them. Her fear suddenly left and was replaced with a kind of airy calm. She felt a hand take hold of hers, and saw that Paul was standing, wide-eyed, beside her.

'It is all of them,' he said breathlessly. 'Can you see?'

She looked again and saw that he was right. The crowd leaving the church was made of soldiers and civilians, side by side, their faces peaceful and impassive. When the last figure had left the church, the bell sounded a final time and then the door swung shut.

They stood for a while in silence. Michelle felt strange, like she had simultaneously been convinced of something but mystified by it at the same time. She could hear Paul's breathing and feel his hand warm in hers. It helped her feel that there was still something real that she could rely on.

'Did you see it too?' his voice was almost a whisper.

'Yes.'

They were silent for a moment. The church looked so ordinary now.

'What just happened to us?'

Paul shook his head. 'I do not know. You read about these things happening, mass hysteria, suggestion. It was the anniversary, we are both personally linked to the events of 1944, we have had wine tonight, smoked dope...'

'But to see the same thing, the people coming out of the church together, how could that be possible?'

'That I do not know.'

'I read about ghosts, a theory, that buildings are like sponges, they soak up memories or emotions; then if the circumstances are right; they play them back, like film projections.'

'Yes, I have heard this too.'

'I want to go in.'

'Are you sure that is a good idea?'

'They've gone, can't you feel it?'

He was silent for a moment. 'Yes, as certainly as I know anything. They've gone.'

For some reason he thought the door would we barred when they got to it, but it swung open easily when he turned the handle. They stepped inside. The candle had burned down, but apart from that, it was deserted and silent. Michelle appeared in front of him and they held each other.

'I feel bad.'

He kissed the top of her head. 'Why would you feel bad?'

'Because I had this awful dream, earlier, that I was caught with all the other women and children in the church, and there was a little girl with me, in the fire, and at first, I thought it was Adele. Then when I realised it wasn't, the sense of relief was indescribable. But;' she made a choking sound, as if a sob had caught in her throat, 'she was still somebody else's little girl, wasn't she?'

Paul stroked her hair and held her tighter. 'Oui. But you comforted her anyway, in your dream?'

'Yes, yes I did.'

'Then there was no more that you could have done.'

Suddenly he was crying too, the sorrow burning in his throat. 'And I saw my Papy.'

'Where? What do you mean?'

'In my dream. He was with the soldiers and the officers, here in the church. He was one of them, screaming, his face was all twisted and his eyes, *merde*, I cannot even say it.'

He felt her breath, hot on his cheek as she wiped his tears away. 'They were in pain too.'

He couldn't speak, his mind had filled again with the sight of their tortured faces.

'That kind of cruelty, it goes against nature. We're just animals, really, but we're the only ones that take pleasure in causing pain. I think it destroyed them, the soldiers and the officers, maybe not straight away, maybe not until the end of their lives, or maybe it happened, bit by bit, day by day, but it caught up with them in the end.'

'That is a terrible thought.'

'But then, when they all left, just now. They left together, and there was a kind of peace, wasn't there?'

'Yes, there was.'

'It reminds me, of when Adele was born. Only a week before I'd been with my gran when she was dying. I had this feeling, it's hard to explain, a feeling of *knowing*; knowing that she didn't need to be afraid. And when I was giving birth to Adele, there was this moment when it felt like I had moved in-between life and death, and it was a similar kind of feeling I'd had with my gran, like I had a kind of knowing, like I was all stripped back to what I started with when I began. I think that's what birth and death feel like, a kind of knowing. That's how I feel now.'

He took her face in his hands and kissed her. 'Yes, I feel it too.'

As they walked back to the cottages Michelle could sense the dawn. The last of the night was slowly draining from the sky and there was a slight sweetness in the air. Imperceptibly she became aware of the birds singing; just a murmur at first, soft and hesitant; but then ripening and swelling with joy as the sun flushed the sky above the trees with pink.

They were still holding hands, and it felt like the manifestation of a new state of being, an irrevocable connection. Michelle's heart felt light and achy, as if it was out of practice at this new emotion, but she resolved to accept it, to let it in. They reached the lake; its surface was blush pink with the reflection of the dawn sky. For a moment, it looked as if the ground had fallen away to reveal the bare flesh of some buried giant. She shivered, despite the warmth in the air, and leant against the reassuring solidity of Paul's arm. He squeezed her hand in response.

As they reached the bottom of the field and could see the hedges that marked the bottom of the cottages' gardens, a movement made Michelle stop. Someone was opening the gate to her cottage, it looked like a young woman. Michelle watched her come through the gate, pushing a bike in front of her.

'Paul, Paul…' she could barely speak; her throat was compressed with shock. The girl mounted her bike, then looked up and Michelle saw her face. It was young but serious, the dark hair pulled back into a ponytail. She started to cycle towards them, looking straight ahead, as if they weren't there.

'Michelle, what is it Michelle?' Paul's voice sounded far away, as if she was inside a bottle. She couldn't move, still the girl came closer. And then, just as she thought they were going to crash into each other, girl and bike moved through her instead. Something trembled inside her, and then there was a sense of pulling, but not just a physical one, an emotional one too, a thread, tugged, somewhere near her heart. A beat later, and she knew the girl had passed through her and suddenly she could breathe again. She whipped round and looked behind her, but the figure had disappeared.

Paul took hold of her shoulders and shook her gently. 'Michelle, what was it? You have gone so white, and you are trembling!'

'Paul, I saw her.'

'Who, saw who?'

'Aunt Michèle, she...she went right through me.'

'What do you mean?'

'Just that, I saw her at the gate, she looked like a girl, a teenager maybe. She got on her bike, and then she cycled towards us. But she wasn't looking at us, just ahead, and then she went right through me and it felt, Oh God, I can't tell you how it felt.'

He held her tightly and she burrowed her face into the warmth of his neck. 'It is like they are all leaving.' He sighed and she felt his shoulder rise and fall against her cheek.

'Yes.'

'And maybe, next, my Papy?'

'You should go and see him.'

'Yes, I must.'

She took his hand again and pulled him towards the cottages. 'Come on then, let's get back.'

They walked more quickly now, both, Michelle imagined, propelled forward by their own sense of urgency.

When they got to the cottage gate Paul stopped and kissed her briefly. 'I need coffee.'

'Good idea, there's no way I'm going to be able to go to sleep, however early it is.'

'Non! And I want to head to Paris before the roads get busy.' He opened the gate and headed down the garden. She watched him go, marvelling at the new emotions that were pressing against her, slowly, tentatively, almost as if they were conscious entities, wary of scaring her away. She found herself thinking of Chris and steeled herself for the rushing onset of guilt; but she was surprised to find that the feeling didn't come. He would have wanted her to be happy again, she realised, it was that simple.

She looked at the back of her new home, and imagined Michèle, as she'd seen her, putting air in the tyres of her bike, packing sandwiches in her back-pack. She imagined the uncle she'd never met, Jacques, looking much like Paul, all tanned and golden. And in that moment, she imagined a different future for them, one where they had gone on their cycle ride, but had decided to go a different way. In this world they have their picnic lunch, a sneaky sip of local cider, then make their way safely home. 'I'm sorry.' she whispered.

She turned and walked through the garden. When she was back in the cottage she could smell coffee brewing and found Paul in the kitchen.

'You want a coffee?'

She felt suddenly exhausted and sank into one of the kitchen chairs. 'God yes.'

He took the expresso pot off the hob and poured her a small, tar-black coffee then sat beside her. She stirred a big teaspoon of sugar into it and cradled it gratefully in her hands. The smell was reviving. She gestured at his ruck-sack. 'You're going straight away?'

'Oui.'

She felt a sudden pang of anxiety. 'Are you sure you're ok to drive?'

'Yes, I am fine. Now I have decided to see my Papy, it is like I am full of energy.'

She started to get up, 'Let me make you a sandwich.'

He laid his hand on her arm and pushed her gently back down. 'I will buy one on the way. It is fine.'

She found her eyes were suddenly brimming with tears and turned her head away so she could wipe them away before he saw them.

'Ma chérie.' She felt him take hold of her and turn her around to face him. She struggled to keep the tears in but it was hopeless. They tumbled out of her, she started to sob. He pulled her to him. 'Please, Michelle, what is the matter?'

'You...' she fought to calm herself and get the words out. 'You will come back won't you?'

He leant away from her and held her face in his hands. 'Of course I will come back! I want to be with you, Michelle, you must know that?'

'I want to believe it, but it's been so long since –'

'Shhh.' He kissed her forehead. 'I am coming back. That is all.'

'Yes.' She looked at him more confidently then and felt something white-hot and urgent swell in her chest. 'I know it.'

As Paul walked down the hospital corridor, the astringent smells of bleach and cleaning fluids made his stomach tighten with anxiety. The nurse at the ward desk had said there had been no change, but now that he was here, now that he had decided to come, he had an irrational fear that Papy was going to die before he got to him.

The door to Armand's room was a couple of inches ajar, and Paul steeled himself for the possibility that a member of his family might be in there. *If there is, please make it Camille* he prayed to himself but when he opened the door he was relieved to find that it was empty, apart from Armand.

He stood there for a moment, numbly, not sure what he was feeling. Part of him, the younger part of him, the Paul that he had been before everything that had happened over the past few weeks, wanted to rush over and embrace his grandfather. The new Paul, the Paul who had witnessed terror attacks, found out his parents had imperceptibly slid into racism; that his Papy, who he worshipped, was a Fascist collaborator; the Paul he was now since falling in love - and yes – his breath caught in his throat – he was in love - this Paul was both tougher and more vulnerable, and didn't know what to do.

He let his body lead him through his indecision and found himself sitting beside Armand with his grandfather's hand in his own. It felt strangely light, as if it could launch itself off and fly away like a butterfly. The old man had lost weight, and his face was gaunt and angular in a way that uncomfortably suggested the skull beneath the thin ageing skin.

Confronting his Papy's fragility, provoked a convulsion of emotion and despite himself, Paul felt the tears running hotly down his cheeks.

'Oh, Papy.' He stroked the old man's face, the slightly silvered flesh soft and papery beneath his hand. He still loved him, it was still there, he could feel it. Despite everything he knew now, every horror he had read about in that terrible month of June, 1944, he still loved his Papy. It wasn't something he could just dissect from himself. Because it was in his flesh, and in his bones, and to kill that love he would, he now realised, have to kill a part of himself.

A sound slid from between Armand's thin lips, something inarticulate but beseeching.

'Papy, Papy! I am here, it is Paul!'

Armand's eyelids flickered then opened. For several seconds they stared out blankly, indiscriminately, but then, slowly they seemed to find Paul and focus on him. 'Paul.' The word was barely a word, it was so vague and scratchy.

'Don't speak, Papy, let me get a doctor.' He started to stand.

'Non!' His grandfather's hand pulled him down with surprising strength. 'Water, Paul.'

He nodded and poured him a glass from a jug on the bedside table. There was a special plastic cup with a straw. He held it in front of Armand's face and guided the straw between his lips. Armand raised his head, an infinitesimal amount, and sucked gratefully on the water. After a few seconds, he released the straw and sank back down with a sigh.

'I will get the doctor, Papy.'

'Non, Paul. There is not much time. Hold my hand again, I'm scared.'

'You don't have to be scared, Papy.' And there it was, that feeling, the one Michelle had described – a singular, focused conviction, a deep and utter knowing – that Armand did not need to be scared. He wished he could tell him, about the church, that he had seen his pain, that in the end everyone had left together, that there had been peace; but he could not find a way to say it, to make it sound like anything other than a fairy story; so he just squeezed Armand's hand and said it again. 'You don't have to be scared.'

'No, not me, not anymore, but you, you must be scared.'

'Why Papy?'

'Because it is back.'

'What, what is back?'

A spasm of effort passed over his grandfather's face. 'You know what.'

Paul nodded, he did.

'You must fight it.'

'I will, I am trying, but what can I do?'

'All anyone can do. Use love, and truth.'

He stroked Armand's hand, his mind felt suddenly heavy and sluggish.

'There is one more thing, and you must answer me honestly, Paul.'

'Ok, I will try, Papy.'

'Can you understand, now? Can you understand me? Why I ended up doing what I did?'

A horrible tightness took hold of Paul's chest. What could he say? The truth, that is what his Papy asked for, so it was what he must give. 'No, Papy, I am sorry, but despite everything I have experienced, everything I have read, I still do not understand.'

Armand nodded, the effort of the action took its toll and his skin visibly greyed.

'Can you...' his voice was barely more than a wheeze now, 'can you, forgive me?'

Paul thought again then leant down and kissed his grandfather gently on the forehead. 'Oui, Papy, I can forgive.'

The trace of a smile trembled at the corners of Armand's mouth. 'Merci, Paul.'

It was the last thing he said.

From their position on her bed, Michelle could see a patch of sky through the bedroom window. A plane cut across the blue of it, languid and tail-less.

'Don't stop reading, Mum.'

Paul had left the book on her bed with a note, *I have got the new edition of Michèle's book in English for you. Read the Prologue and the Epilogue. They are the threads that lead to us. I will be back soon, my love. Paul.* The words had sent a thrill right through her and she still felt light and joyful, despite the tragedy of her Aunt's story. 'Are you sure? It's really sad.'

'Yes, I want to know.'

She picked up the book. 'Ok, sweets.' She started to read again.

"I slowed to a leisurely pace, wondering how far ahead Jacques was, when a lot of things happened at once and my life changed forever - just like that - on a moment as tiny and precise as the point of a pin - the depression of a trigger - or the edge of a knife.

I decided to come off my bike and push, the turning for Argemourt was just around the corner and there was an old gate that we would have to go through. As I came to the bend I could see Jacques, about fifty yards ahead, but something was horribly wrong. A handful of German soldiers and an officer had surrounded him. I backed up, my heart thumping, and pressed myself into the bushes and peeped through the leaves.

'Are you with someone?' The SS Officer asked in jagged French.

'No, I am on my own.' Jacques replied, and it was awful to hear the forced jolliness in his voice. 'It is a beautiful day, Ja? A beautiful day for a cycle that is all!'

And then my brother, my beautiful brother, he fell. But it was a terrible falling, sudden and profound, like he had been crushed. I didn't understand what had happened until, through the fog of my shock, I saw the pistol in the SS Officer's hand. I don't even remember hearing the shot; I think, now, because I did not want to believe it possible.

I didn't cry out, and I don't remember even considering going towards them, and this has haunted me all my life. Instead, silently, I turned, laid my bike down in the bushes, and ran. So, this book, it is for Jacques; to say I am sorry that you died alone, but I have broken my silence at last, and I have never forgotten you."

Michelle let out a slow, trembling breath, trying not to cry. Adele was leaning on her, the little girl's body warm against her chest.

'It wasn't Auntie Michèle's fault though, was it, Mummy?'

'No, darling, of course not.'

'She couldn't have stopped the bad soldiers. And he was trying to help her, wasn't he, Jacques, by telling them he was on his own?'

'That's right.'

Adele was silent for a moment. 'Mummy.'

'Yes?'

'We're not going to leave here are we?'

Michelle bent down and turned her daughter's face towards hers. 'No, of course we're not, it's our home. That's what you want isn't it?'

Adele smiled. 'Yes.'

Michelle leant back again and stroked Adele's hair. Outside, a wood pigeon hooted dreamily.

Adele picked up *Villages des Fantômes* from Michelle's lap, where she had let it drop and pressed it back into her hands.

'Read to me again, Mummy, I want to know how it ends.'

EPILOGUE

Haute-Vienne, 13 June, 1944

As the last man fell, heavily and bloodily onto his neighbour the madness left me. My finger came off the trigger and a sudden convulsion of nausea took me over.

One of the officers waved his cigarette at me. His expression was calm and he barely seemed to register the carnage that lay in front of him, or the screams and wails of the women and children in the church. 'If you are going to be sick, go away!' He turned from me in disgust.

I half ran, half staggered to the back of the church. As soon as I was there the retching started. It was violent, as if my insides wanted to leave my body. When I had spat the last bitter mouthful of bile onto the ground, I wiped my mouth with the back of my hand and straightened up. When I did so I almost cried out. A little boy, about seven, or eight, I suppose, was cowering against the back wall of the church. His face was rigid with terror. For that moment it was as if the world had stopped, to give me time to decide what to do.

I held my finger up to my lips and shook my head. He didn't move. I gestured towards the woods ahead of us and then pointed at us both. I started to move but he stayed, rigidly, against the wall. I realised I would have to carry him, but there was a risk that he would cry out. *So be it*, I thought. *If he cries out they will kill us both. If he stays, he will be killed. If I pick him up, maybe, just maybe, he is so terrified he will stay silent and there will be a chance.* All of this thinking took a fraction of a second. I reached for him, and mercifully, he did not scream, in fact he made no noise at all. I flung him over my shoulder and started to run.

I don't know how long I ran with him, perhaps ten minutes, perhaps it was an hour. I remember having to hide by a dirt track as a group of soldiers on motorbikes went by. I was sure that they would see us, that the boy would cry out and expose us, but they just drove past. Finally, I had nothing left, I could run no further. I put the boy down.

I thought he would run from me, but he did not. Instead he squatted beside me and studied me with big black eyes. Finally, he spoke.

'Maman, Nicole, they are in the church.'

'They will be ok.' I managed to say, though my throat was dry and burning still from the vomit. 'The men, they had to be punished, for helping the Resistance. The soldiers put the women and children in there to stop them from seeing, to stop them being afraid. You will meet them again, you must just be patient.'

The boy's eyes had filled with tears, I couldn't bear it. I had heard the rumours, about Oradour-sur-Glane, about Tulle, but it had suited me not to believe it. The Nazis were notorious for exaggerating their actions, I told myself, it was simple boasting because the Resistance were strong here, and they were running scared. But as soon as our division had rumbled into the village of Argemourt, a terrible foreboding had come over me.

'They shot my papa!' The boy suddenly cried out, as if the truth had only just revealed itself to him. 'They were going to shoot me!'

'Shhh!' I was terrified that he would be heard, that that would be the end of us; but he wouldn't stop.

'Why did you do it? Why did you kill them? I saw you!'

'I had to, I am a soldier, we are at war.'

'But you aren't one of them, you are French.'

Dark stars of pain exploded in my chest. 'Yes.'

The boy hugged his knees up under his chin and started to rock. 'Maman. Nicole.' He repeated miserably.

What could I say. What could I say to this poor, terrified boy. We had just taken everything from him. His whole world. There was only one thing, one way to bear the horror and shame that engulfed me at that moment. I had to save him. I was overwhelmed with a sense of urgency.

'Do you know where we are?'

The boy looked around him blearily then nodded. 'We are near the farm of Monsieur Bujold.'

'Is he...is he a good man?'

The boy looked at me strangely then nodded.

'Then we must take you to him. When you are there, tell him what has happened, tell him they must wait until sunset before they go to Argemourt, and when they go, they must enter from the East to avoid Stellerman's Division. Do you understand what I am saying?'

The boy nodded again.

We walked for another ten minutes or so, the boy leading the way, until we came across a pair of German scouts. They were standing, poring over a map. When the boy saw them he froze, his eyes wide. I motioned for him to stay where he was. I couldn't shoot them, it would give our position away in a second. I knew there was no time for deliberation, I would have to rely on my instincts. Stealthily I moved up behind them. Mercifully, at that moment, one moved off to the left to take a piss. As soon as his back was turned I came up behind the first one and slit his throat. A soft, gurgling sound came from him, enough to make the first turn. His gun was leaning against a tree, and his trousers were still undone. I ran at him. He was almost too shocked to fight back, and only managed to land a couple of chaotic blows on me before I sank the knife into his chest. I almost felt sorry for him, they were normal soldiers, probably simple country boys, torn away from their families, just as I had been.

When I had finished, I wiped my knife on the ground and looked for the boy. I thought he may have run away, but I found him, where I had left him, trembling and pale.

'I had to do it.' I said bluntly. He didn't respond. 'Come on, we need to keep moving. Take me to the farm.'

Silently he got up, then swayed. He was clearly in shock. I took off my jacket, I knew better than to send him into the farm dressed in German uniform, but underneath it I had a cardigan, knitted for me by my fiancé. Giving it up was hard, but he needed it more than me. I threaded his skinny arms through the sleeves and rolled them up; it was so long it trailed the ground and was in danger of tripping him up. He had a belt on, so I took it off then refastened it over the top of the cardigan and pulled it up from the chest to make it shorter. He tolerated all of this with a kind of numb pragmatism.

With a small shout of victory, I remembered that I had a bar of chocolate in my top jacket pocket; won from a Scharführer in a bar room card game. I took it out, unwrapped it and held it out to him. To my relief, he snatched it from my hand and ate it, greedily.

Now some colour had come back into his cheeks I knew it was time to move on again. 'We must go now.'

He was licking the chocolate from his fingers. 'Water?'

'Sorry, I don't have any. Come on, let's go.'

He headed off before me, still a little unsteadily, through the thinning trees. I kept vigilant, looking around us, expecting, any moment to come across a group of soldiers waiting to ambush us. But we made it to the boundary fence of the Bujold farm without incident. When he reached it, the boy turned to me.

I gestured at the field beyond. 'Is this it?'

'Oui.'

'Do you remember what I told you?'

'Oui.'

'Say it to me.'

'I must tell them what has happened, but say when they go, they must go East.'

'They must *enter* from the East. That is important! And they must wait till sunset.'

The boy nodded.

With a sense of sudden, choking loneliness; now that this one, tiny act of atonement had been completed, I saw the rest of my life stretch emptily ahead of me, each of its future actions drenched in shame. Pushing the thought away, I picked the boy up, hoisted him over the fence and set him down on the other side. 'Go! Go on, now!'

But he didn't go, he just stood there, studying me again with those terrible, infinite black eyes. 'What is your name?'

I paused, for a second unable to speak. 'Armand,' I managed to choke through my tightening throat. 'My name is Armand. Now go!'

Thank you so much for reading Argemourt, I hope you enjoyed it.

If you'd like to keep up to date with my news, new releases, events and special offers go to **www.corinnaedwards-colledge.co.uk**. *Everyone who subscribes to my author newsletter will also receive a free eBook of my short story collection, The Ring. You can also find me on Facebook, Instagram and Twitter.*

ABOUT THE AUTHOR

Corinna Edwards-Colledge was born and brought up in Chorlton-cum-Hardy in Manchester. Her favourite pursuit as a child was spending many Kendal-mint-cake-fuelled hours exploring magical local sites like Alderley Edge and Styal Woods. From this she took an enduring love of mystery and the natural world into her writing.

She studied English and Media at the University of Sussex and went on to a diverse working life including running art activities for kids on play-schemes and a few years in a local TV newsroom. The stage also beckoned, the highlight of which being a tour singing and acting in a raucous play written by and starring the late Brian Behan.

Writing has been a lifelong passion, including poetry, short stories, screenplays, journalism and novels. For the past sixteen years she has worked in the public sector supporting people to improve their health and wellbeing. She lives in Brighton with her husband, and a loving if sometimes hectic, patchwork family including two kids each, and a menagerie of pets.

...

If you'd like to find out about other Author's Reach writers visit www.authorsreach.co.uk.

ALSO BY CORINNA EDWARDS-COLLEDGE

THE SOUL ROOM

It's been the worst year of Maddie's life, but the offer of a gardening job in Italy gives her the opportunity to start afresh and takes her back to the Amerena Vineyard, scene of a childhood mystery.

The heat and beauty of an Italian summer and romance with the Amarena's son, Sergio, gives her a new lease of life; but it is destined to come to an unexpected end when Maddie's brother, Dan, goes missing.

Back by the stormy beaches of Brighton, Maddie finds she has brought more back from Italy than she bargained for, as sleep now brings her to a mysterious ocean-bound room, home to something wonderful and unexpected.

The discovery of her dead mother's diary uncovers a terrible family secret and Maddie must now play a dangerous game if she is to find her brother and protect the life of her unborn child.

"A heady mixture of love, loss, intrigue, mysticism and danger, set in Italy and Brighton." (Amazon)

"...an articulate, pacy, intelligent page turner." (Amazon)

"There is mystery, intrigue, heartbreak and renewed hope - all the necessary ingredients for a brilliant read. I loved it." (Goodreads)

RETURN OF THE MORRIGAN

It's the hottest summer on record in the run-down village of Burdon, and someone's coming...

Roaring into town one night on a powerful motorbike, the beautiful and mysterious Mary soon proves she is not what she seems.

For young Niall Costello, Mary becomes an obsession, and within days, her influence has spread across the village. As ancient myth collides with their lives, Niall and his family must defeat their inner demons if they are to defeat the very real one that has decided to pursue them.

'A dark and thrilling read, absolutely fantastic, simply un-put-downable, I devoured it in less than 24 hours!'
(The Book Club)

'A powerful and gripping novel of lives being turned inside out with a brilliant end.' (Amazon)

'Takes you on so many twists and turns before reaching the thrilling ending...complex characters and a gripping storyline...testament to the skill and brilliance of the author.'
(Amazon)

'Intriguing novel, beautifully written. This writer brings the Morrigan myth bang up to date.' (Goodreads)

THE CALL

Fourteen people, fourteen phone calls, one morning, infinite fates.

When Pippa comes across a young man standing on the edge of a deserted bridge, little does she know that her next phone call will be part of a chain of events that will reverberate through the lives of thirteen people she will never meet.

"It is intended to be, and is, truly moving." (Amazon)

"...beautifully observed and stylishly written with flair and energy" (The Book Club)

"This book is like a breath of fresh air, well-written compelling and intelligent. I loved it." (Goodreads)

"Each chapter creates a turmoil of emotion and some of the characters were hard to let go of. A sign of brilliant writing." (Goodreads)